THE FIRST GENTLEMAN

ALSO BY THE AUTHORS

The President Is Missing

The President's Daughter

THE FIRST GENTLEMAN

A Thriller

BILL CLINTON

AND

JAMES PATTERSON

LITTLE, BROWN AND COMPANY

ALFRED A. KNOPF

The characters and events in this book are fictitious. Any similarity to real persons, living or dead, is coincidental and not intended by the authors.

Little, Brown and Company
Hachette Book Group
1290 Avenue of the Americas
New York, NY 10104

Alfred A. Knopf
Penguin Random House
1745 Broadway
New York, NY 10019

First edition: June 2025

Little, Brown and Company is a division of Hachette Book Group, Inc. The Little, Brown name and logo are trademarks of Hachette Book Group, Inc.

Alfred A. Knopf is a division of Penguin Random House LLC. Knopf, Borzoi Books, and the colophon are registered trademarks of Penguin Random House LLC.

ISBN 9780316565103 (hardcover) / 9780316588843 (large print) / 9780316596459 (international) / 9780316597845 (Walmart edition)
LCCN 2025932202

1st Printing

LSC-H

Printed in the United States of America

For Hillary, Chelsea, Marc, Charlotte, Aidan, and Jasper—the real thrills in my life

THE FIRST GENTLEMAN

PROLOGUE

PRESIDENT WRIGHT ADMINISTRATION

YEAR THREE: SEPTEMBER

1

Brentwood, New Hampshire

Cole Wright is sitting in the rear seat of a black up-armored Chevy Suburban, one of three in a convoy speeding its way down Route 125 in the Seacoast Region of New Hampshire.

Two dark green state police cruisers, lights flashing, are leading this no-frills motorcade, scaled down for the occasion. The presidential limousine—the Beast—is back at the airport, along with the Secret Service counterassault team, support personnel, news media vans, and a fully equipped ambulance.

Three years after the election, Cole still gets pumped from seeing traffic part like magic, even though he's well aware that it's for the convenience and safety of the woman sitting beside him—his wife, Madeline Parson Wright, the president of the United States.

He's just the First Gentleman.

A light drizzle spatters against the bulletproof windows. The agent accelerates to seventy along the two-lane highway.

"Two minutes out," says Burton Pearce, the president's chief of staff. Pearce perches in a rear-facing jump seat across from the First Couple. He's pale and serious, wearing one of his many identical gray suits. "The Gray Ghost," staffers call him. The president nods without looking up.

Cole glances over to see the CONFIDENTIAL stamps on the pages Maddy is reading as the convoy hums along. He knows those pages represent the biggest political gamble of her administration—of *any* administration. She should be in the Oval Office working the phones and twisting arms, but instead she's here with him. A powerful personal show of support.

Maddy puts her briefing packet aside. Cole takes her hand and squeezes it.

She squeezes back. "Don't worry," she says. "After all we've been through together, we can get through this too."

The Suburban slows down to make a hard turn behind the police escort. Now the convoy is moving at just forty miles per hour. On both sides of the route, locals hold up crude hand-painted placards.

WE BELIEVE IN YOU, COLE!

STAY STRONG, COLE!

KEEP MOVING, COLE!

He looks out through the tinted side window. Almost game time. He can feel his muscles twitching, his focus narrowing, just like in his days as a tight end for New England—before the blown knee forced him out. He remembers how the tension in the Patriots locker room would build and build almost to the breaking point until the team ran out into the light, and when the cheers of the crowd washed over him, he'd think, *Yeah, we're okay. We've got this.*

But today?

Today he's not so sure.

The redbrick facade of the Rockingham County courthouse comes into view. The road is lined with police barricades holding back hundreds—maybe *thousands*—of onlookers. Up here, some of the signs have a different tone.

SCUM!

MONSTER!

JUSTICE FOR SUZANNE!

"Don't worry about these people," says Maddy. "They don't know what they're talking about."

"I don't care about the people on the road," says Cole. "I'm worried about the twelve people waiting for me inside."

As the Suburban slows to a crawl, two women jump out in front and unspool a long banner.

CONVICT COLE WRIGHT! SEND HIM STRAIGHT TO HELL!

Thanks for the kind wishes, Cole thinks.

2

A thousand demonstrators, media people, and curious locals are crowded into the rain-slick parking lot. The convoy is passing through the tall evergreens flanking the pavement leading up to the courthouse when I realize I left my umbrella in my car. Too late.

Rockingham County has never drawn security like this. Uniforms representing every law enforcement department in New Hampshire—from local cops to Fish and Game—are patrolling the courthouse steps. On the roof there's a detail of men and women in tactical gear and black baseball caps carrying sniper rifles. They're not even trying to hide. That's the job of their colleagues, posted in places nobody can see.

I hear someone calling my name: "Brea Cooke? That you?"

I look at the crowd. Mostly white. No surprise; the Granite State is around 89 percent Caucasian. It's a situation I got used to as a Black student at Dartmouth, about two hours north. Let's just say it's not unusual for me to stand out around here.

I turn around. "Ron Reynolds!"

Ron is a friendly face from the old days when he and my partner, Garrett Wilson, both reported for the *Boston Globe.* He's wearing his standard outfit—tan overcoat, khaki pants, and a tweed cap. His big press pass is dangling around his neck.

I give him a quick hug. "Guess we both forgot our umbrellas."

A guy in a thick camo jacket jostles by us and flicks a finger at Ron's press pass. "Fake news!" the guy shouts. Ron ignores him.

"So why are you here?" I ask. "You could be in one of those gyms right now, dry and toasty. Probably getting a better view than this."

"I get paid to get wet," says Ron. "Even if nothing happens."

But something is happening. I've been waiting for this day a long time. I see flashing lights coming up the drive. Two state police cars and three big black SUVs.

"It's them!"

The lights are getting closer. I'm in the middle of the crowd, but suddenly I feel as alone as I've ever felt in my life.

I close my eyes for a second. My mind whispers, *Garrett.*

I blink hard. Not now! I need to focus. Capture this scene for my book. *Our* book. The one Garrett and I were working on together. Until he...

Ron points to the courthouse steps. "See the podium and the camera stands up there?"

I nod. "What about them?"

"All for show. No way the Secret Service allows the president and First Gent to go through the front entrance."

"The crowd won't appreciate being tricked like that."

"You're right," says Ron. "They came to witness history."

So did I.

The first time in history that a president's spouse is going on trial for murder.

3

The convoy crawls toward the entrance as cops push the crowds back. Inside the six-ton Suburban in the middle, Cole rubs his hands together nervously. Pearce leans forward in his jump seat and says, "The county sheriffs, state troopers, and Secret Service have carved out a path so we can go around to the rear of the courthouse. By the time the crowd and the press catch on, we'll be inside and out of sight."

Hidden away, Cole thinks. "No," he says quietly. "That's not going to happen."

Pearce blinks. "Excuse me?"

"I said no. Going in through the rear of the courthouse signals that I'm guilty, that I have something to hide. Screw that. I'm going to run the ball straight through the line of scrimmage."

The Suburban moves toward the driveway turnoff. Pearce is getting testy. "Cole, plans have been in place for days. Best to arrive via the rear from both a safety and PR viewpoint."

But Cole is firm. "We go through the front door. That's final."

He turns to his wife. "Maddy, will you say a few words on the courthouse steps?"

It's a big ask. Maddy doesn't need to tell him the source of the tension in her eyes. The conflict between being his loving partner while serving as POTUS, leader of the free world, is etched on her face.

Maddy looks at her chief of staff. "Cole is right, Burton. We go through the front entrance, heads held high."

"But, ma'am, we're just about there. Arrangements have been made."

Cole sees Maddy shift into commander-in-chief mode. Cool. Crisp. Decisive. "You've got a phone," she says. "Make new arrangements."

4

They're getting out!" Ron grabs my sleeve.

Sure enough, I hear the slamming of heavy car doors and see movement at the front of the courthouse steps. The Secret Service is scrambling to clear a path to the podium.

"That takes some brass ones!" Ron calls to me above the rising noise.

A ring of dark suits surrounds President Wright and her broad-shouldered husband.

The president walks up the wide steps and pivots to the podium. The crowd surges forward. Cops push back. Secret Service agents watch the sea of faces. And hands. Especially the hands. Looking for weapons.

President Wright squeezes her husband's arm just before she leans into the microphones. "Ladies and gentlemen, my dear friends, I will make this short and to the point."

I hear her voice echo across the parking lot. She pauses after each phrase to let the words sink in.

"I have full faith and confidence in my husband's innocence, and I trust that the good citizens of New Hampshire, who have stood by my side over the years, will also support my husband during this time of crisis."

The president turns and kisses her husband's cheek, making sure the cameras have a good angle. Then, as if it's an afterthought, she steps up to the mics again and says, "I believe in our legal system, and I'm confident justice will be done here."

She takes her husband's hand. The Secret Service team surrounds them. As a unit, they walk up the steps to the courthouse doors.

"Quite a performance," says Reynolds.

"It was a performance all right. Pure theater. They're not a couple—they're a damn criminal enterprise."

My outburst must surprise Ron. A second later, he heads off to gather quotes.

Once again, I'm alone. I scan the masses. Almost every man, woman, and child is looking toward the courthouse, trying to get one last glimpse of the First Couple.

On the far side of the parking lot, I spot the lone exceptions: a man and a woman, looking straight at me.

I've seen these two before. My watchers.

Damn. Not again.

The crowd shifts, and they disappear.

All around me, people are chattering and yelling, but their words are a blanket of white noise. Again my mind whispers, *Garrett.* I hold out my hand, half expecting to see him reaching for me.

I fight back the tears as reality hits home.

The love of my life, Garrett Wilson, is dead. And I believe the man inside that courthouse is responsible for his death.

The First Gentleman.

He might even have pulled the trigger.

PART ONE

THE PREVIOUS JANUARY

CHAPTER 1

Manhattan

In a wide corner office belonging to one of Nottingham Publishing's senior editors, Marcia Dillion, I'm smiling as I watch my man, Garrett Wilson, do what he does best: Sell a project. And himself.

Tall and muscular with short, dark brown hair, he's dressed today in a green oxford shirt, khaki slacks, and brown shoes. As he paces in front of Marcia's desk, which is stacked high with manuscripts, his blue eyes twinkle.

Garrett was born with that special something that commands instant attention. He definitely gets Marcia's when he says, "This book—it's going to change politics forever."

He pauses for effect, then continues. "Think of all the great political stories—Hamilton versus Burr, Kennedy versus Nixon, Carter versus Reagan. But this one, Marcia, this one won't be just a bestseller, it'll be a history-maker. Nothing like it has ever been published, *ever*!"

"Garrett, please, hold on." Marcia raises one hand to the silver hair framing her pleasant face. "You know I love you. But *politics*?"

"Not just politics," says Garrett. "A political bombshell." He walks over to a bookcase and plucks two hardcovers from the middle shelf. His two bestsellers, *Integrity Gone* and *Stolen Honor.* "Way better than these."

I know both of those books by heart. I researched every page.

"What you need, Marcia," says Garrett, "is an international hit that will sell millions of copies and put Nottingham back into the black."

"Garrett, stop. Take a breath," says Marcia, impatience creeping into her voice.

My turn. Time to shift the tone. One of my lawyer tricks.

"Marcia, you know Garrett. When he gets spun up like this, he thinks he's Bob Woodward, Robert Caro, and Ron Chernow all rolled into one."

"That's impressive company, Brea," says Marcia. She turns back to Garrett. "Look, your first two books earned their way onto the bestseller lists with positive reviews and strong word of mouth. But this topic..." Her voice trails off. She's dismissive. We're losing her.

Garrett's smile never drops. I can see him rising to the challenge. He once told me, "An editor is like a thousand-pound tuna, and all I've got is a hundred-pound line. And it's fraying."

Garrett puts his hands on Marcia's desk and leans in. "Marcia, pretend you're an outsider looking at our political system and the corrupt acts—from dark money to contributions in kind and worse—public figures get away with. Nobody can really explain how a congressperson earning a hundred and seventy-four grand a year ends up rich at the end of their term. Do you know how many millionaires there are in the so-called People's House?"

Time for me to tag-team again. "Fifty percent of them are millionaires. Not counting members who hide their money behind their spouses and kids."

Marcia shoots me a little smile. "You're his researcher again, I presume?"

"I am. And this time, I'm a coauthor too."

"Right," says Marcia. She turns back to Garrett. "Books on politics are a hard sell, and books on political corruption are an even harder sell. Your first story was about a mole in the CIA. Very sexy. Your second was about an American hero being screwed over by her superior officers and not getting the Medal of Honor she deserved. Even better. But an exposé about payoffs and dirty public officials? No one interested in those topics needs to read about them in a book. They can switch on MSNBC or Fox any night of the week."

My turn again. "You're absolutely right, Marcia. But this story is a lot deeper and darker than that."

Marcia's smile is tighter now. "Aren't you supposed to be teaching criminal law at Yale?"

"I'm taking a sabbatical. For a story this big, it's worth it."

Marcia sighs. "Okay, Garrett. I'm all yours. Bowl me over."

Garrett glances at me. I know exactly what he's going to say next. And I'm pretty sure it'll put the deal in the bag.

"Marcia," he says, "our book will prove that Cole Wright, the First Gentleman of the United States, is a stone-cold murderer."

CHAPTER 2

Marcia is stunned into silence. I listen to the traffic moving along Sixth Avenue until the editor says, "Garrett, excuse me, but I'm getting along in years. Please repeat what you said, slowly and clearly."

Garrett enunciates every word: "Cole Wright, the First Gentleman, is a murderer."

I can see Garrett warming up for the next stage of the pitch. "Marcia, like you said, people have gotten used to payoffs and political corruption. But we're going to show that those at the highest levels of power in DC have literally gotten away with murder."

I'm reading Marcia's expression and body language. She's getting excited and trying not to show it. "All right," she says. "I'm listening. Who's your source?"

"An employee at Dartmouth College," says Garrett.

"Where you and Brea went to school. Am I right?"

"Correct," says Garrett. "As did President Wright and her

husband. They graduated before we started. Cole was a star on the Dartmouth football team."

"So who's this employee?" asks Marcia. "A professor? A coach? Someone in security?"

"A custodian." Garrett plunges ahead. "Think about it, Marcia. Who knows everyone's dirty secrets? Janitors and other low-level employees—like Frank Wills, the night watchman who foiled the Watergate break-in—they're the ones who see everything, hear everything. And nobody pays them any mind."

Marcia likes the fact that I have a law degree. I can see that I need to play that professional card now. "Judd Peyton is the custodian," I say. "He's legit, Marcia. He's been working on campus for more than thirty years. Straight shooter."

"And you first met Mr. Peyton at Dartmouth and stayed in touch with him all these years?" asks Marcia.

"No. We met Peyton at the campus signing for *Stolen Honor*," I tell her. "He'd actually read the book."

"He cornered me afterward," says Garrett. "And we started talking about secrets. Like the ones I'd written about. Then he told me that he had a secret he'd been keeping for years."

Marcia leans forward. "And that secret is?"

"The secret," says Garrett, "is that Cole Wright allegedly sexually assaulted a girl while he was an undergrad at Dartmouth."

Marcia winces. "That's horrible if it's true." She pauses. "But it's not murder."

"Stay with me," says Garrett. I picture that fishing line getting pulled tighter and tighter. "Peyton was a big football fan. Followed Cole Wright's career after he was drafted by the Patriots."

My turn. "Peyton had a cousin who worked as a landscaper at Gillette Stadium. The cousin told him that Cole was dating one of the Patriots cheerleaders. A twenty-two-year-old named Suzanne Bonanno."

"Which is against team and NFL rules," says Garrett.

"Sounds like a good rule," says Marcia.

"They tried to keep their relationship secret, but it looked like some teammates were about to leak it to the press."

"Which could have tanked his career," I add. "And cost him his pension."

"What then?" Marcia asks. Her desk phone rings. She ignores it.

"Seventeen years ago," says Garrett, "Suzanne Bonanno told her family that she was going to meet up with Cole Wright. She was never seen again. A missing person report was filed, but nothing ever came of it. A few days later, Cole Wright flew to California to have a knee injury treated."

Marcia's phone stops ringing. "There has to be more on what happened to the cheerleader," she says.

"You'd think," said Garrett. "I've kept my contacts from when I was reporting for the *Boston Globe*, and the paperwork on Suzanne Bonanno's case seems to be missing. I think it was swept, Marcia."

I lean in. "By someone working to help Cole Wright."

"Dear God," Marcia says. She taps her fingers against her desktop. "Still, going after the president's husband? You'll be called saboteurs, traitors to the country, operatives for the other political party, and if you've ever had even a sip of Stoli, they'll say you're Russian agents. Are you sure you're ready for that?"

Garrett says, "I'm ready."

"What about you, Brea?" asks Marcia. "You're not scared by this?"

"My activist granddad had his head cracked open in Selma. I've got his DNA in me. I'm more scared that the truth will never come out."

The room is quiet again.

"All right," Marcia says. "Any other editor here would toss

you out on your asses. It's a huge risk. If you're wrong on this, it'll sink you both, and me along with you. Maybe the whole company."

"We're not wrong," says Garrett, eyes blazing.

He has the look of a man who's just landed a very big fish.

CHAPTER 3

When we reach the crowded sidewalk outside the Nottingham building, Garrett lets out a whoop of triumph. He picks me up and swings me around a few times, and when he puts me down, people are staring, but I don't care.

I give Garrett a big, long kiss, then pull back. "You were a damn magician up there! A master word spinner."

Garrett grabs my hips and gives them a loving squeeze. "With you on the job, there's no chance we're going to fail." He takes my hand. "Feel like celebrating?"

"Absolutely!" In my heart, I'm quietly celebrating for Suzanne Bonanno too.

We walk a few blocks to the Times Square subway station, holding hands, taking in the moment. I give his hand a squeeze. I truly love this man.

About twenty-five minutes later, we emerge near Washington Square. I know exactly where he's taking me. Whenever we're in Manhattan for business or pleasure, there's one specific place Garrett insists on visiting. It's like a pilgrimage for him. A sacred site.

Two minutes later, we stop in front of a glass door between two huge display windows. On it is a sign: SAMMY'S MUSIC SHOP. For a musician, this is nirvana.

Guitars of all shapes and sizes are hanging on the walls: acoustics, electrics, even a few random banjos. Glass cases are filled with straps, strings, and accessories. One whole section of the floor is devoted to speakers and amps, from shoebox size to stadium rattlers.

Every inch of wall space is filled with framed photos and letters of appreciation from famous guitar players—Eric Clapton, Jack White, Willie Nelson, and plenty of others I've never heard of.

"Garrett Wilson?" A rotund man approaches us from the other side of the shop, his black Sammy's T-shirt stretched over his belly and tucked into his jeans. He's wearing round-rimmed glasses and he's got a white beard drooping down to his upper chest.

"Hey, Sammy," says Garrett, "good to see you." He gestures to me. "You remember Brea."

Sammy smiles at me through his beard. "How could I forget Brea?" Another great salesman. He turns to Garrett and rubs his hands together. "So, my friend, is this the day?"

Garrett is vibrating with excitement. I can feel it. He lets out a long breath. "Yep," he says, "today's the day."

Sammy grins at me. "So what happened? Did your man just win the lottery?"

I grin right back. "Something like that."

"Do you mind getting it for me?" asks Garrett. He's practically drooling.

Sammy strokes his beard. "Man, I'm gonna miss seeing that beauty around the shop, but since it's going to you, I'll probably get over it." He makes his way through the displays toward a back room. "Five years you've been waiting, right?" he calls out.

"Six!" Garrett calls back. "Since I finished my first book." His face is lit up like a kid's on Christmas morning.

He pulls me toward the main counter, which is topped with green felt. I remember our first date when I touched the tips of his fingers and felt the calluses there.

"From my hobby," he'd told me.

"What hobby?" I'd asked. "Working in a quarry?"

He'd laughed at my joke and wrapped his hands around mine. I knew I was sunk.

Sammy emerges from the back of the shop. He's wearing white cotton gloves, holding a dark brown acoustic six-string. Customers stare as he brings it over and gently lays it on top of the felt.

"There you go," says Sammy, "your 1953 Martin D-28. Practically perfect condition. New tuning pegs. New saddle. New bridge pins."

One guitar looks pretty much like another to me, but even I can tell there's something special about this one. Something that sparkles.

As Garrett runs his fingers along the neck, I notice that the fret markers are not the usual simple white dots. They're inlaid gems, red beryls and green emeralds.

I gasp. "My God. That's beautiful."

Sammy nudges the guitar across the counter. "Go ahead," he tells Garrett. "I've got your credit card on file. She's all yours."

Garrett picks up the guitar and sits on a stool near the counter. He runs his hands over the curve of the body and lets it nestle on his knee.

Sammy winks at me. "I always say you should hold a guitar like you hold a woman—gently, but like you mean it."

Garrett places his left hand on the neck. His right hand brushes the strings over the sound hole. I'm waiting with anticipation, wanting to hear him bring this gorgeous instrument to life.

He strums down hard, filling the shop with sound.

Horrible! The ugliest chord I've ever heard—so harsh it hurts my ears.

Everybody is staring. Especially Sammy.

Garrett looks up and smiles. "Just kidding."

Then, seamlessly, smoothly, he launches into the delicate intro of Mason Williams's "Classical Gas." His left hand dances up and down the neck while his fingers pluck the complicated pattern. Customers crowd in to listen. The melody takes off. The music builds. Garrett closes his eyes—he looks transported. Sammy leans on the counter and nods at me. He can see how impressed and proud I am. I don't want the song to end.

Garrett rolls his fingers over the strings for the final chord to a round of applause. I reach over and hug him. "That was beautiful," I whisper.

A woman calls out, "Encore!" More clapping.

Garrett waves a hand as he gives the guitar back to Sammy, who lowers it into a sturdy black case. "Sorry, everybody," says Garrett. "My love and I need to be going."

"I hope you're referring to me," I say. But he looks so happy that right now, I don't mind playing second fiddle to a guitar.

Out on the street, Garrett waves down a cab, holding the case's handle tight in his left hand. With his free hand, he gives me a strong hug and I kiss him.

"They would have listened to you for hours," I tell him.

"Always leave them wanting more," he says. "Always."

CHAPTER 4

The White House

Burton Pearce, chief of staff to President Madeline Wright, stands behind the desk in his West Wing office. *What goddamn lousy timing!* he thinks as he slowly puts down the receiver.

His earlier call with one of the fifty-two congressional representatives from the state of California had been productive. The topic was confidential—a complicated piece of legislation that Pearce and the president semi-jokingly call the Grand Bargain. But now the day has gone south in a big way.

Pearce glances down at his wide, neatly kept desk to check President Wright's daily schedule. He looks up at the wall clock, then picks up the phone and presses a single key.

This can't wait.

The call is immediately answered by Dana Cox, the president's efficient, hard-as-nails private secretary, seated right outside the Oval Office. It's "Mrs. Cox," not "Dana," to everybody. Including the president herself.

"Yes, Mr. Pearce, how can I help you?"

"I see the president is meeting with a Sierra Club delegation. Can you get them out now, five minutes early? I need to get in there."

"I'll see what I can do," says Mrs. Cox.

And, apparently, she does it.

The last members of the delegation are walking out as Pearce enters. He closes the door behind them. President Wright looks impatient. "You're not on my schedule, Burton. What's on your mind?"

"How did the Sierra Club visit go, Madam President?" he asks.

The two have known each other since college, but Pearce hasn't called her Maddy since just before noon on Inauguration Day.

He flashes back to the ramshackle off-campus student residence in Hanover that he, Cole, and Maddy had all once lived in. Of the three of them, only Cole had his future mapped out. With his college football record, he was one of the few Ivy League players likely to get a big NFL contract.

Pearce had always had more in common with Maddy Parson than with Cole Wright. Sometimes he's still a bit stunned that the wild parties and the all-night talk sessions—the usual college bull about dreams and ambitions and the conviction that theirs was the generation that would finally make a difference in politics—led them both to this room. And now he spends day and night trying to forge their youthful bond into a two-term presidency for Maddy.

She brings him back to the present. "I finally convinced the Sierra Club to stop protesting against the Energy Department's modular nuclear reactor program," she says with a confident smile. "They still oppose it—no big surprise—but when it comes up for a vote, they'll keep their mass emails and phone banks quiet. That'll give us a solid in with the trade unions as we move ahead." The president takes off her reading glasses and puts them on the Resolute desk. "Burton, what's going on that justifies breaking into my morning?"

Pearce takes a breath. "I got a call on my private line. My contact has a connection at Nottingham Publishing in New York..."

The president's eyes slowly harden. Pearce can feel her stare burning right through him. "What was the call about?" she asks.

"It seems they just made a book deal with two writers, Garrett Wilson and Brea Cooke."

"Should I know them?" asks the president.

"No reason you would, though they're also Dartmouth alums like us," says Pearce. He, Maddy, and Cole had all been in the same graduating class, a decade ahead of Wilson and Cooke. "Cooke teaches criminal law. Wilson has written a couple of bestsellers. Investigative journalism stuff, one on the CIA, one on the military."

The president walks out from behind her massive desk and stands in front of her chief of staff. "Burton, you're hedging. Out with it."

"Madam President, I'm sorry to say this, but they're digging into Cole's years at Dartmouth. And his Patriots career." Pearce pauses before delivering the worst of it. "And his relationship with that cheerleader who disappeared."

The president shakes her head and takes a moment before responding. "But there's nothing there, Burton. Never was. What's prompting this renewed interest? What's behind it?"

"That's what I'm going to find out, Madam President."

The president walks back around the desk and eases into her leather chair. She turns away from Pearce to look out at the Rose Garden. "You know, when FDR got Congress to fund the Manhattan Project, there were few questions asked. People knew how to keep a secret. We've managed to keep our Grand Bargain confidential up to now, but it hasn't been easy."

"I know, Madam President," says Pearce. He knows this better than anybody. He's the one who makes the threats, dangles the favors, works the dark angles all over DC—the Gray Ghost doing what he does best.

"You know what will happen if we don't succeed?" says the president. "We're heading for the worst depression in a hundred years."

Pearce listens, head down. He knows the president well enough to understand when she just needs to vent.

"Damn it!" she says, turning to face him again. "We've got one chance, one chance only, to make things right before everything collapses. We can't let two no-name muckrakers sink our efforts."

"I know, ma'am," says Pearce.

President Wright's eyes flash with anger and determination. "Then take care of it. Now."

CHAPTER 5

Seabrook, New Hampshire

Garrett and I didn't waste any time. After stashing his precious new guitar in the Connecticut house we rented, we drove his Subaru northeast to Route 495, then continued an hour to Seabrook, New Hampshire.

Now, three hours later, we're sitting in the living room of a double-wide trailer facing a distressed middle-aged woman. Felicia Bonanno didn't want to let us in at first, but Garrett turned on the charm, and now he's appealing to the memory of her long-lost daughter, former Patriots cheerleader Suzanne Bonanno, who's been missing for seventeen years.

"Mrs. Bonanno, Brea and I have just signed an agreement with a major publisher in New York City to do a book on Cole Wright. And get justice for Suzanne."

Felicia's face reveals a mixture of exasperation and distrust. She's obviously dealt with a lot of pesky reporters over the years. "You're nothing but dirt diggers, all of you!"

"This won't be tabloid trash," I tell her. "We have new information, and the book will be the result of a serious investigation."

"We're building a case," says Garrett, "that will send Cole Wright to prison."

Felicia's modestly furnished trailer is in a planned community called Border Family Homes. I nod at a framed color print of a stunning young woman in a Patriots cheerleader outfit. "That's a beautiful picture of Suzanne."

Felicia glances at the photo. "She surely loved that uniform," she says. Her voice breaks.

I look at Garrett. Time to dig in. He starts off. "Mrs. Bonanno—"

"It's Felicia," she says, reaching for a tissue.

"Felicia," Garrett says, accepting her invitation to proceed on a first-name basis. "As my colleague said, we have new information, but it's not the right time to reveal it to anybody, even you, one of our most important witnesses."

I lean over and touch Felicia's arm. She doesn't flinch. Good sign. I speak softly. "Felicia, you were one of the last people to see your daughter."

Felicia takes a deep breath. "June seventh. I still remember every detail of that night," she says. "Suzanne was here visiting, and she was so excited because the Patriots had asked her to return to the cheerleading squad that fall. She had a new apartment in Boston. One Cherokee Street. I still remember the address. And she was interviewing for a good job at Fidelity Investments that she thought she'd get. That evening, Suzanne told me she was driving to Walmart to pick up a few things for her new place, gave me a quick kiss goodbye, and that was that."

"Do you remember what time she left?" Garrett asks gently.

"Seven p.m., on the dot," says Felicia. "Cole was going to meet her at Walmart and then take her to dinner somewhere."

"How long before you reported her missing?"

"Not for two days. She didn't come back that night, and I assumed she was staying at her new place in Boston until I got a call from her new roommate there. Amber Keenan. Another cheerleader. Amber said Suzanne had never shown up. She wasn't answering her cell, and neither was Cole."

"What was the police response like?" asks Garrett.

"Shitty," Felicia snaps. "I called the local police. They told me to call the state police. The state police looked into it but when they found out Suzanne had just moved to Boston, they tried to hand it over to the Boston cops, and they didn't want to take it. Assholes. They said she was an adult who'd driven her own car to Walmart that night. She could have just driven off. No sign of her car in the parking lot or anywhere in the area. No signs of violence or abduction. It turned into a missing person investigation. Then the case just... dribbled away."

My turn. "Did you or the police ever contact Cole Wright?"

Felicia nods. Her eyes are red now. "A Seabrook detective talked to me. He said that he'd talked to Cole and that he'd been cleared, that he wasn't a suspect in Suzanne's disappearance."

"Did Cole get in touch with you after Suzanne went missing? Ever call to express his concern?" I ask.

"I didn't hear a single word from him," says Felicia. "I saw in the *Globe* a few days after that he was in Los Angeles at some high-end medical clinic having his knee looked at. His precious football knee."

I see the opening and take it, just like I did in the courtroom when I was a public defender. "Felicia, this is a sensitive question, but I need to ask it."

She looks at me and nods.

"Were you aware that it was against the rules for a Patriots football player and a Patriots cheerleader to see each other socially?"

"I was," says Felicia. "So was Suzanne. During the few months they were dating, she reminded me that they had to keep it quiet."

"And did you ever meet Cole Wright?" Garrett asks.

Felicia looks at the floor and nods. "I hated him from the get-go."

Interesting. Cole Wright has a reputation for strong people skills. At least in public.

"Why is that?" asks Garrett.

"Why?" Felicia's face hardens. "When he first walked in, he was all smiles and hugs, paying special attention to my girl. But I saw through that act."

"Did he ever say anything rude or insulting?" I ask.

"To my face? No. But his eyes were cold. Like a snake's. And the minute I realized Suzanne was missing, I knew that bastard was responsible." Felicia breaks down. "I know he had something to do with it. I know it!"

Garrett leans forward. "Felicia, it hurts me to say this, but we think you're absolutely right."

I reach out to squeeze her hand. "And trust me, we're about to tell the whole world."

Suddenly, I hear a car screeching to a stop outside. A door opens, then slams.

Company.

CHAPTER 6

We all look up when the front door opens. A woman in her early thirties with hair dyed deep red walks in, weaving slightly in mid-calf leather boots. Her denim jacket partly covers a stained white turtleneck, and her tight jeans are torn at the knees. She looks at Garrett, then me.

"Hey, Ma," she says. "Who's this?"

Felicia sits up straight. "Teresa, this is Garrett Wilson and Brea Cooke. They're writing a book about Cole Wright and your sister."

Teresa looks drunk and maybe high as she walks across the carpet pocked with cigarette burns. "For shit real?" she asks, slurring the words.

"For shit real," says Garrett.

"You getting paid, Ma?"

"We haven't talked about that," says Felicia.

"Really, Ma? They must be getting paid to write about my big sister and that shit Cole Wright, but they're not gonna pay you?"

"I'm sorry, Teresa," I say. "That's not how it works."

Teresa takes a step toward me, wobbles, and steps back. She glares at Felicia. “Ma, don’t you see how they’re using you? You give them family photos, childhood stories about Suzanne, and they make big bucks on their book—maybe even get a movie deal or a miniseries on Netflix.”

I can see that Felicia is embarrassed and uncomfortable. “Teresa, please don’t make a scene. Not now.”

Teresa wipes a hand across her mouth, smearing her lipstick. “Well, I got a scene for all of you!”

I wonder where the hell this is going.

Teresa goes quiet, then lets out a small belch. She puts both hands on the back of the black vinyl sofa and leans over. I can smell bacon and booze on her breath.

“I know for a damn fact Cole Wright murdered my sister,” Teresa says. She points toward the front door. “Right out there in Ma’s driveway, in the front seat of Suzanne’s car. He came out of the bushes, got into the car, and strangled my older sister with his big fat football hands.”

I look at Garrett. I know he’s thinking the same thing I am: *Did we just break this case wide open with one visit? No way we’re letting this source slip through our fingers.*

I see sweat glistening on Teresa’s brow. Her lips start to tremble. Then she bolts out the door.

CHAPTER 7

"Is that true?" I ask Felicia. "What your daughter just said?"

Felicia looks numb. "She's never said it before. How could she know a thing like that and never tell a soul?"

Garrett and I jump up and follow Teresa. I hear loud retching and the distinctive sound of vomit hitting pavement. Then I hear a car door opening.

Teresa!

We run down the steps and across the driveway.

Teresa is at the wheel now, starting her car. Or trying to.

The engine grinds and grinds.

She sees me coming and fumbles for the lock button but not fast enough. I pull the door open and snatch the key out of the ignition. It's one of many attached to a Jack Daniel's holder.

I pull back, breathing hard. Garrett comes up beside me.

Teresa whirls toward me. "You bitch! I want my keys back."

I stuff them into my pocket. "I can't do that, Teresa. One, you're in no shape to drive. And two, you just confessed to seeing a murder."

"You're not cops," says Teresa. "You got no power."

I pull out my cell. "I'll call. I can have them here in two minutes."

Teresa grabs for my phone. "Hold up, hold up!" She leans out of the seat and spits a stream of saliva. Just misses my shoe. Then she looks straight at me. "What I just told you? Back inside? That was all bullshit. But it was also the truth."

I look at Garrett. Talk about an unreliable witness...

"Gimme the keys," she says. "I won't take off, I promise. And I'll tell you how I know."

I pull the keys out of my pocket and dangle them slightly out of Teresa's reach. "No more lies." She nods. I hand over the keys. "You need a new starter."

"Okay," she says, "here's the story. Not too proud of it, but it's the real friggin' deal. For nearly twenty years now, it's been Suzanne, Suzanne, Suzanne. Ma built a friggin' shrine to her, left her bedroom just the way it was when Suzanne packed up to move to Mission Hill."

"Being a survivor isn't easy," says Garrett.

"I mean, Ma, let it go! Say a few prayers, empty out her room, keep a picture, and move on. Suzanne's gone. She's not coming back. She's dead. Cole Wright killed her."

"How do you know that?" says Garrett. "You just admitted you made it up."

"Well, I heard stuff," Teresa says. "From the man himself."

I lean in close. "What are you talking about?"

Teresa swings her legs out of the car and rests her boot heels on the running board. "One night, I called Suzanne on her cell, and I could hear Cole shouting at her in the background. My sister tells me she has to go. Then I hear Cole up close, telling her to get off the damn phone or he'll break her fucking neck."

I look at Garrett. Is this just another fabrication? The dark fantasy of a jealous sibling?

"Did you tell this to the police?" Garrett asks.

"Sure I did," says Teresa. "But I was higher than hell. And who do you think they'd believe, some messed-up teenager or a New England Patriot?"

CHAPTER

8

The White House

Cole Wright approaches the Oval Office. He runs his fingers through his thick, dark hair and checks his Omega watch, his gift to himself after Maddy's successful campaign for governor of California.

Seven ten p.m.

Maddy's working late.

Strike that. She's working her usual long hours.

He's always amazed at her stamina and focus, especially considering how many problems and questions get tossed at her every day from the moment she wakes up until her head hits the pillow.

Two Secret Service agents, one male and one female, guard the door to the Oval. "Sage to see Sierra," the female agent says into her wrist mic, using the code names for the First Couple.

Cole feels claustrophobic in these fancy rooms with all these people. Even three years into Maddy's first term, he hasn't gotten used to being surrounded by security and staff—and being watched nonstop.

One of Maddy's predecessors said it best: "I don't know whether it's the finest public housing in America or the crown jewel of the prison system."

One of Cole's predecessors, Jackie Kennedy, said of her first night in the White House, "I felt like a moth hanging on the windowpane."

Cole nods to the two agents. He has seen them before, many times, but unlike his wife and her chief of staff, he has no talent for remembering names.

But he brings other strengths to the administration—and to the marriage.

"Is she alone?"

"Yes, Mr. Wright," the female agent says. "For the past half hour." She opens the heavy curved door and Cole steps into the most important room in the country.

And he blinks every time he sees Maddy sitting behind that big oak desk. He can hardly believe this is real life.

His wife. The leader of the free world.

It seems like just yesterday that she was Maddy Parson, a poised and pretty student in his poli-sci class at Dartmouth. From her seat in the row ahead of him, she articulated point after point in class discussions, and Cole knew that she wouldn't have any interest in a tight end on the football team.

But to his surprise, she did.

That was junior year. They dated through the rest of college. Then, like many college couples, they broke up after graduation; she enrolled in a master's program at Stanford and he remained in New England for Patriots training camp.

Three years later, a bum knee ended his career just as Maddy's was taking off. They reconnected back home in California. Maddy was running for assemblywoman with their college pal Burton Pearce as her campaign manager. *Parson for Progress!*

From there, she leaped from success to success, and the two of them married just before her first term as governor of California. And now…

Maddy looks up from her papers and finally notices him.

"Getting close to dinnertime," Cole says. "Ready?"

"Sorry," says Maddy, leaning back in her chair. "Burton should have let you know. I'm meeting Senator Lewis and Senator Lopez tonight. They've both been solid noes for the Grand Bargain, but now they're softening. I called a late meeting so I can wrestle them over the line."

"You want me there, Maddy? I can lighten the mood, tell some football stories. Lopez played semipro ball in Houston, you know. Or I can talk about my fitness council."

Maddy sits up and folds her arms across her chest. Cole knows that posture. It means trouble is on the way. It means she's protecting herself. "Thanks, Cole, but that could backfire. You know Lewis opposed the expense of your fitness council from the beginning."

There's something going on, Cole can feel it. Something besides a negotiation with two low-ranking senators.

"What is it, Maddy?" he asks. "What are you worried about?"

Maddy exhales slowly. "Burton got a phone call today," she says. "Investigative reporters are digging around. Our Grand Bargain might get exposed before we're ready to reveal it. And that will be the end of it. The end of my presidency. We can't let that happen."

CHAPTER 9

After Cole leaves, Maddy rests her elbows on top of the Resolute desk in the Oval Office.

She's thinking.

About the Grand Bargain.

The plan, she hoped, would ensure that the US government could meet its ongoing obligations to the people, seize future opportunities, and maintain the capacity to address any threats.

Right after the midterm elections, Maddy had called a fifteen-minute meeting with the director of the Office of Management and Budget. It turned into what was essentially a two-hour TED Talk. The director's message became Maddy's obsession:

"Madam President, a character in a Hemingway novel said that you go bankrupt two ways—gradually, then suddenly.

"Social Security, Medicare, Medicaid—America's entitlement programs—have grown to consume half the federal budget as people live longer and health costs rise. Those programs, along with Social Security's disability benefits, make life bearable for millions of people. But they aren't sustainable in a country that strongly opposes both cutting benefits and raising taxes enough to pay for them.

"The required spending to preserve the economy and get people through COVID on top of big tax cuts has increased the national debt to ninety-eight percent of the national income. It is projected to reach one hundred and thirteen percent in ten years. Without prompt action, the government will be paying so much interest on the debt, there'll be little left for anything else.

"Madam President, the latest quantum computers at MIT's Sloan School are producing numbers that disprove our long-held assumptions about how much time we have to make tough national-finance decisions. We don't have years. We might not even have months. We're going under, and quickly."

It was a wake-up call.

The dire warning prompted Maddy to begin work on legislation that same afternoon. She called on experts and out-of-the-box thinkers to come up with proposals, and eventually they hammered out a plan that saved entitlements, reduced the debt, and might get through Congress.

Though there have been rumors in Washington of something big afoot, none of the details have been leaked, because only the president and her most trusted advisers have copies of the final plan. The members of Congress have been shown only an outline, but the document contained enough key details to convince them not to discuss it.

Once the plan was developed, the real hard work began for Maddy. First, she had to secure pledges from leaders in the Senate and House that they wouldn't derail her efforts. Then came the long behind-the-scenes battle to line up the necessary votes to get it passed without amendments, lengthy floor speeches, or blockades from various lobbying groups. As soon as it was passed and signed, they could offer ideas to amend it, understanding that Maddy would almost certainly veto those.

So far, they were inching forward on something no one would have thought possible in this era of extreme partisanship.

This, Maddy thinks, *is our last chance to turn lemons into lemonade. If we don't, we'll all be sucking lemons.*

Burton Pearce has been with her through every challenging step. Her chief of staff enters the Oval Office now and takes a seat across from her.

"Well?" Maddy says, her fatigue and impatience showing.

"Here's some unexpected good news," Pearce says. "Put Congressman Monroe from Florida's Twenty-Sixth in the yes column."

"I thought he was a bitter-ender," says Maddy.

"He was," says Pearce, "but I dug deep."

Maddy stretches her arms above her head and yawns. "Where's Cole?"

"He's taking a jog on the Mall."

CHAPTER 10

National Mall

Cole Wright unfastens his seat belt before the Secret Service Suburban comes to a halt on the National Mall in the center of Washington.

On the hard-packed gravel lanes, DC bureaucrats are heading home after long hours at work, and tourists of all nationalities are gawking at the capital's impressive collection of stone and marble monuments to this magnificent country's lofty dreams of democracy. Most of those dreams are routinely dashed, of course—despite the efforts of the present administration.

Cole steps out with his Secret Service detail and leads them in some quick stretches. Then they start running east at a medium jog. A young female agent falls in beside him, matching his pace, her ponytail flipping from side to side. Her name is Leanne Keil and this is her regular assignment, so Cole has made it a point to remember not only her name but her impressive achievements on the NC State track team. There's no chance of his speeding away from an athlete who ran the two-hundred in twenty-one seconds.

As they pass Constitution Gardens, the illuminated obelisk of the Washington Monument looms into view on the right. Behind them, the Suburban is already merging back into traffic on Constitution Avenue to join the other armored vehicles circling the Mall for his protection.

Cole looks like your average middle-aged guy out running with his daughter or his personal trainer, but it's all choreographed. No one sees the carefully positioned special agents among the pedestrians on the Mall and the sniper teams on the roof of the Smithsonian National Museum of African Art and the National Gallery. Four miles away, at Reagan National Airport, a pair of helicopters—one carrying trauma doctors and nurses, the other filled with heavily armed members of the Secret Service counter-assault team—are poised and ready to take off and fly to the Mall.

In the very first days of Maddy's term, Cole had pushed back hard about Secret Service protocols around his evening exercise. "I can walk to the Mall and back in thirty minutes!" he argued, adding that Harry Truman took daily walks outside the White House.

No way, the Secret Service supervisor, mindful of cell phones, tracking software, and terrorists, had told him. Too open, too vulnerable, no quick means of escape. "Sir, you can run any route you want—with our transport and protection."

Now Cole picks up the pace. Despite the January chill, he's starting to sweat a little under his blue windbreaker, and it feels good.

Here and there, people point and whisper. Others hold up their cell phones. Cole nods if somebody waves to him, but he never draws attention by waving back.

As he runs, Cole brushes a round embroidered patch on the front of his windbreaker. It has the seal of the United States with six stars, and the lettering around it reads PRESIDENT'S COUNCIL

ON PHYSICAL FITNESS. It's vintage, more than sixty years old, from the JFK era.

In the early days of Maddy's presidency, Cole had struggled to identify his role. He'd spent hours with Burton Pearce, his onetime college housemate and now the president's chief of staff, trying to determine where he should put his focus.

Cole was clear on one point. "Burton, I want a job."

Burton chuckled. "See all these folders on my desk? Every single one represents a congressperson or senator who says they were mistaken in opposing your wife for president. They're apologizing and making nice because they want jobs in her administration—and jobs for their assorted nieces and nephews. And I'm going to take great pleasure in telling them no."

"Nicely, of course," Cole said. "Now back to me."

Pearce sighed. "You, Cole, already have a full-time job. First Gentleman."

"That's not a job," said Cole.

"Okay, then," said Burton, "what do you want to do? Every presidential spouse I can think of had some kind of special mission." He ticked them off on his fingers. "Jackie Kennedy was a supporter of the arts. Lady Bird was into highway beautification. Nancy Reagan had 'Just Say No.' Laura Bush was all about literacy. Michelle Obama was into nutrition—"

"Right," said Cole. "Here's my mission." He reached into his pocket and tossed a circular cloth patch onto Burton's desk.

Burton picked it up. "What the hell is this?"

"Read it."

Burton held the patch up and squinted. "'President's Council on Physical Fitness.'" He worked it between his fingers. "This is a relic. From the JFK era."

"Exactly my point," said Cole. "A relic. I want to resurrect it. Make it mine, officially. That's what I want as my mission."

Burton tossed the patch down. "Why this?"

"Burton, you and I have been on the campaign trail together," said Cole. "You know that whenever I'm in front of some group, nine times out of ten, they want to talk about my football career. They never ask me about trade balances, voting rights, or foreign affairs. I've got a megaphone now and I want to use it to get America off its collective ass."

Burton passed the old badge back to him. "Doesn't something like this already exist?"

"In name only," said Cole. "JFK was smart enough to focus on physical fitness. Over the years, the program got watered down. Special-interest groups changed its name and mission, and now it's a goddamn mutant—the President's Council on Sports, Fitness, and Nutrition. And it's pretty much dormant. Give it to me and I'll wake it up, bring it back to its roots, and get things done."

Burton rubbed his temples. "There's a certain symmetry to this. Vital, attractive president replaces the stodgy old guard. Gets America moving. Happened in 1960..." Burton sat quietly for a few seconds. "Okay, but you run your programs and speeches by me. Clear?"

Cole waved the badge like a talisman. "This will work. Trust me."

CHAPTER 11

Cole and Leanne follow their usual route, and when they swing around the Tidal Basin, onlookers start clapping and shouting:

"Looking good, Cole!"

"Strong pace!"

"Nice shoes!"

Soon after Maddy's inauguration, the media had seized on the brand of shoes he'd been wearing for years: Where were the First Gentleman's running shoes made? Were the materials recyclable? Was the company ecofriendly? Did it provide humane working conditions? Did its management support the LGBTQIA+ communities?

"Maybe I should just run barefoot!" he'd joked to Maddy during the controversy.

To calm the waves, his assistant, Jason Rollins, had secured an obscure model that checked all the boxes. The shoes were comfortable enough, but after three or four runs they'd fallen apart and had to be trashed. Typical political compromise.

Now Leanne moves between Cole and the crowd.

The people are close enough that Cole can pick out individual faces. He sees folks holding up *Sports Illustrated* magazines with him on the cover, photos, even an old poster from his Patriots days.

"Looks like you've got a cheering section, sir," says Leanne.

Cole smiles and nods as the crowd of people edges closer to the path. There must be twenty of them now. Within seconds, men in running clothes are behind Cole and on both sides of him. More agents, out of nowhere.

"Let's keep moving, sir," says one.

Right, thinks Cole. *Disappear. Pretend I don't exist.*

Cole does just the opposite. He slows down, jogs over to the enthusiastic group, and peels off his windbreaker to reveal a Dartmouth sweatshirt with the sleeves cut off.

"Go, Big Green!" someone in the crowd shouts, bringing Cole back to his gridiron glory days. The faces in front are beaming and excited. Outstretched hands wave scraps of paper and Cole Wright memorabilia.

He sees Leanne step beside him, her head on a swivel. The other agents form a protective cordon around him.

Cole pulls a Sharpie out of the pouch of his sweatshirt. Always good to have one handy. He steps up to the crowd and starts scribbling his autograph on the various photos and magazine covers held out to him.

"Thank you," Cole says over and over. "Great to see you." He bumps a few fists and poses for a few selfies. This is nothing compared to the crowds he used to attract outside Gillette Stadium, but still, the recognition feels good.

"Hey, Cole!" shouts a man from the rear of the pack. "I was at the Bills game!"

Cole flashed back to making the fingertip catch for a TD in

the last second of the fourth quarter, sending the Pats into the playoffs.

"Thanks, buddy!" Cole calls out. "That was a good day!"

A young woman pushes to the front. She's holding out a booklet with a glossy photo spread. "Mr. Wright! Sign this! Please!" She's pretty. Big smile.

"My pleasure." Cole raises the pen as she thrusts the booklet in front of him. Then he freezes.

He's looking at an old New England Patriots yearbook, open to a page showing a beaming blond cheerleader.

Suzanne Bonanno.

The air goes out of Cole's lungs like he's been punched in the chest. He drops the pen and turns to the Secret Service detail. "Let's go."

As Leanne leads the way, Cole hears the young autograph seeker call out, "Good luck, Mr. Wright! You're gonna need it!"

CHAPTER 12

Outside Hanover, New Hampshire

I'm driving Garrett's beat-up Subaru north across New Hampshire as he leans back in the passenger seat, snoring. I've always envied his ability to catch sleep on the go.

Even at twilight, the rolling hills are deep green against the backdrop of the lights marking a few distant farms. I remember the first time I came up here from New York City on the Dartmouth Coach. I was terrified of all the open space. So easy to lose your way.

Up ahead is exit 18, which leads to the state road to Hanover and Dartmouth. I take the exit, tap the brakes at the end of the ramp, and make a right turn.

I see a flicker in my rearview mirror.

Shit.

Flashing blue lights come up behind me. I can make out the shape of a dark blue police cruiser. A Ford Interceptor.

I pull over, praying he'll blow past me on the way to a call.

But he stops.

"Garrett, wake up!" I say, slapping his arm. "We've got a problem."

I flash back to a night when Garrett and I first started dating.

We'd been heading south on the Taconic State Parkway after a day of leaf-peeping. I'd driven the whole way so Garrett could snap pictures. I have no idea how fast I was going, but all of a sudden, I saw police lights pop on behind me. The parkway had a narrow shoulder, so I started looking for a safe place to stop.

It scared the crap out of me when the cop hit the siren. I almost went into a ditch when I finally pulled over, the New York state trooper following close behind.

The trooper came to my window with an attitude, and I gave it right back to him. A few seconds later, I was sprawled on the hood of the car, and the cop was about to cuff me.

I reminded myself of the statistics: About a thousand civilians were killed by cops every year in this country, a lot of them after traffic stops. And many of them had my skin tone. I didn't want to become one of those statistics.

I silently counted to ten, then swallowed my pride and reasoned, pleaded, and apologized. It worked. I got off with a warning.

And a fear of it happening again.

Tonight's cop is a stocky guy, probably mid-twenties. He's a local, not a statie. He hitches up his utility belt as he walks toward my window.

Garrett swivels in his seat and looks. "Don't worry," he says. "Where's your bag? I'll get your ID."

"Back seat." I'm frozen in place, hands at the nine and three positions on the steering wheel.

"On it," says Garrett. He reaches for my bag. I check my mirror. The cop is getting closer. Garrett turns around with my wallet, pulls out my Connecticut driver's license, and hands it to me.

"Garrett," I mutter. "Get your registration!"

"Looking!" he says. He pops the glove compartment and bends his head down to look inside.

I see the cop touching the rear hatch of the car. He's leaving his prints just in case our interaction turns violent.

"Garrett, stop! Sit up and put your hands on the dashboard!" The last thing we need is for the cop to think that he's reaching for a weapon.

Keep cool, I think. *Keep cool.*

The cop raps his knuckles on my window.

I move my hand slowly to the button and lower it.

He peers into the car. "License and registration, please."

The police officer stands at an angle to the car. Bladed, they call it. To present a smaller target. His right hand rests on the butt of his pistol. A nine-millimeter Glock.

I give him my driver's license, then return my hands to the steering wheel. I'm working hard to keep it all under control.

Garrett reaches over me. "Here is the registration, Officer. It was under the owner's manual."

The officer looks at it and grunts. "You Garrett Wilson?"

"I am." Garrett passes over his own driver's license.

"Don't move," says the cop. He takes our IDs and heads back to his car. I close my eyes, trying to manage my breathing.

I open my eyes. The cop comes back and hands over our licenses and Garrett's registration. And a citation.

"What's this?" I ask.

"You failed to come to a complete stop when you exited the highway."

I give him a polite smile. "I don't think that's correct."

"Then I guess it's your thoughts against my dashcam," the cop says, and he leans down and smiles. "You two have a good night."

I watch him leave in my rearview mirror. I take a deep breath.

Still not a statistic.

CHAPTER 13

Walter Reed National Military Medical Center

President Madeline Wright is in a private elevator at Walter Reed in Bethesda, Maryland.

She's riding up to the highly secure seventh floor of the hospital. With her are two Secret Service agents and the ever-present military officer—today it's a young navy lieutenant—carrying the nuclear football.

Maddy had quietly left the White House in a black Suburban, discreetly followed by another Suburban. She could feel the tension among her Secret Service detail. They much preferred the protection of the heavily armored Beast, but she wasn't going to make a goddamn parade out of this. She was heading for a private meeting. And a personal one.

The elevator stops; the doors slide open. The staff at the nurses' station spring to their feet when they spot the president. Maddy nods and makes her way down the hall to the presidential suite. One of the agents pushes the door open, and Maddy walks in, unescorted.

Lying in the hospital bed is Ransom Faulkner, former US senator from Pennsylvania and now Maddy's vice president. The room is filled with flowers, balloons, and dozens of get-well cards for the colon cancer patient.

"Hey, Chief," says Maddy. "How's your day going?"

Faulkner served for years as Philadelphia's police chief, a title he much prefers to his current one, though Maddy has always admired his ability to deliver the Commonwealth of Pennsylvania.

Faulkner struggles to sit up. He looks frail and pasty, with purplish bruises from the IVs, and there's an oxygen cannula under his nose. When he was sworn in as VP three years ago, he'd been on the north side of two hundred and fifty pounds. Now, after a few rounds of chemo, he's lost over sixty pounds and nearly all of his thick brown hair.

"Where's Marianne?" Maddy asks. The veep's loyal wife has been with him day and night since he arrived at Walter Reed.

"She's getting a bite to eat and a treat for me," says Faulkner. "They make a mean chocolate milkshake downstairs, Madam President."

"Call me Maddy—it's just us kids here."

"Speak for yourself," Faulkner says. Then: "How are things going at 1600?"

"About as well as you'd expect." She pats his hand, smiling as she recalls the long, grueling primary fight she and Faulkner had had four years back, when he'd publicly stated that the California governor was too young and green for the job of president.

The battle for delegates went right up to the convention in New York City. Neither had had enough first-round votes to secure the nomination, but Faulkner yielded to party pressure at the last minute. They made peace quickly, although some of the senator's staff and supporters harbored some lingering resentment. Despite concerns that her running mate might feel the top spot was stolen from him, Maddy has found him to be a loyal partner from day one.

"How goes the Grand Bargain?" asks Faulkner.

"It's taking longer than we expected to gather up the votes while we keep the prep work confidential," says Maddy. "Burton tells me we should get there in about a month."

Faulkner smiles again. "Burton's a son of a bitch, but I'd want him in my foxhole."

"Foxhole?" says Maddy. "No way. He'd mess up his nice gray suit."

This provokes a genuine guffaw from Faulkner. And then his bright expression crumples with pain.

"Sorry," says Maddy. "I shouldn't make you laugh."

Faulkner takes a deep breath and settles. "I'm still the president of the goddamn Senate, right? Even if I'm horizontal."

Maddy takes his hand and squeezes it. "Chief, you getting better is all I want. Clear?"

"So tell me about the miracle, Maddy. How have you been able to keep a lid on this program?"

"Simple," says Maddy. "If I hear somebody's lips are getting loose, I threaten to go all LBJ on them."

Faulkner smiles appreciatively. He's a seasoned pol, so he's used the same tactics himself. When somebody gets out of line, highway funds for his district might mysteriously get held up. A promised military base might need to be relocated. A congressman with a safe seat might suddenly see a well-funded primary opponent on the horizon.

"Play hardball, Maddy. We need to get our financial house in order once and for all—before the whole thing collapses."

"I believe it's what we were put here to do," says Maddy. "Me and you."

Faulkner shifts in the bed and brings his head closer to Maddy's. He leans forward.

"Maddy, you need to be careful. Even in this place, I hear things."

"Like what?"

Faulkner eases back down onto his pillow. "Someone might be trying to sabotage you. Someone who wouldn't mind if your first term was your last."

CHAPTER 14

An agent holds the door open for the president. Unsettled by Faulkner's warning, Maddy steps into the corridor and immediately runs into another problem.

Rachel Bernstein.

Bernstein is the VP's chief of staff, formerly his campaign manager, and one of the people who believe that Ransom Faulkner was cheated out of his rightful destiny.

"Hello, Rachel," says Maddy. "Nice to see you." A harmless lie.

"Madam President," Bernstein replies curtly. Behind her are two young staffers and a Secret Service agent from the VP's detail.

"I just saw the chief," Maddy says. "How's he doing, really?"

Citing HIPAA requirements, Bernstein says, "Unfortunately, unless you're a family member or have written permission from the vice president, I can't tell you a thing." She waits a split second before adding, "Ma'am."

Maddy knows HIPAA doesn't apply here, since Bernstein isn't part of Faulkner's medical team, but she nods as if she believes her. "Well, then," says the president, "I'll get on that."

Bernstein heads for Faulkner's door. Maddy grabs her arm and pulls her back. "The vice president is resting," she says firmly. "Let him be."

"Is that what the doctor said?" asks Bernstein.

"No," says Maddy. "That's what *I* said. Remember me? I'm the person you serve at the pleasure of."

"Yes, ma'am," Bernstein says.

Maddy turns to her two Secret Service agents. "Let's move."

Hospital personnel step to the side as the agents clear a path to the elevators. The lieutenant with the football follows close behind Maddy.

Four years ago, in that New York City convention hall, Maddy and Ransom Faulkner had stepped into a private holding room and made a deal: When her two terms were up, she would fully support his run for president. Rachel Bernstein knows about the deal, and Maddy is aware that she can't wait for it to happen.

But after seeing the vice president today, Maddy's not sure it ever will.

CHAPTER 15

Dartmouth College

Campus is just as we remember. It's easy to locate the operations and maintenance department.

Judd Peyton's office is near the Geisel School of Medicine. The janitor is wearing scuffed work boots, jeans, and a khaki uniform shirt stitched with his name and the Dartmouth Lone Pine. His gnarled, callused hands, thinning black hair, and lined face suggest he must be close to retirement age.

Peyton's face lights up when he sees Garrett. "Hey, Mr. Bestseller," he says.

I introduce myself. "Brea Cooke, Garrett's researcher and coauthor. Also his classmate. Fellow alums. I remember you from when we were students."

"Sure, sure, of course!" says Judd, smoothing over any awkwardness. He sits down in an old office chair patched with duct tape and stares at me for a second, and I see the light bulb go on. "You used to study at Baker-Berry Library."

The machine smell inside the building reminds me of the place where my pops worked—the MTA's overhaul shop in uptown Manhattan. The office wall is lined with technical certifications. In the midst of them is a single photo: a smiling young soldier in full battle rattle. Next to it is a folded American flag in a triangular glass and wooden box. Garrett told me all about Judd's son Henry, killed in action in the Middle East. That explained Judd's interest in the military themes of *Stolen Honor.*

But today we're chasing down another kind of injustice.

"Judd," Garrett says, "we're here to follow up on Cole Wright, what we spoke about on the night of the *Stolen Honor* signing."

Judd rubs his chin. "It was Cole's senior year. Couple guys I worked with were cleaning up after a homecoming party. A real disaster zone. Rumor was that during the party, Cole Wright had raped a girl. The underground campus newspaper was supposedly going to run a story about it, but it never got published."

"Do you know why?" I ask.

Judd shrugged. "Word is the reporter was threatened. *If you run that story, you'll have to dictate your next one, because your fingers will be broken.* Something like that."

"What about the student who was assaulted?" I ask. "Did she report it to the campus police or the administration?"

"Not that anybody knows of," says Judd.

Garrett says, "You said you knew somebody down in Foxborough who knew something about the other matter. The cheerleader who went missing."

A nod. "That's right. My cousin Manny York. He worked for me one summer on campus. He had a talent for landscaping that helped him get a job at Gillette Stadium the year after Cole joined the Pats. The pay sucked, but Manny got everything he wanted from the job and then some. Got to know a lot of the players."

"What did Manny think of Cole?" I ask.

"Cole was a first-round pick from a school that's not exactly known for athletics." Judd covers his Dartmouth Lone Pine with his palm and says in a low voice, "Sorry, Big Green. From what Manny said, Cole had a real attitude, got into a few scrapes. Then he decided to sneak around with Suzanne Bonanno, one of the cheerleaders, which wasn't allowed."

I glance at Garrett. "How did Manny know?"

"From what Manny told me, it was an open secret that Suzanne had broken up with her long-distance boyfriend, and Cole swept right in. They'd been dating only a few months when she disappeared."

I ask, "What happened then?"

"The cops told the Patriots front office about the relationship, but the team decided to keep it under wraps. Didn't want the bad publicity. The cops cleared him in her disappearance, but two weeks later, when the team got the report from California on Cole's knee, they released him anyway."

"Any chance you know the name of Suzanne's former boyfriend?" Garrett asks.

"Italian name," says Judd. "Tony something or other."

"When can we talk to your cousin in Foxborough?" I ask, hoping for a primary source. "Can you arrange it?"

Judd shakes his head. "'Fraid not."

"How come?" Garrett asks.

"Manny's dead."

CHAPTER 16

Our next stop in Hanover is an off-campus student residence, a three-story yellow wood-frame house. The president of the United States once lived here? Wow. *Which room was hers?* I wonder.

Students in jeans and sweatshirts are lounging on saggy furniture, staring at laptops and cell phone screens, when Garrett and I walk in. Garrett gently taps a student on his shoulder until he looks up and pulls out his earbuds. "Yeah?"

"Excuse me," he says. "I'm looking for the person who runs this place."

The young man eyes us both, then jerks his thumb to the right. "Office on the second floor of the building next door. Her name is Laurie. Blond. Glasses."

As we leave, I can hear various sounds behind closed doors, from muffled music to a young man's voice repeating a phrase in French. Garrett leads the way next door to a Cape-style house turned administrative building. We walk up a narrow center staircase to the second floor.

A skinny girl with a neck tattoo slips by us on her way downstairs as we reach a door marked OFFICE. It's open.

In the tiny space, a small woman in her thirties with straight blond hair and round glasses is tapping on a laptop at a beat-up wooden desk surrounded by shiny metal file cabinets.

Garrett knocks on the door frame. "Hello? Are you Laurie?"

Laurie doesn't even look up. "Help you?"

"I'm Garrett Wilson. This is my partner, Brea Cooke. We're working on a book about President Wright and the First Gentleman. We hear you manage the building next door where they used to live?"

Laurie reaches out and shakes our hands. "I'm Laurie Keaton. My dad has a bunch of properties he rents to the school for student housing. I help him out."

"Do you get a lot of curiosity seekers?" I ask. "I mean, people who want to know about the education of an American president?"

Laurie rolls her eyes. "Yeah, now and then people show up here expecting Mount Vernon or Monticello. We're not exactly on the National Register of Historic Places. But I told my dad we should charge admission. Make a few bucks." She leans back in her chair. "So you're writing a book, you said?"

"That's right," says Garrett. "Investigative journalism."

"Well, their old rooms are off-limits. Privacy issues with the current residents."

I take a step closer. "Understood, Laurie. Do you have a tenant list for when the president and her husband were living there?"

"*Future* president," Garrett clarifies. "And future First Gentleman."

"What for?" asks Laurie. She's looking at me.

"Background info about what things were like then. Whether Madeline Parson and Cole Wright interacted with the other residents in ways that predicted their great futures. Personal details. Stuff like that."

Garrett leans in, turning on his best smile. “So, Laurie, do you have a list like that?”

“I don’t,” she says. “But my dad might. He’s a real hoarder and he’s doubled down since the break-in.”

Garrett glances at me. This is new.

“What break-in?” I ask, trying not to sound as interested as I am.

“A few days ago,” says Laurie. “When you came in just now, I thought you might be cops following up about it.”

“Somebody broke into your office?” asks Garrett.

“Yeah,” says Laurie. She waves a hand around the tiny room. “This is the scene of the crime.”

Now I understand why the file cabinets look brand-new. All metal. Heavy-duty. With combination locks. Laurie sees me looking at them.

“Yeah. The old cabinets were wood. Looked like somebody went at them with burglar tools, the cops said.”

“What did they take?” asks Garrett. I can almost see his reporter’s antennae shooting up.

“That’s the funny thing,” says Laurie. “Nothing.”

“Nothing?”

“Nope. But they destroyed the cabinets. Good thing our property insurance covered new ones.”

“Interesting,” says Garrett. “Do you think it was students?”

Laurie shakes her head. “There’s nothing in here kids would want. No money. No checks. All the financial stuff gets handled out of my dad’s office.”

Garrett taps one of the file cabinets. “So what *is* in here?” he asks.

“Maintenance reports. Water bills. Inspection certificates. Pest-control contracts…”

“No resident records?”

“Nope. But like I said, my dad might have that stuff. Somewhere.”

CHAPTER 17

We can't resist a nostalgic tour of our own Dartmouth haunts, so we cross the green to the Baker-Berry Library and reenact our first kiss.

After taking in a famous Dartmouth sunset, we decide to try a new place for dinner. At Sunapee Roadhouse, we order cheeseburgers and pints of Sam Adams. We always alternate between burgers and pizza when we're working long hours researching and writing.

When our beers arrive, I look across the hardwood dance floor to a small stage with a round stool and a mic stand. The stage is otherwise empty, so I guess there's no music tonight. Or maybe the mic goes live after the dinner rush.

I slide out of the booth. On my way to the restroom, I see a sandwich board chalked with the words *Amateur Nite Tonight! Newcomers Welcome!*

I know in that moment what I have to do. I spot a young guy lugging some black cases into a small alcove behind the stage.

I'm not proud of it, but what happens next involves a lot of pleading and a little flirting.

When I return to the table, I'm carrying a beat-up six-string acoustic guitar with a sweat-stained leather strap and a broken pick guard.

"What the heck is that?" Garrett asks.

"I believe it's a Gibson. All tuned up and ready to go."

Garrett looks at me like I'm crazy. "Go where? Did you buy that from somebody?"

"Nope. Borrowed it. For exactly twenty minutes."

The overhead lights dim a few notches and the house music cuts off. After a few seconds, the crowd noise dies down too.

A spotlight pops on and hits the empty stool on the stage. I hear a microphone rattling and then a man's voice comes through the stage speakers.

"Testing, one, two..."

I look at Garrett. The man I love. He squints back at me, not understanding what's going on. Not yet.

"Ladies and gentlemen," the voice says. "Welcome to amateur night at the roadhouse!" Shouts and applause all around. And a lot of foot stomping. I do a couple of stomps myself.

Garrett looks confused. Then he turns a little pale. "No way."

The voice continues, dialing up the energy. "We have a new face here tonight, a first-timer on the roadhouse stage all the way from the wilds of Connecticut! Please welcome... *Mr. Garrett Wilson*!"

Garrett's mouth is hanging wide, then his eyes narrow into a squint of disbelief.

I hand him the guitar. No backing out now. He's up.

The crowd is clapping and shouting: "Let's go!" "Showtime!" "Get up there!"

Garrett weaves through the tables and walks across the dance floor. He steps onto the stage and slides the guitar strap over his shoulder.

I perch on the edge of the booth as he takes his place on the spotlighted stool. He gives the guitar a few test strums. The sound comes through the speakers loud and clear.

He greets the crowd nervously. "Hello. I have no idea why I'm up here. But since I am..." For a second, he looks awkward and vulnerable. Then he launches into "Crazy Little Thing Called Love." He strums out the rhythm with conviction and does his best Freddie Mercury on the vocal. By the time he gets to the second verse, the crowd is totally with him, clapping along, having a great time.

I join them. This is great!

He follows Queen with "A Horse with No Name." At first, I worry that it's too ancient and folk-rocky for this crowd, but they're into it. When he finishes, I see our waitress leaning against a partition, whistling and clapping with the others.

"Thanks," says Garrett. "I appreciate it." He adjusts his position on the stool, does a little tuning on the guitar, then fingers the intro to another classic, "The Sound of Silence" by Simon & Garfunkel. At the first chorus, a few people in the crowd start to harmonize, and suddenly I'm in the middle of a roadhouse singalong. Amazing! Better than I could have hoped for.

When Garrett finishes strumming the final chord, he gets the biggest applause yet. I know he hates that I did this to him. But I also know that he loves it.

"I'd like to do one more," Garrett says. "I dedicate this song to the most brilliant, most resourceful, most *diabolical* woman in the room tonight." Damn it. He's looking right at me. "Brea Cooke—please stand up!"

Hadn't planned on payback. I half rise from the booth, give a little wave, and sit right back down again.

"Uh-uh," says Garrett from the stage. "If I'm going to sing about the woman I love, I need her right here beside me."

You son of a bitch...

The crowd starts chanting: "Brea! Brea! Brea!"

I walk toward him. A server grabs an empty chair and sets it next to Garrett's stool, right under the spotlight. I step up onto the stage and sit down.

"Hi, Brea," says Garrett sweetly.

I could kill him right now, but I guess turnabout is fair play. "Hi, Garrett."

The crowd roars.

Garrett looks down at the guitar strings, then up at me, and then he starts to sing an old Joe Cocker hit. But there's no rasp in Garrett's version of "You Are So Beautiful." He sings it soft and sweet while looking straight into my eyes. " 'You're everything I hoped for, everything I need...' "

After a few seconds, my embarrassment fades away and it's just the two of us. In a restaurant full of people, he's the only one I see.

By the time he gets to the last chorus, tears are running down my cheeks.

CHAPTER 18

The man occasionally known as Jack Doohan has his powerful night-vision spotting scope trained on the window of the third-floor room at the Hanover Marriott where his targets are staying. He's been surveilling the two subjects for hours, mumbling his fake name over and over until he believes it himself.

When the room lights go off, Doohan lowers his scope and figures he might as well turn in too. It's been a long two days, first locating the subjects, then following them around town here. Nice school. Pricey. High-class. Stuffed to the gills with snobs.

Doohan had nursed a beer at the roadhouse bar while the subject named Wilson did his little show for his girlfriend. The set list was way too sappy for Doohan's taste. He much prefers thrash metal, which is what's pulsing through his earbuds right now. It clears his mind.

He moves a bit in his position on a roof across the street from the hotel. No need for a full ghillie suit here, just light-gray overalls that blend in with the concrete. He wasn't able to access the hotel room to bug it, and the windows are too thick for his surveillance boom mic. Unfortunately, his lip-reading skills aren't great at night. All he can do is snap a few pics with his telephoto lens for documentation purposes.

Earlier, he'd circled back to campus for a chat with a maintenance supervisor and learned that Wilson and Cooke had talked with Judd Peyton, who'd been working the buildings and fields of Dartmouth for nearly three decades.

That was not good news.

Paperwork could be destroyed or misfiled, but old-timers knew things. And they loved to talk.

Doohan sighs. It would be so simple to track Mr. Peyton down tonight and persuade him to give up everything he'd told the subjects, but that would be outside the scope of the assignment.

Observe and record.

For now.

That could change.

He has his CWS sniper rifle beside him just in case.

Doohan takes one last look at the room through his night-vision scope. Still dark. No activity. Or maybe the subjects are having wild, passionate sex out of view. The bed is hidden behind the half-closed drapes.

Time to get some sleep. Start fresh tomorrow.

He eases up to his knees, packs up his gear, then gets to his feet and heads for the parking garage three stories down. He has another little problem to dispose of before bedtime. Tedious, but necessary. The result of an unfortunate encounter in the woods earlier that day.

Doohan had been testing his scope and sighting his rifle when some crazy bird-watcher popped up out of the bushes and started giving him shit. A kid. Early twenties. And he would not let up: "Who are you? What are you doing here? This is a conservation area. No weapons allowed. I've got sensitive birdcall recording equipment set up all over. I'm working on my master's project here." Then he'd pulled out his iPhone. "I'm getting your face and plate number, buddy."

Wrong time. Wrong place. Too bad. It happens.

Doohan walks to the dark corner of the garage just out of range of the nearest security camera where he'd parked his black Lexus.

He sets his equipment down on the garage floor and opens the trunk. The interior light is disabled, but there's still enough ambient light to see what's taking up most of the trunk—the body of a bearded young man with an unnatural twist to his neck.

Doohan tosses in his equipment and slams the trunk shut.

"Okay, birdman," he mutters. "Let's find you a nest."

CHAPTER 19

I wake up in our room at the Marriott. It's early. Still dark. I yawn. I stretch. I'm feeling warm, relaxed, loved. I reach over to snuggle with Garrett, but he's not there.

I roll over and see him sitting at a desk near the window. His face looks ghostly blue from the dual reflections of his phone and laptop screens.

Garrett doesn't look up. "Judd Peyton texted me. He remembered the full name of Suzanne's old boyfriend, the one she dated before she hooked up with Cole."

"And?"

"His name is Tony Romero. He's from Cranston, Rhode Island."

"What'd you find out about him?"

Garrett rotates in his chair. He's wearing black briefs and nothing else. "He owns a used-car dealership, two gas stations, and a few laundromats around Providence."

"Sounds industrious."

"Yep. But other than the business websites, he's totally dark on social media."

I sit up in bed and hold the sheets over my bare chest. "Got a picture?"

Garrett turns the laptop toward me and clicks to enlarge a photo from the car dealership home page. Rough-looking guy in his forties. Big nose. Small eyes. He turns the laptop back.

"Tony's got a record," Garrett says, typing. "Assault. Loan-sharking. Illegal gambling. Did a couple years in Rhode Island Maximum Security Prison in Cranston."

"At least it was right near home. Was this before or after Suzanne?"

"After," says Garrett. He keeps typing until I tap the bedside clock.

"Hey. Check the time. It's not even five a.m. and they don't serve breakfast until six."

"So?"

I flip the covers down. "So come on back to bed and I'll sing you one of my favorite blues songs."

"Which is?"

I wiggle my eyebrows at him. "'Sixty-Minute Man.'"

Garrett slams his laptop shut and climbs back under the covers, laughing. "Is that a request—or a challenge?"

I pull him down and start kissing his warm neck. "Why not both?"

CHAPTER 20

Two hours later, I'm eating waffles with Garrett in the downstairs lounge.

This is nice. Cozy. Almost makes me forget why we're up here—to dig up evidence that the man married to the president of the country has blood on his hands.

"How many people know that we're working on this book?" I ask.

"Marcia Dillion. Felicia Bonanno. Teresa. And we told Laurie yesterday."

"You think Marcia is blabbing it around back in New York?"

"No way. Not until she sees what we've got." He turns to me with a guilty look. "While you were sleeping, I called in a little backup."

"Not your friend in Roxbury again!"

"Seymour is definitely not my friend," says Garrett.

"One of your hackers, then."

Garrett doesn't say anything. Got him. "The Ukrainian or the Serbian?"

"The Ukrainian. Daryna. She's an expert digital fact finder. Reliable and fast." Garrett sips his coffee. "Here's another idea you won't like. We need to cover more ground. I think we should conduct separate research."

He's right—I don't like this idea either. And I'm sure it shows on my face. "Garrett. We work together. We're a team."

"Just listen," he says. "We need to find out who was writing for the underground student newspaper and who might have known about the story that got killed. Digging out files and records is your strength, so I was thinking you could look for that reporter."

"And you?"

"I'll rent a car and head to Boston," says Garrett. "Meet with a retired police detective who worked the Bonanno case back then, see how the cops handled Suzanne's disappearance."

"Or *didn't* handle it." I can't help inserting that on Suzanne's behalf.

Garrett nods, acknowledging my point. "Afterward," he says, "I'll head down to Providence to look for Tony Romero."

CHAPTER 21

The White House

The phone on Maddy's desk rings and rings. Maddy finally picks up. "Yes?"

"Madam President, Jessica Martin from the *Post* is here for her appointment."

"Very good," says Maddy. "Have someone escort her to the study."

"Yes, ma'am."

Maddy hangs up, pushes away from the Resolute desk, and walks to the door that opens into the president's study. It's much smaller than the Oval Office, with a low wooden desk, bookcases, and three chairs. A coffee service sits at one end of the desk.

Maddy eases down into one of the chairs and thinks about the advice she's gotten from former presidents. There's a consistent thread: Compartmentalize; approach problems one at a time; once a decision is made, never look back.

A knock on the door. "Come in," says Maddy.

And always, always, focus on the big issues. Don't major in the minor, like tracking who's using the White House tennis court or fretting over criticism in a column written by someone who doesn't have all the facts.

Maddy walks over to the door as it opens. A young male aide says, "Madam President, Jessica Martin of the *Washington Post*."

Maddy smiles. "As if we've never met." The president extends her hand. The reporter returns her firm grip. "Thanks for coming, Jessica."

"Thanks for the invitation, Madam President."

"Come, come in," says Maddy as the aide leaves, closing the door behind him. Martin is in her fifties with short blond hair. She's wearing a flannel skirt and jacket with flat, sensible shoes. She shrugs off a large shoulder bag as she enters.

"Two chairs," says the president. "One for you, and one for your bag. Coffee?"

"Yes, please."

Martin sits, and the president pours coffee from a carafe into a cup with the presidential seal on it. She passes it over. "Cream, sugar, Splenda, whatever you need is right here."

Martin takes the cup in both hands. "Black is fine, Madam President. Thank you."

Maddy pours a cup for herself, then takes a seat opposite the reporter. "First time in the study, Jessica?"

"Yes, ma'am."

"What do you think of the room?"

Martin takes a sip of her coffee. "It's smaller than I expected, ma'am."

"I think it's cozy," says Maddy. "A nice place to duck out of the Oval for some quiet time, to focus on an issue, solve a problem, or get a short nap after a long night."

"I hope I'm not a problem, Madam President," says Martin.

"I hope so too," says Maddy.

Martin puts her cup down on the coffee-service tray and reaches into her shoulder bag. She pulls out an iPad, flips it open, and balances it on her knees.

Maddy puts her coffee cup on a coaster on the desk and places her feet flat on the floor. Small talk is over. She can see Martin shifting into reporter mode.

"Madam President, as I told Burton Pearce, we're preparing to run a story about changes your administration is planning to make to entitlement programs, including Social Security and Medicare. *Drastic* changes."

Maddy lifts her chin. "Jessica?"

"Madam President?"

"Here are the ground rules for our little chat, beginning at this moment. Everything I say going forward is off the record. It's not to be used on background or as coming from 'an anonymous official in the White House' or 'someone close to the president' or any combination thereof. To be blunt, what I say here stays here."

Martin closes her iPad. "Then why the invitation?"

"So that you can hear what I have to say, and so I can convince you to delay publishing anything about the rumors you've heard."

"Madam President, with all due respect, that's a tall order."

"That's because we're dealing with very high stakes," says Maddy, "and I'm appealing to you as a citizen first and a journalist second."

"Madam President, you know that's not how it works."

"I'm hoping you can make an exception this time," says Maddy. "There have been a number of cases where journalists agreed to keep some news confidential, like impending military operations or the location or condition of hostages being held overseas."

"Madam President, those were issues of national security," says

Martin. "You can't tell me that making changes to entitlement programs is in the same realm."

"Really?" Maddy opens a desk drawer, removes a sheet of paper, passes it over to Jessica. It's an old black-and-white photograph of an elderly couple in a street in an unidentifiable city pushing a wheelbarrow full of banknotes.

"That's Opa and Oma in a small German town going out to do their shopping with a wheelbarrow full of marks. This was right at the end of the First World War. Inflation at the time was running at three hundred and twenty percent a month. A *month*! The postwar German government eventually collapsed, and you know where that led."

Martin nods with a grim expression. "I do. It led to Adolf Hitler."

Maddy leans forward. "Believe me, Jessica, what we're wrangling with is *definitely* an issue of national security."

Jessica Martin gives her a skeptical look. "But Madam President, previous administrations have issued the same warning— "

Maddy interrupts. "And every one of them knew they were just putting off the pain. Well, the time has come, Jessica. Hard but necessary decisions need to be made."

"What kind of decisions, Madam President? Off the record."

"I can't tell you that now, Jessica. I'm just asking you not to scare people, people like your own parents, by running just part of the story."

Martin puts her iPad back into her bag. "I want an exclusive."

Maddy nods. "Deal."

"A day before the announcement."

"One hour," the president counters. "The world's too wired for me to give you a day."

"All right, one hour," Martin responds. "I also want an exclusive interview with you and key members of your group and a timeline of your decisions."

"Agreed, but all embargoed until the announcement is made."

"I can live with that, Madam President."

"But one more point," says Maddy. "Starting today, if even a hint of our discussion or any rumors about this legislative package appears in the *Post*, it will have a chilling effect between this administration and your newspaper. And when I say *chilling*, I'm talking absolute zero. No more interviews, no sources, no rides on Air Force One."

"I understand, Madam President."

"I'm sure you do," says Maddy. She opens a desk drawer and pulls out a slip of currency with blue markings. "We usually give visitors to the White House a souvenir of 1600 Pennsylvania Avenue," she says. "I'm going to give you this instead. That's a one-hundred-trillion-dollar banknote from Zimbabwe. That's *trillion*. With a *t*. It's currently trading on the currency market for forty cents American."

"I get the point, Madam President," says Martin. She tucks the bill into her bag. "I wish you luck. And I'll be waiting for your call."

CHAPTER 22

Dartmouth College

On the border of the green, I'm sitting against one of the big oak trees soaking up some especially bright winter sun while finishing a takeout burger from Murphy's, one of my favorite campus hangouts. One of Garrett's too. In fact, it's where we went on our second date. Before ending up back in my bed in Richardson Hall.

This morning, I kissed Garrett goodbye in the rental-car parking lot and headed over to the office of the underground student newspaper. The visit was a dead end—until a staffer told me that the back issues were in a collection at the Rauner Library.

I flashed my alumni ID card, and the student behind the desk pointed me toward the student newspaper archive. Some intrepid librarian had amassed printed copies of every back issue. While the reporters for the official campus newspaper, the *Dartmouth*, were governed by the same libel laws that professional journalists had to adhere to, the underground paper pushed the envelope, even investigating stories about campus crimes that otherwise went unreported.

I scanned the bylines of stories about blizzards and protests and new buildings and sports—and campus dramas. Maddy Parson's and Cole Wright's names came up frequently. So did Burton Pearce's. I lingered over a photo of Cole from the homecoming game, his teammates clustered around him. From what Judd Peyton told us, the rape would have happened that night. But the story never ran. Which reporter was threatened? And what did he or she know?

When I was done, I had twenty-nine student reporters to follow up on. Names that are now on a list on my laptop along with notes for my call script.

After lunch, I return to the library and set up my computer in a carrel where I can make calls. I start working my way through Google, Facebook, LinkedIn—my first-resort sites for tracking strangers down. Before long, I've got contact info for nearly all the names on my list.

My phone buzzes with a text from Garrett: Will be in Beantown by 1. Followed by four heart emojis. I emoji him back and add, Be careful! His reply: You worry too much.

He's right. I do. Especially about him.

Back to my list. First up, Colin Abrams, currently a producer for an Omaha television station. I call the number for him listed on the website and get lucky.

"This is Colin Abrams."

I launch into my spiel. "Hi, Mr. Abrams, my name is Brea Cooke. I'm a Dartmouth alum working on a book about incidents that happened on campus about twenty years ago."

Nothing from the other end. Then: "And why did you call me?"

"You were a student reporter at that time, right?"

"Sure, me and about two hundred other people."

"Well, I'm looking for information on a story about a

Dartmouth football player who was accused of sexual assault. I have a source who says the reporter who was working on the story got threatened and the story got spiked. Was that reporter you?"

"Nope."

"Do you remember the incident?"

"No, I don't," says Abrams.

"Is there anybody you know who might be able to help me?"

"Sorry," he says. "I was on the paper for only two months when I realized print was dead. Wish I could help you, but I've got a show to prep." He hangs up.

I'm oh for one.

And so it goes. I call a reporter at the *New York Times*, a spokesman for the Red Cross, a writer for CNN—none of them remembers the story or the threat.

My next try is Ellen Layton, editor, owner, and publisher of the *North Empire News*, a small-town newspaper in upstate New York. I run through my standard intro and hold my breath.

"Let me think," says Ellen. And then: "Yes. Sure. I remember it."

My heart starts thumping hard. I sit up straight.

"It was Floyd Whelan who got threatened," says Ellen.

I tap the name into my notes.

"He was this really nerdy, gawky kid," says Ellen. "His desk was next to mine. He was hoping that a police report would come out, but it never did. And after the threats, I remember him saying he was planning to bulk up, take some martial arts classes."

"Any idea where Whelan works now?" I ask. I'm practically bouncing.

Silence on the other end of the line.

"Ellen? You still there?"

"Yeah. Sorry. Floyd joined the military but didn't survive Afghanistan. KIA."

A shudder runs through me. But I have to focus. I've got two more questions to ask. "Ellen, did Whelan ever tell you the name of the student who was assaulted?"

"No," says Ellen. "He never did. Just that she was a freshman."

"Did he ever tell you who assaulted her?"

"Shit, yes," says Ellen firmly. "It was Cole Wright. You know, the First Gentleman."

CHAPTER 23

Boston, Massachusetts

Garrett Wilson walks to a Dunkin' on Parker Street about three blocks from the Boston police headquarters on Schroeder Plaza.

On my way to meet O'Halloran, he texts Brea. Wish me luck.

She texts back: LUCK. We need it.

Sitting in a booth is retired detective Eddie O'Halloran. He has a stout build and a red face that suggests his blood pressure is somewhere in the stratosphere.

Garrett gets a cup of coffee while O'Halloran works his way through two glazed doughnuts.

"You ask me," says O'Halloran, "Dunkin' started going downhill once they quit making crullers. Then they really fell off a cliff when they dropped the *Donuts* from the name. Morons."

"Maybe they're trying to appeal to a more health-minded clientele," says Garrett. "But yeah, I miss those crullers too."

O'Halloran grins. "Let's get to it, all right? Suzanne Bonanno.

Hard to forget a case involving a Patriots player and a gorgeous cheerleader. What's it been, fifteen years now?"

"Seventeen," says Garrett.

O'Halloran swallows a doughnut morsel, then wipes his fingers on a napkin. "So it started as a missing person case, which was hard when the person supposedly missing was a grown-ass adult."

"Harder still when the investigation wasn't even initiated for forty-eight hours, right?"

"Those first forty-eight hours are critical," O'Halloran says.

"And crimes that are not solved in that critical period are less likely to be solved at all."

"Not impossible, but less likely, yes. By the time her mother reported her missing, and we talked to the cheerleading staff, her roommate—"

"The roommate was Amber Keenan, right?"

"Correct. Another Pats cheerleader. Actually, her *future* roommate. Suzanne was supposed to move in the day she went missing. Since she was still a resident of Seabrook, we kicked it back over to the cops in New Hampshire, thinking they'd have better luck, her being a local. They interviewed the mother, who tipped them to the fact that Suzanne's boyfriend was Cole Wright. Which was supposed to be on the down-low. Did you check with Seabrook? Or the FBI? We asked them to get involved too."

"I called," Garrett says. "No one would talk to me. Same with the FBI. They both said the files were unavailable."

"Meaning 'missing.'" O'Halloran smiles. "I hate when that happens."

"So what went on with the investigation?"

"Even though we gave it to Seabrook, Suzanne's mother kept calling us twice a day," O'Halloran says. "We put out a press release for the *Globe*, the *Herald*, and the local TV stations.

Canvassed the neighborhood. Nothing. Then Suzanne's sister, Teresa, came in—drunk or high—and ups things. She told us she heard Wright making threats against Suzanne just before she disappeared."

"Right," says Garrett. "She told me the same thing. You didn't believe her?"

"Like I said, she was kinda loopy. Unreliable."

"What happened with the Cole Wright interview Seabrook did?" Garrett asks.

"I guess they cleared him," O'Halloran says. "Then he was off to some high-end sports clinic in LA to get his knee rehabbed."

"And we all know how that worked out," says Garrett.

O'Halloran shakes his head. "Yeah. Damn it. Great player. Magic hands. I was hoping we'd get another season or two out of him."

"You never talked to him yourself?"

O'Halloran polishes off his second glazed. "Nah. Like I said, we'd already kicked it over to Seabrook. They didn't need my fat Irish ass interfering."

"What happened then? Did they follow up?"

"You know how it is—burned hot for a few weeks, then died down. No sightings, no body, no new leads. Then a couple of suburbanites got gunned down at Downtown Crossing, and poor Suzanne went into the cold-case file." O'Halloran folds his meaty hands together and leans toward Garrett. "And now you, my friend. After all this time. Why the sudden interest?"

"I've got some new information," says Garrett.

"About what?"

"About Cole Wright," Garrett says. "Some rumors from back in his college days have resurfaced. It's making me want to look at the original case files."

O'Halloran lets out a low whistle. "Good luck with that," he says. "Wright's come a long way since those days. Guy that close to power, you know he's got people protecting him, covering for him."

Garrett nods. "I know."

O'Halloran leans back in the booth. "So you like being on your own, without those assholes at the *Globe* hassling you day and night?"

"I like choosing my own projects," says Garrett. "But I'm not on my own. I've got a partner. She's a lawyer."

"That's good," says O'Halloran, smiling. "Considering the people you're dealing with, you might need one." He slides out of the booth. "Besides, you know what happens to lone wolves, right?"

"What?"

"They get hunted down. And skinned."

CHAPTER 24

Providence, Rhode Island

It's midafternoon when Garrett Wilson rolls into Providence. It takes him twenty minutes to track down the nondescript bar where Daryna told him he would find Tony Romero.

The bar is identified only by a sign near the metal door: RAYMOND'S TAVERN. Maybe the name is in honor of former Providence godfather Raymond L. S. Patriarca? A Mob bar named after a Mob boss. Bold choice. Poetic, even.

There are no neon beer signs in the windows because there are no windows. Only a peephole near a small plaque that reads PRIVATE CLUB. Garrett walks down a short flight of concrete stairs and pulls on the door handle. Locked.

He looks around and sees a rusted doorbell partly obscured by a trail of stringy vines. His fight-or-flight response kicks in, meaning he's on his toes. He presses the button.

After a few seconds, he hears the click of a heavy bolt and a gravelly voice saying, "What?" The door opens about six inches, emitting a waft of stale cigarette smoke.

"I need to see Tony Romero," Garrett tells a looming male figure.

"Who does?"

Garrett assumed that a guy like Romero would be protected by layers of muscle, so he launches into his prepared story. "I owe him money."

"Who doesn't?" says the voice. "Members only."

The door slams shut.

Garrett rings the bell again.

A few seconds later, the door reopens, this time a little wider. "How much money?" Now Garrett can see the doorman more clearly. He's a hulk, muscles bulging underneath a polo shirt.

"That's between me and Tony. C'mon, man. I can't handle another week's vig. I just need two minutes with him."

"Tony's busy. Come back later."

The door starts to close again. Garrett jams his foot in the gap and presses his face into the open space. He decides to roll the dice. "I lied just now. I don't owe Tony any money. Just tell him it's about Suzanne Bonanno."

The hulk hesitates. "Move your foot or I'll break it," he mutters.

Garrett slides his shoe out. The door closes. Longer wait this time. But when the door opens again, it opens all the way.

Garrett steps into a dark vestibule with a pedestal stand holding a reservation book.

"Follow me," says the hulk.

He pushes aside a curtain and leads the way to a polished bar in front of a mirror and rows of up-lit bottles. Club members circulate to the jazz coming from the speaker system. At one table, two men are talking with a young woman in satin shorts and a halter top; in the corner, a man plays a vintage arcade game. Cue sticks lie neatly crossed on two green-felted pool tables.

Garrett follows his escort down a narrow cinder-block corridor stacked high with liquor cases to a simple wooden door marked PRIVATE. The hulk gives two sharp raps on it with his knuckles, then pushes the door open and motions Garrett into a wood-paneled office.

Behind the desk, a well-dressed middle-aged man is sitting in a high-backed leather chair. The face is a match to the photo Garrett saw online. It's Tony Romero.

"Thanks, Donnie," Romero says.

The hulk backs out and shuts the door. Romero looks closely at Garrett as if trying to place him.

Garrett senses movement behind him. He turns and sees that each of the room's back corners is occupied by a man in a suit. One is smoking a cigarette. The other has his arms folded across his thick chest.

"Who the hell are you?" Romero asks, eyes narrowed.

"My name is Garrett Wilson. I'm an investigative reporter. An author. I write books."

"Bullshit. You're a cop. You look like a cop."

Garrett feels his stomach drop. But he stands his ground. "No. Like I said, I'm a writer. Garrett Wilson. You can look me up online. I have a website."

Romero nods to one of his associates, the smoker. The smoker pulls out his iPhone and starts tapping. After a few seconds, he walks over to the desk and holds the screen in front of Romero.

Romero glances at it, then looks up. "Two books. Good for you. They sell?"

"They did all right," says Garrett.

"How does it pay?"

"Not great."

Romero looks down again, scrolls for a minute. "Dartmouth, huh? That your girlfriend in the picture? It says here she's your researcher. Nice."

"We're partners, yes."

"And where is she this fine day?"

"Working on a different assignment."

"I see." Romero flicks his hand at his men. "We're okay," he says. They leave the room. Romero gestures toward an empty chair across from his desk. "Sit, Mr. Writer. Sit."

Garrett perches on the edge of the chair. His mouth is dry. His feet tap against the floor.

Romero leans forward and stares at him. "So. What about Suzanne Bonanno?"

Garrett forces himself to stare right back. "Mr. Romero—"

"Tony."

Garrett resets. "Tony, I'm told that you and Suzanne dated about twenty years ago. Is that true?"

Romero grins, leans back. "In my mid-twenties, man, I played the field as much as I could. Yeah, Suzanne. The Patriots cheerleader. Nice piece." He leans forward and his expression turns earnest. "You have any idea what happened to her?"

"That's what I'm trying to find out," Garrett says. "After you two broke up—"

Romero puts up a hand. "Hold on, hold on. It's not like we were serious. We just hung out here and there, had some fun."

"Okay," Garrett says, "after you two stopped hanging out, she started dating Cole Wright. This was when he was still on the team."

Romero drums his fingers on his desk. His face is grim. "Yeah. I knew that."

"So maybe you know she was supposed to be on a date with him the night she disappeared."

"Right," Romero snarls. "And now that prick is living in the White House, screwing the goddamn president. I guess he moved up in the world. Can you believe that shit? Only in America..."

"Did you and Suzanne keep in touch? Did she ever talk to you about Cole Wright? Ever complain about the way he was treating her?"

"Treating her?"

"Like, was he ever rough with her?"

Romero is silent for a few seconds. Garrett can sense his mind working. "Jesus Christ! Is that what your book is about? You think Cole Wright offed Suzanne Bonanno?"

"So she never talked to you about him?"

"I didn't say that."

"So she did?"

A few more seconds of silence. Then: "She did call me once. She was crying and sniffling and shit. Said Cole had slapped her around. She wanted me to do something about it."

"Like what?"

"What do you think, Mr. Writer? She wanted me to find a couple guys to teach him a lesson."

"And did you?"

"Me? Send mugs after a Patriots player? Like that was ever gonna happen. I told her to break it off with the prick. That was my advice. That was the last time we talked. I swear on my kids." Romero places both palms flat on his desk. Garrett senses impatience. "That it? You get what you want?"

Not by a long shot. But Garrett decides not to press his luck. He stands up. "Yes. Thanks, Tony. Appreciate the time."

"You got balls coming in here," says Romero, grinning. "Good way to get 'em cut off." He stands up too. The door opens. The two thugs reappear.

Garrett feels sweat dripping under his shirt. "I can find my way out." The two thugs move to block him, but a hand squeezes his shoulder from behind.

"No, no," says Romero. "I'll walk him out myself." The two associates step aside.

Garrett starts to breathe easier. Romero hooks an arm through his as they walk out of the office and into the dank corridor. "It's quicker through the back," Romero says.

Garrett's mind is humming. He's trying to fix Romero's quotes in his mind, word for word, in the right order, until he can get to his laptop. He sees a metal door just ahead, sunlight streaming through its wire-mesh security screen.

Tony pushes the door open, revealing a small concrete platform and two dumpsters. Garrett takes a breath. The air smells like garbage.

"Just one thing," says Tony.

Out of the corner of his eye, Garrett sees the fist coming just before it connects with his temple. He collapses to his knees. A kick to his ribs flattens him. His face is on the concrete now. Fingers grab his hair and pull his head up. His brain is spinning with bright light.

"Listen, you Ivy League fuck! If I see one word about me in that book or anyplace else, I'll find you and burn your house down with your girlfriend inside. Do you understand me?"

Even if Garrett wanted to answer, he couldn't; his mouth is no longer working. His head is rammed onto the concrete.

And then everything goes black.

CHAPTER 25

The man occasionally known as Jack Doohan watches the whole thing through his spotting scope as he munches an energy bar. Impressive. He knows a professional tune-up when he sees one—it will cause severe pain and bruising but no permanent damage.

As Doohan zooms in, the guy whips out a cell phone. Jack reads his lips: "Yeah, it's me," he says. "That asshole writer was just here asking about Suzanne. I think it's time our man confesses." He ends the call and ducks back inside.

After about half a minute, the subject Wilson starts moving. Then crawling. Lucky man—looks like he kept all his teeth.

Through his scope, Doohan follows Wilson as he stands up and staggers back to his car.

The question is, what's Wilson doing here in the first place? And whose feathers did he just ruffle? What does this pissant joint in a shit-ass corner of Rhode Island have to do with Cole Wright's shady past?

It's a golden opportunity. Wilson is in a weakened state. With a little encouragement, he'd probably start blabbing the whole story and give up all his leads.

But those are not Doohan's orders.

Observe and record.

He watches as Wilson pulls open his car door and slides inside. The engine starts up.

Doohan gets to his feet and heads for his own vehicle.

Where's this preppy punching bag going next?

CHAPTER 26

Outside Hanover, New Hampshire

After the phone call with Ellen Layton, I get back into Garrett's Subaru and start heading south on I-91. Garrett and I agreed to meet up tonight back home in Connecticut.

I try calling Garrett. No good. His phone must be on DND.

The traffic starts moving. Finally.

My phone rings on the dash. Boston area code, but I don't recognize the number. I accept the call. "Hello, this is Brea."

Static. "Hello?" More static. Then: "Piece-of-shit phone… hello, is this Brea Cooke?" A woman's voice, agitated.

"Yes!" I'm shouting in the car now. "Who is this?"

The woman shouts back, "This is Teresa Bonanno! Suzanne's sister!"

I check my rearview and swing into the right lane. "Hold on, Teresa!" I spot a gas station off the next exit. "Give me a few seconds." I pull into a parking space and turn off the engine. "Teresa, I'm here. What's up?"

"I got something for you," she says. "You know Amber? The girl who Suzanne was gonna move in with before she went away?"

"Right. Amber. What about her?"

"Well, her name's not Amber anymore. But she's back in Boston. I know where she works."

Teresa sounds relatively coherent, if a little edgy. And this seems like a terrific lead. I grab a pad and pen out of the center console. "Go ahead, Teresa. I'm ready."

"Hold on, now," says Teresa. "Finding isn't giving. If you want the information, it's gonna cost you five hundred bucks. You give me that, I'll give you the name."

Right. And violate a basic rule of journalism. I can practically feel my Ethics in Communications professor staring at me from the car's back seat. "Teresa. You know we can't pay for information. It would damage our credibility. And yours too."

Teresa says, her voice steely, "I need that money, Brea. And you need that name."

I rack my brain, trying to find a way to get her to give me the name. Then I flash on a detail from my initial research. "Teresa, I read that the New England Patriots offered a ten-thousand-dollar reward for information that led to the arrest of the person responsible for your sister's disappearance."

The phone is fumbled, then Teresa is back. "They did? Really? That offer still good?"

Who knows? I'm honestly just spitballing now, throwing stuff out there, hoping something will stick. "You tell me, Teresa—do you think the Patriots, noble citizens of New England that they are, would renege on an offer like that? About one of their own cheerleaders?"

Frankly, I don't know what the Patriots would do, but it's enough to convince Teresa.

CHAPTER

27

Boston, Massachusetts

Three hours later, with a name embedded in my brain, I pull up to the curb across from a bar in South Boston, a brick and stone pub called the Lord Mayor's.

I have to admit, my neck hairs are prickling a bit. It's an involuntary response. This used to be enemy territory for people with my skin color. They say things have changed. We'll see.

I step forward and grab the big brass handle on the oak door. Deep breath. I swing the door open and step in.

I'm blasted by a rush of warm air and the sound of loud Irish music. It's coming from a trio in the corner: a tall, skinny fiddler, a small guy with a drum in his lap, and a huge man playing a penny whistle. The six-holed woodwind looks like a toothpick in his large hands.

I scan the crowd as I make my way toward the bar. I'm not the only Black person in the place. We're outnumbered, for sure, but everybody seems to be having a great time. When I sit down, I start to relax. A little.

Working the far end of the bar is a burly redheaded guy in a collared shirt and a green vest. The bartender nearest me is a tall woman wearing skintight jeans and a black tank top printed with the Lord Mayor's logo. Her dark hair is cropped short and streaked with purple. She looks to be around forty but has the figure of a much younger woman.

"Lillian!" A waitress is calling to her from behind the service rail. "I need two Guinnesses!"

Lillian. The name Teresa gave me. This must be her. The former Amber Keenan.

The bartender draws two perfect pints from the tap and slides them down the bar. She sets a coaster in front of me, then leans forward to make herself heard over the music. "What can I get you?"

"Hennessy neat," I call back. She grabs a tulip glass from the overhead rack with one hand and the Hennessy bottle with the other and pours my drink in record time. "Enjoy!"

I swirl my cognac in the glass, take a sip, and let the warmth wash through me. What I need is an opening. And a little quiet. But the Irish music is still pumping from the corner, and the buzz of the crowd is getting louder. I sip my drink and wait.

Just as I take my last swallow, my luck changes.

The music stops. The man with the penny whistle quiets the applause by leaning into the microphone. "Thanks, folks. We'll be taking a short break now. See you soon!"

I turn toward the band and join the applause. When I turn back, the bartender's there.

"Another Hennessy?"

I shake my head. No time to waste. "Actually, I came here to talk to Amber."

She freezes. The smile melts. Her eyes turn cold. She looks up and down the bar, then back at me, and says in a low voice, "Who are you?"

The words tumble out. "My name is Brea Cooke. I'm working on a book. It involves Suzanne Bonanno."

She turns and grabs the Hennessy bottle. This time, her hands shake a little as she pours it into my glass.

I try to stop her. "No, I don't need—"

"Be quiet," she says under her breath. "Pretend you're a normal patron and that this is a normal interaction. In two minutes, take your drink to the booth marked 'reserved' in the back. I'll meet you there."

"You promise?"

"That's what I said."

She turns her smile back on and draws another round of beers. I see her catch the eye of the redheaded bartender and give him a hand signal. He nods. She ducks under the bar's service rail and disappears.

I lay some cash on the bar and pick up my glass. I walk through the crowd until I spot an empty booth with a card reading RESERVED. I slide in. And pray.

A minute later, the former cheerleader slides onto the bench across from me. "Did they find Suzanne's body?"

That's her first question. I definitely have the right person.

I shake my head. "No. To the rest of the world, Suzanne is nothing but a missing person in a cold case. What do you remember about her, Amber?"

"Lillian," she mutters with a tight smile. "Call me Lillian."

"Yes. Lillian. Sorry."

"Sure," she says. "Suzanne was great. A lot of fun. Suzanne dating Cole was an open secret on the cheerleading squad. But we were a sisterhood. Nobody would have said anything. Besides, it's not like she was the only rule-breaker."

"How do you mean?"

She folds her hands on the table. "I mean, you're in your early twenties, young and pretty, and looking to blow off steam with a hunk pulling down a major paycheck."

"And you just hope you don't get caught."

"Right. Just a little innocent fun. Plenty of us did it. Maybe to make up for the fact that we were being paid less than the team mascot. A lot of girls were waiting tables to make ends meet. Most of us were just enjoying the exposure and looking for a way out."

"But Suzanne already had another job possibility, right?"

"Yeah. With Fidelity. After she disappeared, things weren't the same. I took off to Virginia and got my union card. Electrician."

"So why aren't you running wires right now?" I ask.

"Construction dried up. So I went to bartending school in Virginia Beach, got some experience. I always liked Boston. I just needed to come back as somebody else."

"Is that when you changed your name?"

"Yup. New name. Less hair. I had an aunt Lillian. Died when I was five."

"Why didn't you hang around to talk to the police after Suzanne disappeared? You must've known you'd be a valuable witness."

"I always thought Cole was behind it and that the cops would get him. That was before he was released from the Pats, became a famous political figure, and got off scot-free."

"Lillian, what was Cole Wright like? I mean, back when he and Suzanne were dating."

She stares at the table. I can feel her choosing her words. "Ninety percent of the time, Cole seemed smart, funny, kind. A good guy."

"And the other ten percent?"

"If he'd been drinking a lot or lost a game or if the coaches were riding him, his temper came out, along with his prima donna complex. He thought he was entitled to anything he wanted. Anything."

"He get rough with people?"

"Sometimes."

"With Suzanne?"

"They had some fights. I know that for a fact." She looks at the band, who are picking up their instruments for a second set. "I gotta get back to work."

"Lillian. *Amber.* What are you keeping from me?"

She says in a low voice, "Are you really gonna investigate Cole Wright, the First Gentleman of the United States? Are you really after the truth? Because nobody else was."

"I am. That's why I'm here." I see her biting her lip. I lean in. "You know something."

She's quiet for a few seconds. Then: "Near the end of the season, the Pats were supposed to crush the Steelers. Instead, they got their balls kicked in. The after-party turned into a wake. Lots of booze, some guys fighting, really bad energy. Dark. Dangerous."

"You were there?"

She nods. "So was Suzanne. And Cole. But the team brass was around, so they were pretending not to be together. Cole was hanging out more with me."

I hear the drum pounding from the corner. The fiddle answers.

"Lillian!" a waitress calls.

"I gotta go," she says.

"Can we talk again?" I ask.

"Give me your number. I'll call you."

I get the feeling she's been wanting somebody to talk to for a long time. I scrawl my digits on a napkin and hand it to her. She tucks it into her jeans pocket.

I take her arm and squeeze it lightly. "I need you. Suzanne needs you."

She's sniffling now. She says, her voice shaky, "After all this time, I do want justice." She wipes her eyes with the back of her hand. The fiddle music is rising in pitch and urgency. She leans close and whispers in my ear, "That night after the Steelers game?" she says. "That's when I learned the truth about Cole Wright."

CHAPTER 28

Litchfield, Connecticut

Between brutal traffic on the Mass Pike and a slowdown on every back road in Connecticut, what should have been a three-hour drive is closer to four and a half. I text Garrett a few times from the road, letting him know my ETA. All I get back is K.

The little farmhouse we're renting is outside of Litchfield on five acres not far from the Topsmead State Forest. It's an hour drive to the Yale campus, but Garrett felt this need to be isolated from the world, so here we are.

As I turn into our winding driveway—more like a dirt road, really—I can see lights on in the living room. There's a strange car parked by the barn. Oh, right. Garrett's rental.

He's home!

I park the Subaru out front and hurry inside. "Garrett? You here?"

I see a hand wave from the top of the sofa. I walk around and put down my bag.

And then I freeze.

Garrett's lying under a thin blanket. The right side of his face is bruised and swollen. His forehead is scraped. Bloody washcloths are piled on the wood floor.

I drop to my knees and put my hand on his shoulder. My heart is pounding. "Garrett! What happened? Can you talk?"

"I can talk," he says. "But my jaw hurts."

"Jesus! Were you in an accident?"

"Yeah," he mumbles. "My face collided with Tony Romero's fist."

I grit my teeth. "That mother—Did you call the police?"

Garrett shakes his head. I run my hand down his side. He flinches in pain. His ribs! I move the blanket and pull up his shirt. His whole torso is purple.

"You need to get to a hospital. I'm calling 911." I pull my phone from my bag. Garrett grabs it out of my hand.

"No!" he says. "I'll be fine."

"You could have internal bleeding!"

"If I start spitting up blood, I'll go. I drove home like this. Leave it."

"Don't move," I tell him. I grab a roll of paper towels from the kitchen and a bottle of isopropyl alcohol from the bathroom. "You think anything's broken?" I ask.

He shakes his head. "I cracked a rib playing soccer in high school. This doesn't feel like that."

I pour some alcohol on a paper towel and start wiping the crusted blood off his forehead. "Did that son of a bitch Romero say anything useful before he started pounding on you?"

"He did. He gave me another reason to suspect Cole Wright." Garrett pulls my hand away from his head and asks, "What did you find out? About the college reporter?"

"Well, the college reporter died in Afghanistan, but he told a friend about the assault after the homecoming game—and named Cole Wright as the girl's attacker."

Garrett groans as he sits up. "Great. But that's all hearsay. We need something more solid. Something firsthand."

I put down the paper towel. "I might have it."

"How? Who?"

"Remember Teresa? Suzanne's sister?"

"Hard to forget."

"She managed to track down Suzanne's old roommate. Living in Southie."

"You found Amber Keenan?"

"She's Lillian now. Working in an Irish bar. Our talk got cut short, but she promised to call me with more information."

"Brea. This could be it. It would establish a pattern!"

I can see Garrett focusing through the pain. I stroke his cheek—the one that's not all beat up. "You want some Tylenol?"

"I already took twice the daily limit. I just need to lie still." He groans again as he eases back down on the sofa.

Night is falling; I look out the window and see empty fields and the woods on the far side of the road. For the first time, the view creeps me out. I pull the drapes tight.

I didn't see anybody.

That doesn't mean there's nobody out there.

CHAPTER 29

Boston, Massachusetts

Lillian glances at her face in the rearview mirror of her battered Corolla. Sometimes, she's amazed at how completely she's left Amber Keenan, with her twenty-four-inch waist and blond-streaked cheerleader mane, behind.

But now it's time for her to emerge again.

"You hid Lizzie!"

"Did not!"

In the back seat, Lillian's nine-year-old, Susan, is accusing her eight-year-old brother, Shane, of taking her favorite doll.

"We'll find Lizzie tomorrow, I promise," Lillian says when she brakes at a stoplight. "Remember where we're going right now?"

At this, both kids perk up.

The Stop and Run is one of the places that stocks their favorite treat, Hoodsie Cups, a perfect split of chocolate and vanilla ice cream enjoyed with a small wooden spoon.

In spite of all the sugar, Hoodsie Cups calm the kids down. Lillian figures that by the time she gets them home, they'll both be out. All she'll have to do is wrangle them into their beds.

Lillian is exhausted, her feet aching and ears ringing from her double shift at the bar. The music isn't her style, but she likes the crowd. And her neighbor Jasmine is kind enough to look after the kids on late nights.

At the next traffic light, the engine rattles hard enough to vibrate the steering wheel. Lillian smiles.

She won't be driving this shitbox much longer.

In fact, her whole life is about to change.

Thanks to Brea Cooke.

She can hardly believe how it just fell into her lap. After all these years of tending bar, it's easy to sense what people are looking for, what they really need. And Brea Cooke was no different. Lillian knew the kind of stuff she wanted to hear. And she gave it to her, all tied up in a pretty bow.

This has been a long time coming. Her payback.

The facts don't matter anymore. All she has to do is make the accusation. Brea will put it in a bestselling book. Fox and social media will take care of the rest.

When she calls Brea tomorrow, she'll give her some grisly details. Juicy stuff. And then... *boom.*

Cole Wright will sweat and protest and plead his innocence, but in the end, his fancy lawyers will suggest an out-of-court settlement, just to keep things quiet. Even if they never get him for Suzanne, even if Cole never goes to jail, Lillian figures she'll be set for life.

The weird thing is, she doesn't feel guilty about it, not at all. Is it her fault that NFL cheerleaders were, and are, paid crap and treated like sex objects? Is it her fault that work in Virginia dried up? Is it her fault that her asshole ex-husband is months behind with child-support payments?

No, damn it. She's been struggling for years. And the struggle is about to end. For her. And for her kids.

"We're here!" Susan shouts from the back.

Lillian pulls into the nearly empty parking lot. She unfastens her seat belt, turns around, and points first to one kid, then the other. "I'll be right back. You two behave, hear me?"

The kids start chanting, "We want Hoodsies! We want Hoodsies!"

Lillian can still hear them after she closes the door and clicks the lock. She walks to the front door and pulls it open. A little bell chimes.

She heads for the cooler in the corner and slides the cover open. It's filled with Nutty Buddies, Creamsicles, and Snickers Ice Cream Bars. One whole section is stacked with Hoodsies. She grabs two cups and heads for the counter.

Usually, Lillian spends a few dollars on a scratch ticket, but not tonight. Tonight she's already hit the jackpot.

"Hey, Larry, how's it going? Your dad got you working nights again?"

Larry is a pimply teenager who's here almost every time Lillian comes in. Friendly kid.

But now he's not saying a word.

Lillian puts the ice cream on the counter and starts fishing for cash in her purse. When she comes up with a ten, Larry keeps his hands flat on the counter. He still hasn't said anything. Hasn't made a move to ring her up.

Lillian notices that Larry's lower lip is trembling and that his face is pale under the fluorescents. He looks like he's about to throw up.

"You okay there, Larry?"

Two masked men in black stand up from behind the counter. They're both holding pistols, so small they almost look like toys.

"Hi, Lillian," one says.

"Hi, Amber," says the other.

She feels a quick stab of fear. Then a powerful blow.

Then nothing.

CHAPTER 30

The White House

President Madeline Wright and Burton Pearce are on the third floor of the White House in the family quarters.

Early in her administration, the president learned that due to renovations of the gym in the Eisenhower Executive Office Building, Burton had been exercising at a public facility five blocks away.

"Waste of time," Maddy had told him. "Come to the residence. We'll exercise together in the workout room, just the two of us. Cole never uses it." And they've done this almost every morning since; it's become their little ritual.

Still wearing their workout gear, they breakfast on coffee, juice, oatmeal, and cinnamon rolls. Pearce peels off a chunk of pastry and pops it into his mouth. "Damn it. I just burned off five hundred calories, and now I'm putting three hundred right back."

"So you're still ahead," says Maddy. She takes a sip of her coffee. "What's up with our little pot-stirrers?"

"Who?"

"The journalists. The ones writing the book."

"Still poking around, but under control." Pearce pushes the pastry plate away and brushes a few crumbs off his T-shirt. "How's the vice president?"

"Rough," says Maddy. "Still fighting an infection along with the chemo. He's lucid, though he's struggling with pain and fatigue. But something he said concerns me."

"What's that?" asks Pearce.

"He told me to be careful, Burton. That I was in danger of being betrayed by somebody I trusted. *Sabotage.* That's the word he used."

Pearce leans back in his seat. "Disloyalty in the ranks. That's been the worry of every president since Washington. But there's no reason to believe that now. Maybe somebody's planting thoughts in Faulkner's head while he's loopy on pain meds."

Maddy looks up. Something clicks.

Rachel Bernstein.

CHAPTER 31

National Mall

Let Maddy and Burton have their stuffy little White House gym, Cole thinks. He much prefers being out in the open air.

Beside him this morning on the National Mall is Secret Service agent Doug Lambert. Slim, dark-haired, and nondescript, an agent right out of central casting, Lambert's wearing sweats and running shoes, a Yankees baseball cap, and a loose black jacket that conceals a small arsenal and a compact communications system. "Detail is ready, sir."

"Hang on a minute," says Cole. "How's your daughter settling in at Dartmouth?"

Lambert smiles. "Doing great, sir. I want to thank you again for—"

Cole holds up a hand. "I was happy to make the call. Carrie had the grades and everything else. Besides, I figure the trustees at Dartmouth still owe me something for my eleven-and-one season back in the day, don't you think?"

Lambert smiles. “Yes, sir. Thanks again, sir.”

“No problem, Doug.” Cole bends down to tighten his laces. “But now I need a little favor from you.”

“I’ll do whatever I can, sir.”

“That evening run on the Mall the other night? Leanne was with me.”

“Right. I stayed in the vehicle.”

“We ran into some folks near the Tidal Basin.”

“Football fans. You signed some autographs.”

Cole pulls out his iPhone, selects a photo, and enlarges one section. “I took this picture as we were leaving.”

Once, at a campaign stop in Iowa, a woman threw a cabbage at Cole. It was Doug Lambert who’d knocked it down in midair. Cole has had a special connection with him ever since. He knows he can trust him.

“See this young woman, the one right there in the middle? I think she could be a threat.”

“A threat? To you, sir? Or to the president?”

“Maybe both. We need to identify her.”

“Let me get my laptop, sir, and I’ll start the process—”

“No,” says Cole. “Nothing official. I don’t want to worry the president.”

“I can start with facial recognition and see if I get any hits.”

“Good,” says Cole. He pats Lambert on the back. “Start there. I’ll send the picture to your personal phone.” Then he starts pumping his legs on the path. “Now let’s get going!”

“Yes, sir.” Lambert speaks into his collar mic. “Sage on the way.”

Cole feels a sense of relief. At least he’s put things in motion. Better safe than sorry.

The woman in the photo could just be your everyday Capitol nut.

Or she could be the tip of a very dangerous iceberg.

* * *

Cole Wright is slipping into the zone, working up a healthy sweat; his muscles have warmed up and the endorphins are starting to kick in. This is his happy place. Always has been.

Agent Lambert sets a good pace. They're approaching the Tidal Basin. No crowd today. Too early.

Suddenly, Cole hears a flurry of chatter from the agents behind him. He turns his head and sees them talking into their shirtsleeves.

One of the agents catches up with Cole and taps his arm. "Slow up a bit, please, sir."

Cole reduces his pace. "What's the problem?"

Then he looks back down the path and sees another cluster of runners heading their way. He hears his wife's code name, Sierra.

He smiles.

Maddy is running in the middle of the pack, surrounded by her own detail. A few seconds later, she's right beside him. "Hi, stranger. Do you own this park, or is anybody welcome?"

Cole grins at Maddy. "Don't worry. I know the lady who runs the place."

Now the two details blend to form a protective cocoon around them both. It reminds Cole of taking laps with the whole NFL team.

"I need a favor," says Maddy.

"You spent all this hard-earned taxpayer money just to ask me for something?"

"You're in a more receptive mood when you're out in nature."

"Wow," says Cole. "This must be one ugly ask."

"Senator Balquière, Louisiana," she says, her voice slightly lower. "I think he's ready to come over to our side."

"Balquière? He's a party leader for the opposition!"

"It's taken some work," says Maddy, "but he's starting to think like an American, not a politician. Now he needs a sweetener, and that's you."

"How sweet?" asks Cole. "And how far?"

"Baton Rouge," says Maddy. "Small high school. The senator's grandson is on the football team and they're having a god-awful season. One of your inspirational talks could make a difference."

"How bad a season?"

"Eight losses. No wins. Dead last in the league."

"Christ," says Cole, shaking his head. "I'll need my A material."

After another half a mile, Cole hears fresh chatter from the agents around them. When he looks up at the path ahead, he sees the presidential limousine—the Beast—waiting between two armored Suburbans. Agents in dark suits are spaced around the vehicles, scanning the area. One has his hand on the open rear door of the limo.

"My ride's here," says Maddy. "Want a lift?"

"I'm gonna do another couple miles," says Cole. "But thanks for the offer."

Maddy slows down as they get closer to the curb. She grabs Cole's sleeve and pulls him to a stop. "Cole, your visit could help break the last logjam. Getting an old warhorse like Balquière on board is a huge step toward saving this country and making history."

Cole sees a few reporters from the press pool waiting near a van behind the Suburbans. They edge forward as Maddy and Cole get close. Maddy gives them a wave and a smile. "No remarks, guys. Just a friendly run with my husband."

Cole hugs her around the waist and quickly kisses her on the lips. He hears the cameras snapping.

Maddy slides into the car, shielded by three Secret Service agents. She looks straight at Cole and mouths *Thank you.*

Just before the eighty-pound door slams shut, he waves. As the small caravan pulls away with the press van behind them, Cole nods at Lambert. “Let’s go, Doug.” All around him, Cole hears the agents chatter: “Sage on the move.”

Maddy made special arrangements to visit him on his run. His usual response to her requests for these small-time pep talks is “I was a player, not a coach.” But he knows how important this next week is for her. For the whole damn country.

CHAPTER

32

Litchfield, Connecticut

The buzz of a cell phone wakes me. It's not my phone, it's Garrett's. I check the screen—O'Halloran—and pass it to Garrett. "It's your detective friend."

Poor Garrett. He had a rough night. Every move made him groan in pain. The towel I put over his pillow is streaked and splotchy with blood from the wound on his forehead.

He sits up, wincing and grabbing his side. "Eddie! Let me put you on speaker. I've got my partner, Brea, right here." He taps the screen. "Go ahead. What were you saying?"

The voice on the other end is gruff, with a thick Boston accent. "My buddy, a detective who covers Southie, called me about a homicide they caught late last night. Single mom took two to the forehead."

My stomach starts to cramp.

O'Halloran clears his throat. "The victim's license was from out of state. Virginia. Name on it was Lillian Brady. They checked with her neighbor, then with the police down in Virginia Beach.

Court records show a name change. Turns out Lillian Brady was Amber Keenan. They have a witness, a store clerk, who says one of the shooters called her Amber."

Screams rise in my throat and I clutch a blanket. Did my visit with Amber somehow lead to her death?

"Her two kids were outside in the car when it happened," says O'Halloran.

Garrett goes into reporter mode. "So maybe she stumbled into the middle of a robbery."

"No," says the detective. "Clerk says they were waiting for her. This was a hit, pure and simple."

"What about the shooters?"

"Masks. Pros. They even took the ejected cartridges."

I put down the blanket and lean toward the phone. "Detective, this is Brea Cooke. I talked to Amber Keenan yesterday about the Suzanne Bonanno case."

"What? Where?"

"At the bar in Southie where she worked."

"And did you get anything out of her?"

"I did. But not the whole story. She was supposed to call me to follow up today."

"Well, it might not have mattered."

"Why is that?" asks Garrett.

"Because I got another news flash for the two of you," says O'Halloran. "Somebody just confessed to Suzanne Bonanno's murder."

CHAPTER 33

The White House

In his West Wing office, just a few steps from the Oval, Burton Pearce checks his desk clock. Rachel Bernstein, chief of staff for the vice president, is ten minutes late.

Playing the game.

Sitting on Pearce's desk is a framed photo of President-Elect Madeline Wright taking the oath of office. Cole is holding the Jefferson Bible with a big, proud smile on his face. Pearce is two rows back, behind the outgoing president. He remembers how full his heart felt that day. How far the three of them had come since they were Dartmouth undergrads living in a rickety off-campus student residence dreaming of the future.

His intercom buzzes. "Yes?"

He hears the voice of his assistant, Pam Hitchcock. "Ms. Bernstein is here."

"Good," he says. "Wait exactly three minutes, then send her in."

"Yes, sir."

Two can play this game, he thinks. In fact, everybody in Washington plays this game.

Pearce picks up the framed photo. Behind the chief justice is the newly sworn-in vice president, Ransom Faulkner. And right over his shoulder is Rachel Bernstein. Faulkner's former campaign manager—and, as of that bright January morning, chief of staff—knew the powerful symbolism of clothing. Bernstein had chosen a gray dress so dark, it looked like funereal black.

Burton turns the photo so it will be right in Bernstein's face when she sits down. Then he folds his hands and watches his clock. Two minutes...three...

A quick knock. Pam Hitchcock holds the door open as Bernstein storms through, wafting her expensive fragrance. Her burgundy dress and matching manicure complement her shiny dark hair and flashing green eyes. No question she's an attractive woman—and an angry one.

"What is it, Burton?" she asks. "I've got a legislative meeting in ten minutes."

"It'll wait," says Pearce. "Sit."

Bernstein perches on the edge of a cushioned chair. Pearce sees her glance at the photo. It's hard to miss. Point made.

In meetings like this, time is power. And Pearce has all the time in the world. He rocks back in his chair and puts his feet up on his desk. "How's the vice president today?"

Bernstein stares. "You know I can't—"

"Screw that HIPAA bullshit, Rachel. You know it doesn't apply here. How is he?"

Pearce sees Bernstein's cheeks flush. She's mad. But he knows she didn't get this far without being able to control her temper. "He's holding his own," she says curtly. "The infection is better, but the chemo is debilitating. The next few weeks will be key."

"They're taking good care of him at Walter Reed? If there's any problem, I can make a call—"

"Thanks," says Bernstein. "So can I."

Pearce slides his feet off the desk and positions himself so that he and his guest are eye to eye. "Rachel, I've heard that the vice president may be spreading baseless rumors that someone is trying to sabotage the president."

Bernstein's expression doesn't shift. She doesn't even blink.

"Listen, Rachel. I remember the convention, how upset you were when your boss agreed to take the VP spot."

"Agreed? I'd say he was forced."

"Let's play it this way," says Pearce, his voice level and calm. "All rumors, all remarks—whether they're coming from the vice president's hospital room or your office across the street—are to stop."

"I don't work for you," says Bernstein.

"I didn't say you did. But anything and everything that involves this administration belongs to me. I own it."

"You don't own *me*."

"Maybe not. But I can make it hard for you to get your job done. So hard that you might start considering one of those lucrative offers you're getting from the private sector."

Bernstein is smiling now. Pretty smile. Perfect teeth.

"Let's play it *this* way," she says softly. "In my position, I don't know everything, but I know a lot. And from what Vice President Faulkner has said in the hospital, I know that you and the president are working on a legislative deal that's highly compartmentalized. I know it involves entitlements. I know enough to put some activist bloggers on the case. With the right poke, the whole thing will pop like a balloon. So stop threatening me. It makes you look small."

Pearce digs the fingernails of his right hand into his left palm.

A trick for managing his anger. "We're done here," he says. "Go to your meeting."

Bernstein picks up the inauguration photo. She turns it around so it faces Pearce again. "I like this office, Burton," she says, standing up and smoothing her dress over her hips. "And I'll do what I have to do to make it mine."

CHAPTER 34

Rhode Island Maximum Security Prison

According to former Boston PD detective Eddie O'Halloran, an inmate named John DeMarco had confessed to killing Suzanne Bonanno.

Actually, what DeMarco did was brag about the killing to another inmate, so *confessed* seemed like a strong word. That inmate owed a favor to Eddie and tipped him off, after which Eddie got Garrett approved for a prison visit.

So Garrett is here. Only one visitor is allowed, but that's not a problem, since Brea is going back to Seabrook on a mission of her own.

Garrett shows his ID multiple times and goes through two metal detectors, a pat-down, and a wanding. He leaves his keys, wallet, change, and phone in a locker. He tries to hold on to his pen, but a corrections officer shakes his head. "Ever see a guy with a Bic through his brain?"

As he waits, Garrett runs through the facts O'Halloran gave him about the convict he is about to meet. DeMarco is doing time for aggravated assault, weapons possession, and armed robbery. And it's not his first stretch as a guest of the Ocean State.

"Is he connected?" Garrett asked.

"Slightly," said O'Halloran. DeMarco was a soldier in what was left of Boston's Angiulo crime family. "Not really a family anymore," O'Halloran said. "More like a few distant cousins trying to resurrect the good old days. They don't scam a gift card without a nod from the Providence Mob."

Garrett moves through security into the visitors' room, where he's surrounded by gray concrete walls and guards with guns. At octagonal orange tables, inmates in khaki pants and smock-like shirts sit across from wives, girlfriends, children, or social workers in street clothes.

A loud buzzer sounds, and a metal door on the far side of the room slides open. A uniformed corrections officer steps into the room, followed by a thickset inmate with tattooed arms. A second corrections officer points to Garrett. The inmate locks his eyes on him as he walks over. Even from a distance, he projects menace.

When he gets to the table, the inmate stands with legs spread. "You Wilson?"

Garrett nods. "John DeMarco?"

DeMarco sits down heavily across from Garrett, arms on the table. One of the corrections officers steps up and goes through the interview protocol until DeMarco waves him away.

The inmate angles his head for a better look at the right side of Garrett's face. "The fuck happened to you?"

Garrett reflexively touches his stinging cheekbone. "Fell in my driveway."

"Yeah, right," says DeMarco. He smirks.

"Thanks for agreeing to talk to me," says Garrett.

"I'm tired of talking to cops," says DeMarco. "Thought this might be more interesting."

Garrett digs right in. "Mr. DeMarco, I'm here because you talked to another inmate about murdering a young woman named Suzanne Bonanno seventeen years ago. A cheerleader for the Patriots."

DeMarco blinks, then smiles. His teeth are big, blocky, and stained yellow. "I might have."

"Might have said it? Or might have done it?"

DeMarco asks, "Ever move into a new neighborhood, Wilson?"

"Yeah, sure. Many times."

DeMarco waves one inked-up forearm arm around the room. "Well, this is my new neighborhood. And sometimes in a new neighborhood, you say things to impress your new neighbors."

Suddenly, this visit is looking like another wild-goose chase. "So this is all bullshit," mutters Garrett. He starts to signal to one of the guards.

"Put your damn hand down," growls DeMarco. "Lady who took two to the head last night in Southie was what made me think of it. I hear she used to be a Patriots cheerleader too." A pause. "I did see Suzanne Bonanno once."

Garrett leans across the table. "Where was that?"

"Gillette Stadium. Pats were playing the Jets. I had good seats. Great view of the cheerleaders. I noticed her. Suzanne. Fantastic body. Hotter than hell. Later, I got her name off a poster."

"Ever meet her?"

"Meet her? Fat chance. They guard those girls better than they guard us in here. I never got closer than fifty yards from Suzanne Bonanno. Never touched her." He licks his thin lips. "Except in my luscious wet dreams."

That does it. Garrett's bruises are beginning to throb. He shifts in his seat, ready to stand up. "Right. Okay. Thanks for wasting my time."

"You know what?" says DeMarco. "You suck as a journalist."

"Why is that?"

"Because you don't seem to be after the truth."

Garrett is irritated. His patience is drained. "Sorry, I'm not following."

DeMarco lowers his voice and says in a near whisper, "You asked me if I killed Suzanne Bonanno. I said no." He looks from side to side. "You never asked me if I know who did."

CHAPTER 35

What kind of game is DeMarco playing? Garrett thinks, then asks, "You know who killed Suzanne Bonanno?"

"That's right. And I also know where her body is buried."

"Why should I believe you?"

DeMarco smiles again. "*Integrity Gone. Stolen Honor.*"

Garrett feels a weird tingle. This creep knows his books?

"Don't look so surprised, Wilson. I've got nothing but time in here. I read a lot, nonfiction mostly. I recognized your name when I saw it on the visitor request. Figured somebody with your skills might be able to help me."

"Help you how?"

"Help me get out of here."

"And why would I do that?"

"'Cause I think you're working on another book, and I can help you finish it."

"Sorry. I already have a collaborator."

"I'm gonna give you another one. I got a PI in Boston working on evidence to get some of my convictions thrown out. Cut some years off my time. Maybe spring me altogether. You work with him, get me some relief, and I'll give you what you need."

From his time at the *Globe* following cops around for years, Garrett knows every PI from Charlestown to Fenway Park, good and bad. "Who is it?" he asks. "Who do you have working for you?"

"Seymour Washington," says DeMarco.

That's the last name Garrett wants to hear.

CHAPTER 36

Seabrook, New Hampshire

Felicia Bonanno's double-wide looks even smaller than it did the first time I was here. I can smell Lestoil and Pledge, evidence that she tidied up when I called to say I was coming. I wanted to get here early, before she heard the news about Amber. I'm not about to tell her anything that the guy who confessed said, not until I get some kind of confirmation from Garrett.

Felicia puts a basket of muffins on the coffee table, then sits down across from me with two mugs—tea for her, black coffee for me.

"Felicia, have the police called you this morning?"

"No." Then she goes white. She puts down her mug, her hand trembling. "Why? Did they find something? About Suzanne?"

I lean over and rest my hand on her knee. "Felicia, there was a shooting last night in Boston. A murder. The woman who was killed was Amber Keenan."

"Suzanne's friend?" Felicia says, clearly shocked. "I never met Amber. Only talked to her that once on the phone. But I know she and Suzanne were good friends. They looked out for each other. Do they know who did it?"

"There were two shooters last night. The police are still looking for them."

Suddenly, she stands up. "Brea, come. I want to show you something." She reaches for my hand. I put down my coffee and follow her down the narrow hallway to the back of the trailer.

We stop in front of a closed door. Felicia reaches up and runs her hand along the top of the molding. She pulls down a key, puts it in the lock, and turns it. Then she opens the door and flicks on the light.

It's a bedroom, carpeted in blue. The window shade is drawn. The walls are decorated with Patriots cheerleader posters. Over a small desk hangs a bulletin board covered with faded snapshots and newspaper clippings. Pinned in the middle is a publicity shot of Cole Wright in his Patriots uniform, helmet under his arm.

"This is her room," says Felicia. "Just how it was."

A small flat-screen TV sits on a wooden dresser, a DVD player alongside it. Felicia powers it up, then opens the top dresser drawer and pulls out a stack of thin plastic cases. "The police took all these, but they brought them back."

She inserts a silver DVD in the player.

The TV flickers, then lights up. I'm looking at a scene of Patriots cheerleaders performing a routine in an empty stadium. It must be a practice session, but the ladies are in full uniform—red, white, and blue spangled shorts and tops. And they're going full out. Kicking, dancing, strutting, beaming. The camera starts at one end of the line and pans across. These girls are clearly athletes. They also look like specimens from a glamour lab, all variations on a physical theme: Long legs. Toned bellies. Bright smiles. Thick, bouncy hair.

Felicia presses a button to freeze the frame. Then she gently taps the screen. "There she is. My baby."

Just twenty-two. I stare at her beautiful face. I've seen pictures of Suzanne Bonanno, but nothing like this. In the middle of her practice, she's radiant. Almost supernatural.

Suzanne is one of the tallest girls, positioned at the center of the formation. She appears to know exactly where the camera is, because she's looking right into it, her eyes bright and sparkling. It's like she's looking at *me*.

Felicia hits play and lets the video run another few seconds. She freezes it again. "And that's Amber."

It takes a second for me to recognize the woman with the long blond hair as the bartender I talked to yesterday. The one who's now on a slab in a Boston morgue.

The DVD cuts to show a corridor of a children's hospital. In this clip, a smaller group of cheerleaders are in street clothes in Patriots colors. Surrounding them are nurses in scrubs and smiling kids—some in wheelchairs, some holding on to rolling IV stands.

Felicia turns the sound up. Suzanne is talking to whoever's behind the camera.

"We love performing at the games, but we love being here too, with the kids, being part of the community." She turns and passes out kid-size Patriots jerseys to the young patients. She turns back and brushes a lock of hair out of her eyes. Her nails are painted Patriots blue. A tennis bracelet with gleaming red jewels sparkles on her wrist. "Games matter," says Suzanne, "but to me, this is even more important."

The camera pulls back to a wide shot. I can see Amber on the right, handing out mini-footballs, as the other cheerleaders hug the kids. When the camera pans to a local reporter, Felicia turns the video off. "And that's all I have left of Suzanne."

I wrap my arms around the grieving mother and feel her lean into my shoulder, sobbing. I'm probably violating some rule of journalistic objectivity, but screw it. I squeeze her tight. "Suzanne was a very special person," I say. "I know you really miss having her here with you."

I can feel Felicia nodding against me as her voice breaks. "I do."

As we hug in front of the dresser, I hear the front door open, then slam shut.

"Mom, you here?"

Teresa.

Felicia straightens up and grabs a tissue from a box on the dresser. She wipes her eyes and dries her nose. "In here, honey!" she calls out.

Suddenly, Teresa is in the doorway. Her eyes go cold when she sees me.

"You!" she says. I can smell booze on her breath. "What are you doing here?"

"I had more questions for your mother."

"Oh, yeah? Like the questions you had for Amber Keenan? 'Cause I just heard the news on the Boston station. It looks like whatever questions you asked her got her killed!"

CHAPTER 37

It takes Felicia about five minutes to get her daughter settled down. All Teresa can talk about is her reward and how she's not going to get it now.

"Amber gave me some very useful information," I tell Teresa. "We still need to investigate it. You putting me in touch with her was a big help."

"Didn't help me," says Teresa, accepting a mug of black coffee from Felicia. "Or her."

"Brea is trying to solve the case," Felicia says. "It's not like you have any friends down there at the Seabrook police department who are willing to help us."

Teresa is silent, tapping her coffee mug with her lacquered nails.

"I know we're all shocked about Amber right now," I say. "But I need to ask you both about somebody Suzanne was dating before she started seeing Cole Wright."

"You mean fancy Tony?" says Teresa, looking up.

"Tony Romero, yes."

I look over at Felicia. Her expression brightens. "Oh, Tony! What a charmer!"

Charmer, I think. *Right. The charmer who just beat my partner to a pulp.*

"Tony loved to buy me gifts," says Felicia. "And Suzanne too. Even Teresa. I think Teresa had a little crush on him, right, honey?"

"Mom! I was just a high-school kid!"

"Well, didn't Tony take you along on some of their dates? Down to Seabrook Beach? Treat you nice?"

Teresa glances down again. She looks embarrassed. "Yeah. Sometimes."

"For a while," says Felicia, "I thought Tony might be the one, but something happened."

Interesting. "Did Suzanne say anything at the time?"

I can see Felicia searching her memory. "I disagreed with her decision to break it off with Tony. He's Italian, just like our family. That's important."

"Then Cole Wright came along," says Teresa bitterly.

"That's right," says Felicia. "It almost seemed like he was waiting for Suzanne to be free. And a few weeks after they met, Suzanne started looking for apartments in Boston. Amber had an apartment in Mission Hill, and she needed a new roommate. It was supposed to be the start of a new chapter."

There's nothing more to say.

Teresa picks up her car keys and walks out. I need to get back to Garrett, find out what he learned from the inmate in Cranston. It could bring peace to this broken family. "I'm sorry, Felicia. I should go too." I give her a strong hug. "Thank you for showing me the video of Suzanne. That's the way I'd like to remember her."

"Me too," says Felicia.

When I head down the front steps, I see Teresa starting to pull out.

I walk right in front of her car.

She brakes hard. "Hey!"

"Teresa, I need to ask you something. How did you know where I'd find Amber?"

She's irritated, impatient. "I was FaceTiming with a friend from Virginia Beach. Her brother knew Amber down there in electrician school, right before she changed her name to Lillian. My friend heard that she'd been a cheerleader. And she knew that my sister had been one too. That's why she brought her up. Said she was working in an Irish bar in Southie. Eventually, I found a bartender with the right name."

"And did you tell anybody else up here about Amber? About what her new name was? About where she was working?"

"Nope. Just you."

"Well, somebody found out."

Teresa taps the steering wheel. "So. You and your boyfriend getting any closer to nailing Cole Wright?"

What can I say? "You'll know when we do."

"Well, get busy," says Teresa. "Now move!" I step aside. She puts the car in gear and pulls away.

I don't trust Teresa enough to tell her that somebody else just confessed to murdering her sister. If O'Halloran's lead pans out, Cole Wright might be in the clear—at least for that crime.

CHAPTER 38

Connecticut State Route 118

Icy rain pelts Garrett's rental car. For long stretches of the drive from Rhode Island to Connecticut, he's the only one on the road, which is good because the wipers are barely up to the task of keeping the windshield clear. It's the middle of the afternoon, but as he passes through the farmland and woods on Route 118, visibility is so poor, it might as well be night.

Garrett is in a hurry to get home and talk to Brea. In this wintry mix, driving an unfamiliar car, he won't call her and risk distracting himself with a conversation about his visit with DeMarco.

At Rhode Island Maximum Security Prison, he'd been hoping for something solid. Something provable. But all he got was an unpleasant blast from the past; it was like finding a rotten clam in a bowl of chowder.

Seymour Washington.

Garrett has known Washington a long time. The former Boston city council member, activist lawyer, and industrious private investigator whose bread and butter is insurance cases, work injuries, and slip-and-falls has never been averse to working on the dark side of the law. A lot of his clients are attorneys who advertise on late-night cable shows. But the PI is also wired in to the underbelly of Boston and beyond. He knows secrets and he has access. Through pathways unknown.

When Garrett was reporting for the *Globe*, Seymour Washington was often "a source close to the investigation." Washington had even done some research for Garrett, but Brea's distrust of the man had prompted Garrett to employ overseas hackers instead.

An oncoming pickup truck splashes slush against Garrett's side door, then disappears in his rearview. He's alone on the road again.

And then he's not.

Behind him, a car with its high beams on is coming up fast. Too fast for this weather.

Fifty yards. Then thirty.

Garrett edges closer to the shoulder.

The big vehicle is not slowing down. It's throwing off white plumes of water.

Garrett reduces his speed from fifty to forty.

The headlights are right behind him now.

"Go around, idiot!" he mutters. "Go around!"

Bam! He feels the hard jolt to his rear bumper. His car fishtails, then spins. His head bangs against the side window. He sees a blur of sky and trees, then he's flying off the road. His car rams into the side of a ditch. Garrett feels something explode in front of him and hears the loud blare of the car horn.

He takes a breath. Then another. He's covered with powder from the airbag. His cell phone has been knocked off the dashboard. It's nowhere in sight.

But he's alive.

The car is resting at a forty-five-degree angle, pressing Garrett against the driver's-side door. He sees car lights on the road above the embankment. Then, through the rain, he sees two figures stumbling down the slope.

Before he can think or register what's happening, the window on the passenger side shatters. Pebbles of glass hit him. He looks up and sees two dripping faces leaning in. Two men.

"How many hints do you need?" one of the men says. Garrett recognizes the voice. It's the bouncer from Raymond's Tavern. The hulk, Donnie.

"Tony wants this book to stop now." That's the smoker from Tony's office.

Garrett is still in shock. Hard to grasp what he's hearing.

"No more warnings," the smoker says. Garrett sees a black shape in his hand.

The hand stretches toward him. Gun!

Garrett shouts, "No!"

The blast lights up the inside of the car.

CHAPTER 39

The man calling himself Jack Doohan pulls up as the black sedan speeds away.

He steps out of his car into the sleet. Sees the fresh skid marks on the icy gravel. He walks to the shoulder and looks down into the ditch. The subject's rental car is about twenty feet below, on its side. Subject not visible.

Doohan is not sure what just happened. But based on experience, he has a pretty good idea.

For a few seconds, he stands there in the wintry mix, considering his options.

He looks back down the road and sees a vehicle headed his way. An SUV with a light bar. Not lit up. Local cop or state trooper. Probably just on patrol.

But a stopped car in this weather might draw attention. Doohan whips out his camera and snaps a picture of the subject's vehicle. Then he jumps back into his own car and pulls away from the scene.

Don't get involved.

Observe and report.

CHAPTER 40

The White House

Cole Wright is in his East Wing office with Secret Service agent Doug Lambert. It's taken Lambert only one day to determine the identity of the woman who confronted Cole on the Mall.

"Sir," he says, "Joan Cardinal is a twenty-year-old sophomore at George Washington University. Political science major who lives on campus in Thurston Hall."

"Politically active?" asks Cole.

"No, sir."

"Background?"

"Grew up in Klamath Falls, Oregon. Poor community. Father on disability. Mom's a waitress. No siblings."

"How does she afford GW?"

"Scholarships, grants, work-study," says Lambert. "She's been living on a shoestring. Up to last week."

"What happened last week?" asks Cole.

"Until then, her checking account balance was about five

hundred dollars. And she was carrying a credit card debt of about four thousand."

Cole can already see where this is going. "And that changed."

Lambert nods. "Last Monday, she received a wire transfer in the amount of nine thousand, five hundred dollars."

"The magic number," says Cole. Just under the ten grand that requires a currency-transfer report to the IRS.

"Yes, sir. And her credit debt is now zero."

"The poster with Suzanne Bonanno's picture. How did she get it?"

"No way to know, sir. But I found one on eBay for twenty bucks."

"Maybe we can send somebody to talk to her undercover? Say we're doing a student survey or some damn thing..."

Lambert folds his hands and leans forward. "She's not there, sir."

"What?"

"The morning after you encountered her, she took a flight out of Reagan National to LAX. Final destination Cambodia."

"Cambodia? She's gone?"

"Off the grid, sir."

Cole shakes his head. "I guess I shouldn't be surprised."

"I can reach out to the embassy in Phnom Penh, sir."

"Don't bother. Cambodia is a non-extradition country. She's been paid off and tucked away. Thank you, Doug. You can go."

Lambert walks out and pulls the door closed behind him.

Alone in his office, Cole balls his hand into a fist and brings it down hard on his desk. Right now, it's about the only power he can muster.

There's no way to tell who Joan Marie Cardinal was working for.

She's completely out of reach. Unavailable for questioning.

If she's even still alive.

CHAPTER 41

Litchfield, Connecticut

I'm sitting at home in the upstairs alcove I call my office looking at news reports on Amber Keenan's murder. So far, I'm finding nothing beyond what O'Halloran already told us except that her two kids are temporarily in the care of a neighbor, and the store clerk is not a suspect. The killers are still on the loose.

Plink! Plink!

I've got a ten-gallon pot on the floor near my desk to catch the drips from the farmhouse's leaky ceiling.

When Garrett texted me after his prison meeting, he had a two-hour drive ahead of him. He should be home by now.

I hear a car in the driveway.

Finally!

I get up from my desk, look out the window, and see the reflection of blue lights.

I look down. It's a police car. I take the steps two at a time and yank open the front door.

The cop is standing on the porch, ice already forming on his cap and slicker. He's backlit by the headlights of his car. "I'm Officer Blaine, Litchfield Police," he says. "Is this the residence of Garrett Wilson?"

My heart is pounding and my vision narrows. I grab the door frame. "What happened? Where is he?"

"Are you a relative, ma'am?"

"I'm his partner! Girlfriend! My name is Brea Cooke! We live together!"

"There's been an accident, about five miles from here. Car went into a ditch. The Enterprise rental agreement shows the name Garrett Wilson and this address."

"Yes! Yes! He was driving a rental from Rhode Island. Is he hurt? Is he in the hospital? Which hospital? Can you take me? I'll get a jacket!" I grab a raincoat from the front closet.

Officer Blaine holds up his hand. "Ms. Cooke, there was nobody in the car. No victims at the scene. Mr. Wilson is not here?"

"Here? No, he's not here! I've been waiting for him!" I take a breath. "Hold on. The car was empty?"

"Yes, ma'am. We found a cell phone under the back seat."

"Well, he must still be out there! Get helicopters! Get bloodhounds! Start looking!"

"Not much we can do until this rain lets up, ma'am. We've got alerts out to all the hospitals. And patrols are searching the roads in the vicinity."

That's it. I'm done talking. I push past the cop and head for the Subaru. The mud sucks me in with every step. "I'm joining the search."

"Ms. Cooke!" Officer Blaine shouts at me. I stop and turn around. "We can't have amateurs on the road during a storm like this. Stay here. We need to know where to find you when we locate him."

I feel all the strength drain out of me. I nod and watch him get back into his car. He does a quick K-turn and drives off.

I turn to the house, and a figure appears. I stop in my tracks, then back away.

The figure takes a few steps forward until he's hit by the porch light.

Garrett!

CHAPTER 42

I can't believe I almost lost him.

While I pull off Garrett's wet clothes, wrap him in warm blankets, and settle him on the sofa with a steaming mug of tea, he tells me about his meeting with DeMarco, about being knocked off the road by Romero's thugs, about the warning shot two feet from his head, and about his five-mile trek through the woods.

"We need to call the police," I tell him. "You could have died back there!"

"The official story, Brea," Garrett says, "is that I lost control of the car on the icy road. That's what we'll tell the police."

"What about the dent in your rear bumper where they hit you?"

"Dent? Hell, the whole back end got shredded when I went into the ditch. It's just cheap plastic. People can't tell one dent from another unless they call in the FBI. Which they won't. It's Litchfield. The insurance company will declare the car a total loss and it'll get junked for parts."

"So, to be clear, you're saying that you're not going to report a crime that happened tonight just so we can keep working on our book."

"Right," says Garrett. "Something like that."

"And now, because that lowlife Seymour Washington is representing DeMarco, we have to work with him again?"

"Until we find another way to get DeMarco to spill what he knows."

"Or what he *says* he knows."

My phone rings. I don't recognize the number. Probably the police checking in. "Hello?"

"Is this Brea Cooke?" A male voice. Crisp. No-nonsense.

"Who's asking?"

"I've been trying to reach Garrett Wilson, but he's not answering his phone."

"Right. Again, who are you?"

A short pause, and then: "This is Burton Pearce."

CHAPTER 43

Burton Pearce? The president's chief of staff? He's not calling from the White House number. I can't imagine what this could be about—unless it has something to do with our investigation into Cole Wright?

I mute the phone. "It's Burton fucking Pearce!"

"On the level?" asks Garrett. "Not some prank?"

A message pops up—Burton Pearce requesting a video call. We don't really have a choice; we have to accept the call. Garrett nods, and I click on the video function. Two panels appear on the screen. Garrett and I are on the right. On the left, sure as shit, is Burton Pearce, the Gray Ghost himself. He's sitting in an office chair with a bookcase in the background. Could be at the White House. Could be at his house. Could be anywhere.

"Hello, Mr. Pearce. I'm Garrett Wilson."

"Pleasure to meet you both," says Pearce in a low-key, disarming voice. Kind of friendly. Not the total hard-ass portrayed in the news. He pauses, squints at the screen. "Are you okay, Mr. Wilson? You look like you went a few rounds in the ring."

"Fell in the driveway," says Garrett.

"Sorry to hear that," says Pearce. "Okay. It's late. I'll get right to the point. I understand that you two are running down some old stories about the First Gentleman and that you're planning to write a book about your findings."

"How would you know about our book?"

"You've made no secret of it to your interview subjects. I'm concerned about the facts you're finding."

I chime in. "Facts are all we're after, sir."

"Good," says Pearce with a smile. "Glad to hear it. That's where I can help you."

"Help us?" says Garrett.

Pearce leans forward. His close-shaved, balding head practically fills the frame. "Ever since his days at Dartmouth, Cole Wright has been the victim of false rumors. I know. I was there with him."

"*Lived* with him," I add. "And with Madeline Parson, the future president, correct?"

"That's right. And I saw it firsthand. Dartmouth hadn't been much of a football power until Cole showed up. And I think it's fair to say that the team's winning record during his years there was largely due to his efforts."

"He was a star player," says Garrett. "No argument there."

"Right," says Pearce. "And stars generate heat. And heat generates jealousy. I'm sure there were a lot of players, and maybe even some coaches, who felt overshadowed, felt like Cole was hogging the spotlight. And now that he's in a position close to power, those people might exploit those old jealousies to serve what they believe is a bigger purpose."

I lean toward the screen. "Bigger purpose? What bigger purpose?"

Pearce stares directly into the camera. "The purpose of embarrassing the First Family and crippling the president's administration."

"A conspiracy?" asks Garrett.

"Yes. A conspiracy, and people are leading you two around by your noses. Look, we all understand that there's a large slice of the American public that just can't stomach having a woman in the Oval Office. And that includes a lot of politicians, lobbyists, and corporations. Go after the president's husband and you hurt the president, maybe deny her a second term, maybe even get her to quit altogether."

"So, in your opinion," says Garrett, "these stories about the First Gentleman are just rumors being spread by political enemies of the president?"

"Absolutely," Pearce insists. "You think Cole Wright's life wasn't examined, rehashed, and deep-checked back when California governor Maddy Wright was preparing to run for president? You don't think party leaders and donors and PACs made sure Cole Wright was clean before they threw us their money and support? I'm telling you, I've seen everything. Cole Wright may have ruffled some feathers in Hanover and Boston. I know he had a temper then. He was young and cocky. I'm sure there are some comments and incidents he'd like to take back. But nothing like the charges you're looking into. That's all made-up stuff, meant to hurt the president and derail her agenda."

"If you're right," says Garrett, "that's a very big story."

I decide to go for the jugular. "Sir, what can you tell us about Suzanne Bonanno?"

Pearce's smile gets a bit tighter. "I can tell you that she and Cole Wright were in a relationship, against team policy, and that she disappeared shortly before Cole was released from the Patriots due to a knee injury. Cole was questioned by the police at the time and cleared of any involvement."

I push a little harder. "Have you ever talked with the First Gentleman about Suzanne?"

"Why would I? The matter is closed. That was seventeen years ago."

"Right," says Garrett. "Except that it's *not* closed. Suzanne Bonanno is still missing."

"Unfortunately," says Pearce, "a lot of disappearances are never solved. You know that as well as I do. It has nothing to do with Cole Wright."

For a second, I think about bringing up Amber Keenan's murder, but I realize that won't get us anywhere with Pearce. Besides, I'm really curious to hear what he's up to with this call.

"Here's what you need to understand," says Pearce. "I can't stop you from chasing rumors, even though you're wasting your time."

"And if we find out that the rumors are true?"

"All I'm asking is that you give me a chance to comment on or rebut anything you find."

Time for me to speak up again. "We need something in return."

"Such as?"

"If your conspiracy theory turns out to be true, we want an exclusive one-on-one with the president and the First Gentleman and access to your investigation. Before the *Post*. Before the *Times*. Before CNN. Before anybody."

Pearce chuckles. "Where'd you go to law school, Ms. Cooke?"

"Columbia, sir."

"They taught you well. We have a deal."

"All right, then, Mr. Pearce," says Garrett. "Have a good night."

Pearce leans in close to the camera. "Mr. Wilson?"

"Sir?"

"I'd try a warm compress if I were you." The screen goes black.

Garrett and I just stare at each other until he finally asks, "Did we just get bamboozled by the second-most-powerful person in the country?"

"No. I think we just found out how close we are to hitting a nerve."

CHAPTER 44

Roxbury, Massachusetts

The next morning, against my better judgment, we're sitting in the second-floor office of Seymour Washington, private investigator.

On the drive from Litchfield to Roxbury, Garrett logged phone time with Liberty Mutual insurance and Enterprise Rent-A-Car, explaining his so-called accident and arranging for an appraisal of the wrecked vehicle.

I kept quiet, thinking about Suzanne Bonanno and Amber Keenan, two innocent young women who did not deserve their fates.

Seymour Washington, by contrast, is anything but innocent.

I've met Washington only once before, a few years back, when we were working on *Integrity Gone*. He gave me the creeps then. Still does now.

I glance around the office. The walls are lined with framed photos of Washington posed with national leaders, like Jesse Jackson, Al Sharpton, Cory Booker, and Barack Obama, and local Boston politicians like Mel King. An older picture shows a much younger Washington—huge 'fro, multicolored dashiki, and a raised clenched fist—standing in front of the John Harvard statue in Cambridge.

Today, he's in a three-piece suit and ready to get down to business. He leans across his desk and looks at Garrett. "So you and John DeMarco came to an understanding."

"Stop right there," I say.

Washington turns to me. I hold out my hand. "Give me a dollar."

Washington's brow furrows. "What for?"

"Don't ask. Just do it."

He reaches into his pants pocket and pulls out a crisp single.

I grab it. "Mr. Washington, you have just paid me. Unless you object, I am now your attorney in the matter we're about to discuss. All conversations related to this matter are privileged."

"My first question," says Garrett, "is how you turned into a one-man Innocence Project for a guy like John DeMarco."

"Two reasons," says Washington. "First, I genuinely think his assault charge was a miscarriage of justice. Unreliable witnesses. Possibly a tainted jury. Second, he once did me a favor. A big favor. And I owe him."

"Do I want to know what that favor was?" I ask.

"You do not," says Washington.

Garrett speaks up again. "DeMarco was willing to talk with me only because he knew I was an investigative reporter. He wanted my help with his case. And he offered something in return. Something he said he left in your possession."

I slide my chair closer. "DeMarco told Garrett that you have information about the location of a murder victim from seventeen years ago. And the identity of her killer."

"That information would come from him, not me," says Washington. "I'm merely a conduit."

"But you have it," says Garrett.

Washington folds his hands under his chin. "I have half of it."

Garrett looks confused. "What do you mean?"

"I have the supposed location of the body. A good-faith offering. Mr. DeMarco is withholding the name of the alleged killer until he sees evidence of progress in his appeal."

I look over at Garrett, then ask the obvious question. "If John DeMarco has information about a murder he didn't commit, why wouldn't he trade on that information? Make a deal with the DA and get his sentence reduced?"

"Because," says Washington, "that would make him a snitch."

Garrett nods. "And snitches get stitches."

"Or worse," says Washington. "Mr. DeMarco prefers alternative channels."

I shake my head. "We're heading down a very dark tunnel here."

Washington stares at me. "Do you want the information or not?"

I glance at Garrett. He looks at Washington. "We do."

"I want to be clear," says Washington, "that this information was provided to me in confidence and comes with no guarantee. I cannot vouch for its accuracy."

"Understood," says Garrett.

Washington swivels around in his chair and opens a panel in the floor. Inside is a safe. He shields the lock dial with his left hand as he works the combination with his right. In a few seconds, he brings out a gray legal-size envelope.

"Do you know what's in that?" Garrett asks.

Washington shakes his head as he hands the envelope to Garrett. "Came to me taped shut. I never looked."

"As your attorney," I tell him, "I'd say you made the right decision."

"Why don't I give you two a minute," says Washington. He rises from his desk, walks into a small bathroom attached to his office, closes the door, and turns on the faucet. Primitive white noise.

I pull my chair closer to Garrett's. He grabs a slim letter opener from Washington's desk and slices through the tape on the envelope. He pulls out a single sheet of paper and unfolds it, then stares at it. "You've got to be kidding me."

I lean over to see what's on the page.

It looks like a treasure map drawn by a mental patient.

CHAPTER 45

Seabrook, New Hampshire

After we deciphered the map, we thought about driving directly to the police station in Seabrook to turn it over. But then we realized they would ask where we got it. Garrett said he wasn't ready to unravel that knot.

Not yet.

"Let's see where the map leads us," he said. "Then we can decide."

The big fat arrow pointing to a location in Seabrook was the obvious part. It was only an hour's drive from Boston. The map was very specific about a particular landmark, but Garrett insisted on waiting until most people would be asleep, then taking a roundabout route to the spot.

We rented a motel room where we could keep the equipment we'd need, then drove to a small feed and grain store—one with no surveillance cameras—and paid cash for two shovels, a couple pairs of heavy-duty work gloves, industrial-strength flashlights, and a forty-foot tape measure.

When we suited up to head out, I thought, *I became a lawyer for this?*

I decide now the question is not worth answering. My gloved hands hurt from carrying the shovel along the wooded paths. I've got burrs stuck in my hair. I'm as far out of my comfort zone as a city girl can possibly get. I like my nature in small doses and in broad daylight when I can see what's coming at me, not in the New Hampshire backwoods in darkness.

Garrett puts black tape over the lenses of our flashlights, leaving narrow slits to light our way as we bushwhack through brambles and low branches. He shines his slit beam onto the map. Its visual markers are crudely drawn, yet identifiable: Rock. Picnic tables. Stream.

"We should be there any minute," Garrett says.

By now, my night vision is pretty sharp. We push through another tangle of bushes and into a small clearing. On one side are two beat-up picnic tables. On the other is a large boulder.

"This is it," says Garrett.

He leads the way to the boulder and shines the light onto a weathered brass plaque. I can barely make out the words:

ON THIS SPOT THE REVEREND BONUS
WEARE PREACHED HIS FIRST SERMON
AFTER THE ARRIVAL OF THE FIRST
COLONISTS IN 1638

ERECTED BY SEABROOK
HISTORICAL SOCIETY 1938

Garrett checks the map and puts down his shovel. He pulls out the tape measure and places the start of it at the base of the boulder, right under the plaque. Then he walks backward, letting the tape out as he moves through a tangle of brush at the edge of the clearing. The foliage closes around him and he's out of sight.

"Garrett!"

A few seconds later, he calls out in a low voice, "Brea! Over here!"

For a second, I flash back to the video of Suzanne, that gorgeous young woman with her whole life ahead of her. And I realize that I might be standing on her grave.

After all these years, there'd be little left but bones. Though we knew that when we came here, I'm overcome with emotion. My cheeks are suddenly wet with tears. *Suzanne, we're going to find you.*

Garrett extends the forty-foot tape until it's at its limit, then grabs a stick and jabs it into the ground to mark the spot. He reels the tape back into its case.

"This is where we dig," he says.

CHAPTER 46

Garrett shines his flashlight around the edge of the area. "Hold on," he says. "The soil is loose, not hard-packed."

He bends down under a bush and comes back up with a handful of soil. "This is recent."

"Somebody was here, Garrett. Somebody got here first!"

Garrett wipes his brow. "Maybe we read the map wrong."

I grab his arm. "Stop. We're in the right spot. Somebody dug a hole. And recently, somebody dug it up again. If there was anything here, it's gone. Somebody took it. Took *her*."

Garrett blades his shovel through the loose soil. "There has to be something here."

I shine my flashlight where he's working. Then my foot slips and I fall. My nose is so close to the dirt, I can smell it.

Shit. What's this? I rip the tape off the flashlight so I can actually see. I brush away the fresh dirt. *A flash of red. It could be evidence! Or it could be trash left over from a picnic.*

Garrett kneels next to me. "What is that?"

While he holds the flashlight, I use my shovel to comb through the dirt. A shape appears. A small clump of something. Not dirt. Not a rock. My chest is pounding. I reach down between my feet and pick it up.

I hold it in front of the flashlight beam and rub the dirt away, just enough to see what I'm holding.

A piece of jewelry.

Oh my God.

I'm looking at a tennis bracelet with red gems.

Like the one Suzanne was wearing at the children's hospital.

"DeMarco was right, Garrett. She was here. Suzanne was here."

But where the hell is she now?

CHAPTER 47

Portsmouth, New Hampshire

In the northbound breakdown lane on Interstate 95, Steve Josephs of Troop A of the New Hampshire State Police stretches and yawns in the driver's seat of his dark green Ford Interceptor as the digital clock on the dash changes from midnight to 12:01. He's waiting for Morneau Towing to show up from nearby Greenland.

New day, same old shit, thinks Josephs. The flashes from his grille lights and roof light bar reflect off the rust-red Sentra parked on the shoulder just in front of him. The driver of that car, Herb Lucienne, is sitting in the back seat of Josephs's cruiser, cuffed and woozy.

"How much longer?" Lucienne asks. "I don't feel so good."

Josephs looks at him in the rearview. "Do *not* vomit in my vehicle. Do you hear me?"

Josephs had been patrolling the northbound lanes when he got a call from dispatch about a red Sentra weaving on the highway about five miles ahead. He'd caught up, hit his lights, and pulled the car over. As soon as the driver's window came down, Josephs smelled the beer.

He gave Lucienne the standard field sobriety tests—the horizontal gaze nystagmus test, the one-leg stand, and the walk-and-turn—and the Breathalyzer test, all of which Herb Lucienne failed in spectacular fashion.

His license showed one previous DUI from two years back. The Sentra was registered to Ken MacDonald of Portsmouth. Lucienne claimed that MacDonald was his friend and had lent him the car. Since a check showed the car hadn't been reported stolen, that seemed like a reasonable story.

"Shit!" mumbles Lucienne from the back seat. "If it wasn't for bad luck, I wouldn't have any fucking luck at all."

"Well, sir," says Josephs, "sometimes you make your own luck. If you hadn't been drinking tonight, we would never have met."

He glances at his side-view and sees the amber lights of the tow truck approaching. The wrecker pulls in front of the Sentra and into position.

As Josephs exits his vehicle, another state police Interceptor pulls up behind him. His supervisor, Sergeant Evan Tasker, turns on his flashers, opens his door, and climbs out.

"Hey, Sarge," says Josephs. "Slow night?"

Tasker puts on his trooper hat as he walks over. "You know me, always looking for excitement." He glances into the rear of Josephs's car. "That your DUI? I heard the call."

"Yep. Caught him bobbing and weaving, just like they said."

"Local?"

"Yeah. Herb Lucienne, from Hampton Falls. Failed every test."

"Yo! Troopers!" The tow-truck driver is calling from the side of the Sentra. "You want to inventory this thing before I hook it up?"

This is one reason Josephs likes working in New Hampshire. In most parts of the country, cops can't search a car without the owner's consent or a warrant. But if a driver gets arrested in the Granite State, the car gets inventoried before being towed. Very efficient system. Especially if the inventory turns up drugs or stolen property or unregistered firearms.

Josephs and Tasker walk over to the Sentra. Tasker sticks his head through the open driver's-side window. "All I see is a duffel bag in the back seat."

"I'll grab it," says Josephs. He opens the rear door and pulls out the worn denim bag. He puts it on the trunk and unzips it, then rummages around inside.

"Just some work clothes and tools," he says. The tow-truck driver writes it down on a clipboard. Tasker walks around to the passenger side and checks the glove box. Nothing but manuals and a flashlight. He grabs the flashlight and peeks under the seats. "All clean," he calls out, "except for candy wrappers."

Josephs reaches into his pocket for the Sentra's keys. "I'll pop the trunk."

Tasker and the tow-truck driver meet him at the back of the car. He sticks the key in the slot and turns it.

The lid pops open; the interior light flashes on.

"Jesus Christ!" The tow-truck guy takes two steps back.

"Fuck me," says Tasker.

Josephs feels his stomach turn. But he leans in to get a closer look.

Alongside a set of jumper cables and some road flares is a bundled-up filthy blue sheet.

Staring out through a gap in the fabric is a grinning human skull.

CHAPTER 48

Seabrook, New Hampshire

In the motel shower, I press my hands against the tile, hang my head, and watch the dirt swirl down the drain. The soap and water sting my blistered hands. I breathe in the steam and imagine it seeping deep into every pore. Cleaning me out.

I'm exhausted. From digging all that dirt out of the hole and then putting it all back.

I cannot believe this night.

And I cannot believe what this investigation has turned me into:

Brea Cooke, attorney-at-law and grave robber.

On the way back from the woods, Garrett wanted to dump the shovels in a lake.

But the lawyer in me said no. That felt like cognizance of guilt.

But guilt about what? Trying to solve a crime that everybody else had given up on? Trying to bring closure to a family after seventeen years? Trying to find out what really happened to

Suzanne Bonanno? Or are Garrett and I thinking more about our damn book than about solving the crime?

A quote from Sir Walter Scott comes into my head. My law professor Dr. Graham kept it pasted above his whiteboard at Columbia. He said it was a good caution for aspiring lawyers:

Oh, what a tangled web we weave / when first we practice to deceive.

When the bathroom fills with enough steam to overwhelm the exhaust fan, I turn off the water and step out of the shower. I do my best to wrap the ridiculously small motel towel tight around me before I leave the bathroom and make sure the room's drapes are all the way closed before putting on a pair of boy shorts and a Columbia Law T-shirt.

Garrett is lying on the bed in his briefs, his hair still wet from the shower. He looks over at the nightstand. On top is a plastic bag. The tennis bracelet is inside.

"You're sure that bracelet belongs to her?"

"It looks exactly like the one she was wearing in the video I saw."

"So what do we do now? Maybe we should just take the bracelet to the police and come clean about where we got the lead."

"Of course we should. Garrett, we're on thin ice here, legally speaking."

"I don't want us to get charged with anything, Brea, but I also don't want what we've learned so far to go nowhere."

"If we hand it over," I say, "we could be considered murder suspects ourselves—or accessories after the fact. Who the hell are we protecting? John DeMarco, a convicted felon? Seymour Washington, a crooked fixer? And what are we going to tell Washington?"

"That's easy," says Garrett. "No body, no deal."

CHAPTER 49

Portsmouth, New Hampshire

Detective Sergeant Marie Gagnon of the state police's Major Crimes Unit slows her unmarked Chevrolet Impala and pulls over into the breakdown lane.

At the scene are two state police cruisers, a tow truck, an orange highway department pickup truck, and a sad-looking Sentra with its trunk half open. Two workers in orange vests are setting out traffic cones to cordon off the area.

Gagnon exits her vehicle, hoping her young son has gone back to sleep by now. He's been running a fever since dinnertime. For a minute, she'd thought about letting somebody else take this call, but her husband waved her out the door. "Go, go. I got it. I'll call you if he gets worse."

When Gagnon walks by the second cruiser, she sees a man in handcuffs in the back seat slumped against the window, sleeping with his mouth open.

Gagnon knows both troopers. "Which one of you boys caught this?"

"It was Josephs's stop," says Tasker.

"Hi, Sarge. Right. Dispatch got a report of an erratic operator. I caught up with him here at mile marker fourteen and pulled him over at midnight. He failed all three field sobriety tests and a Breathalyzer."

"I don't suppose he mentioned anything about transporting human remains?"

"He did not."

"Okay," says Gagnon, "let me see what you've got in that Sentra."

She pulls a pair of purple disposable gloves out of her coat pocket and slips them on. When she looks up, she sees a big MCU scene truck pull up behind her car, lights flashing. "Let's wait for Vicki."

The passenger door on the truck opens. A young woman with dark hair that's pulled into a ponytail hops out. She's wearing a blue windbreaker and carrying a digital camera.

"Sergeant Gagnon," she says in greeting. Quiet. Respectful.

Gagnon turns to the two troopers. "You guys know Vicki Barnes? Best crime scene photographer we've got." She knows a few compliments go a long way this early in the morning.

Barnes exchanges nods with the two troopers.

"Sorry to wake you up, Vicki," says Gagnon.

"I wasn't asleep, Sergeant. What're we looking at?"

"We're about to find out." Gagnon walks to the back of the Sentra and lifts the trunk so it's all the way open. Josephs shines a flashlight into the interior.

Gagnon sucks in a quick breath as if she's been stung. She'll never get used to this part of the job.

"Female," she says, pointing at the skull. "Delicate glabella, and the suborbital rims are really light." She turns to Vicki. "Shoot this before I move anything."

The photographer leans in and clicks off a series of shots. Her flash illuminates the trunk in quick bursts.

I see you, Gagnon says to herself. *Whoever you are*, *I see you*. Her private mantra.

She pulls a pen from her pocket and gently teases the blue fabric away from the skull. A few spidery strands of hair still cling to the cranium. The skull is resting on a cluster of other bones. Ribs, femurs, tibiae, patellae.

"It's a whole damn skeleton," says Tasker.

"Hopefully nothing's missing," says Gagnon. She holds the fabric aside as Barnes clicks another series of shots.

"Josephs, pass me the flashlight," Gagnon says, using two fingers like tweezers to tease out a small packet of red vinyl from among the bones. A wallet. The seams are loose, and the contents are poking out.

"New Hampshire license," she says. "Old one."

Through the crusted grime, she can make out an image of a young Caucasian woman with a headful of wavy blond hair. Gagnon squints at the faded print next to the ID photo. "'Bonanno, Suzanne L.'"

Vicki Barnes leans in, eyes wide. "Bonanno? Holy crap. Isn't that the cheerleader who..."

Gagnon nods. "Welcome back to the world, Suzanne."

CHAPTER 50

Greenland, New Hampshire

The man still calling himself Jack Doohan walks out of the massive TA truck stop off I-95, extra-large coffee in his hand. The place is a city unto itself. Seventy-two truck bays, a diner and a fast-food joint, a mini-market, showers, and a laundry facility.

It even offers ministry services. Doohan can't remember the last time he set foot in a church, but if he did feel the need for spiritual comfort, a truck-stop chapel would suit him just fine. No pretentions. No dress code. He climbs back into his rented SUV, rips his fresh burner phone out of its package, activates it, and dials an out-of-state number.

It rings twice before a man picks up. "Did it happen?" he asks.

Not even a hello.

Doohan can tell that the guy on the other end is electronically disguising his voice. He sounds like a robot version of one of the gangsters on *The Sopranos.* Doesn't matter to Doohan as long as the funds keep flowing into his numbered Cayman account.

"The package has been intercepted," says Doohan.

"You sure?"

"Affirmative," says Doohan. "I watched it happen."

For this kind of money, he wasn't taking any chances.

He'd followed the Sentra when it left the Walmart parking lot and headed north on I-95. The driver made the rest easy for him. As soon as Doohan saw him weaving from lane to lane, he'd placed a quick, anonymous call to the state police. Just a concerned citizen reporting a possible danger to the driving public.

A few minutes later, he saw the Sentra pulled over near the Greenland town line. When he made another loop past the scene, a second trooper had arrived.

Doohan didn't wait around, but he knew it wouldn't be long before Major Crimes showed up too. Because the troopers were definitely about to discover a major crime.

"We might have more jobs for you in the future," the voice says.

"You know how to reach me," says Doohan. "And you know my rate."

He hangs up, then pulls out the phone's SIM card. He steps outside and places the phone in front of his left front tire. When he drives off, it makes a satisfying crunch.

CHAPTER 51

Seabrook, New Hampshire

I carry two hot coffees from the self-serve station in the lobby to our motel room. Garrett takes his and says, "Let's review our notes."

We pull two chairs together, but before we can power up our laptops, Garrett's phone rings. The caller ID says Nottingham. "Eight thirty a.m.? Marcia must be an early riser."

He answers and puts it on speaker.

"Is this Garrett Wilson?"

I recognize the voice. It's Lynn LuBrano, a Barnard grad who's Marcia's latest assistant.

"Hi, Lynn," says Garrett. "Brea and I are both here. What's up?"

"Hi, Mr. Wilson. Hold on a sec, I'm going to connect you with Mr. Hamilton."

"Wait!" says Garrett. "Where's Marcia?"

Lynn's already put us on hold. Over the first few bars of Nottingham's hold music, I whisper to Garrett, "Marcia's boss?

Reginald Hamilton, the head of Nottingham Publishing and a half a dozen other media operations?"

Garrett shrugs. We've never met Hamilton. Neither have most of the people who work for him. He's a cranky seventy-five-year-old Brit and a total recluse.

The hold music abruptly stops. "Hamilton here."

"Mr. Hamilton, this is Garrett Wilson and Brea Cooke. We work with Marcia Dillion—"

He cuts Garrett off. "She's no longer with Nottingham. Now, about your project. We're pulling the plug."

CHAPTER 52

Partial transcript of interview of HERBERT LUCIENNE by Detective Sergeant MARIE GAGNON, New Hampshire State Police, Major Crimes Unit

GAGNON: I want to again confirm that you've been read your Miranda rights, that you have not requested an attorney, and that you are aware that we are recording this conversation.
LUCIENNE: Yeah, I want to get this shit over as soon as possible.
GAGNON: Good. So do I. Please state your full name and address.
LUCIENNE: Herbert Lucienne, fifteen Mast Lane, apartment four, Hampton Falls, New Hampshire.
GAGNON: And your age?
LUCIENNE: Forty-three.
GAGNON: What is your current employment status, Mr. Lucienne?

LUCIENNE: I'm on disability from a construction accident three years back. Cheapskate cousin of mine owns the building I live in, and basically, I got a room, a bed, a minifridge, and a hot plate.
GAGNON: According to state records, Mr. Lucienne, you've supplemented your disability income by other means. Including burglary, drug peddling, and shoplifting.

[*Pause in audio*]

LUCIENNE: Sorry, was that a question?
GAGNON: My question is this, Mr. Lucienne. Can you explain to me how you came to be driving a vehicle with skeletal remains in the trunk?
LUCIENNE: I have no idea. It's not my car.
GAGNON: The vehicle is registered to Ken MacDonald of Portsmouth, New Hampshire. Do you know Mr. MacDonald?
LUCIENNE: No, I don't. I don't know who that is.
GAGNON: If you don't know Mr. MacDonald, why were you driving his car?

[*Pause in audio*]

LUCIENNE: Look, this is what happened, God's honest truth: Three days ago, I found an envelope under my door. Note inside said if I wanted to make five hundred bucks, go to the far end of the Walmart parking lot and pick up a red Sentra. It gave me the plate number and time—last night at eleven forty-five.
GAGNON: And you didn't question why you were being asked to undertake this task?
LUCIENNE: Shit, no. The envelope had five one-hundred-dollar bills, but they were, like, cut in half. No good by

themselves. The note said that taped inside the right front fender there'd be another envelope with the car keys and directions and a hundred bucks for expenses.
GAGNON: If you were making so much money for such a simple job, why would you risk it by drinking before you started your trip?

[*Pause in audio*]

GAGNON: Mr. Lucienne?
LUCIENNE: Because I was being stupid, that's why. I had a couple of cold ones before I left.
GAGNON: How many is a couple, Mr. Lucienne? Your blood alcohol level was point one six.
LUCIENNE: Maybe more than a couple. I guess I was celebrating in advance.

[*Pause in audio*]

GAGNON: And where were you taking the car?
LUCIENNE: Up to a cottage on Lake Marie, near Meredith.
GAGNON: And then what were you going to do?
LUCIENNE: I was supposed to drop the car off and walk to a local motel about a mile away. Come back the next morning to get the other half of the cut-up hundred-dollar bills. Then drive the car back to where I found it.
GAGNON: And you never saw or spoke to anybody about this little mission? No phone calls? No texts? No secret meetings?
LUCIENNE: Nope.
GAGNON: Do you know who gave you the money and instructions?
LUCIENNE: Nope.
GAGNON: Were you aware of the contents of the trunk?

LUCIENNE: No! Why would I look? Shit, if I'd known there was a bag of bones back there, I wouldn't have touched that car. No way.
GAGNON: Mr. Lucienne, you're being charged with aggravated DUI, which carries a two-month jail sentence. You're also going to be charged with New Hampshire statute six forty-four colon seven, abuse of a corpse. Do you have anything else to tell me?
LUCIENNE: Hell yes! Look. I got a record. Not proud of it. And I drink sometimes. I admit that. But I'm no grave robber!

[*End of partial transcript*]

CHAPTER 53

Seabrook, New Hampshire

Screw Reginald Hamilton! If Nottingham won't publish our book, we'll find somebody who will. Or we'll publish it ourselves. Or we'll do a podcast. Or we'll call Anderson Cooper. Or maybe Oprah Winfrey.

Garrett is a lot cooler and more composed than I am. I admire that about him. He just squares his shoulders and keeps working.

Right now, he's headed back down to Boston in a new rental car. He wants to talk to his buddy Detective O'Halloran and see if he's heard anything about the Amber Keenan case. And about Tony Romero. Garrett wants to follow up on the lead we found, that the FBI and Providence authorities have been interested in Tony for years.

I'm thinking about all the enemies we seem to be making, but I'm determined not to be scared off. The more forces there are against us, the more solid I get.

Maybe it's genetics.

I think back to my grandfather, nearly beaten to death on the Edmund Pettus Bridge in Selma. I think of Mama and Pops talking about the discrimination they suffered at their jobs.

I can't lie. The slights hurt. Always have. I overheard people at Dartmouth calling me a "quota gal," suggesting that I hadn't been good enough to get there on my own merits. But it's also toughened me up and made me sensitive to injustice, no matter where it lives.

Even if it lives in the White House.

My phone buzzes with a text. *Probably Garrett.* I grab the phone. It's from an unknown caller. It's a warning.

Your book is dead. Leave it be. Or you will be too. You and Garrett both.

A Brother

What the hell is this about? Whoever this is should know that warning me away from something has the opposite effect. If there's nothing to any of this, why are people trying so hard to stop us? The more they try to stop us, the more determined I become.

Still, I don't feel right about having a crucial piece of evidence in my possession. I need to put the bracelet back where I found it and direct the police to it.

CHAPTER 54

Concord, New Hampshire

In the chief medical examiner's office, Detective Sergeant Marie Gagnon gets a text from her husband. Their son's fever has broken. *What a relief.* Her mind is now clear to review her notes on the interview with Herb Lucienne.

To Gagnon, Lucienne seemed like the kind of simple, desperate man who would do just about anything for a buck, let alone hundreds, no questions asked. A thorough search of the Sentra had not turned up any digging tools, and Lucienne's shoes and clothes were not soiled with dirt. Gagnon is convinced that Lucienne was telling the truth. He is no prime mover, just an unwitting deliveryman. Which means whoever actually dug up Suzanne Bonanno's remains is still out there.

On the other side of the room is a plain metal door leading to the morgue and autopsy room that serve the entire state. Gagnon was present for the delivery of the skeletal remains and had stood alongside deputy chief medical examiner Dr. Alice Woods in the autopsy room, as she had done many times before.

But today, there was no Y-shaped incision down the center of the chest. No weighing of organs. No sightless eyes. No body at all.

Gagnon feels something like relief that she's dealing with a long-dead victim who had been reduced to calcium and hardened collagen instead of the pale corpse of a teenager who'd OD'd on fentanyl or been ripped apart by bullets.

The metal door swings open. Alice Woods emerges in scrubs, her face mask dangling from one ear. "You'll get my preliminary report in a couple of hours. Dental records confirm the identity. Age and size of the bones correlate. With that and the driver's license, there isn't any doubt."

"Cause of death?"

"In my opinion? Strangulation. The hyoid bone was broken. Tiny little thing. We're lucky whoever gathered the bones didn't leave it behind. I believe that Suzanne Bonanno was strangled."

Gagnon lowers her head. Not that she'd been expecting to hear that the cheerleader had died of natural causes, but still, a horrible image. And a slow, painful way to die.

"Marie, I did some other tests," says Wood. "That's what took me so long."

"What tests?"

"Detailed analysis of the pelvic bones showed reabsorption of bone at the ligamental attachment points."

"Meaning what?"

"Look, the remains were buried in bare dirt for seventeen years, and this kind of analysis is not an exact science—"

"Alice, what are you trying to say?"

"What I'm trying to say is that there's a good chance that your victim was pregnant when she died."

CHAPTER 55

Seabrook, New Hampshire

It's a one-hour drive from the morgue in Concord to Suzanne Bonanno's former residence, where her mother, Felicia, still lives. Detective Sergeant Marie Gagnon could have called officers on local patrol to make the notification, but this is something she wants to do. In person.

Mother to mother.

The whole way there, she turns the case over and over in her mind. So many questions. So many loose ends.

So many *dead* ends.

When she checked the files on Suzanne Bonanno's disappearance the morning after her remains were found, both in Seabrook and at the FBI office in Bedford, she got the same answer: The files were missing, maybe misplaced. It happens with cold cases. But in two different offices? And why would somebody be moving bones after seventeen years anyway? If you want to hide the crime, why not just leave the bones buried forever?

She parks her unmarked Chevrolet Impala in front of Felicia's place and sits there for a few moments, observing and absorbing. Run-down trailer homes. Small, scrubby lawns. Narrow lanes. A far cry from Gillette Stadium.

Gagnon walks up the trailer's steps, knocks, and raises her badge when a woman opens the door. "Felicia Bonanno? I'm Detective Sergeant Gagnon, New Hampshire State Police. I need to talk with you about your daughter Suzanne."

The middle-aged woman gasps, then buckles at the knees. Gagnon catches her before she can fall. Felicia looks up, her eyes filled with tears. "You found Suzanne. You found my daughter."

"Yes, Mrs. Bonanno. We did."

"Where have you been?" Felicia wails. *"Where have you been for seventeen years?"*

CHAPTER 56

The White House

Cole Wright sits alone in his East Wing office. He's decided, to borrow a phrase from his football days, that it's time to call an audible.

Cole presses the intercom buzzer. His assistant, Jason Rollins, instantly enters the office, legal pad in hand.

"Listen carefully," says Cole. "Cancel all my appointments for the rest of the day. Contact the White House travel office and the military liaison. I want a plane ready to go within the hour. Half-day trip. Quick turnaround. Tell Lambert I want a minimal detail, and make sure he's on the flight with me."

"Yes, sir."

"One more thing," says Cole. "And this is the tricky part. I don't want one word, one *syllable*, of this to get to the West Wing, especially to the president or Pearce. This is between you, me, Lambert, and the flight crew. My wife is tied up in meetings on the Hill all afternoon anyway. I should be back before she's done."

"Understood, sir," says Rollins. "Destination?"

"Hanover, New Hampshire."

CHAPTER 57

Outside Boston

The meeting with O'Halloran was a bust. The former detective had done an about-face. He'd previously been one of Garrett's top sources, but now he seemed to be warning him off the investigation. "This case is bigger than you, Garrett. It's bigger than both you and your partner. Watch out."

Garrett's on the road when a black Suburban roars past, then pulls in front of him. Garrett hits the brakes, then his horn. "Asshole!"

He signals to move into the left lane, but when he checks his side-view mirror, he sees another Suburban moving up next to him. He's boxed in.

The Suburbans slow down gradually. They're working as a unit, forcing Garrett to ease onto the shoulder and stop his car. Why the double-teaming? His heart is pounding. Is it Romero's crew again? Maybe he decided the last message wasn't strong enough. Maybe this time there won't be a warning shot.

A rap comes at the window. A professionally dressed woman

signals for Garrett to lower it. “Mr. Wilson, I’m Special Agent Leanne Keil, Secret Service.”

Secret Service? Garrett places both hands on the wheel. No sudden movements. “Why are you stopping me? What did I do?”

“Hold on. Don’t move. Somebody wants to talk to you.”

Keil pulls a cell phone in a heavy-duty case from her inside breast pocket. She taps a code, then puts the phone to her ear. “Yes, sir. We have him.” She hands the phone to Garrett. The screen is blank except for the time. “Hello, this is Garrett Wilson.”

“Hi, Garrett. This is Cole Wright.”

CHAPTER 58

Mr. Wright?" Garrett asks.

"I'll get to the point, Garrett. You and Brea Cooke are writing a book about me. How would you like an in-person interview with your subject?"

"With *you*?"

"Yes, with me. It'll be just the two of us. No handlers in attendance." Wright sounds cordial, warm. Like a pal.

"Brea's not here at the moment, sir. Can we wait until—"

"Sorry. It has to happen today. Come by yourself. You can fill her in later."

This is the scoop of a lifetime! Garrett thinks. Everything they've been working for. More than they ever hoped for.

"This would be on the record?" Garrett asks. His head is spinning.

"Absolutely," says Wright. "Put Agent Keil back on."

Though Keil steps away from the rental car to take the call, Garrett can hear her say, "Yes, sir. Understood, sir."

At the Suburban in front of him, Keil has a quick exchange

with the agent behind the wheel. Garrett sees her nodding, then pointing at him. She sticks her phone back into her pocket. She walks over to the rental car and opens the door.

"I'm driving."

"Where are you taking me?"

"You'll know when we get there."

Garrett exits the vehicle and goes around to the passenger seat. The Suburban ahead pulls out of the breakdown lane, lights flashing, and speeds away. Keil puts the car in gear. "What is this, a Corolla?"

"Yeah. A rental."

Keil jams her foot down on the gas. Garrett's head is thrown back against the seat. The Corolla accelerates and moves in behind the Suburban. The second SUV pulls up behind them. Garrett looks out the passenger side. Within ten seconds, the passing countryside is a blur.

"These things can move," says Keil, "if they're handled right."

Garrett tilts his head to peek at the speedometer. Eighty-five and climbing.

"Can I use my phone?" asks Garrett.

"No, you can't," says Keil, maneuvering to within three feet of the Suburban's rear bumper and locking in at ninety miles per hour. "Just relax and enjoy the ride."

CHAPTER 59

Concord, New Hampshire

"Sad outcome, Marie. But I'm glad it was you who finally found her."

Deputy Attorney General Hugh Bastinelli is sitting behind his desk in his book-lined office. Across from him is Detective Sergeant Gagnon. Dark suit, white blouse. Her handbag is stashed under the cushioned chair.

"I was hoping for a happier ending," says Gagnon, "but after seventeen years..."

Bastinelli finishes the thought. "We all knew the odds were against that."

The pretty Patriots cheerleader disappeared the same year he graduated from law school. It was big news back then. But for almost twenty years, it seemed like the coldest of cold cases. It's not surprising that the younger attorneys on his staff have never even heard of Suzanne Bonanno.

"So it was a random traffic stop?" asks Bastinelli.

Gagnon nods. "Somebody got stupid. We got lucky."

"Well, like I said, I'm glad it was you."

Bastinelli has worked murder cases with Gagnon before. He knows her as a precise, no-nonsense investigator who never forgets the collateral damage of a homicide—the anguish of the victims who are still alive. Mothers, fathers, siblings, friends...

But Bastinelli's job is to convict the killer and put him in jail. Right now, he has nobody to charge. And Gagnon has nobody to offer. This is just an update meeting. Colleague to colleague. A heads-up.

"What about the driver?" asks Bastinelli, glancing down at his legal pad. "Mr. Lucienne?"

"A patsy, from what we can tell," says Gagnon. "Claims he was paid—anonymously, in cash—to pick up the vehicle, drive it up to Lake Marie, leave it there overnight, then drive it back to where he found it."

"Stolen vehicle?" asks Bastinelli.

Gagnon nods.

"And what's up at Lake Marie?" asks Bastinelli.

"Nothing obvious at first look. But it's a big property. I've got some troopers doing a follow-up search right now."

Bastinelli glances down at his notes again and reads off a few cold facts. " 'Cause of death likely manual strangulation'... 'ID from dental records and driver's license.' " He looks up. "Where the hell has she been for the past seventeen years?"

"That's what we're trying to find out," says Gagnon. "Lab is working on soil samples to see if they can narrow it down. The bones were wrapped in a blue polyester sheet. We're seeing if we can find a manufacturer and a distributor, maybe figure out where it was sold."

"Polyester never dies," says Bastinelli.

"There's one more thing that's not in the preliminary report," says Gagnon.

"What's that?"

"The ME thinks Suzanne Bonanno might have been pregnant."

Bastinelli winces. "So we're looking at a double homicide?"

"Not sure. The ME is doing more analysis. There are no fetal remains."

"That won't make my job any easier," says Bastinelli.

"I'm afraid I'm about to make it even harder," says Gagnon.

"How's that?"

"Back when the case first broke, it was a hot potato between Seabrook cops and Boston PD. FBI got tangled up in there too. Somehow in all the handoffs and confusion, it looks like the original files got lost or dumped. They're nowhere to be found."

"Jesus. So we're starting from scratch?"

"We're reaching out to some of the original investigators. But a lot of them are retired. In fact, a lot of them are dead."

"Refresh my memory," says Bastinelli. "Who were they looking at back then?"

"One of the last people to see her was the Pats player she was dating."

Bastinelli sits up straight. Now he remembers. Not just any football player. "You mean..."

"You got it," says Gagnon. "The same one who's now the First Gentleman of the United States."

"But they cleared him, right?"

"Seabrook did. Yeah."

Bastinelli hears a dull vibration.

Gagnon grabs her bag from under the chair, pulls the phone out, and looks at the screen. "Sorry," she says, "do you mind if I—"

"Go ahead," says Bastinelli.

"Gagnon here." As Bastinelli watches, Gagnon's face tightens. "Wait. Hold on," she says. "I'm putting you on speaker." She taps the screen and places the phone on the edge of Bastinelli's desk.

"Okay. Trooper Hess? You're on speaker with the deputy attorney general."

"Right. Like I was saying, myself and two officers from Troop E are here at the Lake Marie location at the edge of the property, secluded area. And we just found a freshly dug hole."

Bastinelli asks, "How big a hole? Could it be for irrigation?"

"I'd say eight feet long, six feet deep."

"Is the hole empty?" asks Gagnon.

"Looks clean," says Hess. "Like there's never been anything in it. Hold on, I'll send a picture."

A few seconds later, Gagnon gets the image. Bastinelli leans in close. *That's no irrigation ditch*, he thinks. *That's a grave site.* "Trooper Hess, who owns this property?"

"Caretaker says it's an LLC with a conservation easement. Tight End..."

The connection is staticky. Gagnon shouts into the phone, "What's that, Trooper?"

"Tight End Limited. That's the name of the LLC."

Gagnon picks up the phone, takes it off speaker. "Thanks, Trooper Hess. Good work."

Bastinelli is already tapping away on his laptop. As soon as Gagnon hangs up, he has the listing on the New Hampshire Secretary of State website. He flips his screen around so Gagnon can see it too.

The registration for Tight End Limited LLC shows just one name.

Cole Wright.

CHAPTER 60

Outside Hanover, New Hampshire

Garrett Wilson is driving south on I-89, trembling with excitement.

He's alone now in the rented Corolla. He left the agents and their guns and their Suburbans behind at the airport—the airport where he spoke for two hours with Cole Wright.

After the interview, he drove to a Starbucks and spent the rest of the day consolidating his notes from memory. No taping devices had been allowed. The laptop holding all his notes is on the seat beside him.

Pure gold.

The story is going in a direction Garrett never expected. Mind-blowing! When this manuscript is finished, there will be a bidding war for sure. *Bite me, Reginald Hamilton!*

Garrett glances at the speedometer. Eighty-five in a fifty-five zone. Careful. This is no time to get caught by a radar gun. He eases his foot off the gas, grabs his phone, and calls Brea.

After three rings, it goes to voicemail. Again. "Brea! Call me!" he shouts into the phone.

She's going to be so disappointed to have missed out on a chance to be face to face with the First Gentleman himself. I could have used her intuition back there—and her legal brain.

He was surprised to find the First Gentleman so down-to-earth. Straightforward. Even with all Garrett's suspicions, even with his reporter's guard up, he actually liked the guy.

And he was blown away by what Cole Wright had to say.

CHAPTER 61

Seabrook, New Hampshire

They definitely did not cover what I'm about to do at Columbia Law. I'm trained as a lawyer but thinking like a damn criminal. *What the hell has happened to me?*

I need to put a crucial piece of evidence back where I found it—then make sure the police find it.

It's barely twilight and I'm trying to follow the same path Garrett and I took through the park last night. I don't see any hikers, but I freeze every time I hear skittering in the underbrush. I duck down behind a tree and watch for moving shadows. I hear it again. Too light to be human. Probably a squirrel, right?

This is no place for a girl from Bed-Stuy.

When I get to the big memorial rock, I orient myself and plunge through the thicket into the small clearing. I'm wearing my work gloves, but I didn't bring a shovel. I didn't want to draw attention to myself. All I brought was an ice scraper from the trunk of the Subaru.

I kneel down and brush a section of leaves aside, then use the ice scraper to dig down through the soft dirt. Six inches . . . twelve inches . . . I cannot believe I'm doing this. Two feet now. My forearms are covered in dirt. At three feet down, I lean back, breathing hard. Enough. I sit there for a moment looking around, listening for sounds, watching for shapes.

I pull the plastic bag out of my pocket and take out the tennis bracelet. I drop it into the hole I just dug.

Suzanne, I hope this helps bring you home.

CHAPTER 62

Transcript of 911 call

DISPATCHER: Seabrook Police Department. What's your emergency?
UNIDENTIFIED CALLER: I need to talk to an investigator with the state police.
DISPATCHER: What is your emergency, please?
UNIDENTIFIED CALLER: I have information concerning a homicide.
DISPATCHER: Ma'am, what is your location?
UNIDENTIFIED CALLER: Look, I know this call is being recorded. Connect me with a state police investigator right now, or I'll hang up and you can explain to your supervisor why you didn't help a citizen report a murder.
DISPATCHER: Hold, please.

[*Pause in audio*]

GAGNON: New Hampshire State Police, Detective Sergeant Gagnon. Can I have your name, please?
UNIDENTIFIED CALLER: My name doesn't matter. Just listen. Suzanne Bonanno was buried in the woods in Seabrook, forty feet west of the Reverend Bonus Weare memorial rock.
GAGNON: Ma'am, can I get—
UNIDENTIFIED CALLER: No, you can't.

[*Call ends abruptly*]

CHAPTER 63

Litchfield, Connecticut

I smash the burner phone and toss the parts into a drainage pond—and accidentally drop my own phone in with it.

"Shit!" I fish my phone out and power it down, knowing I won't be able to dry it out until I get home.

At the farmhouse, I sit in the living room with the lights off and drapes pulled shut. If I had a gun, it would definitely be loaded and on my lap right now. I'm wishing I'd bought one in New Hampshire. Every few minutes, I get up to peek through the drapes, hoping to see the headlights of Garrett's rental car.

Hoping I don't see anybody else.

I stare at my dark phone sitting in a tub of rice. Screw it. I press the button and the Apple symbol glows as the phone comes back to life.

I have one voicemail from Garrett: "Brea! Call me!" He sounds nervous. Excited.

I also have half a dozen texts from him. And another one from an unknown caller.

The danger is getting deeper. Stop now.

A Brother

A chill runs down my body all the way to my feet.

That does it. I'm calling Garrett.

He picks up on the first ring. "Brea! Why haven't you been answering your phone? I have to tell you about a meeting I just had at an airport near Hanover. I don't want to talk about it over the phone except to say that it was with the subject of our investigation."

"How is that possible?" I ask. *And what does this mean?*

"Let's do a rendezvous," says Garrett. "Meet me at our place."

CHAPTER 64

Seabrook, New Hampshire

As the night deepens, Detective Sergeant Marie Gagnon leans on the Reverend Bonus Weare memorial rock. She's wondering what his sermon on this spot was about. Brotherly love? Do unto others? Thou shalt not kill?

Forty feet away, under a battery of lights, a small backhoe is excavating a section of loose soil. The forensics team wanted to wait until morning, but Gagnon pulled rank. If this really is Suzanne Bonanno's grave, it's already been disturbed once.

She wanted the area secured and searched pronto.

Gagnon is usually not big on anonymous tips, but there's a lot about this case that doesn't fit normal patterns. She and a couple uniforms found the spot the caller had pinpointed, and they could see it had been dug up recently. That's when she mobilized the crime scene team.

A few yards from the rock, two state police investigators in white coveralls gently sift the excavated dirt through screens. Vicki Barnes from MCU is documenting the whole process with her camera. Seabrook cops poke through the bushes with flashlights looking for anything that doesn't belong.

Gagnon looks up as a tall man in khaki pants and a plaid shirt lopes up the path toward the site. One of the cops steps forward to stop him.

"It's okay," Gagnon calls out. "He's with me."

It's not every night that a deputy attorney general shows up at a crime scene dig, but Hugh Bastinelli lives just twenty minutes away, and Gagnon gave him a call. She figured he'd be interested.

"I know this spot," Bastinelli says as she waves him over. "I hike here on the weekends. I've taken selfies with my kids in front of this rock!"

"I checked the municipal records," says Gagnon. "The summer she went missing, this part of the park was closed for renovation and regrading. The ground was all torn up. Wouldn't have been hard to make a fresh grave seem like part of the work." She points to the backhoe. "When the foliage was replanted, the site over there was pretty much hidden."

Bastinelli looks at the members of the forensics team, hard at work. "Have they found anything useful?"

Gagnon leads him over to a folding table and holds up an evidence bag. "Well, they found this right off the bat."

Inside the bag is a dirty tennis bracelet with red gems.

Bastinelli leans in for a closer look. "Think it's hers? Was she wearing it when she went missing?"

"We *would* know that," says Gagnon, "if gremlins hadn't made off with the case files." She puts the bag back on the table. "The bracelet was just a few feet down, so maybe it's not connected at all. Could be somebody dropped it recently. They also found some fibers that might be from the sheet the bones were wrapped in. Same color."

"Who called this in?" asks Bastinelli.

"Wish I knew. Female. Thirties, maybe. Wouldn't give her name, but her directions were on point."

"Somebody who was involved?"

"Maybe somebody who knows who was. Maybe somebody who wants closure—without the liability."

Vicki Barnes walks over with her digital camera. Gagnon makes the intros.

"Sorry we're ruining your night," says Bastinelli.

"No worries," says Barnes cheerfully. "Detective Gagnon does it all the time." She holds up her camera so the digital screen faces up. "Take a look at this."

At first, the frame looks just like a square of dark dirt. But when Barnes zooms in, a small whitish-gray shard comes into view. "Is that what I think it is?" she asks.

"The ME will know for sure," says Gagnon. "But I'd bet on a phalanx or a metatarsal—a toe or a piece of the foot."

Bastinelli shakes his head. "Jesus."

Gagnon gives him a tight smile. "See what you miss sitting in that fancy office?"

"Detective!" one of the forensics sifters calls. "You need to see this!"

Gagnon walks over with Barnes and Bastinelli. The young woman in the white suit is holding something in her gloved hand above the sifting screen. Gagnon snaps on a fresh pair of gloves and takes the object carefully between two fingers. It's a man's wristwatch with a broken band.

"Squirt it, please," says Gagnon. "Gently."

The woman in the white suit picks up a small squeeze bottle from the table and sprays a fine mist across the face and back of the watch. Dirt drips off in small muddy trickles.

Gagnon angles the watch toward one of the scene lights. "Look. There's something on the back..."

The woman in white does another quick misting.

Gagnon gently wipes the back of the watch clean. Barnes

clicks away with her camera, her lens just inches from the object. Bastinelli leans in. "Look at the date!"

June. Twenty-four years ago.

Below the date is a filigreed inscription:

TO CW

FROM BC,

WITH LOVE

"Bag!" Gagnon calls out. Another member of the forensics team hustles over with a transparent sleeve. Gagnon carefully lowers the watch in, then removes her gloves.

She leans toward Bastinelli. "CW," she whispers. "Cole Wright?"

Bastinelli shrugs. "Or Christopher Walken. Or Charlie Watts. Let's not jump to conclusions."

"Okay," says Gagnon. "I won't if you won't." She's doing her best to keep an open mind. But she can't help making connections. It's what she does.

Gagnon rubs her hand across the bagged tennis bracelet. Call it intuition, but she has a strong feeling now about who was wearing it.

I see you, Suzanne. I see you.

CHAPTER 65

Brattleboro, Vermont

In cabin 19 at Montcalm Acres, Garrett is in a great mood. He was able to snag the same unit where he and Brea had their first off-campus date years ago. What better place to tell her the news and reignite their project?

Back then, they had planned to spend a long day exploring local trails, but a late-autumn cloudburst cut their hike short. Not a bad outcome, as it turned out. They'd spent the rest of the day in bed making love while their clothes dried in front of a roaring fire.

That was the day he'd first told Brea that he loved her. Right there, in that saggy, squeaky bed. Garrett can still remember the sound of the rain hammering on the tin roof over their heads. It was perfect.

Tonight, it's chilly in the cabin. Garrett pulls a wool blanket from a shelf and drapes it around his shoulders for warmth, then puts his laptop on the table near the fireplace. He paid for a load of firewood when he checked in, but it's not here yet.

Garrett pulls up a stool and opens his laptop to reexamine his notes. He's thinking that today's events could make a dramatic prologue: Kidnapped on the open road by the Secret Service. Taken to a small airport for a clandestine interview with the First Gentleman of the United States.

Hell, that's better than Woodward's damn parking garage.

Garrett checks his email. The internet service here is iffy. Google takes forever to load.

No reply yet from Ukraine. Not unusual. Daryna works her own hours. And her internet service is spotty too, thanks to Russian missile attacks. It's not unusual for her to be off the grid for days at a time. She always resurfaces. At least, she always has so far.

Garrett rubs his hands together under the blanket. All they really need is a solid proposal and a few killer chapters to kick off the auction and make the Nottingham people sorry they tore up their contract.

Garrett gets up from the chair, nervous energy flowing through him. He starts pacing. He checks the time on his phone.

Brea should be here any moment.

There's a knock on the door. A muffled voice. "Mr. Wilson?"

Must be the guy with the firewood. Garrett closes his laptop. "Hold on."

He walks across the wide-plank floor and pulls the door open.

Two men are standing there. Dark slacks, short black jackets, plain black baseball caps.

First impression: No firewood. One man is in his thirties; the other is a little younger. The men push into the room.

"Hey!" says Garrett. His mouth suddenly goes dry.

The younger man shoves him in the chest, forcing him back. The older one says, "Now."

The metal end of the silencer is cold on Garrett's forehead.

Brea! His last thought.

CHAPTER 66

I make it to Brattleboro in record time. My last text from Garrett said that he'd booked cabin 19, our place. After all, that's where he first told me that he loved me. As if I hadn't known it already. I told him I loved him too.

I round the last curve through the pine trees.

What the hell?

The woods are lit up with flashing red and blue lights.

I brake hard. Everything comes at me like freeze-frames every time I blink.

Garrett's rental car. An ambulance. Two police cars. Uniformed cops standing on the porch of a cabin.

I put the Subaru in park and jump out. I start running. One of the cops jumps off the porch and heads straight for me.

"What happened?" I call out. "I'm meeting my boyfriend here!"

The officer has the sturdy build of a lacrosse player. She stops me cold. "Honey, you can't go in there."

My ears start ringing, and she keeps talking but her words

sound like they're coming from underwater. "What's your boyfriend's name?" She's staring right into my eyes. "Sweetheart! Listen! Who were you meeting here?"

I try to push past her, but it's no use. She has her legs planted wide.

There's a glow coming from the cabin. Bright lights. Brighter than a fire.

"Garrett!" I shout. "Where are you?"

"Garrett? And what's the last name?" The cop is in my ear. She's half holding me, half hugging me.

"Wilson! Garrett Wilson!"

"Okay, honey. I need you to come sit down with me." She pulls me toward a wooden bench under a pine tree. My eyes are fixed on the cabin door. The number 19 is carved into it.

No!

I don't know how, but I tear myself away from her and run up the steps to the cabin. Two more cops grab me.

But it's too late. I can see inside.

A blanket on the floor. Blood.

Garrett!

PART TWO

ONE WEEK LATER

CHAPTER 67

Brooklyn, New York

I wake up slowly in the small room that was mine from infancy to age eighteen. Bed in one corner, small desk and chair in another. Bookcases along every wall.

For a few brief, merciful seconds, everything feels right. Normal. Then the heavy wave of grief rolls in again. It picks me up and swallows me. I pull my sheet and blanket up around my chin as if they can protect me. But they can't. Nothing can.

Over the desk is a bulletin board with thumbtacked-on color photos, from my formal first-grade picture to the high-school graduation photo where I'm flanked by Mama and Pops, all of us smiling, me looking like I have a whole bright, shiny future waiting.

That confident young girl is gone. So is the confident young woman she grew into. And so is that bright, shiny future.

A soft knock. "Brea, can I come in?"

"Sure, Mama."

My mother comes in and sits down gently on the edge of the

bed. She reaches over to stroke my hair. "So you just planning on staying in bed forever?"

"Why not?" I feel her strong fingers against my scalp, then her warm hand on my shoulder. "Mama? Is this what it was like for you when Pops died?"

It had been so sudden. Pops died of a heart attack at work.

She leans over and kisses my forehead. "I know that time was hard for you too. Don't forget, you learn to live with the pain and love the memories." She pulls my hand out from under the covers and squeezes it. "Put your worries and your trust in the Lord, Brea. You'll get through this, I promise."

I know my mother would be hurt if I told her that I don't have much belief in the Lord anymore. Not after being a public defender and seeing how His children got used and abused. Not after what happened to Suzanne Bonanno. And Amber Keenan.

And Garrett.

It's been one week today.

Three days after he was murdered, his body was released to his family in Swarthmore, Pennsylvania.

I think Garrett's parents were a little surprised that Garrett made me the executor of his will, but they were okay with it. It's not like he had a huge estate to settle. It took me only a few days to pay off his credit cards and close his bank accounts. He'd made the will himself on LegalZoom. He left me the Subaru, his precious guitar, his book royalties, and, as he wrote in the codicil, "anything in the house that's not nailed down."

At the funeral service, Garrett's folks were polite, but I think they blame me for what happened.

For all I know, they're right.

"Oh, Mama, I miss him so much!"

"I know, I know. Just try to think of better times."

I try. But right now, that hurts too much.

CHAPTER 68

Concord, New Hampshire

Detective Sergeant Marie Gagnon takes a chair across from the deputy AG's desk. It's been a week since their nighttime chat at the grave site, and Bastinelli wants an update. He doesn't waste any time.

"So, Marie, where do we stand?"

"Without the original records, I'm mostly working blind," Gagnon says. "I've been able to put together some bits and pieces from talking to a couple of the old investigators, but you know how that goes."

"I do," says Bastinelli. "Memories get porous."

Gagnon glances down at her laptop. "I talked to a retired detective named Foster down in Fort Lauderdale. He sounded a bit wonky, but he'd kept some of his original notes. Said he interviewed a stadium attendant who said she heard Cole Wright talking rough to Suzanne once. Saying, 'I'll wring your neck,' or something like that."

"Did his memory include the attendant's name?"

Gagnon nods. "Stacey Millett. She's a coach at a girls' school in Milwaukee. I called her. She still tells the same story. But she doesn't know if Cole was serious. She says he might have just been talking tough. And she volunteered that she's a big supporter of President Wright."

"That doesn't help," says Bastinelli. "Easy to impeach her testimony. What about the watch?"

"We found a serial number stamped along the ridge of the watch face. Traced it back to a New York manufacturer, Zahn Fine Watchcraft. Nice watch, but hardly a Rolex. It was shipped to a jewelry store in Hanover, New Hampshire, twenty-four years ago."

"So the timing lines up."

"I can do better than that," says Gagnon. "The store was Schmitt's Jewelers. Still in business. Third-generation German family. Meticulous recordkeepers."

"So they know who bought the watch?"

"They do. Brenda Connelly. She was a Dartmouth student at the same time as Cole Wright. Now she's a successful tech exec, though she came from family money."

Bastinelli lights up. "Brenda Connelly. BC! Those were the initials on the back of the watch, right?"

"Yes. It's Brenda Monroe now. I tracked her down through the alumni association. She said she and Cole dated for a few months freshman year."

"So why the watch?"

"She says Cole was always late. It was a little joke between them. And it was a very nice watch. Even after they broke up, she remembers seeing him wear it. It's not like it was a wedding ring," says Gagnon. "And it sounds like Brenda might have dumped him, not the other way around."

"Any threats or violence with her?"

Gagnon shakes her head. "Brenda says he was a perfect gentleman. Just habitually tardy. Even with the watch."

Bastinelli leans back in his leather chair. "So let's paint the picture. Theoretically, Cole Wright keeps a watch from an old girlfriend, Brenda. Later, he dates Suzanne Bonanno. They fight. He strangles her and loses the old watch in the dirt while he's digging her grave. Seventeen years later, somebody exhumes Suzanne's bones and pays a driver to bring them to a property Cole Wright owns nearby."

"I assume the bones were headed there," says Gagnon. "Until Herb Lucienne overserved himself."

"That's a twisted little tale," says Bastinelli. "Anything to place Wright or Suzanne together in the park while she was alive?"

Gagnon shakes her head. "Her mom said the last time she saw Suzanne, she was heading to the Walmart to buy some stuff for her new apartment, and Wright was going to meet her there and take her out for dinner someplace. She doesn't remember the name of the restaurant. No other record of their movements that night. I don't even know where they interviewed Wright or if they checked his car. Like I said, I can't find the original case files. Property records say he lived in North Attleboro at the time."

"What about the bracelet?"

"It was Suzanne's for sure. Her mother confirmed it the day after we found it. She gave me a DVD showing her wearing it."

"Anything on the sheet she was wrapped in?" asks Bastinelli.

"We sent some fibers to a lab in Boston. Nothing yet."

Bastinelli slaps his hand on his desk. "Goddamn it! We need something I can take to Jen. You know she'll be under the microscope on this."

New Hampshire attorney general Jennifer Pope is Bastinelli's boss. Gagnon knows her reputation as a tough prosecutor. But she was appointed by Madeline Wright's predecessor, the head of the opposing party. Law enforcement and politics are supposed to be kept separate, but they never are.

"We can't afford to be sloppy on this, Marie. We need something solid to rest this case on. We need to connect some of this evidence. When you shoot this high, you get only one chance."

Gagnon rises to leave. "I'm on it. Don't worry."

Strong words. But the truth is, Gagnon is very worried. She's working without the original case files. Her evidence is inconclusive. And the potential target of her investigation is literally in bed with the most powerful person in the world.

Right now, her case isn't even a hill of beans.

It's a pile of sand.

CHAPTER 69

Brooklyn, New York

In the kitchen, I'm poking at a plateful of fresh waffles and crisp bacon. I think I'm done with coffee for a while, but Mama's on her third cup of the morning.

"Good to see you eat, girl." She's sipping from an MTA mug that belonged to Pops.

My father worked on the parts of the trains that nobody ever sees. Sometimes he'd sit me in the cab of one of the railroad cars and I'd pretend that I was driving the train into a deep long tunnel. He said I always wanted to run things.

"Thanks, Mama. Delicious, like always."

Actually, I can hardly taste a thing. It's like all my senses have been dulled or turned off. For a while there, I was afraid that I would shut down completely and never recover. But Mama's waffles are starting to bring me back.

She smiles and pats my hand. "Good to know I still have the touch." She eyes me over the rim of her coffee mug. "What about your work?"

"I'm still on sabbatical from Yale."

"No, I'm talking about your book, the one you and Garrett were working on."

I put down my fork and push my plate away. "The book is dead, Mama. It died with Garrett. Anyway, Nottingham canceled the contract."

She gives me a quiet nod.

"Besides, I'm afraid working on that book is what got Garrett killed."

The first few hours after I saw his dead body are a blur. The Brattleboro police questioned me twice, once at the scene, once at the station.

Of course I told them about Tony Romero, the thug from Providence. About how he'd beaten up Garrett over a book we were writing. They took down his name and contacted the Providence police. Naturally, Romero had an alibi. He had been in his private club, Raymond's Tavern, the whole day.

I had as many questions for the cops as they had for me. For one thing, where was Garrett's laptop? He never went anywhere without it. Were there any tire prints by the cabin? Did anybody else see anything? And even though it hurt me to ask: Exactly how had Garrett died? They told me it was a single gunshot. Said it would've been over in a second. I've chosen to believe that. I can't bear the thought of him suffering.

They asked if Garrett did drugs. I said nothing stronger than Tylenol. They told me that there were drugs on a table in the cabin. High-grade coke. Looked like it was being cut and repackaged for distribution. I told them it was obviously a setup, which meant it had been a planned execution. They ordered a tox screen anyway.

I didn't tell them about Garrett's meeting with the First Gentleman. I believed that it had happened, but I didn't have any proof, and I was afraid of coming off as some kind of government conspiracy nut. I was worried that they'd sic the Secret Service on me. When the detectives asked what our book was about, I told them it was about politics. A work in progress. I said we didn't even have a publishing deal.

Enough.

After breakfast with Mama, I toss my sweats in the hamper, take a shower, and put on a pair of jeans and a blouse. I don't feel normal. But at least I kind of look it. One step at a time.

CHAPTER 70

Walter Reed National Military Medical Center

Walter Reed may be one of the world's finest medical institutions, but it's still a hospital, and the scents and sounds make Burton Pearce queasy. For good reason.

Five years ago, he watched his younger sister waste away from kidney disease at Union Memorial in Maryland. His mother died from stomach cancer at Georgetown University Hospital three months later. Not long after, his dad went to Mount Sinai in New York for a routine angioplasty and died on the table.

He gets off on the seventh floor and heads for Vice President Ransom Faulkner's suite. This is a solo visit, timed right after morning rounds. Thanks to a couple of well-placed phone calls from Pearce, Rachel Bernstein is on her way to a conference of Virginia mayors. She'll be gone all day.

Pearce nods to the two Secret Service agents outside the suite. He pushes the door open—and almost walks right back out.

He didn't realize it had gotten this bad.

Faulkner is gaunt, his chin coated with gray stubble, an oxygen cannula below his nostrils. The metal stands at his sides are filled with monitors, humming and beeping. An IV bag hangs at the head of the bed. One of the most dynamic men he's ever known—a generational political force—reduced to fluids in, fluids out.

Pearce drags a chair over and sits down.

The noise wakes the VP. He blinks and turns his head on the pillow.

"Burton," he says weakly. "Nice surprise."

"Good to see you, Chief. Can I get you anything?"

A wan smile. "About six feet of clean colon, if you can spare it."

Pearce laughs. "I was thinking more like ice chips."

"Only if they're floating in a tumbler of scotch," says Faulkner. He coughs. "What's up, Burton?" he croaks. "You've got better things to do than visit the sick and infirm."

Pearce rests one hand on the bed rail. "We're getting close, Mr. Vice President. I want to keep you in the loop."

Faulkner's furry eyebrows lift. "The Grand Bargain?"

Pearce nods. "Things are reaching the critical point, sir. We need to make sure you have all the help and support you need. All the right people."

Faulkner rests his hand on Pearce's. "Don't worry. The doctors here are great. Nurses too." He smiles. "The best a nine-hundred-billion-dollar military budget can buy."

"I'm talking closer to home, Chief." Pearce leans in. "I'm just here to help you reach the right decision."

CHAPTER 71

Brooklyn, New York

My iPhone chimes with an incoming text. I look down.

Sorry to hear about Garrett's death.

A Brother

I've been getting condolence calls and texts all week from everyone I know. Even Burton Pearce expressed his sympathies. I was touched by the outpouring of messages. This one pisses me off. I sit down on my bed and text back:

Who is this, you son of a bitch?

So far, this has been a one-way communication. I've never responded until now. I don't know what to expect.

Within seconds, there's a reply.

You're still in danger. Suzanne. Amber. Garrett. You could be next.

A warning or a threat? Either way, I'm over it.

No more texting. Meet me in person.

I send it and wait. My head is throbbing, and my heart is pounding. This better be good.

It is.

Grand Central. Today, 3 p.m., the information booth clock. Alone.

I throw open my bedroom door and stomp into the kitchen. "Mama, I changed my mind."

"What's that?"

"I'm going back to work."

"You mean teaching?"

"No. I mean the book. I'm going to finish it myself."

CHAPTER 72

Grand Central Terminal, Manhattan

When I was little, train rides put me to sleep.

Today, I'm wide awake.

Pops used to take me on train rides all the time, all over New York City and up and down the Hudson River. He was proud of being part of a system that moved millions of people every day. He told me to always be polite to the engineer and the conductor. They usually gave us a special nod when he flashed his MTA ID.

My train pulls into Grand Central and I follow the crowd to the main floor with its shiny gold clock and 125-foot-high ceiling mural illustrating the constellations of the zodiac.

I stop at the edge of the concourse and scan the people walking by. I see cops patrolling. I assume I'm watching for a Black man, since the texts came from "A Brother." That's all I know.

A young woman with locs falling over her shoulders stops in front of me like she's about to ask for directions. She's skinny and tall and can't be more than nineteen or twenty.

"Looking for Brother?" she asks.

The expression on my face is all the confirmation she needs.

"Let's go," she says. With a strong stride, she crosses the terminal, turning back to make sure I'm behind her as she climbs the marble staircase on the west side of the concourse.

I hustle to keep up.

At the Vanderbilt entrance, a battered Hyundai is parked illegally, hazard lights flashing. Standing on the far side of the car is a Black man wearing a long tan coat, frayed at the collar. His eyes are darting left and right.

Is this the man behind the ominous texts? Is this Brother?

The young woman goes around to the driver's side. I see her slip a folded bill into the man's hand, and he leaves—she must have paid him to watch the car.

Guess that's not Brother.

"Ride up front," she says. "I'm not your Uber driver."

She works her way through Midtown, then Hell's Kitchen. When we're in the northbound lane of the Henry Hudson Parkway, I ask, "Can you tell me where we're going?"

"Nope." Her eyes never waver from the traffic ahead.

She takes the 125th Street exit, and things start to look familiar. *Very* familiar.

I don't believe this. We're heading for Jerome L. Greene Hall, a blocky building better known as "the Toaster."

It's the home of my alma mater Columbia Law. When I walk through the main door, powerful sense memories bring me back to when I first set foot in here.

We ride the elevator to the sixth floor, then I follow the young woman through a wide corridor. We stop abruptly in front of an office door I know well.

She leaves, and I step forward and knock beneath a plaque reading DR. CAMERON GRAHAM.

"Enter!" booms that familiar voice.

It's him, all right. My old mentor. Also my tormentor and inquisitor. And a father figure after Pops died.

I push open the door, and there he is. Behind his wire-rimmed glasses, Dr. Cameron Graham's brown eyes are twinkling. Above his expressive face is a fringe of white hair.

"Brea Cooke," he says, standing up with a broad smile. "It's been too many years." He must be in his seventies now and wearing the same outfit as always: black slacks, white shirt, blue necktie that's tight to the collar.

"Dr. Graham, I'm glad to see you. But I'm not sure why I'm here."

He turns serious. "Close the door," he says softly, dropping his smile. "And call me Brother."

CHAPTER 73

Concord, New Hampshire

Behind her desk at the New Hampshire Department of Safety, Detective Sergeant Marie Gagnon is rubbing her temples, frustrated by the meager contents of Suzanne Bonanno's murder book.

Even though it's been seventeen years, the file should be bulging. But she's had to rebuild it from practically nothing. She has the autopsy report, of course, complete with digital photographs and precise anatomical measurements. She has Dr. Alice Woods's opinion that Suzanne might have been pregnant. But both she and the ME know that a defense expert could easily cast doubt on that theory. If there had ever been fetal remains, they're long gone, dissolved into the dark Seabrook soil.

She has Suzanne's bracelet and the DVD that shows her wearing it at a Boston children's hospital back when she cheered for the Patriots.

But all that does nothing but support the conclusion that the body in the pit was Suzanne's. Gagnon is still nagged by the fact that the bracelet was found near the top of the grave and not with the bones below. But as she and Bastinelli had discussed, the bracelet could have been disturbed by whoever dug up the bones and deposited them in the trunk of the Sentra.

Gagnon rereads the interviews she conducted with Felicia Bonanno and the Foxborough worker, Stacey Millett. Both women talked about Cole's overbearing manner, but a football player with an aggressive personality isn't exactly a shocker. And of course, Felicia has a reason for blaming Cole for her daughter's death. She admitted that she'd never trusted him. Besides, Brenda Connelly Monroe, the coed who'd gifted Cole the watch at Dartmouth, said he was a total sweetheart. Not exactly a convincing pattern.

Gagnon clicks through archival photos of Cole Wright after he joined the Patriots, looking for pictures of him wearing the watch. But most of the photos show him in his football gear, no fashion wrist wear permitted. And in the few shots she can find of him in a suit, his cuffs cover his wrists.

The watch could have been lost or stolen sometime after he graduated. That would be an easy thing for Wright to claim, anyway. And who could prove him wrong?

And now there's a new file on her desk, about a murder in Boston last week. Amber Keenan, onetime squad mate of Suzanne's on the Patriots cheerleading team. No leads there so far, according to the Boston detective Gagnon talked to.

Two dead cheerleaders, seventeen years apart. Is there a connection, Gagnon wonders, or is it just coincidence that Suzanne's body was found around the same time?

Gagnon's desk phone rings. She picks up. "Detective Gagnon, Major Crimes."

"Detective, this is Jan McHenry, from Icon Labs in Boston."

For a second, Gagnon can't place the name. Then it comes to her. "Right! The sheet fibers."

"Correct. Sorry it's taken us so long, but we were able to trace the dye and the fabric to Formosa Industries in Taipei, Taiwan. They have a proprietary weave and confirmed that that specific blue dye was used in a limited run of sheets and pillowcases about twenty years ago. And they offloaded the whole supply to one buyer, Walmart. Under the name Regal Soft Touch Bedsheets."

Fueled by two cups of office coffee, Gagnon can feel her synapses firing. Some days, detective work is like the children's card game concentration. You turn over cards, two of them each time, trying to find a matching pair. The trick is to turn over the first card and remember where you saw its match.

"Thanks! Gotta go!" Gagnon doesn't even wait for a goodbye from Jan. She grabs her files and starts shuffling through her interview records. *Felicia Bonanno! Where is Felicia? Here!* She runs her hand down the transcript pages, flipping through until she finds what she wants, right near the end.

GAGNON: So, just going back once more—you're sure you don't remember the name of the restaurant Cole and Suzanne were going to that night? Even the type? Italian? French?
BONANNO: No, I'm sorry. Someplace on the shore. I just know they were meeting at the Walmart so Suzanne could buy some apartment supplies first.

Gagnon grabs a yellow highlighter and circles the exchange. With her other hand, she reaches for the phone. She taps the extension of Beth Condon, an analyst at police headquarters, fresh out of MIT.

"This is Beth."

"Beth, it's Detective Gagnon upstairs. I need a favor. I need you to find all the Walmart locations within twenty miles of Seabrook."

CHAPTER 74

Columbia University

As I walk with Dr. Graham through Morningside Park, I realize that during my three years as his student, I never once saw him outside a lecture hall or his office.

He points to a bench facing a wide sidewalk lined with trees. "Right here is good." He sits down heavily and turns to me. "I'm so sorry about Garrett. I only met him once, that afternoon when he picked you up after class. Nice young man. Talented too. I've read his books."

I remember that day. We'd just found an apartment in Washington Heights and were so happy to be moving in together and starting our professional careers. I also remember how tough Dr. Graham's classes were. He pushed us hard but always stayed after the lectures to answer questions.

I'm bursting with questions now. "Dr. Graham, why the cloak-and-dagger? Why call yourself Brother? And why were you watching us in the first place?"

"You've been gifted with a piercing mind and a knack for challenging authority—even mine, from time to time."

Dr. Graham never made a secret of the fact that he had worked at the FBI before he became a federal judge and long before he retired from the bench to become a law professor.

"How did you find me? How did you know what Garrett and I were working on?"

"I may be old, Brea, but I still hear things. When I found out about the book you were writing, I knew how important it was and how dangerous the investigation could be."

"So you were deliberately trying to scare me."

"I was."

"What do you know about the old accusations against Cole Wright?" I ask. "The rape of a freshman girl at Dartmouth? The disappearance of Suzanne Bonanno? Did you know that on the day Garrett was murdered, he was coming from a private meeting with Wright?"

Dr. Graham sits up a little straighter. "A private meeting with the First Gentleman? Where?"

"I never found out. Garrett mentioned an airport near Hanover."

I can see that Dr. Graham is wrestling with a decision. Eventually, he says, "Brea, there are two groups who've been following your investigations. One group wants very much to stop you. The other wants very much to help you."

"And it was the first group that had Garrett killed?"

Dr. Graham nods. "I'm sorry. Looks that way. I have information that might help you track down his killer—and keep you alive."

"Information from where?"

"From Seymour Washington."

I shake my head. Him again. "You know Seymour Washington?"

Dr. Graham smiles. "Brea, *everybody* in the FBI knows Seymour Washington."

"So what does he have for me now?"

"He has the name of a Mafia button man who's dying."

"Did he kill Garrett?"

Dr. Graham shakes his head. "No, no. This man is my age. He's been out of the game for a long time. But he knows things. And apparently, he's feeling some remorse about his life choices."

"So give me his name. I'll call the police. Let's have him picked up and questioned."

"Brea, think. This man has been dodging the law his whole life. Now he's dying, and he's not about to talk to the police on his way out. But he might talk to you."

Dr. Graham pulls out a folded piece of paper and puts it in my hands. I open it.

The page has a single handwritten name: *Leo Amalfi*. Underneath that is *Cranston, RI*.

I look up at Dr. Graham. "Never heard of him."

"That means he was good at his job."

CHAPTER 75

Concord, New Hampshire

Deputy attorney general Hugh Bastinelli has faced down tough judges and ruthless criminals in court, but nothing intimidates him more than sitting across the desk from his boss, New Hampshire attorney general Jennifer Pope.

Pope is in her mid-fifties with a stylish haircut and even smarter clothing. The AG is known for driving hard on homicide investigations and clamping down even harder on leaks. But what she's hardest on is evidence.

Or the lack of it.

Pope is reading through a rough draft of Bastinelli's prosecution memo, the framework of the case against Cole Wright. It's the core of the argument that will be made to a grand jury when the AG's office seeks an indictment of the First Gentleman for the murder of Suzanne Bonanno.

Pope finishes the last page and purses her lips. She looks up at Bastinelli. "Hugh, just between us—are you shitting me?"

"No, Jen. I think he's guilty."

"Well, this sure as hell doesn't prove it." Pope shakes her head and flips through the pages again. "Look, the medical forensics and ID are solid. No reason to doubt that the bones belong to Suzanne Bonanno. Alice Woods is a good ME and even better on the stand. She might even be able to convince the jury that Suzanne was murdered. But the rest is loose. You've got Seabrook and a Lake Marie property that belongs to Cole Wright but nothing to connect them except a watch."

Bastinelli squirms a bit.

"What do we know about the Lake Marie property?" she asks.

"Wright bought it when he signed with the Patriots. Planned to build a camp there."

"And did anybody see him dig the hole? Did he order the hole to be dug?"

"Not that we know of. The caretaker didn't even know it was there until the troopers found it."

Pope isn't done. "You've got a few people from twenty years back who say Wright used to talk tough to women. I'm sure the defense will find a dozen other people to say that he walked on water. The White House will bring out the best lawyers to fight this, Hugh. They'll drive a bus through these cracks."

"Jen, this case has been on ice for seventeen years. The original records are missing. We've had to rebuild everything."

"Cry me a river, Hugh. Records go missing all the time. Where's your motive?"

"It's right there," says Bastinelli, on the defensive. "The relationship between a player and a cheerleader was against team policy. It could have cost Wright his position with the Pats. Millions in potential income and endorsements. Maybe Suzanne was threatening to go public with the relationship. Maybe because she was pregnant with his child."

"And so he lost his temper and killed her in a fit of rage?"

"Happens every day. I don't need to tell you that."

"Okay," says Pope, leafing through the document. "Where's the fetal DNA?"

Bastinelli scratches his chin. "There is none. No fetal remains at all."

"The results of a pregnancy test? Interview with her ob-gyn?"

"Not that we can find."

Pope stops turning the pages. "So we're basing the pregnancy theory on an analysis of buried pelvic bones?"

Bastinelli nods. "Osteoclastic formation due to ligamental changes in preparation for childbirth. It's a frequent finding."

"Right. A finding I could find a dozen experts to piss all over."

Bastinelli can't argue with that. He could locate a few himself.

"Before I stick you in front of a grand jury," Pope continues, "you need to convince me that you can place Cole Wright with Suzanne Bonanno after she left her mother's trailer. Some indication that he *was* actually the last person to see her alive. And I need some direct connection between that night and what was in that grave. Until you have that, we're wasting our time. And don't forget," says Pope, "I'm going to have to brief the governor on this."

"What kind of pushback can we expect?"

"Lots of sound and fury, I'm sure," says Pope. "The media will go apeshit, seeing how he supported Faulkner during the primaries."

"Right, he did," says Bastinelli. "All the way to the convention floor."

"And I was part of the opposition. Look, I can claim I'm neutral until the cows come home, but a lot of the media and Wright's supporters will think this is a hit job."

"Okay," says Bastinelli. "I'll see what else Gagnon can find."

He stands up to leave. Pope picks up a small commemorative

medallion from her desk and points to an inscription. "See this? *Fiat justitia ruat caelum.*"

"Sorry," says Bastinelli, "my Latin's a little rusty."

"It means 'Let justice be done though the heavens fall.'"

"Noble thought."

"I agree," says Pope. "Just don't let them fall on me."

CHAPTER 76

Everett, Massachusetts

In the parking lot of the Encore casino, the man still calling himself Jack Doohan is getting some fresh air when his phone vibrates.

Not his iPhone. The other one. "Yeah?"

"Good job in Brattleboro." It's the same electronically masked voice with the same Jersey-mobster vibe.

"No problem," says Doohan. "Appreciate the bonus."

Which was well earned. This time, he'd done more than observe and report.

Up at the Vermont hideaway, he'd watched from the trees as two men entered cabin 19. He heard the soft pop that told him their job was done. Watched them take off into the woods. As soon as they disappeared, he put on his paper booties and disposable gloves and slipped through the half-open door. Subject on the floor; laptop on the table. Just as he'd expected.

He'd taken the laptop and replaced it with a kilo of his finest cocaine, some pharmaceutical utensils, and a bag of baking soda.

A poor man's drug lab. Actually, not so poor. The coke was worth at least twenty-five grand on the street.

The cost was covered, of course, along with his other expenses.

"We might need you again," the voice says. "What do you think about killing women?"

Doohan shrugs. "I think about it all the time."

CHAPTER 77

Hanover, New Hampshire

I go to gas up Garrett's Subaru at a Circle K. I guess it's my Subaru now, but in my mind, this car will always be his. It's as much a part of him as his ratty sweatshirts and beat-up tennis shoes. And that precious Martin guitar.

I wish to hell Garrett could talk to me right now. Garrett said that he met with Cole Wright at an airport near Hanover. You'd think it would be easy to find the right one in a state with fewer than thirty airports, but it's not.

My first stop was Lebanon. The manager checked the records but found nothing. She said she'd been there six years and had never seen an incoming flight from DC.

Next I'd checked out a private airport in Canaan, but it was little more than a grassy field. I couldn't imagine anything bigger than a Cessna landing there, and I doubted the Secret Service would let the president's husband travel in a plane that small.

When I get to the pump, I notice the handwritten sign: *Please Pay Inside.*

Pain in the ass. That's how my day is going.

I lock up the car and head inside to pre-pay at the register.

I grab a bottle of Pepsi from a cooler and put it on the counter. "I'll take this, and forty bucks' worth of gas," I tell the gray-haired cashier who rings me up. I hand her a ten and a couple of twenties. "Can I ask you a question?"

"Questions and answers still free around here," she says.

"I'm a writer and I'm looking for some background on the area. I need to talk to somebody who knows the local history, especially the kind that doesn't get into the history books."

"Local history? You mean like Revolutionary War stuff? They've got a historical society over at the library."

"I'm thinking more recent history. This century or last."

She hands me my change and a receipt. "Then you should talk to the Romeos."

"The Romeos?"

"Yeah. 'Retired Old Men Eating Out.' They hang out at Olie's, a coffee shop about five miles down the road." She points east. "Wind 'em up and they'll talk your goddamn ear off."

Olie's turns out to be a run-down brick building with a counter covered with coffee urns and glass pastry containers. I get a cup of black coffee.

In a back corner, six white men with the lined faces of seventy-somethings are clustered around two tables pushed together, talking and laughing. The three men facing the door give me the eye. The others just keep on yakking.

I gather my nerve, drag a chair over, and give the men my brightest smile. *My* secret weapon. "Morning! I heard you gentlemen know everything there is to know about this area."

At first, the faces are stern. Suspicious. Then one of the guys grins back. "Ain't no gentlemen here." The others guffaw at the joke. Can't blame them. The delivery was spot-on.

One of the other guys shifts his chair to the side to make some room. "Slide in, honey. What do you want to know?"

"She's not your honey," another man says, wagging his finger.

"You *wish* she was," says a third. He chuckles into his coffee mug. The others laugh.

I feel like I'm at a Friars Club comedy roast. "My name's Brea Cooke. I'm working on a book about airplanes, and I'm looking for some local history."

"What kind of history?" Judging by his looks, this is the oldest guy in the bunch. Bald head. Bushy white eyebrows. All the others are wearing caps—Hanover FD, Caterpillar, John Deere, and two with Vietnam patches.

Veterans.

In an instant, I have my spiel. And the first part is totally true. "My great-grandfather was a Tuskegee Airman. A fighter pilot. Before the war, he was a mechanic with the regular Army Air Corps."

The bald guy gives me a nod. "Those Tuskegee men kicked ass."

I nod right back. "They did. My great-grandpa was part of a transportation wing that flew planes up to Canada so they could be transferred to the RAF and the RCAF."

"Sure," the man on my right says. "I heard of that."

From here, I'm just winging it, so to speak. Pure invention. "So there's a family story that on one flight, my great-grandpa's plane lost an engine, and he landed at an emergency strip somewhere around here. I already checked with Lebanon, and I looked at Canaan—"

"The grass strip?" says one of the vets. "They call it Triumph now."

"And it wasn't even there in the forties," says the other. "Opened around 1962."

The guy in the John Deere cap hasn't said much. I wonder if he resents my intrusion. He narrows his eyes and looks at me.

"Etna Drags," he says.

Silence all around. Then the bald guy slaps the table. "Shit, yes! Etna Drags. It was a refueling stop and emergency depot during the war. After that, they turned it into a racetrack for cars. A drag strip. Went bankrupt about sixty years ago."

The guy in the Caterpillar cap leans toward him. "About the time your balls dropped, right, Lou?" Uproarious laughter.

"Hey, hey!" one of the vets shouts. "There's a lady present!" He looks over at me. "Apologies, Brea."

I wave my hand. "No worries. I've heard worse." I grab my coffee and get up from the chair. I look right at Mr. John Deere. "Etna Drags. Thank you!"

He nods and tips his cap. "Do right by your great-grandpa, now."

"I will."

That's one more person I need to do right by.

CHAPTER 78

Seabrook, New Hampshire

Detective Sergeant Marie Gagnon walks into the Seabrook Walmart, one of three Walmart stores that existed in the area seventeen years ago and the one closest to Suzanne Bonanno's former address.

She glances around and wonders how the store looked back then and if Suzanne spent the last few minutes of her life picking out housewares here.

A stout gray-haired woman in a blue vest gives Gagnon a cheery wave. "Welcome to Walmart!"

Gagnon holds up her badge. "State police. Where can I find the manager?"

The greeter's smile dissolves. She's suddenly flustered. "Oh, my heavens! That's, uh, Gayle Brennan. She's usually on the floor somewhere..." The greeter turns and looks anxiously down the aisle. Then she turns back to Gagnon and points. "Yes! See that lady in the red top? Halfway down on the right? That's her. That's Gayle."

"Thanks." Gagnon keeps her badge by her side. The woman with the red top is scanning barcodes with a handheld reader that beeps like a hospital monitor. "Gayle Brennan?" The badge comes up again. "Detective Gagnon, Major Crimes Unit."

Brennan's ruddy face goes pale. "Oh my God! What is it?"

Gagnon sees it all the time. As soon as the badge appears, people assume that they're in big trouble or that somebody's dead. They're often correct.

"Do you have an office where we can talk?" says Gagnon, sliding the badge back into her pocket. "I just have a few questions about the store."

The color comes back into Brennan's face. "Sure. Of course." She drops the scanner on a utility cart and leads Gagnon down an aisle and up a metal staircase to a mezzanine. "Right in here," says Brennan, opening the door to a small room with a narrow window overlooking the vast sales floor.

"Let's sit," says Gagnon, taking one of the chairs in front of the glass desk while Brennan makes a stab at straightening some papers.

"Sorry for the mess," she says.

"Don't worry about it, Gayle. You should see *my* office. Tell me, how long has this store been open?"

Brennan lowers herself into her desk chair. "I'm gonna say...twenty years? I've been here fifteen. Started on the floor."

"Long time," says Gagnon. "That's exactly the era I'm interested in. I'm investigating a homicide from seventeen years back, and I'm trying to determine if the victim stopped in here on the night she was last seen."

"Dear Jesus," says Brennan, then covers her mouth with one palm.

"I know you have surveillance cameras all over the store. Was that system in operation back then?"

"Oh, I'm sure it was. Maybe not as sophisticated and high-res as it is now, but yeah, I expect the whole store would have been covered."

"And is there any chance you'd have the footage for this date and time?" Gagnon hands her a slip of paper.

"That far back?" Brennan shakes her head. "I'm sorry. We wipe the files every three months unless there's been an incident, like a fight or shoplifting or a slip-and-fall. Then we'll save it for as long as we need to, for legal or whatever."

"And you control the surveillance from here? Do you have a security room?"

"We do now," says Brennan. "It used to be centralized, but I guess that didn't work out."

"When was it centralized and for how long?"

"Not sure. Before my time."

"Is there anybody around who would know?"

Brennan drums her fingers on her desk for a moment. "Hold on." She presses a button on her phone console. "Paul? Gayle. Listen. What was the name of that woman from IT, the one who was here a few months ago about the checkout scanners?" Brennan rolls her eyes and says, "Right, the really hot one." She scrawls on a pad. "Okay, Paul, thanks." A pause. "What? No. Don't worry. She didn't complain about you. Relax."

Brennan hangs up, tears the page off the pad. "Lindsay Farrow. She works out of the supercenter in Salem. Should I tell her you're coming?"

"Please don't," says Gagnon. "It just makes people nervous."

CHAPTER 79

Etna, New Hampshire

Now I know why the name Etna rings a bell—it's where two Dartmouth professors were murdered in their home. Two teenage boys came looking for money, stole about three hundred dollars, then stabbed the professors to death. The Dartmouth Murders, they called them.

That was years ago, before my and Garrett's time at school here, and although Etna—POPULATION 870, according to the sign at the town limits—is just a few miles from campus, neither of us ever visited. Not much here to visit.

Etna Drags wasn't coming up on my GPS, so I had to stop at the post office and ask for directions, and that led me here, to the end of a narrow dirt road. I get out of the car and look through a chain-link fence. Two NO TRESPASSING signs are shot through with rusted bullet holes. Birds cry in the distance.

From where I'm standing, I can see a long strip. The paved surface looks pretty sound even though grass is growing through the cracks. Set back from the strip are two structures, an open-air

Quonset-type hangar and a two-story brick building with broken windows that might once have been a control tower.

Is it possible that this is the place Garrett met the First Gentleman?

I squeeze my way through the sagging gate and past a clump of crushed and rusted car bodies. Drag-strip casualties, I suppose.

"Hey! What are you doing?"

I turn and see a man with a chest-length black beard coming from the hangar. He's in a grease-stained denim jumpsuit, and he's holding a pistol in his right hand, though his arm is at his side.

By instinct, I turn my palms forward and open my arms wide. I try my smile. "Hi! Are you the manager?"

The smile doesn't work this time. "Manager of what?" he asks. "I sort through the junk, if that's what you mean." He wiggles the gun but doesn't lift it. Not yet. "You here from the government again?" he asks.

Again? I feel a flutter in my gut. "No. I'm an attorney looking for information. Somebody told me there was an airfield here, not used much anymore."

"That's true. Technically decommissioned in 1945. Haven't had anybody come through recently—until a week or so ago."

"What happened then?"

"Lots of shit. Late one afternoon, a big black SUV pulls up. Two big dudes in suits get out. They tell me there's an emergency government drill. Ask me the length of the runway. Walk around on it a little."

"And then what happened?"

"Then they take my gun and my phone, put me in one of their SUVs, and lock me in." Just remembering the events makes him outraged. "Half hour later, out of nowhere, this black military passenger jet comes in for a landing, low and smooth. Five minutes after that, three more cars pull up, two SUVs and a brand-new Corolla. Guy and a gal get out of the Corolla and walk up the steps into the plane."

"What did they look like?"

"The lady was in a suit. All business. The guy was dressed casual with messy hair, like he was goin' out for pizza or something. Looked a little spooked, though."

"Who was on the plane?"

"No idea. After about two hours, the guy comes back out and drives away in the Corolla. In no time, the plane taxis around and takes off. Right after that, they give me back my stuff and let me loose. Then all the SUVs head off toward the highway."

"The guy, the one with the messy hair. You get a good look at him?"

"Yeah. He walked right past me. Right where you're standing."

My heart is pounding so hard I can hardly breathe.

I pull out my phone. I scroll to a picture of Garrett, one of my favorite close-ups. I hold it up in front of the man.

"Yeah. That's him," he says. "You know him?"

"I do." I can feel myself crumbling inside. "I did."

CHAPTER 80

Salem, New Hampshire

"Have a seat, Detective. Let me see what I can find."

Lindsay Farrow, the Walmart IT director, is in her late twenties, wearing stylish jeans, a silk blouse, and a fitted jacket. Definitely designer.

"I really appreciate it," says Gagnon, even as she's thinking, *Probably a waste of time.*

They're sitting in Farrow's office at the back of the mammoth Walmart supercenter in Salem. Unlike Gayle Brennan's workspace, Farrow's is pristine—white tables, Aeron chairs. Banks of monitors show every corner of the Salem sales floor and warehouse.

"Seabrook store, right?" Farrow is bent over a sleek laptop, clicking furiously. "Sorry. I need to go down a bit of a wormhole here..."

"Take your time," says Gagnon. "I *live* in wormholes."

Farrow focuses on one panel and zooms in. "Yes. Gayle was right. The year you're talking about, the company rolled out

Operation Harvest, a system that consolidated the security data and linked it to a central database. Probably some consultant sold them on it. From what I can tell, the software was pretty advanced for its time." She turns the laptop around.

Gagnon examines the screen. "Gayle told me that the surveillance files get wiped every three months. Is that true?"

"True now," says Farrow. "But not back then, it looks like."

Gagnon feels the first slight lift since the investigation began. "You mean those files still exist?"

"Like I said, the program was a test, so they might have saved the data in Bentonville for research purposes."

"Bentonville?"

"Bentonville, Arkansas. The mothership. Walmart headquarters. I spent a week there when I was training. Had fun." She smiles at the memory, then goes back to her keyboard. "I think I can pull the files up." She types. "Hold on. I need another authorization code..."

Gagnon closes her eyes and thinks, *Please, please, please don't tell me I need a search warrant.*

"Hey! I'm in!" Farrow sounds genuinely surprised. Long rows of digits and letters spill down her screen. She glances down at the slip of paper with the date Gagnon gave her, June 7. "What time are we talking about?"

Gagnon pulls her chair up close to Farrow's. She thinks back. Felicia said Suzanne left to go to the store at seven p.m. on the dot. "Try from seven fifteen p.m. forward."

"Where should we start looking? Aisles? Checkout?"

"Try checkout."

"Which register?"

How the hell would I know? Gagnon lets out a long breath. "Do you have a view of the whole front of the store?"

"Hold on." Farrow clicks on one of the files. "There we go."

Unbelievable, Gagnon thinks as a bird's-eye view of the checkout section in the Seabrook store appears on the screen. Given that the footage is from seventeen years ago, she was expecting archival black-and-white. But she's looking at full color. Farrow has her video player set at double speed so the images of customers filing forward are jerky and blurry.

"Can you tell me who we're looking for?" asks Farrow.

"Stop!" Gagnon shouts. "Go back." Farrow rewinds at slow speed. "Now freeze!" Gagnon points to the screen. In the line for register 2 are a tall man with an athletic build and a woman with a mane of wavy blond hair.

Gagnon sits back in her chair. "Right there. In the middle. That's who we're looking for."

I see you, Suzanne. I see you.

CHAPTER 81

The White House

Cole Wright walks the halls of the Eisenhower Executive Office Building. Located next to the West Wing, this part of the White House compound is an architectural marvel built in the Second Empire style. It's also a power center, housing the offices of key administration employees.

Like the vice president's chief of staff.

Wright has business with Rachel Bernstein. Business that must be conducted in person.

The door to Bernstein's office is open but there's nothing in the room other than a bare desk. He has a feeling Burton Pearce knows why.

He goes to the West Wing. Pearce's assistant, Pam Hitchcock, is at her desk outside the chief of staff's office. She holds a hand up like a traffic cop. "He's on the phone, Mr. Wright."

"Hey, Pam," says Cole. "I was just over in the EEOB. Rachel Bernstein's office is empty. Did they move her?"

"They did. To Berlin."

"Berlin?"

"Yes. She's joined Ambassador Eastland's staff."

"When did this happen?"

"A couple days ago." Hitchcock glances down at her phone console. "He's off the phone, Mr. Wright. You can go in."

Cole realizes that he shouldn't be surprised about Bernstein.

Cole pushes the door open and sees Pearce behind his massive desk, crossing items off a list with vigorous strokes of his pen and muttering as he goes. "Duffy! Baynes! Price! Morlock! *Idiots!* Every single one!" He slams down his pen. "You know, they say the Senate is the most exclusive club in the world, but sometimes I think we'd be better off picking a hundred names at random."

Cole ignores the tirade. He's heard it all before, every time an important piece of legislation is on the line. Like now. "Problems with the Grand Bargain?" he asks.

Pearce waves a hand dismissively. "Nothing a few dams and tax abatements can't fix."

Cole takes a seat in one of Pearce's cushioned antique armchairs. "What happened with Rachel Bernstein?"

Pearce stacks some folders on his desk. "She went to Berlin."

"I heard that. Why?"

Pearce folds his hands. "Truth? I think Faulkner was tired of her bossing the doctors around at Walter Reed. Another few days and she would've been wearing a white coat."

Cole cocks his head. "Faulkner got rid of her?"

"Let's say he offered her a chance to broaden her résumé."

Cole knows how much Bernstein grated on Pearce. He grins. "Miss her?"

Pearce grins back. "I'm devastated."

He gets up from his desk, walks around, and takes a seat across from Cole. He leans forward and looks him right in the eye. "What in the hell were you thinking, sneaking off to Hanover like that? You had to know I'd find out."

Pearce has always had a way of finding things out. That's why Cole is here. He learned a few things about Garrett Wilson's murder last week from the news. But he has a feeling that Pearce knows more. "Of course I did. I just didn't want you to stop me."

"And what was so important that you had to burn two thousand gallons of government fuel and land at an unsecured airfield?"

"I wanted to talk to Garrett Wilson face to face."

"And what did you talk about?"

Cole can feel his temper rising. "That was between him and me. I don't need your permission to talk to a reporter, Burton. You're not my handler."

"Cole, you've always needed me, even at Dartmouth. Do I have to remind you how I helped when those rumors started about you?"

"That was then. This is now."

"And now is an even more delicate time. Anything *any* of us does can affect the president's agenda! How do you think it would look to the inquiring public? First Gentleman meets with reporter; reporter ends up dead. So yes! You should have asked my permission. And you'd better damn well hope nobody on the outside finds out about your little excursion. This is bigger than you, Cole!"

"You know I wouldn't do anything to hurt Maddy."

"Not on purpose, no. But think about the risk you took!" Pearce inhales deeply and settles down. He eases back in his chair and says in a lower voice, "In four days, the president will address the nation and announce the Grand Bargain. The challenge is to keep a lid on this while we prepare her remarks and work with the majority and minority leaders in both houses so that they will all appear with her when the announcement is made. No matter what we might have promised along the way, we're not leaking anything. We're not tipping off anybody. Not the press. Not the Supreme Court. Not Wall Street. The networks will get ten minutes' notice. In the meantime, I can't have the president's husband taking random undisclosed trips."

"Okay, Burton, I promise I'll put myself on a leash until the announcement is made. Now tell me what you know about Garrett Wilson's murder."

Pearce shrugs. "From what I hear from Brattleboro, Wilson was holed up in a cabin with a kilo of high-grade coke. Way too much for personal use. Looks like he was getting ready to cut it and distribute it."

"So why would his killer leave the kilo of coke behind?"

"Who knows? Maybe he was in a rush. Maybe he didn't want to double his felonies. Look, I don't want to talk about Garrett Wilson. I need you to make a trip for me. Official. On the record."

"Where to?"

"Back to New Hampshire. Manchester."

"For what?"

"You know Bracken, the mayor up there?"

"Dale Bracken? I've heard of him. Didn't he play for Yale?"

"He did. All-America linebacker. He wants to run for Congress next year, and Maddy wants you there for a fundraiser."

Cole gets it. "Jock to jock, right?" His typical campaign shtick.

"It sends an early message to the party that the president's made her choice. Helps eliminate infighting and wasted funds come primary time. You can plug your fitness program in the remarks."

Cole sighs. "Fine. No problem. I'll do it."

"Good. The travel office will set it up." Pearce grins. "My people. Not your band of sky pirates."

Cole feels Pearce's hand on his knee. A brotherly gesture, meant to welcome him back into the fold. Also his traditional signal that a meeting is over. They both stand. Cole is ushered toward the door. Pearce pauses with his hand on the doorknob.

"Cole, my old friend." His voice is low. "We've been through a lot together. And now we're on the cusp of doing something really great. We've got more important things to worry about than some second-rate reporter with a side hustle in drugs. The silver lining for you is that his book is now as dead as he is."

Cole winces at Pearce's last remark, delivered with casual coldness.

Like only the Gray Ghost can.

CHAPTER 82

Concord, New Hampshire

Gagnon huddles over the flat-screen monitor at police headquarters as data analyst Beth Condon works on the screenshot from the seventeen-year-old Walmart video.

"You're lucky," says Condon. "No lossy compression."

"Explain, please," says Gagnon.

"Usually, stored files are compressed to save space on a hard drive or server. When you do that, you lose data. Looks like this file is intact. You said this was some kind of experimental program?"

"Yeah. It lasted only eighteen months."

"That's probably why it's not compressed. If it had gone on longer, they probably would have condensed everything. This file is huge. There's a lot to work with."

As Condon talks, her eyes never leave the screen. Her fingers dance over the keypad. The image is currently blown up so that two figures almost fill the frame. The checkout clerk's vest forms a soft blue edge in the foreground.

"What are you doing, exactly?" asks Gagnon.

"Motion deblurring. Focus sharpening."

"I don't see any difference."

"That's because I haven't re-rendered it yet. Hold on." She taps one more key and sits back. "There."

Gagnon watches as the blurred, pixelated image turns crisp and sharp. Condon points to the man on the screen; his face is now clearly visible. "Hey, that looks like— "

"That's exactly who it is," says Gagnon.

"Cole freaking Wright? Who's the girl? Looks like a model."

"Her name was Suzanne. She was a Patriots cheerleader."

In the sharpened image, Suzanne Bonanno's face is almost as clear as it was in Felicia's video. Her makeup is perfect, and her hair is blown out and flowing. She's wearing a sleeveless V-neck top and jeans. Her left hand is resting on a pile of merchandise on the checkout counter. "Zoom in there," says Gagnon, pointing to Suzanne's right wrist.

Condon moves two fingers across a trackpad. The image enlarges.

And there it is. The tennis bracelet.

"Save that, please," says Gagnon.

Condon clicks a screenshot.

"Now move left." Condon crawls the image slowly until Cole Wright's lower arms are visible. He's wearing a long-sleeved button-down shirt.

"I want to see if he's wearing a wristwatch," says Gagnon.

Condon zooms in even tighter. "Hard to tell," she says. "Those cuffs look pretty crisp and new. If there's a watch underneath, the contour doesn't show. There might be something under there, might not."

"Okay," says Gagnon. "Move down to the checkout counter."

Condon shifts back to the merchandise.

"Can you get that any clearer?" says Gagnon.

"I'm just about at the limit. What are we trying to see?"

Gagnon points to a soft package Suzanne's fingers are resting on.

"Towels?" asks Condon, squinting at the screen.

"I hope not," says Gagnon.

"Give me a sec." Condon places a digital grid over the package, then rotates the image to reveal a black label with gold script. "I can't make it out perfectly, but I see an *R* and an *S* and something like *bedsheets*?" She looks up. "Does that help?"

Gagnon consults her notes from her call with Jan McHenry from Icon Labs in Boston. *Regal Soft Touch Bedsheets.*

"Is that anything?" Beth asks.

Gagnon nods. "It's everything."

Suzanne Bonanno was buying her burial shroud.

CHAPTER 83

Cranston, Rhode Island

I'm parked on a narrow residential street about ten minutes from Providence. The neighborhood is made up of single-family homes with neat fenced-in yards, many containing shrines to the Virgin Mary, Saint Joseph, and a lot of other Catholic saints I don't recognize.

Before I get out of the car, I take a deep breath and exhale slowly. *You can do this, Brea.*

I wish to hell that Garrett had kept his work files on an external hard drive. But everything was on his laptop. And the laptop is gone—along with everything the First Gentleman told him. I know he kept his computer double-password-protected. But with the right tools, whoever has it might be able to crack it. Or maybe no one has it and it's lying at the bottom of some lake.

At least it wasn't hard to find an address for Leo Amalfi, the dying Mafioso whose name Dr. Graham gave me. Apparently, Amalfi doesn't feel the need to conceal where he lives. It's just down the road from the correctional center where Garrett interviewed John DeMarco.

I approach the house. If Amalfi has security, it's not obvious. No guard dogs. Nobody watching except a statue of Jesus and two small stone lions with their eyes painted red.

I open the fence gate and walk through. The tiny porch is edged with a white metal railing. I ring the doorbell. The door opens. An elderly woman with a worried face nods and waves me in like she's been expecting me.

"I'm Brea Cooke. I'm here to see Mr. Amalfi."

The house smells like garlic and onions and antiseptic. The woman leads me to what looks like a dining room that's been converted to medical use and leaves. A wrinkled, wasted man lies in a narrow hospital bed, staring out the window. In here, the medicinal smell is stronger. But it can't mask the sickening odor of decay.

Under an arch at the far side of the room, several men are standing watch. Sons? Nephews? Bodyguards?

I step up to the bedside. "Leo Amalfi?"

The man in the bed turns his head. His eyes are rheumy and red. For a second, I'm not sure he sees me. Then he blinks and raises one hand, so thin and pale it looks like light could pass through it.

"You're the attorney. And you're late," he says.

"I'm here now, Mr. Amalfi. I understand you have something to tell me."

Amalfi glances over at the young men. At his look, they melt away down the hall, out of sight. Now it's just the two of us.

"Before I begin," he says, "if you bring cops into my house, I'll turn silent as a statue. I'm speaking only to you."

"Why? Why me?"

"I know it's personal for you. I want to make amends."

Why should I believe a single word this man says? If what Dr. Graham told me is true, he's a liar and a killer.

And no one can make amends for taking the love of my life.

"Okay, Mr. Amalfi. Go ahead. I'll be your confessor. Tell me what happened. Why did Garrett Wilson have to die?"

I can see Amalfi's pale lips working before he speaks. "There was a contract," he says. His voice is weak. "You understand?"

"I know what a contract is, Mr. Amalfi. In my business and yours."

"The contract was to issue a warning. A kneecap. Cripple him, but don't kill him. I sent two men. Easy job."

"Give me their names."

"Hold on," says Amalfi. "Let me finish. When they came back, they told me the contract had been changed to a hit."

A hit. Just hearing the word makes me feel like I've been punched in the stomach. I turn away from the bed. My eyes are clenched shut as I picture Garrett's final moments. *Don't cry*, I tell myself over and over. *Do not fucking cry!* I turn back slowly. "I thought you were the man who gave the orders."

"Somebody cut the chain," Amalfi says. "Somebody above me."

Suddenly, I realize why I've been summoned here. "You work with middlemen, cutouts. Isn't that right, Mr. Amalfi?"

"Yeah. That's how it's done."

"That's how you've managed to stay out of that ugly prison down the road all these years."

He nods. "I protected myself. I protected my family. I never did any time."

"Okay. So what's to stop me from having you arrested now for conspiracy to commit murder?"

Amalfi stares out the window for a few moments. "You're an attorney. You know how long an investigation takes. By the time they bring charges and set a court date, I'll be done."

Now I understand. I squeeze the bed rail so hard, my knuckles turn white. I try to stay objective, use my left brain. Like Garrett taught me.

I lean in, close enough to smell his rotten breath. "You know who cut the chain, Mr. Amalfi, don't you? And it was a violation of your code. That's why you called me here. You didn't call me to apologize or to wipe your soul clean. You didn't call me here to ask for my forgiveness. You called me here because you wanted to tell me that you weren't the one who gave the order to kill Garrett—and you know who did."

"That's right," says Amalfi. "And you can put it in that book you're writing."

"Why should I believe you?"

"Because I'm a dying man with nothing to gain by lying."

"I'm listening. Say it, Mr. Amalfi. Say it! Tell me who ordered Garrett Wilson killed."

"It was the man in the White House," he says.

Holy shit. We were right. This noble First Gentleman act is just that—an act.

Suddenly, Amalfi lets out a load moan. He lurches on the bed. His hands claw at the covers. He gasps for air in loud, wet wheezes. Drool dribbles from the corners of his mouth. The men he sent out earlier come running in.

I back away from the bed.

I hear footsteps behind me. The woman pushes me aside. "Leo!" she cries, leaning over him. "What happened?"

I look on helplessly as Amalfi's body spasms. His face twitches.

One of the men comes around and grabs the woman's shoulders. He holds her tight as she sinks to the floor, wailing. "Call the doctor!" he says.

The old man's chest rises and falls. His breaths come harder. Then, suddenly, he's frozen still, mouth and eyes wide open.

One of the other men takes a step toward me. "You need to leave."

Suddenly I feel a cold, dark chill in the pit of my stomach. Were these the men Amalfi sent? Were these the last faces Garrett saw?

My mind is spinning with all kinds of dark thoughts as I back out of the room and hurry to the Subaru.

I just watched Leo Amalfi die and I don't know how I feel about it.

I reach into my pocket and grab my iPhone. I click to the voice-memos app. Yes. It's all there. The whole precious five minutes. I press the red button to stop recording and save the file.

A dying declaration from a hit man.

Garrett would be proud of me. At least I hope so.

CHAPTER 84

Manchester, New Hampshire

From his seat on the Air Force C-37A, the First Gentleman glances down at the office buildings and old brick factories of Manchester, New Hampshire. In the seat across from him, Secret Service agent Doug Lambert types on his iPad.

Cole Wright is jumpy and anxious. Not about making a stump speech for a local mayor. From the California governor's mansion to the White House, he's done countless similar events.

What he's nervous about is being out of DC while Maddy prepares for her big address. He's long been her favorite sounding board when she tries out key phrases and closings. Not this time. The only person who's heard her rehearse is Burton Pearce.

They're all hoping the power play will work. The plan is for Maddy, with core senators and House leaders at her side, to roll over any opposition and secure popular support. She's been banking goodwill with legislators and constituents for years. This is when it needs to pay off—big-time.

A uniformed airman makes his way down the aisle. "We'll be landing shortly. Seat belts, please."

One of Cole's aides, Maeve Fusco, come over and hands him an index card.

"Any changes?" Cole asks, tucking the card in his breast pocket.

"No, sir," Fusco says, sitting down. She reviews the itinerary and key event participants on her iPad. "You'll meet Mayor Bracken on the apron. His wife's name is Amy. Schoolteacher. Welcome remarks from the mayor. Then you. You're happy to be in New Hampshire, and in Manchester, the Queen City. Then we convoy to the Bedford Village Inn. Cocktail reception for donors. Then dinner in the great hall. You speak. Bracken speaks. No Q and A. Convoy back to the plane. We should be wheels-up by midnight."

"Surgical strike," says Cole. "I like it."

Fusco leans back in her seat. Cole hears the shift in the engine noise, then the rumble and thud of the landing gear coming down and locking into place. He rubs his eyes and feels the jolt of the wheels hitting the runway at Manchester-Boston Regional Airport. Through the window and across the tarmac, he can see the greeting party and press gaggle. A half a dozen New Hampshire state troopers stand guard nearby.

The jet taxis to a stop. Fusco jumps out of her seat, pulls out her cell phone, and starts nailing down last-minute logistics with her counterpart on the mayor's staff. When the plane door opens, Fusco looks back at Cole and gives him a thumbs-up.

Game time.

Doug Lambert walks ahead of Cole down the aisle. "Sage deplaning," he mutters into his lapel mic. The agent stands in the doorway and surveys the area as another agent positions himself by the belly of the plane. Lambert hangs tight to Cole's side while two more agents scan the greeters.

Cole's smile gets broader with each step he takes. By the time his shoes hit the tarmac, he's beaming like a movie star—or at least a beloved character actor.

The mayor and his wife are at the foot of the aircraft steps. Cole grabs Bracken's extended hand and moves in for a man hug, slapping the mayor's back soundly. The mayor returns the gesture and whispers in his ear, "Thanks for coming, Cole."

"My pleasure, Dale. Honored to be here." Cole releases the hug and turns to the petite woman by Bracken's side. "Amy! What grade are you teaching now?"

She takes Cole's hand and grips it firmly. "Middle school, Mr. Wright. Preteens."

"Please—it's Cole. Preteens? That must take a lot of energy." He moves in and gives her an air-kiss about half an inch from her cheek.

Amy Bracken nods. "All the energy I've got!"

From there, it's another quick round of handshakes and backslaps. Then Mayor Bracken taps Cole's arm and points him toward a bank of microphones on a patch of red carpet. Behind a rope barrier, members of the local media are poised with broadcast cameras and upheld phones.

Bracken steps up to speak. He's got a deep, rolling voice and a folksy, off-the-cuff delivery. "Amy and I are so pleased to welcome the First Gentleman to Manchester. And we're happy to pledge our unwavering support for the Wright administration's agenda. As I've said many times, the president's plans are good for Manchester, good for New Hampshire, good for America!" The mayor nods to Cole, claps enthusiastically, and steps back. The rest of the welcoming party join in, giving Cole a small ovation.

Cole squares himself in front of the mics and locks his eyes at the level of the camera lenses. He notices two people standing to the side of the press scrum. A man and a woman. Badges around their necks.

More local security, he assumes.

"Thank you, Mayor Bracken. We are glad to have you on our team! I'm happy to be back in New Hampshire and in the Queen City. New Hampshire is a state that means so much to Maddy and me. As you know, this is where it all started four years ago, with Dale Bracken's support. And I'm honored to be here to help him as he plans his bright future. You'll hear more about that tonight!"

The administration's endorsement of the mayor is in the bag, of course. This is pure theater. Leave 'em in suspense. Cole steps back from the mics and shouts, "Thank you!" He gives the press a brisk wave.

"Mr. Wright!" a reporter shouts. "What can you tell us about the Grand Bargain?" Other reporters join in. "Is the president really getting ready to blow up entitlements? Is she about to touch the third rail?"

Cole turns to Bracken. His smile is gone now. "Let's move."

The troopers form a cordon leading to a row of sedans and SUVs. A police car with flashing lights idles at the front with motorcycle cops on both sides.

Bracken places his hand on the small of his wife's back and hurries her toward the first SUV. An agent by the side of the second SUV holds the rear door open.

As Cole heads toward the car, he sees two people approaching to intercept him. A tall man and a woman with dark hair parted in the center. The same pair he saw standing near the press.

The next few seconds are a blur. Cole sees Agent Lambert step in front of him. He feels another agent's hands on his shoulders, pushing him to the ground. A third agent sprints toward the pair from the greeting area as he pulls an automatic machine pistol from his jacket.

"Friendly!" the man shouts, holding his badge high. The woman at his side holds up her badge too, and they both extend their other hands, palms open.

Lambert yells, "Stay back!" He has his Glock out now.

"Official government business," the guy calls. "Stand down!"

Cole grabs Lambert's arm. "Doug! Stay cool! Let's not get anybody shot out here."

The woman steps up and looks directly at Cole.

"What's this about?" Cole asks.

"Mr. Wright, I'm Detective Sergeant Gagnon, New Hampshire State Police. I'm placing you under arrest for the murder of Suzanne Bonanno. This man is Deputy Attorney General Bastinelli, and he will read you your rights."

"Like hell," says Lambert.

The agent behind Cole pulls him toward the cars. The reporters are straining at the rope barrier. Cole plants his feet and twists free of the agent. "Stop!" He turns to face Gagnon. "Detective, I don't know what this is about, but let's not have a battle out here on the runway."

"I agree, sir," says Gagnon. "Bad look for everybody. We don't need to cuff you, and you can bring your detail. But as of this moment, you're in our custody."

"We can delay the reading of the rights until we're in the vehicle," says Bastinelli.

Cole cannot believe this is happening. He turns to Lambert. "Call the president, then call Burton Pearce—in that order."

Lambert nods. He holsters his gun and pulls out his phone.

Cole keeps his face composed for the cameras, but his fists are clenched tight at his sides. He'd thought this nightmare was far behind him.

But now, after seventeen years, it's back.

PART THREE

SEPTEMBER

CHAPTER

85

Rockingham County Courthouse, New Hampshire

The rain is falling harder as I reach the courthouse entrance and present my admission pass—one of only sixty available and more precious than a Super Bowl ticket. I have Dr. Graham to thank for that. The pass was delivered to my condo by certified mail, with a note enclosed.

My student should see this trial live and in person.

A Brother

The line moves slowly up to the main entrance of the courthouse. From every direction, I hear whispered conversations:

"He's totally guilty!"

"He's an American hero!"

"He's a government puppet!"

"He's being railroaded!"

A few more steps and I'm finally out of the drizzle and into a bright corridor. I pass through a metal detector and a bag search station. Then I'm in.

That's when it really hits me.

All the months of pretrial hearings, motions, and counter-motions are over.

Multiple requests for change of venue denied. One superior court judge recused himself; another was assigned.

I closely followed the many evidentiary hearings and motions to dismiss and the bail hearing that ended in Cole being allowed to wear an ankle monitor while living in the White House instead of having to wait for his trial in a cell like every other murder suspect. At first, I couldn't believe it. But I shouldn't have been surprised. Power means privilege.

Now all the preliminary legal bullshit is over.

The jury and alternates have been seated.

Today it begins.

The end of Cole Wright.

CHAPTER 86

The courtroom is humming with energy.

I spot Garrett's former *Boston Globe* colleague Ron Reynolds sitting among the reporters in the back row. He gives me a little wave. Ron was one of the first people to reach out after Garrett died. When I worried that I could never finish the book on my own, he gave me a shot of confidence and a little tough love. "Don't let Garrett down," he said.

I won't. I can't. It's what keeps me going.

A wooden barrier separates the gallery from the business end of the courtroom—the tables for the defense and prosecution, witness stand, lectern, jury box, and judge's bench.

I look around for the couple I think of as my watchers, but they're nowhere in sight. Ever since Garrett and I started investigating, I've seen these same people over and over. I keep wondering who sent them. Tony Romero? Burton Pearce? Cole Wright?

If they want to kill me, I don't know why they haven't done it yet. They've had plenty of chances. But maybe they're just waiting for the right moment. If so, I hope I don't see it coming.

Two people who should be here in the courtroom are noticeably absent: Felicia and Teresa Bonanno. As a witness for the prosecution, Felicia is barred from the proceedings. I don't know where Teresa is.

I'm several rows behind Cole Wright, who is sitting at the defense table with his lawyers. His hair is thick and full, and his shoulders are broad. Even in middle age, he still projects the aura of a jock, the career that made him famous.

I can't stand the sight of him.

Beside Cole sits Tess Hardy from Virginia, his lead defender. She's one of the country's most powerful and influential defense attorneys. The judge decided to allow cameras in the courtroom, which plays to her strengths, as she's a legal analyst on CNN and a regular guest on Sunday-morning news shows.

By state law, only members of the New Hampshire Bar can appear in court here, but Hardy has a *pro hac vice* admission, meaning she's been sponsored by a local attorney. That attorney is Carole Clifford, sitting to her left. The optics deliver an obvious message: If these smart, accomplished women trust Cole Wright, then the jury should too.

I hope the jury is smart enough to see through it.

At the prosecution's table on the opposite side, the deputy attorney general, Hugh Bastinelli, is busy stacking binders. He's handsome. Distinguished-looking. Even sitting down, he's taller than the two other attorneys sitting beside him.

Compared to camera-ready Tess Hardy, with her statuesque figure, perfect makeup, and chic short blond hair, Bastinelli seems unenthusiastic about facing the media. But he's got a good reputation as a prosecutor. And he has a high conviction rate.

That's the only statistic I really care about.

CHAPTER 87

At some silent signal, the clerk near the judge's bench gets up from his chair and commands, "All rise!"

All of us in the courtroom obey, like a church congregation.

The twelve jurors and four alternates come in and take their seats. I'm a little surprised to see three faces of color—two middle-aged Black women and one young Asian man. That's more diversity than I expected in New Hampshire.

From here on in, they'll be sequestered in an information bubble, isolated from news about the trial. But bubbles burst every day.

Superior court judge Walter Dow strides in from chambers. I can see a blue shirt and red necktie peeking from beneath his black robe. Dow is sixty, tanned, with close-cropped white hair and black-rimmed glasses. He settles into his large leather chair on the bench and nods to the room. "Please be seated."

I've already got three pages of notes on Walter Dow for the book. Born in Michigan. High-school basketball star. BU undergrad. Cornell Law School. Worked in the New Hampshire attorney general's office for a decade. Has been on the superior court for sixteen years.

Since Dow was assigned to this case four months ago, his personal life has been dissected in the press. Divorced, now remarried, son and daughter in college. He enjoys mountain climbing and takes his Coca-Cola with ice cubes.

When the *New York Times* reported that Judge Dow was considered a moderate in New Hampshire, the *Washington Post* fired back that a moderate in New Hampshire would be considered to the right of Genghis Khan in more progressive states.

I could not care less about the judge's politics. I just want a fair trial. And in my heart of hearts, I'm hoping for a conviction so airtight that it can't be overturned on appeal.

Dow turns to the clerk. "Mr. Begley, please swear in the jurors."

The clerk faces the jury box. "If you would please stand and raise your right hands." The jurors obey. "And when the oath is concluded, respond, 'I do.'" The clerk stands up straight and asks the long-winded question: "Do you solemnly swear or affirm that you will carefully consider the evidence and the law presented to you in this case and that you will deliver a fair and true verdict as to the charge or charges against the defendant?"

There's a chorus of "I do" from the jury box, some muttered, some full voice.

The judge adjusts his glasses. "Mr. Begley, you may read the indictment."

The clerk turns to the defense table. "The defendant will please stand."

I've been waiting a long time for this moment—ever since the day Garrett told me about the rumors swirling around Cole Wright since his college days. I may never be able to pin Garrett's murder on the First Gentleman, so seeing him sent away for Suzanne Bonanno's will have to do.

Cole Wright stands up behind the table. I see Tess Hardy place one hand on his back—a show of support for her client and a bit of theater for the rest of us.

My brain fogs out for a few seconds during the reading of the charges.

Focus, Brea!

I clench my fists. The fog clears. I hear the next part clearly.

The important part.

"Cole Wright, with force and arms, did commit the crime of second-degree murder, RSA six-thirty, one-b, in that Cole Wright caused the death of Suzanne Bonanno, age twenty-two, under circumstances manifesting an extreme indifference to the value of human life, to wit, strangling Suzanne Bonanno in a manner resulting in her death. Said acts being contrary to the form of statute, in such case made and provided, and against the peace and dignity of the State."

I think of Suzanne being wrapped in a sheet and dumped in that miserable hole in the dirt. If there was ever an act against peace and dignity, that was it.

The next few minutes are all legal housekeeping. Dow reminds the jury of what being sequestered means. They are not to talk among themselves or to members of the news media or even with their families, and they are not to do any independent research on the case.

In his instructions to the jury, one part stands out.

"The fact that the defendant has been arrested and charged is not evidence of guilt. It is up to you and you alone to reach a verdict based on the evidence presented here."

I hope these jurors pay attention. I hope they hear the truth. All of it.

Dow nods to the deputy AG. "Counselor, we're ready for your opening."

Nobody's more ready than I am.

CHAPTER 88

Thank you, Your Honor," the prosecutor says as he steps up to the lectern. He sets down the thick blue binder in his hands and walks over to the jury box.

"Ladies and gentlemen of the jury, I'm Deputy Attorney General Hugh Bastinelli. I am here to prove to you, beyond a reasonable doubt, that Cole Wright murdered Suzanne Bonanno."

Music to my ears. He pauses to let the charge sink in.

"Before I get into the details of the case, I want to take just a few moments to discuss the extraordinary nature of this situation." His voice is clear and confident. I can feel warmth and empathy in his delivery. His tone says *We're all in this together.*

I look at the faces of the jurors. They seem alert, like students who know they're being graded on class participation.

"First," says Bastinelli, "we need to acknowledge the proverbial elephant in the room—or the donkey, depending on your political persuasion." This gets a small chuckle from a few jurors.

"Of course I'm talking about the defendant's famous name, his past glory as an athlete, his honored position as the First

Gentleman of the United States, and his personal power and influence in the country."

Bastinelli pivots and points directly at Cole Wright. "But in this room, he's a defendant, nothing more, nothing less."

He turns back to the jury. "You've all heard the phrase *equal justice under the law*. And it's important to remember what it means as this trial begins. It means that every defendant—rich or poor, doctor or factory worker—must be treated the same when they are accused of a crime."

Bastinelli pauses. When he speaks again, his tone shifts. "But we all live in the real world. And we all know of many, many instances where the scales of justice have been tipped to favor people with money or influence."

He's got the jury hooked now. I see a few heads nodding.

Bastinelli rests his hands on the rail of the jury box and leans forward. "But not here, not in New Hampshire. Every four years, this state welcomes men and women with fame and power—people who are seeking the highest office in the land. And we meet them eye to eye, as equals. That's what I'm asking you to do here, as good citizens of New Hampshire. For the duration of this trial, you must ignore Cole Wright's fame and power and focus on his words, his actions, and his deeds. Then, and only then, can justice be done."

Bastinelli looks each juror in the eye, then turns, walks back to the lectern, and opens his binder. "Your Honor, State's exhibit one."

With a click of a controller, Bastinelli lights up a large video screen with an image of Suzanne Bonanno in her Patriots cheerleader uniform and full makeup, looking poised and glamorous.

The jurors go wide-eyed, as if they've glimpsed a Hollywood starlet.

"This is the victim, Suzanne Bonanno," says Bastinelli. "By all accounts, Suzanne was warm, personable, and friendly to everyone.

She was a professional cheerleader for the New England Patriots but was already thinking beyond her cheerleading career and had a potential job with Fidelity Investments in Boston. Suzanne Bonanno's future was bright, full of promise.

"But that future was tragically and criminally cut short—at a time when she was the girlfriend of a New England Patriots football player. That football player was Cole Wright."

Bastinelli leaves the image of Suzanne on the screen as he crosses back to the jury box.

"Ladies and gentlemen, in this trial, the State will prove beyond a reasonable doubt that the defendant, Cole Wright, did in fact threaten Suzanne Bonanno prior to her disappearance, that he had the means and opportunity to harm her, that a personal item belonging to him was found at her burial site, and that he was the last person to see her alive."

Bastinelli clicks the controller again. The image of Suzanne slowly fades to black. I can almost feel a sad collective sigh in the room.

"This crime occurred seventeen years ago last June. Seventeen years is a long time, ladies and gentlemen. Memories can get fuzzy. Evidence can be lost or overlooked. This case won't be as simple or as clear-cut as what you see on *CSI* and *Law and Order*. But trust me when I say this—the State has a strong case for Cole Wright's guilt. We have witness testimony, physical evidence, and visual evidence that will prove Mr. Wright's responsibility for her death.

"We will produce witnesses who will testify that they heard Cole Wright threaten to strangle Suzanne Bonanno. The State's medical examiner will testify that Suzanne Bonanno in fact was murdered by manual strangulation."

At the defense table, Cole Wright has his head bent over a legal pad. I'd give anything to see his face right now, but all I can see is his lawyer's. Tess Hardy's expression is relaxed and neutral. Not giving anything away.

"Now, do we have a confession from Mr. Wright?" says Bastinelli. "We do not. Do we have a photograph of him committing the crime? No. The defense will argue that the evidence against Mr. Wright is circumstantial, as if that somehow means that it's weak or not credible.

"The truth is, ladies and gentlemen, criminal investigations are not as neat and perfect as they are on TV. And it is also true that most criminal convictions are obtained through circumstantial evidence alone. It is enough. It is *more* than enough."

Bastinelli walks back to the lectern. He clicks the controller again. The screen lights up with a new picture of Suzanne. This one shows her sitting on a couch in gray sweats and a black T-shirt, head back, laughing. She looks innocent and vulnerable. And so very, very young. Bastinelli is going for emotion, and I think it's working.

"After a thoughtful and careful review of the evidence we present, you will, I believe, deliver a verdict of guilty against Cole Wright to bring a measure of peace and closure to Suzanne Bonanno's family and to show that equal justice under the law is still alive and strong here in the Granite State."

If I were allowed to applaud, I would.

Instead, I let out a long breath, thinking about the one important player who's not in the room: President Madeline Parson Wright. Ron Reynolds told me she's upstairs in a secure location, watching on a closed-circuit link.

Like everybody else, I wonder what President Wright is thinking.

CHAPTER 89

He's solid, this Bastinelli," says Maddy, looking at the screen across the room.

Burton Pearce nods. "I hope Tess Hardy ate her Wheaties this morning."

They're in a nicely furnished office one floor above the crowded courtroom, surrounded by shelves full of legal books. The office's usual occupant, another superior court judge, is vacationing in Aruba.

It took the Secret Service only a day to sweep the place for bugs, add bulletproof windows, and install a battery of secure phone lines. The office is now a fully functioning remote White House.

Maddy is sitting in the leather chair behind the judge's desk. When Judge Dow declares a short recess after Bastinelli's opening, she hits the Mute button and goes back to reviewing the latest memos and counts from her congressional liaisons. Like most leaders, she possesses an exceptional ability to compartmentalize.

Across the room, a Secret Service agent stands at the door. Melanie Smith, the president's travel aide, perches on a sofa with an iPad on her lap and an iPhone held between her cheek and shoulder.

With all the pretrial publicity and legal maneuvering over the past eight months, the Grand Bargain has been on hold. But Maddy won't let it slip away. Even with her husband facing murder charges, she needs to keep her focus.

"This is better news than I anticipated," she says, flipping through the pages.

Pearce is reviewing the same paperwork, a cup of coffee in his hand. "I agree. So far, the key parties are keeping their pledges. I don't want to jinx it, but maybe this is an idea whose time has come."

Maddy rocks back in her chair. "In the 1700s," she says, waxing philosophical, "people in different parts of the world suddenly and independently started working on steam engines. Why then? Why steam engines? Why not something else? As one of my economics professors said, 'When it was time for steam engines, it was steam-engine time.' "

"Well," says Pearce, "I endorse that theory. Let's hope it's Grand Bargain time. And let's hope we can hold it together until this insanity is over."

"Burton, we *have* to," says Maddy. "And we will."

Pearce puts his coffee cup down and moves his chair closer to the desk. "Madam President, are you planning to stay another night in New Hampshire?"

"Of course. I'll stay as long as it takes."

"With all due respect, ma'am, I think that's a mistake."

"Burton, this is Cole we're talking about!"

"And that's why we hired Tess Hardy. The best in the business."

"You're saying I should absent myself from the trial? Leave my husband alone under house arrest over there at the inn?"

"Every hour you're not in DC, there's a chance that things will start slipping. Phone calls and video conferences are one thing, but this project requires a lot of hand-holding. That means you. In person. One-on-one. We've come too far to let a distraction sink us."

"You call supporting my husband a distraction?"

Pearce shakes his head. "No, no, of course not. You made a strong statement on the courthouse steps today. I think the country saw that as a wife defending the man she loves. Totally appropriate. But you know as well as I do that you can't appear to be putting your thumb on the scale here."

"And you think my presence creates that impression?"

"You're here. In the courthouse. And the press knows it. And every day you attend the trial, they're going to be shouting questions about the testimony, trying to get a rise out of you, maybe get you to say something that will be grounds for a mistrial. Meanwhile, the Grand Bargain is in a holding pattern, and a lot of people would love to shoot it down."

"Enough, Burton. You've made your point."

Pearce leans back in his chair, hands raised in surrender. "Okay, Madam President, it's your decision."

The court recess is over. Maddy turns up the sound again. "Damn right it is."

CHAPTER 90

Judge Dow raps his gavel to quiet the room. "All right, we're in session."

I'm staring at the back of Tess Hardy's perfect blond head. She's up next.

The judge shuffles some papers, then looks her way. "Ms. Hardy, we're ready for the defense's opening statement."

Hardy nods, but for a few seconds, she doesn't move.

Just when the judge seems about to give her a verbal nudge, she stands up slowly and deliberately, head held high and empty-handed. No notes. Heels clicking on the floor, she walks past the lectern and stops in front of the jury box.

"Good morning, ladies and gentlemen. My name is Tess Hardy. I'm here to disprove all the so-called evidence Mr. Bastinelli talked about and show you that the man at that table"—she turns and points at Cole Wright—"is here because of who he is and not because of anything he's done." She turns back, giving the jurors a warm smile.

"But first, I'd like to extend my thanks to the good people of New Hampshire for welcoming a lawyer 'from away,' as the New England expression goes."

I see some of the jurors smiling back. Some even angle toward her.

She's good.

"Over the past few weeks, I've spent a lot of time preparing my opening remarks, writing, practicing, memorizing—but you know what? After what we heard from the deputy attorney general this morning, I've decided to toss my presentation and try something else."

Now even the judge is leaning forward.

"Who here has seen *My Cousin Vinny*?" Hardy asks.

Judge Dow clears his throat. "Ms. Hardy, this is not a quiz show."

Hardy smiles. "It was a rhetorical question, Your Honor. We've all seen it."

Nods from the jurors confirm that.

"So we all recall how Joe Pesci's character, the attorney defending the two young men—'deese two yutes'—responds to the local prosecutor's opening statement." She alters her body language and actually does a pretty solid Pesci impression: " 'Everything that guy just said is—' " She stops there. "I can't finish the line in this courtroom, but you all remember it."

Smiles and nods from the jury. Chuckles and a few laughs from the gallery.

Judge Dow raps his gavel again, and, like everybody else in the room, I add the final word in my head.

The word is *bullshit.*

"Did you know, ladies and gentlemen, that the American Bar Association's own publication, the *ABA Journal*, ranked *My Cousin Vinny* as number three on its list of the greatest legal movies ever made? That's because it got so much right in its portrayal of the legal system, including when a prosecution attorney tries to make a case out of...well, you know."

The jury's with her now. I can feel it.

Hardy turns serious. "It saddens me to say that, because I have so much respect for prosecutors and what they do. But this case should never have come to trial, ladies and gentlemen. The truth—the real truth—is that the government has no case against Cole Wright."

She starts ticking off points on her fingers. "There are no witnesses to this alleged crime. There is no DNA evidence connecting Cole Wright to this alleged crime. There is no physical evidence connecting him to this crime. There are no video or audio recordings of my client threatening or injuring Miss Bonanno."

Now she steps even closer to the jury box. "Yes, there are a few witness statements alleging some harsh or aggressive words from Cole Wright at a time when he was in a very aggressive line of work. Might some of that aggression have spilled over into his personal life? It would be surprising if it didn't.

"And let's all remember that this was over seventeen years ago. When you hear these witnesses, ask yourself: How confident are *you* of exactly what you heard or saw nearly two decades ago? Would you bet on it? Would you send an honorable man to prison based on it? Or might you have some reasonable doubt?"

Damn. I see why the Wrights hired her. As a talking head on TV, Hardy can sometimes seem a bit glib. But here, in person, she's a force of nature.

She walks to the lectern for the first time and picks up a glass of water from a shelf in the back of it. She takes a long, slow sip like she's got all the time in the world. Then she puts the glass down and goes on.

"Now, I'm sure most of you are thinking, *Why would the State bring such a weak case against the First Gentleman?* For what purpose? Is it for justice?" She turns toward the prosecution table with raised eyebrows, then turns back to the jury box. "Or could it be something else? Let's think about it. Earlier, Mr. Bastinelli referred to New Hampshire's traditional position as the first-in-the-nation primary state." She points to the jurors one by one. "In fact, all of you probably know more about politics than most people in this country. Every four years, you see it happen on your front porches, in your living rooms, in your neighborhood diners.

"Now, I don't know what your personal politics are, and I don't care. But you all know that President Wright barely won this state in the general election three years ago. That's not a partisan statement—it's a statistical fact. And you all know that the next election isn't far off. The timing of this trial is no coincidence."

She points back at Cole Wright.

"My client played NFL football for three years. He has the battle scars to prove it. And I believe he would tell you that it was *nothing* compared to the blood sport of national politics, where people will do anything and everything to gain an advantage over the competition. Like rehashing old rumors. Trolling for coincidences. Playing on sympathies for a beautiful young woman who died too soon. Somebody has to pay, right?

"Ladies and gentlemen, ask yourselves—would a case this flimsy be brought in any other state? Is it any mystery why it was brought here in New Hampshire, where President Wright will once again be in fierce competition for votes?"

Hardy folds her hands in front of her skirt.

"Members of the jury, the simple fact is, New Hampshire is a political state. And this is a political trial. You can think whatever you want about President Madeline Wright. Vote for her or not. But you must find her husband—the First Gentleman—not guilty."

CHAPTER 91

"What is this to you—a *joke*?"

Cole Wright and his attorneys are spending the recess in a small conference room. The defendant is furious. He can feel his jaw tightening. Cole paces around the table, clenching and unclenching his fists.

The junior attorneys cower at his sheer intensity. Tess Hardy stands tall and straight against the wall. "I called an audible," she says. "You of all people should know how that works."

Cole glares at the others. "Give us the room, please."

Carole Clifford and the two junior attorneys scurry out the door. The Secret Service agent follows. "I'll be right outside, sir." Cole slams the door in the guy's face. Then he walks up to Hardy until they're nose to nose.

"Tell me why the hell we spent two weeks going over your opening statement if you were just going to wing it this morning? *Joe Pesci?* Are you kidding me? I was about to jump out of my chair! It was reckless, inappropriate, totally off the wall."

Hardy is unintimidated. "Are you done?"

Cole forces himself to take a few deep breaths. He counts to ten in his head. "Yes. I'm done. Now you talk. And explain."

Hardy walks to the head of the table and takes a seat in one of the rolling office chairs. "Sometimes I read the room and get a sense of what will work. Sure, I could have fed these jurors a complex legal argument like the one we practiced. But I went for the gut, and I think I was right. I think I got to them. Sometimes humor works, even when the topic at hand is tragic. And sometimes simple is better than complicated."

Cole slumps into another office chair. He places both palms on the table and leans forward.

"Tess. Listen. Maybe I'm overly sensitive. You need to understand that for the past three years in the White House and the four years before that in the California governor's mansion, every word I've said in public has been scripted, scrutinized, and sanitized."

"Right. Because you're speaking for the administration. I get it."

Cole rises partway out of his chair. "And you're here to speak for *me*!"

Tess stays calm. "That's exactly what I'm doing. I've studied Walter Dow. I know how much rope I've got with the judge."

"Tess, I'm the client. You're my attorney. You work for me."

"That's right, I do," says Hardy. "For two thousand dollars an hour. Including the billable hours accruing right now."

"That can all change," says Cole, his voice suddenly low and cold. "I had a dozen firms pursuing me, dying to represent me in this."

"Fine. Call them. We'll just say we had a disagreement about trial strategy and compensation. Happens all the time." She picks up her briefcase and starts stuffing files into it.

Cole tries his best to center himself. Both Maddy and Burton Pearce say that Tess Hardy is the best. He doesn't want to lose her.

"Wait!" he says, standing up.

"For what?" says Hardy. "I thought you just fired me."

"Did I say those words?"

"Not verbatim."

Cole Wright places both hands on the back of a chair and softens his voice. "Then stop. And stay. Please."

Hardy puts her briefcase down.

"But starting from this point on, no more surprises, okay? You are going to be fully open and transparent with me. I do not want to be caught off guard. And I don't want the president to be caught off guard. You know as well as I do that she's on trial here as much as I am."

"All right, Cole—Mr. Wright—fair enough. But I need a promise from you in return."

"What's that?"

"If you want to remain a free man, don't ever, *ever* raise your voice in this courthouse again."

CHAPTER 92

I slide back into my seat in the courtroom just as the deputy attorney general calls his first witness, a state trooper named Steve Josephs.

Josephs is wearing a pristine uniform—green shirt, tan pants, both neatly pressed. He looks calm and cool on the stand.

Bastinelli leads him through the events of the winter night when Josephs stopped a red Sentra weaving down a New Hampshire highway.

The trooper's answers are brief and to the point. Bastinelli takes him through his encounter with the inebriated driver, the arrival of the tow truck, and law enforcement's decision to search the vehicle before it was taken away.

"And when you opened the trunk, what did you see?"

"I saw dirty blue cloth wrapped around a human skull."

I hear a gasp from the jury box.

"Your Honor, this is State's exhibit two A." Bastinelli clicks his controller and the screen fills with an image of the Sentra's open trunk. A filthy blue bundle sits next to a spare tire. And where the bundle has come loose, sure enough, a skull is peeking out.

Even though I knew it was coming, I'm not ready for it.

That beautiful girl, reduced to bones.

The courtroom is completely still. I see some of the jury members lowering their eyes. Cole Wright stares down at his legal pad. Bastinelli lets the silence hang for a few seconds before continuing.

"Trooper Josephs, is this the trunk of the Sentra as you remember seeing it on that night?"

"Yes, sir, it is."

Bastinelli takes Josephs quickly through the rest of his testimony. The trooper describes the arrival of a detective from the Major Crimes Unit.

"And who was that detective?"

"Detective Sergeant Marie Gagnon."

I sit up straight in my seat. *Marie Gagnon.* The first time I saw her in a press conference, her name hit me right away. She was the one I spoke to after I reburied Suzanne's bracelet and called 911.

The bracelet was never mentioned in the news. I'm still waiting to learn if my strategy paid off.

Now Josephs is explaining how the remains were eventually transferred by van to the medical examiner's office.

Bastinelli walks back to his table. "Thank you, Trooper. No further questions."

Now it's Tess Hardy's turn. She walks to the lectern and introduces herself to Josephs. Seems calm and courteous. And really curious.

"Trooper Josephs, when you made that traffic stop that night, how long had you worked?"

"That shift? About nine hours."

"So nine hours until the point where you stopped the Sentra?"

"Yes, ma'am."

"And then you followed the tow truck with the Sentra to the impound lot and guarded the car until the remains were transferred to the medical examiner's van, correct?"

"Correct."

"How long were you there?"

Josephs has to think for a couple seconds. "Around . . . five hours."

"And this was the middle of the night—actually, the wee hours of the morning at this point, am I right?"

"Yes, ma'am."

Hardy tucks a strand of her neat blond hair behind her ear. "So, after working fourteen hours, more or less, what were you doing while you were guarding the vehicle and waiting for the ME van to arrive?"

The trooper seems puzzled. "I was just sitting. In my cruiser."

"How long did you sleep?"

Josephs looks puzzled. "Not at all."

Hardy leaves the lectern and walks forward until she's standing about four feet from Josephs. He's a big guy, but in this configuration, Hardy is looking down at him.

"Are you sure? Isn't it possible that you dozed off and that, during that time, somebody might have tampered with the contents of the trunk? Removed or added something?"

"The trunk was locked, ma'am. I had the key in my pocket."

"Was the Sentra alarmed?"

"No, ma'am. It wasn't."

"Trooper Josephs, how many vehicle break-ins have you investigated in your career as a law enforcement officer?"

Bastinelli jumps up. "Objection! Relevance!"

Hardy turns to the judge. "Your Honor, I think chain of custody with regard to human remains is *extremely* relevant."

Dow nods. "Overruled. I'll allow it. But let's not make this a long detour, Ms. Hardy."

"Thank you, Your Honor. Trooper, do you need me to repeat the question?"

"If you don't mind."

"How many vehicle break-ins have you investigated?"

"I can't say, ma'am. I'm not sure."

"Less than fifty? More than fifty?"

"Probably more, but..." Josephs looks a bit rattled.

"So you know that professional thieves with the right tools can unlock a car door or a car trunk quickly and with very little noise. Am I right?"

"They can, yes."

"And if you *had* dozed off, after fourteen straight hours of work, in the wee hours of the morning, you might not have seen it happen. You might not even have known it had happened. Isn't that right?"

"But I wasn't sleeping!" Josephs shifts in the witness chair.

"So you said, Trooper." Hardy looks at the jury. She raises her eyebrows slightly. "No further questions."

A seed of doubt, nicely sown.

Tess Hardy is *very* good.

CHAPTER 93

The next witness is clearly uncomfortable in the courtroom. Herb Lucienne, the Sentra driver whom Trooper Steve Josephs pulled over—the guy who was driving a car that turned out to have human bones in its trunk—looks like he would rather be anywhere but here.

When Bastinelli runs Lucienne through his background, I understand why. He has been in and out of jail since he was sixteen. Petty crimes. Nothing as serious as murder.

"Mr. Lucienne, what is your employment status, may I ask?"

Lucienne hunches his shoulders. "Currently unemployed, on parole."

The deputy AG gets Lucienne to tell the jury about the night an envelope containing cut-up hundred-dollar bills was slipped under his door. To collect the other half, all the witness had to do was pick up a car in a parking lot and drive it to a specific location on Lake Marie, in the White Mountains up north.

"Mr. Lucienne, did it occur to you that you were being asked to do something illegal?"

Lucienne tugs at his collar. "I guess it seemed a little shady," he admits.

"Is that why you had six beers before taking on the mission? To calm your nerves?"

"I guess so. Maybe so I wouldn't worry so much."

"But you really needed that five hundred dollars, didn't you?"

"Shit, yes!" He glances up at the judge. "Sorry about the language, sir."

Dow gives him a tight smile. "Proceed, Mr. Lucienne."

Lucienne doesn't seem to know anything beyond what he was told that night. Obviously, Bastinelli knew what he would say on the stand. And there's not much he can do to link him to Cole Wright. But I can't blame him for trying.

"The truth is, you don't know who sent you that message, do you?"

"Nope."

"It could have been somebody acting on behalf of somebody else, correct?"

"I guess so."

"It could have been somebody with a strong motive to make sure those bones were never discovered, correct? Someone who wanted them to disappear forever."

"Objection!" Tess Hardy shouts. "Your Honor, Mr. Bastinelli is weaving his own little fairy tale here."

The judge nods. "Sustained. Mr. Bastinelli, anything else for Mr. Lucienne?"

"Not at this time, Your Honor."

From where I'm sitting, I figure the AG needs to cut his losses. He looks over at Hardy. "Your witness."

This time when Hardy walks across the courtroom, she looks like a cat eyeing a canary. I can see Lucienne squirming in his seat as she begins.

"You have to admit that that's one wild story you just told us.

Mysterious note slipped under your door. Clandestine payment for driving a vehicle up to a remote lake. Is that the kind of thing you normally do to make money?"

"No, ma'am," says Lucienne. "This was the first time."

I can tell that some of the jurors are trying not to laugh.

"So when you got the promise of several hundred dollars in payment, that was appealing to you, correct?"

Lucienne nods.

The judge leans over. "Mr. Lucienne, you have to speak for the record. With words."

Lucienne leans into the microphone on the witness stand. "Yeah, yeah, that's right. I took the job. Went to the parking lot. Found the car, the directions, the key, a little spending money for the trip."

Hardy walks up close to the witness stand. I keep waiting for the judge to tell her to back off, but he seems to be giving both attorneys free rein.

"Mr. Lucienne, did you know there were human remains in the trunk of the car you were driving?"

"That skeleton? No! If I knew that, I would never have gone anywhere near it. Not for a *million* bucks!"

"So for all you knew that night, you were just driving a vehicle from Seabrook to Lake Marie."

"That's right."

"Did you know who owned the property that you were driving to?"

"No."

"Have you ever heard of a company called Tight End Limited?"

"Nope."

Herb Lucienne might not be the sharpest knife in the drawer, as my mama used to say, but he seems to be answering truthfully. Hell, I believe him.

"Mr. Lucienne," says Hardy, "you've been very patient. I just have a couple more questions for you."

"Okay."

"Do you know Cole Wright?"

"Sure," says Lucienne. "He's sitting right over there."

Everyone in the courtroom looks to the defense table. Cole Wright is staring at Lucienne.

"Yes, he is. My fault. I wasn't clear. I mean, do you know him personally?"

"Personally? No."

"You've never met him? Spoken with him? Texted with him? Exchanged email?"

Lucienne shakes his head. "No!"

"So, to be clear, during this entire mysterious process, you never got any communication from Cole Wright telling you to drive skeletal remains up to his property on Lake Marie?"

Lucienne is animated now, practically jumping out of the witness chair. "Never! I mean, that'd be *crazy*!"

Hardy gives him a little smile. "I couldn't agree more. No further questions."

Looks like the cat just swallowed the canary.

Impressive.

CHAPTER 94

Kingston, New Hampshire

It was a long first day at trial. At the end of it, I grab a Domino's pizza and a six-pack of Sam Adams and head to my hotel.

The day Cole Wright's trial was announced, I snagged a hotel room in Kingston, a few miles south of the Rockingham County courthouse. From what I hear, locals are now renting out rooms and basements for five hundred dollars a night.

This entire day has reminded me of Garrett. Drafting the manuscript over the past eight months has distracted me from his death. In a way, it's also kept him alive.

With each page I write, I can feel him standing over my shoulder—editing my grammar, correcting my syntax, and always pushing for clarity. No literary or legal flourishes allowed.

"Don't write to show off," he always told me. "Write to make the reader understand."

After a bit of wrangling with the landlord of the Litchfield house, I got him to let me out of the lease. I lost the security deposit, but that was a small price to pay. For the past six months, I've been renting a nice condo in New Haven within walking distance of Yale Law School, and soon I'll be back to teaching classes three days a week.

When I moved, I put most of Garrett's stuff in storage—his books, his clothes, his notes from *Integrity Gone* and *Stolen Honor.* The one thing I keep in the condo is his guitar. It brings me comfort to see it leaning in the corner of the bedroom. Sometimes, if I close my eyes, I can still hear him playing. Like he did the day he bought it at Sammy's.

Naturally, I played my recording of Leo Amalfi's confession for the detectives in Brattleboro, Vermont. But it wasn't the bombshell I expected. They thought the White House angle was just hearsay or maybe the ravings of a dying man. But at least they started looking for some of Amalfi's known associates in an attempt to track down the actual shooters.

They're still looking.

Personally, I believe Amalfi was telling the truth. I think the First Gentleman ordered Garrett's murder because he was getting too close to finding out about the murder Cole Wright himself had committed. The one he's on trial for now. I think Garrett learned something that day at the airport—and I think he died because of it.

I realize I haven't called Dr. Graham to thank him for the pass yet. Truth is, I wanted to wait until I was sure it would actually get me in. And it did. Good as gold.

I send a text to Brother, but my phone says it's not deliverable. I decide to do a little probing on LinkedIn to get his contact info.

Interesting. I find an email address, but no phone number. He probably doesn't want students pestering him at all hours.

At this point, I think most people would just shoot off an email.

Not me. Not since Garrett taught me the wonders of the dark

web. Just for fun, I click on my Tor browser and go down the rabbit hole on Dr. Cameron Graham. There has to be a phone number in here somewhere.

At first, I'm just scrolling through the usual junk—pictures of him at conferences and seminars, links to papers he's written and books he's edited, civic awards and speeches. Then suddenly, I'm reading an obscure political blog linked to Dr. Graham.

We should have listened to Doc Cams. Maddy and her sports-lug spouse have been a nightmare!

Doc Cams? *Cameron?*

I dig deeper. A lot of these posts are from three or more years back, some from before the election. Now I'm finding posts from Doc Cams himself.

Electing Wright, with her muscle-headed hubby, and the fascist ex-cop VP will be a disaster.

If Wright dies in office, you know who becomes president? Faulkner, that Philly police chief who crapped all over BLM.

Holy Jesus...

More scrolling. More vitriol. Then this:

If you want to get rid of Wright before her second term, go after her jock husband. Easy to weaken her by taking down Cole W.

I close my laptop. What was it Dr. Graham told me?

One group wants very much to stop you. The other wants very much to help you.

Now I know which group Dr. Graham belongs to. Now I

understand his motives. But what about his methods? I'm not sure I understand that. This stuff sounds pretty dark.

I give up looking for his personal number and check the Columbia Law School directory.

It's almost ten. Should I wait until morning? Screw it. I need to know what's going on.

I call his office, and as I expected, it goes straight to voicemail: "This is Dr. Cameron Graham. Please leave a message."

No way I can ask him about this Doc Cams thing on a recording. I need to talk to him, preferably in person. So, for now, I just make nice. "Hi, Dr. Graham. It's Brea Cooke. The courthouse pass is great, so thank you. Need to talk to you when you have a minute. Bye."

I hang up and turn on the television. I scarf down two slices of pizza while I watch Court TV's recap of today's testimony.

Another New Hampshire state trooper testified about finding a grave-size hole on property belonging to Cole Wright on Lake Marie. The prosecution tried to suggest that Wright was attempting to get the bones buried there to hide them away. But Tess Hardy got the trooper to admit that the property wasn't secure and that anybody could have dug that hole.

The next person on the stand was a woman named Stacey Millett. She'd worked at Gillette Stadium during the time Cole and Suzanne had dated and confirmed it was an open secret that they were together. Everybody there also knew about Cole's temper, she claimed, backing it up with a memory of hearing him talking rough to Suzanne after practice one day, saying something like "Suzanne, I'm gonna wring your pretty little neck!"

Tess Hardy poked holes in Millett's memories. Then she asked her why she'd never reported these threats to the police if she was so concerned. Stacey's answers weren't great. I turn up the sound as they show the same clip for the third time.

The camera is focused on the witness box. Poor Stacey looks a little bewildered and tired. Not used to this kind of pressure.

Tess Hardy's voice comes from off-camera. "Ms. Millett, have you ever been angry at someone?"

"Yes, of course."

"I mean *really* mad."

"Sure."

"In the heat of the moment, have you ever said anything like 'I could kill you right now!' "

"Well, yeah," says Millett, "but I didn't really mean it. I was just letting off steam."

"So you've never actually killed anybody?"

"Objection!" Bastinelli's voice.

"Overruled," says the judge. "Ms. Millett, you may answer the question."

"No! Of course not!"

"I didn't think so," says Hardy.

Another point scored for the defense. But the game clock has just started.

CHAPTER 95

Cole Wright's private cell phone buzzes on his nightstand.

He grabs it. Only two people in the world have this number. "Hello?"

"Hey there, it's me. Did I wake you?"

Cole rubs his eyes with one hand. "Hey, Maddy. No problem. I'm up. Good to hear your voice."

"Good to hear yours too."

He jams a pillow behind his back and sits up against the headboard of his bed at the inn in Kingston, New Hampshire.

"I'm sorry I had to leave before court was adjourned today," Maddy says. "Serbia's threatening Kosovo again, and the Chinese are expanding their territorial waters."

"So I heard," says Cole. "You worried?"

"I just got off the phone with the new British PM. He thinks both situations could escalate. But we'll see." A pause. "How are you?"

"Holding up."

"I saw some of the trial replay. Looks like Tess is doing a good job. You two getting along?"

"Better now," says Cole.

"I'm sorry I'm not there at the inn with you."

"Don't be. Room service is terrible."

"I'm serious. I miss you. And I want to support you. But I can't run things from up there. Burton made me realize that."

"Maddy, I understand."

"I want you to know that we're working on the announcement of the Grand Bargain."

"I thought that was on the back burner."

"We can't hold this coalition together much longer, Cole. And if it collapses, we'll lose the whole thing—forever."

Cole grimaces. "I hate being a sideshow. I'm the reason things are being held up."

"Not your fault. We're planning to announce the day after you're found not guilty. A one-two punch to set us up for the next term."

"But what if—"

"No what-ifs. That's how it's going to be. You win. We win. The country wins." Maddy shifts into a comical British accent. "Defeat? I do not know the meaning of the word."

Cole laughs. "Winston Churchill?"

"Close. Margaret Thatcher."

"Burton says you and the Iron Lady had a lot in common."

"Right. Except she got eleven years in office, and I only get eight, tops."

Cole sighs. "I'm just hoping I won't get twenty years to life."

"Stop it! That's not funny. You're an innocent man and the jury will see that."

"I hope you're right, Maddy. I really do." Cole hears the voice of an aide whispering urgently.

When Maddy comes back on the line, she says, "I have to take a call. So sorry."

"Go ahead—save the world."

"I love you."

"Love you too."

She hangs up.

In the silence, the worry he's been keeping at bay until now floods in. Cole knows that he's got the most powerful person in the world on his side.

But she's not sitting on the jury.

CHAPTER 96

Manhattan

Dr. Cameron Graham eases into his black Audi A8 in the parking garage across the street from the Metropolitan Club in Midtown East.

Dinner with old friends was a rare treat, but it's after eleven and he's starting to feel the effects of the booze—a vodka martini to start, two glasses of cabernet with the meal, then an Armagnac. He probably should have passed on the digestif, especially since he has to make the drive home to Westchester. His steak dinner is sitting heavily in his belly.

Graham pats his jacket pocket, feeling for his cell phone. He'd followed club rules and turned it off at the table. Nice to be off social media for a few hours. Now it's time to reconnect.

Graham's stomach is churning as he checks his work voice-mail. He listens to a message from Brea Cooke.

About time.

It's time for Brea to know everything. She needs to understand. Sometimes you pretend to befriend the enemy in order to learn their tactics and vocabulary, earn their trust, figure out how to predict their actions.

He starts the Audi and pulls out of the parking garage. Just as he merges into Manhattan traffic, a cabdriver cuts in front of him. Graham hits the brakes to prevent a collision. A car horn blasts from behind him. He puts down the phone and picks up speed.

He's feeling chilly. Is the AC on? He checks. Nope.

In the middle of the next block, Graham feels a prickle shoot down his left arm. His stomach feels even more sour.

Graham leans over and opens the glove box. He fishes for a foil packet of Pepcid. *Got it!* Grabs it with two fingers. *Damn it!* It slips out of his grip and drops into the footwell.

Now the pressure in his belly is moving up to his chest. He feels a sheen of sweat on his forehead and wipes it off with the back of his hand. He blinks twice to refocus. The taillights ahead are blurry. Those drinks must have been stronger than he thought. *Concentrate on driving!*

Suddenly, a gap opens up in the far-right lane. Graham cranks the wheel and veers into the opening. He can't feel his hands. His chest is exploding in pain.

He jams his foot down on the brake. It slips off. He thrusts his foot down again. His leg is shaking. He hits the gas pedal instead.

There's a loud metallic bang as the Audi rams through a barrier.

A flash of green. Then it's gone, like someone flipped a switch.

Dr. Cameron Graham is dead before the Audi's hood hits the tree.

CHAPTER 97

Rockingham County Courthouse, New Hampshire

I get to court early to snag a good seat for the second day of the trial. The media people are already in place. I wave to Ron Reynolds, and he tips his tweed newsboy cap at me.

As the defendant and his team of attorneys file in, I catch a glimpse of his ankle monitor, well hidden beneath his somber bespoke suit.

The cameras light up. So does the tension in the room.

Testimony opens with the deputy attorney general calling the deputy chief medical examiner Alice Woods to the stand.

Bastinelli takes her through a review of her educational credentials and forensics experience. As she starts to explain how she positively identified the remains, Tess Hardy stands up and interrupts.

"Your Honor, in the interest of time, the defense is willing to stipulate that the remains found in the trunk of the Sentra are in fact those of Suzanne Bonanno."

Smart move. Hardy looks like she's being accommodating but

she's actually taking control. The defense attorney wants Bastinelli to hurry up with Woods so she can get a crack at her.

The strategy throws Bastinelli off his game; it takes him a few seconds to adjust and skip down his question list. He grabs a controller from the lectern and turns on a video screen.

"Your Honor, State's exhibit eleven C."

The monitor shows a full set of human bones laid out on an exam table in the rough shape of a human—the human who was Suzanne.

I look over at Cole Wright. His head is bowed. He's the only person in court not looking at the screen.

Bastinelli hands Dr. Woods a laser pointer. Under the deputy AG's questioning, the expert witness highlights ribs, vertebrae, femurs, radii. She shows the landmarks that identify the skeleton as female. She tells him how she determined the approximate age of the bones and length of time they'd been buried.

There's one bone Bastinelli seems particularly interested in.

"Dr. Woods, can you explain the location and function of the hyoid bone?"

"Yes," she says, using the laser pointer to highlight a small U-shaped bone. "The hyoid bone is crescent-shaped, thinner on the ends, thicker in the middle. It's about two inches across. It sits in the neck, about here." She places two fingers on her own throat. "It supports the tongue and helps with speaking and swallowing."

"And what bones does it attach to?"

"None," says Woods. "It floats."

"It floats?" says Bastinelli. "Please explain."

"The hyoid bone is the only bone in the body that's not attached to another bone. It's connected to cartilage and ligaments only."

"Does that make it easier to isolate and identify?"

"It's a very distinctive little bone, yes."

"And were you able to locate the hyoid bone in the skeletal remains of Suzanne Bonanno?"

"I was."

"Your Honor, State's exhibit fourteen A." Bastinelli clicks to a close-up of a grayish curve of bone lying on a blue surgical towel. It's split on one side, and the rough edges are overlapping.

"Dr. Woods, is this a photograph of Suzanne Bonanno's hyoid bone?"

"Yes, it is."

"And can you tell the court what you found significant about it as you examined it?"

"It was broken."

"And in your extensive experience examining the victims of violent crimes, Dr. Woods, does a broken hyoid bone have any special significance?"

"Yes. It indicates strong external pressure on the throat before the victim's death."

"Dr. Woods, is the hyoid bone easy to break?"

"Well, bones get more brittle as we age. In a young person, it would be quite flexible."

"So the force required to fracture the hyoid bone of a twenty-two-year-old woman would be pretty intense, am I correct?"

"Yes."

"Requiring considerable pressure."

"Considerable force, yes."

"And did the fractured hyoid bone in this case lead you to a conclusion about Suzanne Bonanno's cause of death?"

"Yes. In my opinion, she was strangled."

I look over at the jurors. Some of them have their eyes down. One woman is biting her lip. Bastinelli chooses to end here.

"Thank you, Doctor. No further questions."

Judge Dow turns to Tess Hardy. She's already on her feet. The first thing she does is click off the video screen.

"Good morning, Dr. Woods."

"Good morning."

"Dr. Woods, let's return to this mysterious little hyoid bone. Isn't it true that a hyoid bone can be fractured by impact in a car accident, by hard contact in an athletic event, or even by violent vomiting?"

"Yes, but I saw no evidence of—"

"Violent vomiting? There would be no evidence of that in skeletal remains, correct?"

"Vomiting? No."

"So when you make an educated guess that the victim was strangled–"

"Objection!" Bastinelli interjects. "Defense is mischaracterizing the witness's testimony."

"Sustained," says Dow.

I watch Hardy shift gears in a flash. "So when you came to an *opinion* that the victim was strangled, you did not consider other possibilities, is that right?"

"I used my best judgment," says Woods.

"But it's possible that the victim's hyoid bone was fractured in a manner *other* than strangulation, correct?"

"Yes. It's possible," Dr. Woods concedes.

"Thank you, Doctor. I'm glad we could put that to rest."

Hardy goes over and whispers to her client. I watch him give an almost imperceptible nod. The defense attorney walks to the lectern and picks up a stapled set of pages. "Now I'd like to turn your attention to your preliminary autopsy report. Your Honor, this is defendant's exhibit twelve B."

She flips through the pages until she reaches a highlighted section. I can see the neon-green color from where I'm sitting.

"Dr. Woods, you offered an opinion that the victim was pregnant at the time of her death."

An undercurrent of surprised murmuring rolls through the

courtroom. It's not the first time I've heard this pregnancy theory, but I'm surprised that Hardy is the one to bring it up. What does this mean for the defense's trial strategy?

"That's right," Dr. Woods says.

"But there were no fetal remains? No way to check for fetal DNA?"

"Correct."

"And you were unable to extract placental DNA from the bones?"

"True."

"So what, in your expert opinion, makes you think that the victim was with child?"

Dr. Woods doesn't immediately respond. She seems to be organizing her thoughts. She looks over at the jury, then speaks directly to them.

"When a woman becomes pregnant, the body undergoes physical changes to prepare for delivery. By the start of the second trimester, ligaments attached to bones in the pelvis start to loosen. That causes changes in the composition of the bones in those areas that we can see under a microscope. I saw evidence of those changes in the pelvic bones of the victim."

"Conclusive evidence?" Hardy asks.

"That might be overstating it."

"So do you know for certain the victim was pregnant at the time of her death?" asks Hardy.

"No. As the report states, it's my opinion."

"And would these compositional changes give you an indication of who the father was?"

"No. That would require fetal DNA."

"And if I understand you correctly, you've just told us that there was no fetal DNA."

"Well, after seventeen years underground—"

Hardy holds up her hand. "Dr. Woods, sorry to interrupt, but what I asked was if there was any detectable fetal DNA present in the remains. Yes or no?"

"No."

"So you cannot say with certainty that Suzanne Bonanno was pregnant?"

"I cannot."

"And even if she *had* been pregnant, establishing paternity would be an impossibility without fetal DNA."

"Correct."

"So, from your testimony, you can conclude only that the skeletal remains recovered in Seabrook belong to Suzanne Bonanno. Everything else is purely theoretical. Suzanne could have died in any number of ways. Speculation beyond that seems to border on fantasy."

"Objection!" Bastinelli calls out. "Defense is again mischaracterizing the witness's testimony."

"Sustained," says the judge. "Ms. Hardy? Any more questions for this witness?"

Hardy tosses a glance at the jury. "No, Your Honor, I think we've all heard enough."

CHAPTER 98

Your Honor, the State calls Detective Sergeant Marie Gagnon," Bastinelli announces from the prosecution's table.

The double doors at the rear of the courtroom swing open, and Gagnon walks down the center aisle. She's dressed in a simple black suit and white blouse. Nothing fancy.

The clerk swears her in. She takes her seat in the witness box. Bastinelli steps up to the lectern.

"Good morning, Detective."

"Good morning, Mr. Bastinelli."

"Detective, please give us a quick recap of your experience and background in law enforcement."

Gagnon seems solid and dependable. And her responses are short and concise. She recites her employment history, from the National Guard to the police academy to her years on patrol duty and then to her present position as a lead detective in Major Crimes, in about thirty seconds flat. It's clear that she's gone through this routine many times, and she's got it down pat.

As with any criminal case, the lead prosecutor and the lead

detective work closely together. Still, Bastinelli keeps his questioning formal and proper. To the jury, it seems as if they've never met.

Bastinelli thanks her, then dives into his questions regarding the police investigation.

"Let me take you back to last winter and the night you responded to a traffic stop at mile marker fourteen on Route 95 in Portsmouth, New Hampshire. Were you first at the scene?"

"No. Trooper Steve Josephs and Sergeant Evan Tasker were already there, holding in custody the driver of the Nissan Sentra that Trooper Josephs had pulled over."

Bastinelli takes Gagnon through the officers securing the scene. She tells him that they opened the trunk and discovered its cargo of human remains.

"Your Honor, State's exhibit two A, already in evidence." He clicks the controller and an image jurors saw earlier appears on the screen: a dirty blue bundle in which the skull is visible.

"Detective, is this what you saw then?"

"Yes, it is."

"So what told you that the contents of the trunk were previously buried and recently unearthed?"

"There was dirt all over the bottom of the car's trunk, the blue fabric, and the bones themselves. The dirt was moist and fresh, indicating that the exhumation had happened within a day or so."

"And did you at some point discover a grave in the area?"

"We did. It was in a wooded area near the Reverend Bonus Weare memorial rock in Seabrook."

"And what did you find there?"

"We found evidence of disturbed ground and excavated it."

"And what were you searching for at that time?"

"We were looking for more bones. Another skeleton or skeletons or any further evidence connected to the bones we'd already found."

"Did you find any weapons? A gun? A knife?"

"No, we did not."

"And did you find any other items relevant to the case?"

"We did."

"Can you describe them, please?"

My heart is thumping hard. I've heard nothing on the news or from Felicia about whether the bracelet I reburied was found. *It must have been, right?*

"We found several metatarsals—foot bones—which later proved to belong to the skeleton found in the Sentra."

"Anything else?"

"Yes. We found a woman's tennis bracelet."

Mission accomplished. I give myself a little internal fist pump. *Here we go.*

Bastinelli introduces the item into evidence and puts a photo of it up on the screen. The red jewels gleam in the enlargement.

"And have you identified the owner of this bracelet?"

"From video evidence, we conclude that it belonged to Suzanne Bonanno."

"Did you find anything else, Detective?"

"We did."

I freeze in place. *Oh, shit. Did I leave something behind?*

"Can you describe it, please?"

"We found a man's watch."

Where did that come from? At least I know it wasn't left by me or Garrett. It's been years since either of us wore a watch as we used our phones to check the time.

Bastinelli clicks to another image. "Your Honor, State's exhibit sixteen. Is this the watch you found, Detective?"

"Yes, it is."

"And how deep in the ground was the watch buried?"

"About three feet below where the bracelet was discovered," Gagnon answers.

Damn it! I knew *I should have dug deeper!*

Bastinelli clicks to a close-up. "There's an inscription on the back of the watch. Detective, can you tell us what the inscription says?"

"Yes," says Gagnon. "It says, 'To CW from BC, with love.'"

I don't know who BC is. It doesn't matter. I just know it's not Brea Cooke.

All I care about is CW.

Because CW is Cole Wright.

It *has* to be.

CHAPTER 99

Tess Hardy's turn. The defense attorney strides forward and stops a few feet short of the witness stand.

"Sergeant Gagnon, good morning."

"It's *Detective* Sergeant. Detective is fine."

Hardy adjusts smoothly. "Detective," she says, folding her hands in front of her. "Could you tell the jury how you learned the location alleged to have contained the remains of Suzanne Bonanno?"

I'm riveted—this is the police testimony of my 911 call.

"State police dispatch received an anonymous phone call that was transferred to me. The caller gave specific directions as to where Suzanne Bonanno was buried."

"Have you identified the caller?"

"No. The call was short and not easily traceable. Probably from a burner phone."

"Anything distinctive about the caller?"

"Female. That's all we know."

No link to my identity. Thank goodness.

Tess Hardy says, "Your Honor, defendant's exhibit ten B. This is an audio exhibit." She presses a button on the controller and a recording starts.

Oh, crap. That's my *voice booming through the speakers!* I shift uncomfortably in my seat, hoping that Ron Reynolds, the only person in the courtroom who knows my voice, won't recognize it.

"My name doesn't matter. Just listen. Suzanne Bonanno was buried in the woods in Seabrook, forty feet west of the Reverend Bonus Weare memorial rock— "

Hardy stops the playback. "Is that the voice you heard?"

"It is, yes."

"Detective, are you aware that the Department of Homeland Security, NSA, and other government intelligence agencies can sometimes trace burner phones?"

I feel a twist in my gut. To my relief, Gagnon is quick to answer.

"I am aware of that," the detective says. "But by the time we considered contacting them, we'd already arrested a suspect with longstanding ties to the victim."

Hardy gives a disapproving look, then moves in another direction. "Isn't it true, Detective, that criminals often return to the scene of the crime?"

"Sometimes they do, yes."

"And have criminals been known to plant evidence?"

"Of course. It happens."

"So it's possible that those items were buried at a different time than the remains were? Maybe at a later date?"

I can tell Gagnon doesn't want to answer this question, but she has no choice. "Yes. It's possible."

"Thank you. No further questions for the witness at this time."

CHAPTER 100

The man still calling himself Jack Doohan is attempting to do a recon of the Rockingham County courthouse, but the crowds make it impossible for him to assess the sight lines.

Right now, Doohan is about thirty yards from the courthouse steps, getting bumped and jostled. He ducks as a JUSTICE FOR COLE sign almost knocks him in the head. From what he can tell, about a third of the crowd are pro–Cole Wright, another third want him locked up, and the rest are just random nonpartisan nutjobs, the kind who show up at every protest no matter the cause.

When it comes to the question of Cole Wright's innocence, he could go either way. Doohan is loyal only to whoever's paying him.

Ever since his deployment to Iraq, crowds make him twitchy. Over there, a mass of civilians could suddenly turn violent. Guns could appear out of nowhere. Sometimes it was hard to tell the good from the bad from the totally innocent, and things got mixed up. Fog of war. Price of doing business.

Today he's dressed to blend in with the locals. Khaki pants,

L.L.Bean jacket, aviator sunglasses, black baseball cap. He holds up his Nikon camera and snaps a few shots of the protesters and the cordon of state troopers just to make the press pass around his neck look legit. He's careful not to point his camera directly at the Secret Service agents. No need to attract their attention.

A podium is fixed at the bottom of the courthouse steps in case somebody important decides to make a statement. Doohan weaves through the crowd-control barriers, assessing his options.

He doesn't like any of them.

His sponsor wants the hit to be public, which makes no sense. Why not just let him follow the subject to a dark street or empty hotel room? No witnesses. Easy exfil.

But for this kind of money, he's not asking questions.

He could make the shot from here, easy. A high-powered pistol would do it. But all it would take is one solid citizen or plainclothes agent to spoil his getaway. And he can't let that happen. Not on this job.

Doohan looks up at the roof of the courthouse. Too many professional snipers up there already. No other tall buildings in view. A bunch of trees line the parking lot, but most are evergreens. Not great for climbing. He sees a cell tower a few hundred yards back, but that's a long shot with windage and an exposed position to boot.

Forget it. This whole place is negative for the operation.

Although he can't wait to put crosshairs on a forehead again, it has to be someplace else.

No worries.

He'll have no problem spotting his target.

In New Hampshire, a Black woman stands out.

CHAPTER 101

The State calls Felicia Bonanno."

Every head in the courtroom swivels around as Felicia comes through the doors and walks down the center aisle. She's wearing a plain blue dress and her hair is done up in a neat bun. I try to catch her eye, but she just stares straight ahead, biting her lip, looking sad and afraid.

I don't blame her. What happened to Suzanne is something no mother should ever have to endure, let alone relive. Since Garrett's murder, sadly, I empathize with her even more than I did when we began our investigation.

As a witness for the prosecution, Felicia hasn't been allowed in the courtroom until now. I'm grateful that she hasn't been here to see the photos of her daughter's remains and burial spot projected on the large screen.

The clerk swears Felicia in. She sits down in the witness stand, then shifts forward in the chair until she's a few inches from the microphone.

"Good morning, Mrs. Bonanno," says the deputy attorney general.

"Good morning." Her voice sounds shaky and nervous and very soft.

The courtroom stills as we all strain to hear her.

"I'm sorry you have to go through this. I know you'd rather not be here," says Bastinelli. "I'll do my best to finish this as quickly as possible."

"Thank you," Felicia says. "And you're right, I'd rather not be here."

"Understood, ma'am." Bastinelli walks over to a side table and picks up a plastic evidence bag. I can see what's in it. He holds it in front of Felicia.

"Mrs. Bonanno, can you confirm for the jury what this item is?"

Felicia nods. "It's a tennis bracelet. It belongs . . . it belonged to my daughter Suzanne."

"Mrs. Bonanno, I can imagine that your daughter had a lot of jewelry. I know my daughters do. Why do you remember this piece in particular?"

"I remember it because I got it repaired for her."

"Can you explain that to the jury, please?"

"The clasp got broken," says Felicia. "A couple weeks before Suzanne . . ." Her lips are trembling now.

"Take your time," says Bastinelli.

Judge Dow leans over. "Mrs. Bonanno, I need you to speak up a little."

Felicia straightens in the chair and clears her throat. "A couple weeks before Suzanne disappeared, she asked me to take the bracelet to a jewelry store because the clasp was broken and she didn't have time to get it fixed. She was too busy getting ready for her move."

"And did you get the clasp fixed for her?"

"Yes, I did. I brought it to Manfred Jewelers."

Bastinelli introduces an exhibit and projects an image of a receipt from the jewelry store in Seabrook, New Hampshire. Digitally circled are the date and notation of a charge for replacing a clasp on a tennis bracelet with red stones.

"Mrs. Bonanno, is that your signature on the receipt?"

"Yes, it is."

"When Suzanne asked you to get the bracelet repaired, did she tell you how it got broken?"

Here it comes...

"Yes. She told me she got in a fight with her boyfriend and he tore it off her wrist."

"And who was her boyfriend at the time?" asks Bastinelli.

Felicia looks directly at the defendant before she answers in a confident voice, "It was Cole Wright!"

No problem hearing her now.

CHAPTER 102

Judge Dow calls a five-minute recess. He asks Felicia if she wants to step down, but she says all she needs is water. A bailiff brings her a bottle.

At one point, she looks in my direction. I give her a little smile and a nod.

She doesn't nod back. I think she's afraid to. I can sense how alone she feels.

I wish I could run up and hug her.

Tess Hardy whispers to Cole Wright during the whole recess. When Dow raps his gavel again, she gets up from her chair and walks slowly over to the lectern. I can see that she's keeping a respectful distance from Felicia. Giving her some space.

"Good morning, Mrs. Bonanno. First, I'd like to echo what Mr. Bastinelli said. I'm very sorry that you have to be here."

"Thank you, ma'am."

I'm hoping Bastinelli warned Felicia that while Tess Hardy might project warmth and sympathy, her job is cutting prosecution witnesses to shreds.

"Mrs. Bonanno, can you confirm that Cole Wright gave your daughter this tennis bracelet?"

Felicia nods her head. "I assume he did."

"You assume? So you weren't there when she received the bracelet?"

"No, I wasn't."

"Did you see a gift box or a note from Mr. Wright?"

"No. I just saw the bracelet on Suzanne's wrist. And she told me it was a gift."

"Did she tell you it was a gift from Mr. Wright?"

"No, but Cole Wright was her boyfriend— "

"Sorry, Mrs. Bonanno. This is important. If you didn't see Cole Wright give Suzanne the bracelet, and she didn't tell you it was from him, how can you be sure he gave it to her?"

She's got Felicia rattled now. It's painful to watch.

"Mrs. Bonanno?"

"I don't know."

"Meaning you're not sure? Isn't it possible that somebody else gave her the bracelet?"

"Objection!" Bastinelli rises from his chair. "Counsel is trying to confuse the witness!"

Hardy waves her hand over the lectern as if she's a magician making something disappear. "I'll withdraw the question, Your Honor." She pulls out a sheet of paper and walks toward Felicia.

"Mrs. Bonanno, are you familiar with any of these names?" She glances down at the paper and reads, "'Darrel Masterson, Gus Blair, Manuel Jennings, Tony Romero.'"

"I... yes, I've heard of them..."

"You've heard of them because these are all men your daughter *dated*, isn't that right?" Hardy's inflection makes *dated* sound like a filthy word.

I can see Felicia trying to correct the impression. "My daughter was very popular with boys. But she— "

"I can see that," says Hardy, interrupting her. "*Very* popular. And any of those boys, as you call them, could have given Suzanne that bracelet at any time."

Felicia is clearly starting to lose it as she defends her daughter's honor. "Suzanne was a good girl!"

Aware that she's just created a hostile witness, the defense attorney dials it back. "Nobody's questioning that, Mrs. Bonanno," Hardy says. "All I'm suggesting is that your daughter could have been wearing a bracelet given to her by one man while she was dating another man. Or two."

"Your Honor! Objection! Badgering!" Bastinelli interjects.

I can tell that Hardy is getting in his head, which is exactly where she wants to be.

Judge Dow looks down over his glasses. "Sustained. Ms. Hardy, you know better."

"I'll stop there, Your Honor. No further questions."

CHAPTER 103

Judge Dow adjourns early. I look for Felicia Bonanno, but she's already gone.

After the proceedings, the road is shut down for thirty minutes while the Secret Service extracts Cole Wright and shuttles him, ankle monitor and all, back to the inn where he's staying.

The convoy can't avoid the TV trucks and demonstrators that have taken over the parking lot. I hope Felicia figured out how to bypass them.

When the road reopens, I hike back to where I parked the Subaru. I'm just about to open my car door when my phone chimes with an incoming text. It's from an unknown sender. Just a link to an article from the *New York Times* headlined "Columbia Professor Dies in Car Crash."

Holy shit!

I enlarge the text and absorb the story in quick nuggets. *Cameron Graham, JD. Heart attack. Lost control of vehicle. Midtown East. No pedestrians injured.*

I lean back against the car. I'm stunned. But I'm not totally surprised. Dr. Graham underwent a quadruple bypass my second year of law school.

Now what?

Garrett—gone. Amber—gone. Amalfi—gone. Dr. Graham—gone.

At this point, I've got more dead ends than good leads. And now I'm wondering about all the secrets that died with him. Especially about his alter ego, Doc Cams.

The news has me rattled. I can't shake the feeling that I'm being followed. I take a circuitous route back to my hotel, but when I arrive, I see an unnerving sight: My watchers sitting in a car in the parking lot. Clearly they're waiting for me.

Enough. My adrenaline is pumping. *I want answers.*

I start marching toward them. Before I can get there, the car peels out.

Who the hell are these people?

As I open the door to my room, my phone rings.

The name on the caller ID is Laurie Keaton.

I've got so many names flying around in my head, it takes me a second to make the connection. I take the call. "Hello, this is Brea."

"Hi, Brea. This is Laurie, from the off-campus student residence in Hanover. You and your partner were here in January—you wanted a list of people who lived in the house at the same time as the Wrights. Sorry it took me so long to dig it up. Did you get it?"

"Oh, I moved about six months ago. When did you send it?"

"I mailed a copy about two months ago to an address in... let's see... Litchfield, Connecticut."

Shit! My old address. I'd had my mail forwarded, but who knows what happened to that envelope.

"I've been watching the trial on TV and I remembered you

saying those names might be important. That's why I called to check."

"Laurie, could you scan it and email it to me now?" I give her my email address, then run out of the room and fly down the back stairs to the hotel's business center—a small carrel with a Dell desktop and an inkjet printer. I hold my phone between my cheek and shoulder as I log into the computer with my room number, then open my email account.

I sit there and wait, refreshing my inbox every few seconds until it shows up.

"Did you get it?" Keaton asks.

"Got it! Thank you so much!" I open the document but don't bother to read it before I send it to the printer.

"How about you?" asks Keaton. "Have you been watching the trial?"

"I've got a front-row seat."

"Well, if you ask me," she says, "I think Wright might walk."

Not if I can help it.

CHAPTER 104

Kingston, New Hampshire

It's two a.m. and Cole Wright is running free.

Unfastening the ankle monitor was unexpectedly easy. All it took was a metal nail file and the right leverage on the clasp. He told the agent on guard that he was going down the hall for ice. From there, it was a quick dash down the back stairwell and out the rear door.

For the first time in months, he's stretching his legs and feeling his heart pound in a healthy way. The dark street is empty. With every stride, he feels lighter. He can hardly even tell his feet are hitting the pavement. It's almost like he's flying. Then he hears an odd jangle, like loose change.

Louder with each step.

He pulls up short on the sidewalk and looks down. He tugs up the right cuff of his sweatpants.

There. Around his ankle.

A tennis bracelet!

A helicopter roars overhead and hovers in front of him. A searchlight hits him with a powerful beam.

Suddenly, Secret Service agents move in all around him. Agents from his detail at the hotel. Agents from his detail in DC. Doug Lambert approaches in a suit and running shoes. Leanne Keil is wearing her tracksuit from North Carolina State.

The chopper dips lower, almost touching the pavement. Cole shields his eyes against the searchlight. Then the pilot leans out of the cockpit. Female. No flight suit. Just jeans and a V-neck. Thick wavy hair.

Cole drops to his knees on the sidewalk.

Suzanne!

He wakes with a start. He reaches down in bed and touches the steel and Kevlar electronic device fastened around his ankle.

Ever since the trial began, Cole can't get Suzanne out of his mind.

He'll never speak to her again, but he wishes he could. Just like he wishes he could speak to each and every person on the jury and tell them just one thing.

The truth.

He didn't kill Suzanne Bonanno. But he thinks he knows who did.

CHAPTER 105

Twenty names. Twenty students who rotated through that ramshackle house during the years when Cole Wright, Maddy Parson, and Burton Pearce were there.

I spent last night cross-referencing the names on the list Laurie Keaton sent me with the online Dartmouth alumni directory. But a lot of people slip through the cracks in alumni records. Maybe they never graduated. Maybe they changed their names when they got married and never updated their profiles.

I've already made six calls this morning. I work my way down the list. There are three names left. I'm thrilled to get an answer when I dial Caleb Stringer. His wife, Helen, answers—but she quickly tells me that her husband is unavailable.

"I'm sure he'd be happy to talk to you," she says. "He always has stories about his Dartmouth days. But that's not going to happen today. He's away on a six-month grant to study the grizzly bear population in Alaska's Katmai National Park and Preserve. But I'll pass your message along next time I talk to him."

Just my luck: The one guy who might actually be able to help me turns out to be a wildlife biologist who's somewhere on the tundra with apex predators.

I walk over to my minifridge and grab a bottle of water. I've got Court TV on in the background. As I pass by, I get a flash of a man's face on the screen. I stop.

Jesus Christ!

It's Leo Amalfi!

I grab the remote and turn up the sound just in time to catch the end of a reporter's intro.

"And now his handiwork may have surfaced again. Providence police report finding two fifty-gallon metal drums partially submerged off Rock Island in the Providence River. Those drums reportedly contained human remains suspected to be those of Anthony Puglisio and Enzo Lucia, two low-level associates of the Providence crime family, missing since just before Amalfi's death."

The video cuts to side-by-side mug shots of two men, one much older than the other. Both with cold eyes.

I drop my water bottle and sit down on the edge of the bed to catch my breath.

Could these be the two men Amalfi told me he sent after Garrett? The ones who said someone above him cut the chain and turned a contract into a hit?

If they are, I'm not sorry they're dead.

I'm only sorry they can't talk.

CHAPTER 106

Rockingham County Courthouse, New Hampshire

I'm late to court, but thanks to last night's Court TV preview, I recognize the witness for the prosecution on the stand: Detective Herman Fleming.

Since I missed Bastinelli's questioning, I'm not entirely sure how he's connected to the case. I'm about to find out.

Throughout the trial, I've been jotting down capsule descriptions of people I'll need to describe in the book. For Fleming, I scrawl, *Brown hair, thick as a teenager's but gray at the temples. Brown suit.*

I put down my pen and look up.

Herman Fleming is about to meet Tess Hardy.

"Good afternoon, Detective."

"Good afternoon, Counselor."

"So, to confirm what we heard in your testimony with Mr. Bastinelli, you were not part of the Suzanne Bonanno missing person investigation seventeen years ago, correct?"

"That's right. I was a patrolman in Seabrook then."

"And now you're retired. No longer active in law enforcement."

"Correct. I'm a contractor."

"In your testimony with Mr. Bastinelli, you indicated that you did have knowledge of a jurisdictional dispute regarding the case at that time, true?"

"Yes. It was much discussed in local law enforcement circles."

"What was the nature of that dispute?"

"The victim was in the process of moving between residences. She had legally changed her address from Seabrook, New Hampshire, to Boston, Massachusetts, but hadn't physically moved. It wasn't entirely clear where she officially lived. So Boston PD and Seabrook pushed the case back and forth until it was determined that the victim was still a resident of Seabrook. We ended up catching the case."

"Sounds like a bit of a mess."

"It was, yeah."

"Now, Detective, you're aware that most of the original case files are no longer available, is that right? Based on your knowledge and experience, can you offer an opinion as to where those files went?"

"Objection!" Bastinelli says. "Calls for speculation."

"Sustained," says Dow.

Hardy smiles. "All right. Let's take a different tack. Who was the lead detective once the jurisdiction finally got sorted out?"

"That would be Detective Isaac Collins, ma'am. Seabrook PD."

"And where is Detective Collins now?"

"Deceased, ma'am."

"Do you happen to know if Detective Collins interviewed my client, Cole Wright, in the days following Suzanne Bonanno's disappearance?"

"He did, yes."

"And how do you know that?"

"I was—I *am*—a big Patriots fan. So was Collins. Probably bigger than me. And Cole Wright was, you know, on the Pats back then, which was a huge deal. And so I asked Collins about him after the interview."

"And what did Collins tell you?"

"Said Wright was pleasant, cooperative, friendly."

"Did you and Detective Collins discuss the substance of the interview?"

"No. Collins was about to write up his report."

"Did you ever read that report?"

"No, I did not."

"And now that report is missing, along with all the other paperwork connected with the initial investigation apparently."

"Objection!" Bastinelli calls out. "Counsel is testifying."

"Sustained," says Dow. "Ms. Hardy, please, ask the questions, don't answer them."

Hardy doesn't even react to the scolding. "Detective Fleming, did Cole Wright request a lawyer before talking to Detective Collins?"

"Objection, Your Honor!" Bastinelli is on his feet. "Hearsay!"

Dow pauses for a second. "Sustained."

"All right, then, Detective. Let me ask you this: Based on your personal knowledge of the case, was Cole Wright detained after his interview?"

"No."

"Was he arrested?"

"No."

"Was he charged?"

"No."

"And was he allowed to travel to the clinic in Los Angeles, California, for treatment for the knee injury he sustained while playing professional football?"

"Yes."

"And what did Detective Collins personally say about Cole Wright with regard to this investigation?"

"Collins said he didn't like him."

I can see the jurors are confused.

But I'm not.

And neither is Hardy. "Can you explain that, Detective?"

"Yeah. Okay. It's like cop slang. When he said he didn't *like* him, he meant he didn't think he was a suspect. He thought he was clean."

From Hardy's smug expression, I know what's coming next.

"No further questions."

CHAPTER 107

The next witness the deputy attorney general calls is Jan McHenry. I perk right up. I don't know who she is or where this is going, but I know an expert witness when I see one.

The clerk swears her in and Bastinelli gets started.

"Ms. McHenry, can you please tell the jury your name and occupation?"

She turns toward the jury box. "My name is Jan McHenry. I am a forensic textile analyst at Icon Labs in Boston, Massachusetts."

Blank stares from the jury.

Bastinelli walks over to the evidence table. "Ms. McHenry, I'm going to ask you to look at a sample that is already in evidence." Bastinelli picks up a clear plastic bag with a patch of dirty blue fabric inside. "Your Honor, State's exhibit twenty—a sample of the fabric in which Suzanne Bonanno's remains were enclosed." Bastinelli shows the bag to McHenry. "Did you have an opportunity to examine this sample?"

She looks closely at the bag. "I did."

"And can you briefly describe how you examined it?"

"Certainly. I observed it visually, microscopically, through Raman spectroscopy, and through chemical analysis."

"And without going into scientific detail, were you able to determine the composition of the fabric to a high degree of certainty?"

"Yes. It is ethylene polyester. Very common fiber. But a proprietary weave."

"Proprietary? Meaning what, exactly?"

"Meaning it came from one specific manufacturer."

"And were you able to identify the manufacturer?"

"I was. Formosa Industries in Taiwan."

"And were you able to determine the approximate age of the fabric?"

"Yes. The factory told me that that specific run of sheets was produced for only a short while, about twenty years ago."

"Are you able to be more specific?"

McHenry nods. "Formosa used an experimental dye accelerator to speed up the diffusion of color into the fabric. That accelerator has a specific chemical profile. After the test run, it was discontinued because it was too expensive. So we know when the sheets were made."

I can always tell how impressive an expert is by how quiet the gallery is. When Jan McHenry speaks, I can hear a pin drop. The jury is paying strict attention.

"And how many colors of fabric were produced in that test run?"

"Only one. Light blue, pattern BL three-zero-zero-nine X." She points at the bag on the table. "That's the color of the sample I examined."

"Thank you, Ms. McHenry."

Bastinelli looks at the defense table. "Counselor, your witness."

I'm not sure what kind of damage Tess Hardy can do to Jan McHenry on cross, but I'm sure she'll do her best.

Hardy walks briskly to the lectern like she's in no mood to waste time.

"Good morning, Ms. McHenry."

"Good morning."

"Ms. McHenry, are you an expert in soil analysis?"

For a second, McHenry seems thrown by the question. "Soil? No."

"You seem certain that you can pinpoint the date that this fabric was manufactured, correct?"

"Yes. As I just said—"

"I'm not asking you to repeat your testimony, Ms. McHenry. My question is: Can you tell us with any degree of certainty how long that fabric sample was buried—or if it was buried at all?"

"I evaluated the fibers. Not the dirt."

"I'll take that as a no. So the sheet could have been buried a year ago, correct? Or left in somebody's crawl space for the past two decades?"

"Objection!" says Bastinelli. "Calls for speculation."

"Sustained," says the judge. "Move along, Ms. Hardy."

"Let me approach it another way, Ms. McHenry. For the moment, let's stipulate that this fabric is, in fact, the age you say. However, based on your expertise, you cannot say with certainty that it has been buried underground for the past seventeen years, is that correct?"

"No, I cannot."

"Or that it enclosed human remains for that entire time or any portion of that time."

McHenry speaks directly into the mic. "I cannot say that."

"Thank you, Ms. McHenry. No further questions."

I see what Hardy is doing. She's undermining the prosecutor's gains with this witness.

More important, she's sowing the seeds of doubt.

CHAPTER 108

Washington, DC

President Madeline Wright sits in the rear of a black up-armored Suburban parked on N Street in Georgetown. Secret Service agents in plain clothes are stationed at both ends of the cross streets. Another agent stands by the back door of the vehicle.

It's ten p.m. Two hours ago, Burton Pearce interrupted Maddy's daily call with Cole to tell her about a serious problem with the Grand Bargain. He described it in three simple words.

"Trent. He's wavering."

Now Maddy's here to solve the problem.

Congressman Aaron Trent of New Jersey is the minority leader. Powerful and influential. If he cracks in his support for Maddy's landmark legislation, it could start an avalanche. Even inviting him for a sit-down in the Oval could be risky. Who knows what he might say to the press gaggle continuously clustered in the West Wing's James S. Brady Press Briefing Room?

No. This problem requires immediate, personal, after-hours attention.

At this very moment, Pearce is knocking on the front door of the congressman's elegant brick home.

The door opens. Maddy is close enough to see the shocked look on Trent's face. His eyes get even wider when Pearce points to the Suburban. Maddy watches as Pearce practically grabs Trent by the elbow, pulls him through the doorway, and walks him down the brick steps to the curb. The agent by the car steps aside as Pearce opens the rear door.

Maddy looks at Trent from the left rear seat. "Get in, Congressman."

Trent hesitates for a second as if he thinks he has a choice. Then he ducks his head and slides into the right rear seat. From the street, Pearce closes the heavy door with a thud.

"Madam President, I didn't expect..." Trent is wearing chinos and a dark blue pullover. Both are dusted with flour.

"Sorry to interrupt your baking," says Maddy.

Trent starts to brush off the flour, then stops when he realizes he's dusting the president's expensive leather seats. "I was showing my daughters how to make scones. Can I ask why—"

Maddy holds up her hand. "Don't insult me, Aaron. Bad way to start off a meeting. I know you're backing away from our legislation."

"Madam President—"

"And if you do, some of the squish members of your party might decide to come with you. What's going on?" Maddy can sense Trent making mental calculations. "For God's sake, Aaron, don't strategize, just talk."

Trent turns to face her. "Madam President, I have concerns about how this legislation was prepared. Too many closed-door meetings. Too many outside advisers. Not enough involvement from my side of the aisle. If this bargain is going to get the full support of the American people, we need to take another look at it, schedule some open hearings, and—"

"Bullshit, Aaron."

This gets Trent flustered. Good.

"Ma'am?"

"I said bullshit. Here's what's going on. You've learned that your good friend Congressman Bragg is planning a leadership challenge. A challenge to you. He thinks you're too cooperative, too willing to play ball with the other side. So, to show him and his gang of misfits that you have the balls to stand up to the bitch in the Oval Office—that would be me—you want to break your promise and take the whole plan down."

"Madam President, I don't want to kill it. I just want to improve it!"

"Spare me," says Maddy. "You know perfectly well that if this plan stalls, it dies. And if we start nibbling away at the edges, it loses its power. Most Americans already think you guys on the Hill just run your mouths and get nothing done. Congress now has an approval rating of nineteen percent. Are you seriously shooting for single digits?"

"No, ma'am, it's just—"

"Listen to me, Aaron. I like you. You're smart. I don't like Bragg. He's a pain-in-the-ass bomb thrower, and he's been nipping at your heels for the past year."

Trent says nothing.

"Have you met Bragg's wife, Celine?" asks Maddy.

"Celine? Of course I have."

"You know she's from France, right? Do you know how desperately she wants to go back there?"

"She's never said anything about that."

"She wouldn't. Not in front of her husband. But I know for a fact that she hates DC. She's threatening to leave Bragg if he runs for reelection."

"I don't believe that—"

"You should. Because it's going to work in your favor—and mine."

Trent looks puzzled. "How's that?"

"In two days, I'm going to announce that I've asked Congressman Bragg to accept the position of US ambassador to France. He'll spare himself a messy separation and he'll be out of your hair. No longer a threat to your leadership."

"But the ambassadorship is filled," says Trent nervously. "We confirmed Arthur Carew six months ago."

"Let me worry about Arthur. When we announce the legislation, I expect you to be standing beside me, leading the applause. Now get back to your scones."

Trent nods. "Yes, ma'am. Thank you, ma'am."

"You want to know a secret?"

"Ma'am?"

Maddy makes a kneading motion in the air. "Make sure the butter is cold when you mix it into the dough."

"Thank you, ma'am. I will."

Trent opens the door, and Pearce is there to help him out. "Have a nice night, Congressman."

Pearce doesn't wait for Trent to reply; he slides into the still-warm seat. The agent shuts the door after him. Pearce looks at Maddy. "So?"

"I need you to find a prestigious, high-paying position for Arthur Carew. Something that doesn't require congressional approval. Do it fast. Make it juicy."

"Arthur Carew? Isn't he in Paris?"

Maddy nods. "For the moment."

CHAPTER 109

Number One Observatory Circle

It's just after eight a.m. when Burton Pearce walks into the nineteenth-century house at Number One Observatory Circle, the home of Vice President Ransom Faulkner.

He nods to the Secret Service detail guarding the VP.

For the past six months, Faulkner's colon cancer has been in remission, and he's been well enough to work from home. He moves like molasses, but his eyes are bright, and his mind is as sharp as ever.

"I've been watching the trial," says Faulkner. "Looks like your boy is still in the fight."

"So far, so good," says Pearce. "The prosecution's case is circumstantial. And Tess Hardy is earning her exorbitant fee."

Faulkner sinks farther back in his armchair and gestures for Pearce to take the one opposite. "So, Burton, when do I get my chief of staff back?"

Pearce smiles. "Rachel? She's happy in Berlin."

Faulkner snorts. “She *hates* Berlin and you know it. Almost as much as she hates you for sending her there.”

“Look, Chief, Rachel’s a smart kid, but she rubs a lot of people the wrong way, one of those people being the president. A little time in the foreign service will smooth her edges.”

Faulkner looks skeptical but changes the subject. “Are all your ducks still lined up on the legislation?” he asks.

Pearce nods. “The minute the First Gentleman gets acquitted, we move. National address from the East Room. All data and projections released to the press.” He reaches over and places his hand on Faulkner’s. “We need you there, Chief.”

“Gladly,” says Faulkner. “This working-from-home shit is for the birds.”

“Those drugs they’ve got you on mess with your immune system. You know that. Right now a case of the sniffles could bring you down. We need you healthy.”

“No,” says Faulkner. “You just need me presentable.”

“Maddy appreciates your loyalty,” says Pearce. “Always has.”

“I think she appreciates having me out of the way, not making waves. And what if this Grand Bargain idea goes to shit? What if Wall Street crashes? What if the governors revolt? What if the electorate turns against us? We’re taking a big risk. There’s a reason why no other administration has gone this far.”

“It’s a moon shot for sure,” says Pearce. “But it might just save the whole system.”

Faulkner lets out a long sigh. “Okay, Burton. I know my place. When you’re ready, just let me know when and where. I’ll show up—like Lazarus back from the dead.”

Pearce smiles. “I like that image, Chief. Excellent optics.”

CHAPTER 110

Rockingham County Courthouse, New Hampshire

"Your Honor, the State calls Lindsay Farrow."

The courtroom doors open and a young woman walks in. She's wearing a forest-green pantsuit, and she's movie-star beautiful.

She's sworn in, then sits down in the witness chair.

"Ms. Farrow, could you tell us your full name, title, and employer?"

"Lindsay Anne Farrow. Manager of digital services, northeast division, Walmart."

"And can you describe the scope of your job, please?"

"Yes. I supervise the technical aspects of the stores in my region. Scanners, computers, routers, modems, surveillance systems."

"Ms. Farrow, are you familiar with an initiative called Operation Harvest?"

"I am."

"Can you describe it?"

"Yes, though it was before my time at the company. It was an experimental program for the centralized storage of surveillance content that Walmart briefly implemented. During that time, security footage from all our locations was collected and logged on a server at headquarters in Bentonville, Arkansas."

"Ms. Farrow, were you asked to retrieve surveillance footage from that period from a specific store on a specific date and time?"

"I was, yes. Detective Sergeant Marie Gagnon requested it."

"Your Honor, State's exhibit thirty-two." Bastinelli clicks the controller. The screen lights up.

On the screen is a video. He freezes the image.

I almost jump out of my seat at the sight of Cole Wright and Suzanne Bonanno standing together in a checkout line. I realize that I've never actually seen an image of Suzanne and Cole together. I stare intently at the screen, searching their faces and body language for clues. One thing I can see clearly is the tennis bracelet on Suzanne's wrist. I hope the jury sees it too.

A buzz runs through the room, followed by gasps and whispers throughout the gallery. The judge bangs his gavel. "Order!"

Bastinelli ignores the disturbance. "Ms. Farrow, can you decipher for us the digital code at the bottom of this image?"

"Of course. The first part is the store location. In this case, the Seabrook location. Then the date, June seventh. Then the time code, nineteen thirty-two, which is seven thirty-two p.m."

The night Suzanne Bonanno disappeared!

Bastinelli unfreezes the video. The bustle in the front of the store comes to life. At register 2, Cole is in front, with Suzanne just a step behind him. Nothing odd or strained about their expressions. Just two normal shoppers, except that he's a famous football player and she's a professional cheerleader.

The checkout clerk's hand reaches over to pick up an item Suzanne is touching—a blue package with a gold and black label. Bastinelli freezes that image.

"Ms. Farrow, were you able to determine what that item is?"

"I was. It's a set of blue polyester bedsheets."

"Were you able to trace the vendor?"

"Yes. It was Formosa Industries in Taiwan."

Bam! Connection made.

I hope the jury is connecting the dots too. Suzanne and Cole were together that night. Suzanne bought sheets. She disappeared later that night. Then she ended up buried in those sheets.

That cannot all be mere coincidence.

The screen is black now, but the images are burned into my brain. The last known images of Suzanne Bonanno alive.

Right now, those images don't look great for Cole Wright.

CHAPTER 111

Concord, New Hampshire

It's been another long day in court, and now Hugh Bastinelli sits across from Jennifer Pope as she pours two fingers of single-malt scotch from a bottle on a small side table.

The attorney general hands him the glass and pours one for herself. She swirls the liquid in it slowly. "How are your feet holding up, Hugh?"

Bastinelli shakes his head. Trying a case requires long hours of standing before the court. "Nobody told me being a prosecutor would be so hard on my arches."

Pope laughs. "Yeah. Try doing it in heels." She lifts her glass. "To justice."

Bastinelli returns the toast. "To justice." He takes a sip and feels the warmth in the back of his throat. Pope's office is dark and cozy, lit only by a pair of antique banker's lamps on her desk. Nobody has smoked in here for decades, but the carpet and leather furniture still retain an essence of last century's tobacco, lightened slightly by the scent of Pope's perfume.

"Are the protesters still going strong outside the courthouse?" Pope asks.

"They never seem to stop," says Bastinelli. "They must work in shifts." Bastinelli cradles his scotch in both hands. He stares across the desk, almost fearful about this first sit-down with his boss since the trial started. "How are we doing, Jen?"

Pope takes another sip. "It would be a lot easier if we had a bullet hole and a gun."

"A *smoking* gun," says Bastinelli.

"Seriously, though," says Pope. "You're doing a great job with the hand we've been dealt. But Tess Hardy is tough. We knew she would be. If there's a crack, she'll find it."

"Right. Then she'll make it wider."

"I'm worried about a hung jury," says Pope. "I think you're getting to most of them, but all she needs is one strong holdout."

Bastinelli sets his jaw. "Then we'll retry him."

Pope shakes her head. She points toward the window. "Those protesters at the courthouse are expanding their reach. They're showing up outside the governor's mansion. Also on the front lawns of the state senate's president, the state's speaker of the house, and a couple of executive councilors. Nobody will be in any mood to start this circus again."

"God, I would love to get Cole on the stand," says Bastinelli.

"In your dreams," says Pope. "Tess will never allow it. She's afraid he'll give a nominating speech."

"Right. Or call a football play."

Pope's intercom chimes. She answers. "Ruthie? What are you still doing here? It's ten o'clock."

A young woman's voice comes through the speaker. "Just answering some emails, ma'am. You've got a visitor. Insists on seeing you right away. Security's holding him downstairs."

"Who's on duty?"

"Kevin, ma'am."

"Put me through."

Ruthie switches Pope to the security guard downstairs. Pope keeps the call on speaker.

"Kevin? Who's the guest?"

"His name's Donovan. Used to work for the Patriots. He has an envelope with him. Says he might have a bombshell."

"Does he seem sane?"

"Yes, ma'am."

Pope lifts her eyebrows at Bastinelli. "Okay, Kevin. Make sure it's not an actual bomb, then escort him up."

Pope hangs up and looks at Bastinelli. "Feeling lucky?"

CHAPTER 112

About two minutes later, there's a knock on the attorney general's office door.

"Enter!" Pope calls out. She stands up. Bastinelli does too.

The heavy oak door swings open. A uniformed security guard is standing next to a man in his sixties dressed in baggy jeans and a flannel shirt.

Pope glances at the security guard. "Thanks, Kevin. Just wait in the outer office with Ruthie if you don't mind."

"Yes, ma'am."

Pope extends her hand to the visitor. "Mr. Donovan? I'm Attorney General Pope, and this is Hugh Bastinelli, the deputy attorney general."

Bastinelli shakes Donovan's hand. It's warm and damp. The visitor looks a bit intimidated.

"Come in," says Pope. "Please sit." She pulls an extra chair from behind a small conference table and moves it over beside the desk.

Donovan takes the seat. "Thank you." He's clutching a large

manila envelope in his hands. "I'm Craig Donovan. Nice to meet you both."

Bastinelli pulls his chair closer to the guest. "You said you were a longtime employee of the Pats?"

"Yes, sir. I was a staff photographer."

Pope is back behind her desk, rocking in her leather office chair. "And what did that job entail?"

"I basically shot behind-the-scenes stuff. Not for publication, just for organization records. I shot practices, trips, celebrations, charity visits, you name it."

"And now?"

"Oh, I retired ten years ago. Moved up here to be near my daughter."

"So why did you ask for this meeting, Mr. Donovan? What was so important that you had to see me right away?"

Donovan looks down at the envelope. "Watching the trial has been bringing back memories. Everybody knew Cole and Suzanne, but not the way I did."

"You knew Cole Wright and Suzanne Bonanno?" asks Bastinelli.

"Sure I did," says Donovan. Then he seems to backtrack a bit. "Let me explain. I knew them the way a photographer does. I took pictures of them. I'd talk to them, get them to move this way or that for a shot, that kind of thing."

"You photographed both of them?" asks Pope.

"Yeah, but not together. I'd usually shoot the cheerleaders when they were rehearsing their routines or when they made appearances at community events. And the players, like I said, I'd shoot mostly during practices and around the facility. And at team celebrations. Like parties after a win."

Bastinelli glances at the envelope in Donovan's hands. He's holding it so tight, the edges are crinkled. "So what's in the envelope, Mr. Donovan? What is it you couldn't wait to show us?"

"Look," says Donovan, "you gotta understand. I liked Cole

Wright. He was always polite to me. Never gave me any attitude. But when I heard that lady on the witness stand, the doctor..."

"The medical examiner?" says Pope. "Dr. Woods?"

"Yeah," says Donovan. "Her."

"What about her?" asks Bastinelli.

"Something she said about Suzanne being strangled," says Donovan. "It reminded me of some pictures I took back when Cole was playing, and I found this." Donovan fingers the clasp on the envelope and opens the flap. He pulls out an eight-by-ten color print and lays it on the desk.

The photo appears to have been taken in the harsh fluorescent lighting of a sports facility—in a locker room or training area. A bunch of male athletes are in towels or workout gear. A few have their arms raised. Others are pumping their fists.

Bastinelli's heart lifts.

At the right side of the image is Cole Wright—with his hands around the neck of a cheerleader.

CHAPTER 113

Rockingham County Courthouse, New Hampshire

Early the next morning, long before the trial is scheduled to begin, opposing counsel are gathered in Judge Walter Dow's chambers just behind his courtroom.

The former Patriots photographer's photo is between Dow and Tess Hardy on a conference table. Since leaving the attorney general's office, Hugh Bastinelli hasn't slept. He rubs his eyes.

"Your Honor," Hardy says, "this is inflammatory—a last-minute desperation play on the part of the prosecution. You can't allow it."

Dow is in his dress pants and shirtsleeves. His black robe is hanging on a hook behind the closed door. "Calm down, Ms. Hardy. I haven't had my coffee yet." He turns to Bastinelli. "Could this have been Photoshopped?"

"The photographer can produce the digital file, Your Honor. I wouldn't have brought it in if I didn't think it was authentic." He looks at Hardy. "I'm not that stupid."

"And the photographer checks out?" asks Dow. "Craig Donovan?"

"We made some calls this morning, Your Honor. He's no crackpot. He was on the Patriots organization payroll at the time the photo was taken. He retired on good terms. I've got two former executives so far who will vouch for him."

"Your Honor, this man was not on the witness list," Tess Hardy argues.

"Right," says Bastinelli, "because we didn't know he existed."

"That's not my problem," says Hardy curtly. "You didn't do your job."

Dow picks up the photo and studies it closely. "Ms. Hardy has a point, Hugh. This could be highly prejudicial."

Bastinelli feels his anger rising. "Your Honor, the jury deserves to see this! It goes to Cole Wright's state of mind and his pattern of prior aggressive behavior toward women."

Dow turns to Hardy. "Is your client aware of this photo?"

"How would I know, Your Honor? I'm seeing it myself for the first time."

"Listen," says Dow, putting down the photo. "I'm going to grant you a twenty-four-hour continuance. But I agree with Mr. Bastinelli. If the picture's for real, I'm inclined to allow it."

The deputy attorney general feels like hugging the judge right there in his chambers. But he keeps a poker face. "The People appreciate it, Your Honor."

"Don't thank me yet." Dow points first at Bastinelli and then at Hardy. "I'm warning you both. If I see this picture show up anywhere in the papers, on TV, or online before I make my ruling, I'll be inclined to change my mind."

CHAPTER 114

Kingston, New Hampshire

Doug Lambert stands in the doorway of Cole Wright's suite at the inn. "Tess Hardy here to see you, sir."

"Already?"

Tess called earlier to tell him that court would be in recess for the day but she needed to speak with him in person. That was just twenty minutes ago.

Since then, Cole's been distracting himself by reviewing the new home page of the fitness program's website. He notes his list of changes on a pad of inn stationery.

Lambert barely has time to step aside before Hardy barges in. She tosses an envelope down on the table. "What is this?"

"Good morning to you too," says Cole. When he opens the envelope and sees what it contains, his mood instantly shifts. "Oh, shit," he mutters. "This is not good."

Hardy leans over until she's right in his face. "What the hell is going on there?" She points to the photo. "Is that really you?"

"Yeah," says Cole. "It's me. Where did you find this? I never knew it was out there."

"I didn't find it. The prosecution did. And Dow is thinking about allowing it into evidence."

"That's nuts," says Cole. "This doesn't mean anything. I remember exactly what happened. The picture was taken in our training room in Foxborough after practice the night before we traveled for a Sunday game against the Atlanta Falcons."

"Cole. Do I need to remind you that you're being accused of strangling a cheerleader to death? And now I'm looking at a picture of you with your hands on a cheerleader's throat!" Hardy taps the image. "Cole, who is this girl? Please, please, *please* tell me it's not Suzanne Bonanno."

Cole looks up. "Tess, take a breath. This isn't what you think it is."

CHAPTER 115

Seabrook, New Hampshire

I pull the Subaru into a spot at Seabrook's Harborside Park, a thirty-minute drive from my hotel.

I'm not sure why the trial got delayed for a day, but that meant I was free when I got the call from Teresa Bonanno saying she needed to talk to me. This morning. Somewhere safe. She suggested this park. So here I am.

Only a couple other cars are in the parking lot on this cloudy day with beach season officially over. I can see the gray Atlantic stretching out past a scrubby green lawn.

But no Teresa.

I pick up my phone to see if she left another text while I was driving.

Suddenly, I hear knuckles rapping on my window. My heart jumps.

It's her.

Teresa seems calm, not as edgy as I've seen her in the past. She's puffing on a cigarette, taking deep drags. "Thanks for coming," she says as I get out of the car. She points toward the beach. "Let's walk."

I don't know quite how to deal with Teresa. I believed her when she told me about Cole Wright threatening her sister. But the police clearly didn't find her credible. And she hasn't been called to testify at the trial, which means the AG didn't find her credible either. But she seems straight today. Her eyes are clear and she's walking steadily.

"How are you doing, Teresa?"

She pulls a small medallion out of her pocket. "Six months sober today."

Wow. That's a change. "Teresa, that's great. I'm proud of you." I really am.

She nods. "Thanks." Then she puts her hand on my shoulder. "I'm sorry about your partner."

"Thank you. I miss him."

I think about what Teresa and I have in common now: Cole Wright was one of the last people to see Suzanne alive. And one of the last people to see Garrett alive.

"So you've been at the trial?" she asks.

"Every day."

"How is it? How did my mom do?"

"Your mom did great. I know how hard it must've been for her."

"Yeah. It was. I wish I could have been there for her," Teresa says, "but I just can't make myself go to the courthouse."

As we walk, I'm wishing I'd brought a heavier jacket. The wind is really whipping off the water.

"Did they show pictures of my sister?" Teresa asks softly. "Her bones and everything?"

"They did, Teresa. They had to. But they also showed pictures of her in her cheerleading uniform, and she looked really, really beautiful."

I immediately sense that this is not what Teresa wanted to hear.

"I was so jealous of that uniform," she says, looking out over the water. "Suzanne had everything. Pretty face. Perfect body. Great job. Famous boyfriend. Me? I had *shit*."

"You were mad at your big sister, I get it. She seemed to have it made. It was natural to feel a little envious."

Teresa nods. "I wanted what she had so bad. At least a piece of it." She takes a drag of her cigarette and blows out the smoke. "I wanted a piece of Cole Wright."

"I remember your mom saying you had a crush on him."

"Oh, it was more than a crush," says Teresa. "We were all here one day, the three of us." She points to a spot on the sand. "It was right there. I could tell Suzanne didn't like me tagging along so much, but Cole was cool with it. It was really hot that spring, and when Suzanne went into the water to cool off, that's when I told him."

"Told him what?"

"That I wanted to have sex with him."

"Teresa! How old were you?"

"Old enough. But I was no virgin."

I'm nervous to hear where this is going. But I have to ask. "What did Cole do?"

"He kissed me. Right on the nose. Like I was some puppy dog or something. And that was it. I was so embarrassed. I hated him from that day forward."

A thought occurs to me. "Teresa," I say, "were you trying to get back at Cole when you told me what happened? Did you make up that story about Cole threatening your sister because he rejected you back then?"

Teresa looks down at the ground. "I know there was yelling, but I'm not sure what I heard. I was pretty drunk most of the time back then."

"Is that why you made me drive all this way, Teresa? So you could come clean about trying to seduce Cole Wright?"

"No, there's something else." Teresa flicks her cigarette into the sand. "I heard that a doctor testified that Suzanne might have been pregnant."

"Right. But there was no scientific proof. No way to be sure."

"I'm sure," Teresa says. "She was."

What?

I need to get to the bottom of this. I see a bench a few yards ahead and suggest we sit down. "Teresa," I say, looking her in the eye. "How do you know Suzanne was pregnant?"

"Because she told me—the night before she disappeared. She said she was gonna break up with Cole because of it."

"Why? Because it would get him kicked off the team?"

"No. Because it wasn't his baby. It was Tony Romero's."

CHAPTER 116

The White House

President Madeline Wright is sitting in the crowded Situation Room, one floor down from the Oval, watching a situation in the South China Sea unravel. It turns out the world doesn't stop just because your husband is on trial for murder.

Around the table are Secretary of Defense George Flanders, Chairman of the Joint Chiefs of Staff Buck Franklin, Chief of Naval Operations Rick Boone, and Maddy's national security adviser, Lydia Carmichael. Junior staff and liaisons are crowded against the walls behind them.

"Can we get any closer?" asks Maddy.

On one of the large screens in the front of the room, an electronic map zooms in on Bajo de Masinloc, also marked as Scarborough Shoal, a small atoll two hundred and twenty kilometers west of Luzon, the largest island in the Philippines. The tiny scrap of land in the middle of the sea has been a smoldering issue for years. And now it looks like it's ready to ignite.

China has claimed sovereignty over the atoll, and crews have constructed floating barriers to block Filipinos from accessing local fishing grounds, areas where they've fished for generations.

A few hours ago, a Philippine navy frigate, the BRP *Antonio Luna*, crossed the area, tearing out the floating barriers and taking fire from two lightly armed Chinese coast guard vessels in the process. The *Antonio Luna* crew returned fire with rifles.

"Any casualties?" asks Maddy.

"Unknown, ma'am," says Flanders. "The shooting has stopped, but our problem is the Chinese navy."

Maddy looks at Admiral Boone. "What's the latest?"

"Chinese destroyers CNS *Guilin* and CNS *Changsha* moving at flank speed to the disputed area. We expect them to be on station within the hour."

"And our assets?" asks Maddy.

"The USS *Ronald Reagan* carrier group is about two hundred miles south, but well within air cover of the location. And we also have the USS *Jefferson City*, a Los Angeles–class attack submarine, on patrol nearby. The *Jefferson City* could be moved closer, Madam President. I wouldn't consider that a direct provocation."

"Give the order," says Maddy.

"The Chinese destroyers are the issue, ma'am," says Boone. "We're not sure what they're up to. Maybe they're just coming to show the flag and make a point."

"Let's hope that's all it is," says Maddy. "Just some muscle flexing."

She knows the Philippine frigate is no match for two Chinese warships. She also knows that if the frigate is attacked or, worse, sunk, a century-old mutual-defense treaty with the Philippines requires a response from the United States. And once the missiles start flying, there might be no turning back.

"I assume we're working our back channels," says Maddy.

"Yes, ma'am," says Flanders. "So far, nobody in Beijing is picking up the phone."

An aide steps forward and slides a slip of paper in front of Maddy. She flicks her eyes down and reads the note: *First Gentleman, line 2.*

Maddy glances at the console in front of her and sees the blinking hold light. She rubs her temples. *Compartmentalize! That's what this job is all about.*

She makes a split-second decision. She scrawls *Not now* across the paper and hands it back to the aide.

About ten seconds later, she sees the light blink off.

First prevent Armageddon. Then return Cole's call.

Maddy closes her eyes for a moment to clear her head. When she opens them, she turns to the secretary of defense. "Get in touch with Manila again. Tell them we advise them to turn their frigate toward the nearest Philippine port—immediately."

"Yes, ma'am."

She looks at Boone. "Can our carriers communicate directly with the Chinese destroyers?"

"We can try, ma'am."

"Do it. Make it perfectly clear that if they attack the *Antonio Luna*, we'll send them to the bottom of the sea."

CHAPTER 117

Rockingham County Courthouse, New Hampshire

The next morning, Ron Reynolds whispers to me as I pass him going into court, "I hear the deputy AG has a bombshell."

I'm still trying to absorb the one Teresa Bonanno dropped on me yesterday. Had Suzanne really been pregnant with Tony Romero's baby? Despite her newfound sobriety, Teresa had admitted to lying before. And I'm not sure if I can trust her.

The court clerk's voice breaks into my thoughts. "All rise!"

Judge Walter Dow enters and sits down behind the bench. "Be seated." He shuffles some papers, then looks at Bastinelli. "Is the State ready to proceed?"

"Yes, Your Honor."

Dow lowers his glasses and looks out over the courtroom. "I am going to caution the gallery, as I have before, that I will not tolerate any expressions of approval or disapproval or outbursts of any kind. If you can't control yourself, the bailiffs will eject you."

Whatever the prosecution has, it must be pretty juicy.

Dow waves his hand at Hugh Bastinelli. "Go ahead, Counselor."

"The State calls Mr. Craig Donovan."

A nervous-looking guy in a corduroy jacket walks through the doors and the clerk swears him in.

It takes Bastinelli only a minute or two to establish the man's credentials. Donovan, now in his sixties, is a retired professional photographer who spent many years working for the Patriots. He took pictures of the cheerleaders and the players, including Suzanne Bonanno and Cole Wright.

Why is he here? What does he know?

"Mr. Donovan, do you see Cole Wright in the courtroom today?"

"I do."

"Can you point him out for the jury, please?"

Donovan points to Cole Wright sitting at the defense table.

"Let the record show that the witness has identified the defendant." Bastinelli continues. "Mr. Donovan, was there an occasion before an Atlanta Falcons road game when you observed the Patriots players in the training area of Gillette Stadium?"

"Yes, sir."

"And were you taking photographs of that occasion?"

"Not on assignment. I just happened to be passing through the facility on my way to my car. I always had my camera with me, so I took a few shots."

"Were these photographs meant for publication or publicity?"

"No, that wasn't part of my job. Just some candids."

"So you never got front-office approval to make these pictures public?"

"No. I never showed them to anybody."

"And the picture I'm about to show the jury has been in your possession since you took it, is that right?"

"Yes."

"Nobody else saw it until you brought it to the attorney general's office, is that correct?"

"That's right."

"And it's your testimony that the image is authentic? It has not been Photoshopped, cropped, or manipulated in any way?"

"It has not."

Bastinelli picks up the controller. "Your Honor, State's exhibit thirty-eight."

Hardy jumps to her feet. "Your Honor, I again object to the introduction of this evidence as inflammatory, prejudicial, and not probative!"

"Noted, Ms. Hardy. And overruled. Proceed, Mr. Bastinelli."

Bastinelli takes a step closer to the witness. "Mr. Donovan, is this one of the pictures you took at that event?"

He clicks the controller and a color photo appears on the screen.

Everybody gasps. Jurors. Spectators in the gallery. Me.

Dow raps his gavel. "Order!"

I cannot believe what I'm seeing. I'm looking at a blond cheerleader from the rear. She's leaning backward. Cole Wright is in front of her, arms extended, with a shit-eating grin on his face. His hands are around the cheerleader's neck.

Another gavel from the bench. "I said order!"

Bastinelli points to the picture. "Mr. Donovan, do you see Cole Wright in that photograph?"

"Yes, he's the one in the blue sweatshirt in the lower right."

"The man with his hands around the cheerleader's throat."

"Yes."

"Mr. Donovan, did you believe that you were photographing an assault in progress?"

"No, sir. Mr. Wright was just fooling around."

"Fooling around." Bastinelli looks at the jury. "Or do you think maybe he was working out some aggressions?"

"Objection!" Hardy practically jumps across the table.

Bastinelli glances at her. "I'll withdraw the question." He walks slowly back to the prosecution table and sits down. "Your witness."

Hardy is out of her chair like a shot.

I would be too.

"Mr. Donovan, we haven't met. I'm Tess Hardy, Mr. Wright's defense counsel."

"I know," says Donovan. "I've seen you on TV."

"Then you probably know why I objected to Mr. Bastinelli showing that picture, don't you?"

"I don't think I— "

"Because it's totally misleading."

"Objection!" shouts Bastinelli. "Counsel is testifying."

"Sustained," says Dow. "Ms. Hardy, frame a question if you have one."

"Yes, Your Honor, I do." She takes a few steps toward the screen and taps the image of the cheerleader.

"Mr. Donovan, from this angle, the jury is not able to see the face of the individual in the cheerleader's uniform. Were you able to identify that individual as you took the picture?"

"Yes, I was."

"And who was it? Tell the jury whose backside we're looking at here."

"It's Timmy Gervin."

The gallery erupts in nervous laughter but quiets when the judge glares. I can see Bastinelli's red face from here. I feel his pain and embarrassment. So much for the "bombshell" the reporters were predicting.

"And who's Timmy Gervin?" Hardy continues.

"He was an assistant equipment manager for the Patriots."

"Can you tell me why a male equipment manager would dress himself up as a cheerleader?"

"I don't know. I wasn't there when it started. He was just playing around, I guess."

"Playing around. I see. And did Mr. Gervin make a habit of dressing in a cheerleader's uniform?"

"Not as far as I'm aware."

"Did it look like Mr. Gervin was being injured in any way?"

"No. I remember he was laughing the whole time."

"So whatever was going on here, he seemed to be in on the joke?"

"Seemed that way, yes."

"So you knew, when you produced this picture, that it showed a bunch of male coworkers just playing around?"

I can tell what Hardy's doing. The jury can't unsee that image. All she can do is try to disarm it. When your client is on trial for murder, the last thing you want the jury to remember is a picture of him pretending to kill somebody.

"I did know."

"So why bring it forward now, Mr. Donovan? Why did you feel compelled to rush it to the attorney general's office?"

"I heard trial coverage about Cole Wright strangling Suzanne Bonanno and I didn't want anybody to think I was hiding something."

Hardy steps toward the bench. "Your Honor, move to strike! This witness is not a medical or forensics expert!"

"Sustained." Dow looks at the jury. "The jury will disregard the witness's last response."

Hardy collects herself before asking her next question.

"Mr. Donovan. A photograph captures one instant in time, isn't that right?"

"One split second, that's right."

"And you've admitted that you don't really know what led up to this picture, right?"

"Not really."

"Meaning no?"

"That's right. I don't know what came before."

"But from what you witnessed, it seemed a harmless joke, right?"

"I think so, yes."

"No further questions."

Bastinelli stands up and buttons his jacket. "Your Honor, the State rests."

His strategy is clear. That picture is *exactly* what he wants the jury to remember.

CHAPTER 118

The White House

In the Oval Office, the president of the United States is staring at a photo of her husband that she's never seen before. It shows him pretending to choke a young man dressed as a young woman.

The couple's daily phone call has been a time for Maddy to show Cole her unwavering support. Not today. They're on a conference call with Tess Hardy.

"Cole, what the hell were you thinking?" Maddy demands, knowing how bad this makes the First Gentleman look.

"It was a joke taken out of context," says Cole. "Harmless fun. Nobody was upset about it at the time."

"Well, they're upset about it now! And why am I hearing about this from the news?"

"I tried to warn you," says Cole.

"I'm sorry," says Maddy. "I was tied up downstairs." *I was a little busy with Armageddon.*

What Tess Hardy says next plunges her right back there.

"Madam President," says Hardy, "Cole wants to testify to explain the picture."

"You want to take the stand, Cole?" asks Maddy. "That's a big risk."

"It's a bigger risk if I don't. The prosecution has painted me as a violent guy. I need to show them I'm not."

"What do you think, Tess?" asks Maddy.

"The prosecution's case is wholly circumstantial and entirely lacking in solid proof. They're just trying to string together a set of unconnected circumstances. A watch. A bracelet. A sheet. A photograph—"

"And I can explain it all!" says Cole.

"You don't have to," says Hardy. "Innocent until proven guilty, remember? The burden of proof is on them. And I think we've done a pretty good job of poking holes in their evidence. Enough to secure at least one holdout on the jury. That's all we need."

"I don't want a hung jury!" says Cole. "That's a cloud hanging over me forever. Not to mention the risk that they can come after me again. Maddy, we need this to be over! For your sake as well as mine."

"I hear you, Cole," says Maddy. "I know you want to be exonerated. We all want the same thing."

Maddy looks at the two-foot-high stack of paper on the side of her desk, the latest draft of the Grand Bargain. Her crowning achievement. Her legacy. If she can ever manage to get it on the congressional floor.

And if she can ever get clear of this trial.

"Tess," Maddy says, "do you think you can coach him so he's ready?"

"I'm very coachable," says Cole. "Ask any of my coaches."

Maddy consults her schedule. "I've got a meeting on China in two minutes. Cole, I love you and I trust you. If you want to testify, it's your call and your call alone. Is that understood, Tess?"

Hardy replies respectfully, "Yes, Madam President. Loud and clear."

CHAPTER 119

Rockingham County Courthouse, New Hampshire

Word is out that Cole Wright has decided to testify. Maybe this afternoon. Maybe tomorrow.

I stand with Ron Reynolds on the courthouse steps as he finishes tapping out an update for the *Globe* on his phone.

"So, Ms. Criminal Attorney, how do you think Hardy is prepping him?" Ron asks me.

"What's most important is that Tess coach him on what he has to say on the stand. Word for word. And then her client has to follow through."

"Do you think it's a mistake for him to testify?"

"If he were a normal murder defendant, I'd say yes. But Wright's playing to a bigger audience. And remember, he was a football player. A tight end. He has faith in a Hail Mary."

My phone buzzes in my bag. Ron gives me a nod and goes back to his texting. I walk up the steps and find an empty spot near the gallery entrance.

I don't recognize the number but I pick up anyway. "Hello, Brea Cooke here."

"Brea. It's Daryna." A pause. "Calling from Ukraine."

Garrett's hacker contact!

Daryna has a heavy Eastern European accent, and she sounds like a teenager. "What kind of phone are you using?" she asks.

I have to think for a second. "It's an iPhone. Umm... an iPhone sixteen. Why?"

"I'm going to send you a link to an app. Tell me when you get it."

I look down at my screen. A message arrives with a simple black icon—looks like a *K* from the Russian alphabet. "I have it."

"Now open the app and install it."

"What's this for?"

"Don't speak. Do it."

I click the icon and follow the prompts. It takes about ten seconds. "Okay, it's done."

"Good. We're safe. This connection is now encrypted. My end and yours. Can you talk?"

I make sure no one is in earshot. "Yes. I can talk."

"My sympathies about Garrett. I miss hearing his voice."

"So do I."

"And I'm sorry that I haven't been in touch. My server got taken out in a drone strike. My whole network was compromised. I've been a nomad for the past few months. I finally found a safer location."

"Where are you?"

"Not important."

"I know Garrett trusted you, Daryna. He said you were the best."

"He trusted you too. More than anybody. He said if anything happened to him, I should give my report to you."

"What report?"

"He asked me to look into an operation that's trying to subvert the Wright administration. He said he had a lead from a very high source."

A very high source?

The airport! Cole Wright!

Does Daryna know about Garrett's meeting with the president's husband? I decide to keep it to myself. "And what did the source tell him?"

"The source just pointed Garrett in the right direction. And then Garrett pointed me. I've discovered that there's an active cabal disseminating disinformation about the president's husband as a way of undermining the administration, trying to bring it down. The cabal was centered in DC, but now the nexus is in Berlin."

"Berlin?"

"Are you familiar with Rachel Bernstein, the vice president's chief of staff?"

"Sure. I read the news."

"She is an enemy of the president. She wants her own man in place. Vice President Faulkner."

Is that who Doc Cams was communicating with? If so, the VP's chief of staff was spreading dirt about the First Couple. Sounds like that's where this is leading.

"And you should know this, too," says Daryna. "The files in the Suzanne Bonanno case weren't misplaced. Somebody in the federal government confiscated them three years ago. There were leads in this case that they did not want followed. It looks like they're covering for the Providence Mob or in collusion with it."

Leo Amalfi. Tony Romero. The Mob connections keep coming up.

"Daryna, I need more information on this. Can you help?"

"I'll keep searching," the hacker says. "I'll do it for you. And for Garrett."

CHAPTER 120

A TV camera is set up on the courthouse steps and a reporter is broadcasting live. "It's not every day that the spouse of the president of the United States gets called to the witness stand to defend himself in a murder trial," the reporter says. "In fact, it's never happened before in American history."

Courthouse security is the tightest it's been yet.

Outside, demonstrators are acting out the conflict of the trial. A couple of state troopers are called in to break up a fight between members of the pro-Cole and anti-Cole camps.

As I pass through the security checkpoints, I'm thinking about what Daryna told me. *Who authorized the removal of the case files? Why is the Mob involved? Could there really be a covert movement to use Cole Wright as a tool to oust his wife from the White House?*

I don't know when I'll next hear from Daryna, but I hope it's soon.

After Judge Dow calls the court to order, he turns to the defense table. "Ms. Hardy, is the defense ready to proceed?"

Hardy stands up. "Yes, Your Honor."

It's happening. I can feel the electricity crackle all around me.

"The defense calls Cole Wright."

The defendant walks to the witness stand. The First Gentleman is wearing a navy-blue suit, well tailored to ensure that no bulge from his ankle monitor is visible.

Cole stands in front of the clerk, raises his right hand, and swears to tell the truth, the whole truth, and nothing but the truth.

Will he?

He takes his seat and smooths his tie.

Tess Hardy walks over to the lectern. She's wearing a red skirt suit and a white blouse. Together, she and Cole present a unified vision in red, white, and blue.

Can't be coincidental.

"Good morning, Mr. Wright."

"Good morning."

Confident. Polite.

Hardy has drawn the toughest legal assignment there is. A celebrity client and murder suspect testifying on his own behalf.

"Mr. Wright, twenty years ago, you became a professional football player, is that correct?"

"Yes. I played tight end for the New England Patriots."

As if anybody in the room doesn't know that. It's like Paul McCartney saying he used to sing with the Beatles.

"And you considered yourself a competitive athlete?"

"Definitely. I played for three seasons. You don't survive in the NFL without being competitive. If you're not competitive, you don't win."

"Mr. Wright, were you an aggressive player?"

"Again, in football, you don't succeed without being aggressive. It's part of the culture. It's part of the game. You hit people. You knock them down. You run over them. They do the same to you. It's a contact sport."

"A brutal sport."

"It can be."

I see a couple of the men on the jury nodding.

"So much so that you tore your quadriceps tendon and patellar tendon playing it, correct?"

"Among other injuries, yes."

The stoic wounded warrior. It's a good image for Cole, and Hardy knows it.

"Mr. Wright, you sat here in court a day ago when Mr. Bastinelli showed a photograph of you at the Patriots facility in Foxborough, correct?"

"Oh, yes, I remember."

Perfect delivery. Sincere. Regretful.

"And you heard testimony from Mr. Donovan, the photographer, that the person in the photograph you appear to be choking was an assistant equipment manager named Timmy Gervin."

"Yes, that was Timmy. And no, I wasn't choking him."

"Thank you for the clarification. Now, Mr. Wright, I'm going to put up that picture again. And I'd like you to explain to the jury in your own words what everybody in this courtroom is probably asking themselves: What in heaven's name was going on?"

She clicks the controller and the photo appears on the screen.

Bold move. Instead of working to erase that image from the jury's mind, she's emphasizing it.

Cole doesn't need to look at the screen. He turns directly to the jury box. Hardy must have told him to make direct eye contact. *Act like you have nothing to hide.*

"That picture was taken at night after a practice," says Cole. "We were leaving the next day for a Sunday game against the Atlanta Falcons. They'd beaten us badly the last time we played them, and it was getting close to the playoffs, so we were fired up—the whole team. We wanted revenge, payback. That was our mood."

"And what would a cheerleader have to do with that?"

Cole looks at Hardy, then turns right back to the jury. "Well, the head cheerleader of the Falcons at the time was a young woman named Lucy Carson. She was also the niece of the owner of the Falcons. A couple days earlier, she had appeared on a morning sports show talking smack about the Pats and how she expected us to choke—"

Hardy interrupts. "Can you explain what *choke* in this context would mean?"

"To an athlete, *choking* means getting nervous, making mistakes, blowing opportunities, and so forth."

"And do professional cheerleaders typically criticize opposing teams?"

"No, not usually," says Cole. "But in Lucy's case, maybe because she was related to the owner, she engaged in a lot of trash talk."

"And was the whole team aware of Ms. Carson's comments?"

"Definitely. We all talked about it during practice that day. It gave us an extra... incentive."

"And what happened after practice, when you went to the training area of Gillette Stadium?"

"The first thing we saw was Timmy dressed up in a cheerleader outfit and a wig. You can't see it, but there's a big Falcons logo taped to his chest."

"What was your reaction?"

"Everyone thought it was hysterical."

"Did you know who Mr. Gervin was trying to portray?"

"Yes. I assumed that he'd overheard us talking about Lucy Carson, so he dressed up as a Falcons cheerleader to make fun of her."

"And what did you do next, Mr. Wright?"

"I walked over and made a show of putting my hands around Timmy's neck, just to make the other guys laugh."

"Did you say anything?"

"I can't remember exactly, but I think I made a joke like 'Who's choking now?' "

A murmur from the gallery. Dow shoots a look that way but doesn't bang his gavel.

"Were you angry at Mr. Gervin?" asks Hardy.

"Of course not. We were just messing around."

"And were you actually choking him?"

"No. I was barely touching him. It lasted for about two seconds. And, unfortunately, that's when Mr. Donovan snapped the picture."

"Mr. Wright, what are your thoughts as you look at that photograph today?"

Cole sighs heavily. "I'm embarrassed by it. It's sexist. It's disrespectful. It's inappropriate. I wish it hadn't happened."

"No further questions."

As a lawyer, I take my hat off to Tess Hardy. I'm staring at Cole Wright, the man who I'm convinced has done terrible things, and she's almost making me like the guy.

CHAPTER 121

During recess, in the conference room at the back of the courthouse, Cole Wright is pumped. The young associates are too.

"I just heard from Maddy," says Cole. "She thinks it went really well."

"So do I," says Tess. "You were solid on the stand. Likable even."

Cole smiles. He feels like he used to feel during a big play, when he'd see an opening in the backfield and blow right through it. Cole can't wait to get back into the courtroom, tell the rest of his story, convince the jurors of his innocence.

He looks across the table at Tess. "So when do I go back in?"

Tess stares back. "Never," she says. "You're benched."

Cole cocks his head. "What do you mean? We're just getting started!"

Tess glances at the other attorneys around the table. "Give us a minute."

Cole asks his Secret Service detail for the same.

Tess gets up from her chair and closes the door after everyone files out. She crosses the room and takes the chair right next to Cole's.

"Cole, I kept my word. I agreed to put you on the stand, and I did. You did a great job of neutralizing that photograph. So good that Bastinelli didn't even want to cross-examine you."

"Exactly. Isn't that a win? Shouldn't we capitalize on it?"

"Listen to me. If I put you up there again and get you to testify to what you've told me—that the watch was yours and that it was stolen, that the hole was on your property but you didn't know about it, that Suzanne's bracelet got broken in an argument but it was an accident—it opens up all those subjects to cross by the prosecution. Bastinelli will keep you up there for days, trying to make you look bad, and he'll find every little inconsistency in your story."

Cole is clenching his fists, trying to suppress his anger. He feels betrayed by the person he's paying to defend him. "I'm innocent!" he shouts. "I want people to know it!"

Hardy stays cool, which makes him even more furious.

"Cole. This was nearly twenty years ago. At some point when you're on that stand, your memory will slip, and you'll get caught—maybe not in a lie, but in something that sounds like one. And it will take days for me to rehabilitate you."

Cole is frustrated, burning with a need to talk, to tell his side. It all spills out in a torrent.

"I told you what happened! I met Suzanne at the Walmart. We were supposed to go out to dinner, but she didn't want to. She told me that there was something going on. That she wanted some time away from me to think. I was surprised, but I didn't push it. Technically, we were breaking team rules by dating in the first place and I didn't know if someone had come down on her about it. So when she got in her car and drove off, I didn't follow her. I never saw her again, but I didn't know that she was missing until I heard from Detective Collins."

"Cole, I know. You've told it all to me many times. You've never wavered. And if we had your original statements, it would be easier to corroborate the facts. But we don't. What the jury *does* know is that Collins was a major Patriots fan and that you were a Patriots star. That could be enough to make the jury think he let you slide."

Cole feels his jaw tightening. "Collins let me go because he knew I didn't do anything wrong."

"But do you really want to give Bastinelli that opening? To dig into every time you lost your temper or made a careless joke? I'm telling you, as your attorney, that's a losing strategy. Their case is circumstantial. No witnesses. No fingerprints. No DNA. My job is to make those circumstances seem ambiguous or irrelevant. I think I've accomplished that, and I'll do it again in my closing.

"Cole, this is not a football game. This is a *legal* game. And we need to quit while we're ahead."

Cole looks down at the table. His instinct is to put himself out there and fight, but he's savvy enough to understand that would only undercut his own case. Make things harder for Maddy. He promised not to lose his temper again. And he's trying. He's really trying.

Hardy reaches over and puts her hand on top of his. "Cole, I need you to be okay with this. When we go back in there after recess, I'm going to speak only five words: 'Your Honor, the defense rests.'"

CHAPTER 122

Kingston, New Hampshire

Stunned! Gobsmacked!" That's how the talking head on CNN starts off his evening commentary.

I'm sitting on my hotel bed doing another Domino's carb load, listening to the pundits' interpretation of Cole Wright's testimony.

"Tess Hardy took a big swing with her strategy today," says the commentator, a gray-haired man in a pin-striped suit. "And I think it just might work. By resting her case early, she basically said to the prosecution, 'We don't think your evidence is even worth discussing. The burden of proof is on you and you haven't proven a single thing.' "

The camera cuts to a legal analyst, a woman with a blond bob and thick-framed glasses. "I disagree. She had to put him up there to undercut the power of that disgusting photograph. But she should have left him up there to declare that he didn't kill his girlfriend. The jury wanted to hear that."

The camera cuts back to the first commentator. "If Tess Hardy had opened that door, Hugh Bastinelli would have kept Cole Wright on the stand for the next two weeks explaining every detail of that relationship. You could see that he was ready to pounce."

The blonde again. "You don't think the world wanted to hear Cole Wright declare his innocence? Shout it from the mountain-tops?"

"Tess Hardy will argue that he didn't need to," says the commentator. "She put him on the stand just long enough for the jurors to see that he's a nice guy, a charming guy. To remind them of his days as a football star. She's betting that she'll be able to handle the rest in her closing argument and plant enough reasonable doubt to get an acquittal."

The camera switches to the clean-cut anchor, a fill-in for Anderson Cooper. He looks right into the camera. "And we need to leave it there for now. When we come back, more news on the flash floods in California."

I click off the TV.

I admit it. I, too, wanted more fireworks in court.

So it all comes down to tomorrow. Two closing arguments, back-to-back.

I hope Cole Wright gets what he deserves.

CHAPTER 123

The White House

In the East Room of the White House, President Madeline Wright walks past the full-length portrait of George Washington to the podium. She opens the leather binder with the presidential seal on the cover. She looks out over the room.

The space is empty except for Burton Pearce.

"What about flags?" asks the chief of staff.

"Flags?" asks Maddy.

"What flags do you want behind you for the announcement? Stars and Stripes?"

"Can we fit the flags of all fifty states and the territories?" asks Maddy. "I want a message of unity—common purpose."

Pearce thinks for a minute. "It would take up the whole back of the room, but sure."

"As long as there's still room for Ransom," says Maddy.

She runs her finger down the first page with a pencil in hand. Her speech isn't quite ready. Neither is the Grand Bargain. This is just a very early rehearsal. The East Room is a stand-in for the chamber of the House of Representatives, where the actual speech will be delivered, assuming everything comes together. But for Maddy, just running through the language in a big room helps make the program feel real.

"The words need work, Burton," says Maddy, flipping through the pages. "Still sounds too political. Not grand enough."

She and Pearce have been working and reworking the details and wording of the announcement. With every new convert to the plan or tweak to the program, language needs to be altered and polished. Maddy considers editing one of her strongest skills, but she's having a hard time concentrating.

The lack of sleep isn't helping.

The crisis in the South China Sea has been a forty-eight-hour roller coaster, eased slightly when Admiral Boone managed to get hold of his counterpart in Beijing. The territorial dispute with the Philippines was not resolved—it's still smoldering—but at least the Chinese navy allowed the Philippine frigate to slip back to its port near Lian. No missiles or torpedoes fired. No casualties on either side.

But right now, Maddy's mind is on her husband.

"Should I be up in New Hampshire tomorrow for the closing arguments?"

Pearce shakes his head. "No, ma'am. It could be seen as trying to influence the jury. You need to stay put. Wait for the verdict."

"I feel like I'm leaving Cole alone at the worst time of his life." Maddy puts down her pencil and grips the sides of the lectern to hide the fact that her hands are trembling.

"He's not alone, ma'am. He's got a top legal team with him. Led by Tess." Pearce steps up onto the riser and leans in close. "Madam President, think back to when Cole was playing football at Dartmouth."

He shifts his gaze into the distance, as if he's staring into the past. "I tell you, there were times when he caught a pass at midfield and it looked like he had nowhere to go. No way out. Cornerbacks chasing him. Safeties coming at him. Somehow, he always found a way through to the end zone. It was a beautiful thing to watch."

Maddy takes a deep breath. "It was." She closes her binder and steps off the podium. "Refresh me—how many cornerbacks and safeties are there?"

Pearce steps down and follows close behind. "Usually four on a team, ma'am."

Maddy turns to face him. "Well, imagine if there were twelve! There could be twelve people against him in that jury room."

"I doubt that, ma'am." The Gray Ghost lowers his voice. "And remember, all we need for a hung jury is one undecided."

Maddy knows that Cole wants a clean not-guilty verdict. She does too. But her old friend and chief of staff is right. If just one juror holds out on a guilty conviction, the judge will have to declare a mistrial.

Not a perfect outcome. But the Grand Bargain is already hanging in the balance. It can't wait much longer.

And in the course of American history, that's what matters more.

CHAPTER 124

Rockingham County Courthouse, New Hampshire

Dozens of TV cameras track the deputy attorney general, Hugh Bastinelli, as he walks to the lectern for his closing argument. He consults his notes, then flips the binder closed.

He doesn't look nervous, but he must be, Brea thinks. *No pressure. Just the whole country watching.*

"Ladies and gentlemen, I told you at the beginning that this would be a circumstantial case, and I think you now have a better idea of what that means.

"The evidence tying Cole Wright to the killing of Suzanne Bonanno did not come tied up in a neat bow. It required you to listen. And I know you have. Now it requires you to *think*—to weave together the strands of evidence for yourselves. When you do, you will reach a conclusion so strong that even Cole Wright's power and fame cannot overcome it.

"We know Cole Wright was in a tense relationship with Suzanne Bonanno at the time of her death. Suzanne's mother, Felicia, confirmed it on the stand. And we have that from stadium worker Stacey Millett as well. We also know that the relationship was forbidden—that fraternization between players and cheerleaders was against the rules.

"We know that Cole was with Suzanne on June seventh, the night she disappeared. We all saw the two of them together on the Walmart surveillance video, the last known image of Suzanne alive. And what did she buy that night? Bedsheets. The bedsheets that ended up wrapping her dead body.

"We know that Cole Wright threatened Suzanne, spoke roughly to her. We know Suzanne told her mother that he once tore a bracelet off her wrist. That same bracelet was later found near where Suzanne's remains were buried. As was a watch we know belonged to Cole Wright."

As Bastinelli speaks, I see Cole scribbling on a legal pad. Hardy has her hands folded under her chin. She's looking past the deputy AG at the jurors, reading their faces to see when Bastinelli's points are hitting home and when he's off the mark.

Bastinelli talks about the hole near the Reverend Weare memorial rock. He shows a map marking its distance from Suzanne's house and from the Walmart where she and Cole were last seen. He clicks back to photographs he showed during Gagnon's testimony, showing the foliage surrounding the hole and how dark the area was at night. He even quotes from a weather report stating that there was no moon the night Suzanne disappeared. He paints a picture of a dark sky, a shovel in the dirt, a dead woman's body hastily wrapped and buried. Like something out of a horror movie.

Bastinelli is clear and deliberate. When it comes to physical evidence of the crime, he doesn't have much to work with, but he does what he can.

"We've talked about the way things happen on TV, ladies and gentlemen. We've all seen how proficient CSI techs are at measuring wounds and detecting poison. But we don't have any of that here. As Dr. Alice Woods testified, Suzanne Bonanno was killed in the most primitive and personal way—by strangulation. Done by somebody strong enough to snap a supple hyoid bone." Bastinelli points to the defense table. "That person was Cole Wright.

"We don't know what might have set him off that night. Only two people were there, and only one is alive. The judge will tell you in his instructions that second-degree murder does not require planning or intent. Cole Wright might not have *intended* to kill Suzanne. It might have been a spontaneous act of passion or anger. We just don't know."

Bastinelli speaks at length. Finally, he concludes: "Ladies and gentlemen, Cole Wright was a famous football player. Today, he is married to the president of the United States. In this country, sometimes we equate fame and celebrity with goodness and positivity. But don't be fooled. There is darkness there. Suzanne Bonanno saw it. In fact, it was the very last thing she saw.

"So whatever your thoughts are about Cole Wright in his public roles, you must put them aside. Based on your judgment of the evidence presented here, circumstantial though it may be, you must find him guilty of murder in the second degree."

To that, I quietly whisper, "Amen."

CHAPTER 125

After a ten-minute recess, it's the defense's turn.

Having seen how good a defense attorney Tess Hardy is, I imagine she's saved her best for last.

She takes her time approaching the lectern. She smiles at the jury. Like Bastinelli, she looks each one in the eye.

"Ladies and gentlemen, I first want to thank you for your work on this trial and the close attention you've paid to it. I understand that jury duty is an inconvenience and, in your case, an actual hardship. You've put your personal and work lives on hold and endured isolation from your friends and families. And for that, we are all grateful. I hope that the hardship will not last much longer. And I don't think it will. Because the verdict in this case is so simple and clear."

Hardy walks to the center of the courtroom. "Let's start with the obvious and sad fact that Suzanne Bonanno was killed. That is a tragedy. A promising life cut short. And there is a feeling—it's a human reaction—that somebody must pay. And that feeling can be even stronger when the victim is young and innocent and beautiful. I get it, ladies and gentlemen. I feel it too."

She turns to look directly at Cole. "But you will not find Suzanne's killer here on trial. There is *no* direct evidence linking my client to this young woman's death. No fingerprints, no DNA, no witnesses, no murder weapon.

"Now, we did see a surveillance video of Suzanne Bonanno and Cole Wright together on the night she disappeared. And the prosecution has insinuated that my client was the last person to see her alive. But we don't know who Suzanne saw last. We can't even say with certainty exactly how or when she died. All we know is that after she and Cole Wright parted that evening, there is no known record of her further movements or contacts.

"Ladies and gentlemen, the prosecution spent a lot of time on those mysterious blue sheets. Where they were made, how they were made, who made them, who sold them, who bought them—as if that formed some chain of evidence. It does not.

"Suzanne's bones were wrapped in a sheet when they were found in the trunk of a car. That sheet was sold by Walmart. Beyond that, we know nothing for certain. Mr. Bastinelli wants you to draw a direct line from a checkout counter to a grave, but the connection is not there. We don't know who bought the sheets those bones were wrapped in. Or when."

Hardy continues dismantling the arguments about the bracelet and watch, arguing that their presence in the dirt did not directly link her client to Suzanne's death.

"I'm sure you'll remember, ladies and gentlemen, that the prosecution ended their case with a photograph showing my client with his hands on a person pretending to be a cheerleader. Again, they're trying to get you to draw a line—in this case, from that unfortunate prank to an actual murder. The link is not there. My client acknowledged he was in that photograph. He explained it.

He apologized for it. In my opinion, it should never have been shown, but I was overruled. It has no connection to what happened to Suzanne Bonanno. None whatsoever."

Hardy looks at each of the jurors again.

"Later today," she says, "the judge will give you your instructions. He will remind you of the legal definition of *reasonable doubt*. He will remind you that a defendant must not be convicted on suspicion or speculation. It is not enough for the State to show that the defendant is *probably* guilty. The State has the burden of proving guilt beyond a reasonable doubt. The State has not met that standard. Not even close."

The defense attorney continues, speaking soberly. "At the beginning of this case, I told you that I believed that this was a political trial, and nothing we've heard here in this courtroom has dispelled that belief. You'll recall that the prosecution talked about the advantages of fame and celebrity. I'd like to suggest that there are *dis*advantages. I believe that Cole Wright is sitting in that defendant's chair not because of anything he did, but because of who he is. An easy target. A big prize. A head for somebody's wall. Don't fall for it, ladies and gentlemen."

She walks over to the defense table and points directly at Cole Wright.

"This is a famous man, no doubt. An influential man. A powerfully connected man. But he is also an *innocent* man."

Hardy gives the jury one final nod, then walks behind the defense table and sits down. In full view, she reaches over to squeeze Cole's hand. He looks somber and grateful.

Bastinelli hasn't been left much room to maneuver in his rebuttal.

"Ladies and gentlemen, you've heard from me, you've heard from Ms. Hardy, you've heard from Judge Dow. You've heard from expert witnesses and state troopers and detectives. You've heard from people whose lives intersected with this case. You even heard, very briefly, from the defendant. But the one person you haven't heard from is Suzanne Bonanno."

He clicks the controller and puts up the picture of Suzanne— not the one in her cheerleading uniform; the one where she's sitting at home laughing.

"As you begin your deliberations, please keep Suzanne alive in your minds. You're the only ones who can speak for her now."

CHAPTER 126

The judge gives his instructions to the jury, then adjourns the trial around five p.m.

I walk out of the courthouse and look for a quiet corner to cry in. After all these months, after all Garrett and I went through together, after all I've been through alone, it's finally hitting me.

This part of it is over. Out of my hands.

All I can do is tell the story—the whole story—as best I can.

My eyes are burning, and tears are streaming down my face. God, I wish Garrett were here! I wish I could talk with him just once more. We were supposed to be sharing this together!

I sit on a bench and keep my head down so none of the other spectators will notice me. I probably look like a mess.

A figure stops in front of me and bends down. "Are you okay, honey?"

I look up. It takes me a second to place the face.

It's Detective Sergeant Marie Gagnon, New Hampshire State Police. She reaches into her purse and hands me a packet of Kleenex.

I take it and pull out a few tissues. "Sorry. I didn't know I would be this emotional."

"Don't be embarrassed. It's an emotional case."

I hand her back the packet. "Keep it," she says. "I've got plenty."

Without thinking, I blurt out: "You must see a lot of crying in your line of work."

"I've seen my share," says Gagnon.

"Well, anyway, thanks for stopping. That was thoughtful of you."

"No problem," says Gagnon. "You take care."

I watch her walk down the steps and get into an unmarked car a trooper has pulled up to the curb.

I get a little jolt when I remember it's the second time Gagnon and I have spoken. The other time was on the phone. I'm trusting she doesn't have a long-term echoic memory for voices—especially those of anonymous 911 callers.

I need a drink.

CHAPTER 127

Kingston, New Hampshire

The minute I walk into my hotel room, I open my minifridge and pull out a cold beer. I take a long, deep gulp from the bottle. For some reason, the beer hits me like a shot of tequila. Maybe because I haven't eaten anything since last night. In a few seconds, I'm all warm and buzzy.

My phone vibrates; the screen says Unknown Caller. Those are the only people I seem to hear from these days. I answer anyway.

"Is this Brea? It's Caleb Stringer! Can you hear me okay?"

The Dartmouth alum from Laurie Keaton's list.

"Loud and clear, Caleb. I guess you survived the Alaskan grizzlies."

He laughs. "Still here. Staying safe so far."

"So your wife, Helen, probably told you that I'm working on a book. I assume you're aware of the Cole Wright trial. I'm looking into the years when he and the future president were at Dartmouth."

"Right. Cole, Maddy Parson, and I all lived in the same house senior year. You know Burton Pearce? He lived there too."

"So you knew them all?"

"You bet. Not many secrets when you share a hall bathroom."

"What were they like, the three of them?"

"I'd call it a tension convention," says Stringer. "Or maybe a soap opera. For one thing, Burton wasn't all that thrilled about Cole moving in."

Interesting. I'd been thinking of them as the Three Musketeers. "Why not? Wasn't having a football star in the house a big deal?"

"Not if he cut in on your romance."

"I'm sorry?"

"Burton was head over heels in love with Maddy Parson."

New angle. I get out my notebook and scrawl furiously. "Were Maddy and Burton a couple?"

"Not as far as Maddy was concerned. And definitely not once Cole came into the picture."

I'm writing so fast my fingers are cramping. "Caleb, I need to ask you about an assault that happened at a homecoming party. One that Cole Wright was at."

Silence.

"Caleb? You still there?"

"I'm here." His tone has changed from chatty to reserved. "What about the party?"

"I heard that somebody on the underground paper was about to write a story about a freshman girl getting assaulted during the party. And there were rumors that the reporter was threatened. And then the story got killed. But it's been hard to get confirmation from anyone who was there."

Another pause. Then: "I was."

Suddenly, it's looking like Caleb Stringer was worth waiting for. I turn the page in my notebook and write *Party* at the top.

"Brea," Stringer says, "I'm not gonna say anything more about this. You need to understand. My project gets government funding."

My lawyer's antennae shoot up. I can't let this lead slip away. "What happened?"

His voice is hesitant. "I only know what people said about Cole. And that's just hearsay."

"Caleb. This is important! What did you hear?"

Another stretch of silence. This time, I think the call might have actually dropped. But then he comes back.

"Look, I haven't talked to anybody about this in twenty years. I didn't think it was my place to speak up, but the person you want to talk to is Eva Clarke. She should be in the alumni directory. Please don't use my name."

"Who's Eva? Was she at the party that night? Will she remember it?"

Another pause.

"She'll remember it," says Stringer. "She's the girl who was raped."

CHAPTER 128

I hang up with Caleb Stringer and immediately check the alumni directory. I find an Eva Clarke and then search for her on LinkedIn. I'm surprised to see she's a Black woman and even more surprised to learn that she lives nearby. Clarke runs a dance studio in Manchester, New Hampshire, only about a thirty-minute drive west on Route 101.

My GPS leads me to a small two-story retail strip just outside of town. The first level is occupied by a Taco Bell, a bike shop, and a dry cleaner. A metal staircase leads to the second level. That's where I see the sign.

DANCE SISTERS

It's just past seven p.m., and through the glass I can see students packing up and exiting the studio.

I ring the bell in the now empty reception area. Through an arch, I can see a hardwood dance floor, a mirrored wall, and a ballet barre. A giant speaker sits in one corner.

"Be right there!" a woman calls. When Eva Clarke comes around the corner, I recognize her immediately from her profile pics. Tall. Elegant. Black. She's wearing a leotard with a ballet skirt and a sweatshirt tied around her waist. Her hair is braided and piled on top of her head.

"Eva?"

"If you're here to pick somebody up, they all just left."

"Actually, Eva, I'm looking for you." I step up to the counter. "My name is Brea Cooke. I'm writing a book about Cole Wright."

Her smile fades. "Isn't he on trial up in Brentwood for killing that local woman?"

"He is. The case just went to the jury."

"Then I don't understand. What kind of book are you writing?"

I reach into my backpack and pull out copies of the books I helped Garrett research, *Stolen Honor* and *Integrity Gone*. "This kind. The kind that gets at the truth. Sometimes after everybody else has given up. Sometimes decades later."

She looks at the books I've placed on the counter and taps them nervously. "Who's Garrett Wilson?"

"He was my partner. We met at Dartmouth. He died looking into the truth about Cole Wright."

I can tell Clarke is trying to figure me out, deciding if she can trust me. "What happened to him?" she asks. "How did he die?"

I shake my head. "Not now. I'm here to talk about what happened to you."

Clarke comes around from behind the counter. "I'm not sure why you're here," she says.

"Eva, please. You don't have to carry this by yourself."

She apparently makes a decision. "Come with me," she says.

I follow Clarke into a small office that looks out onto the dance space. There's a vanilla-scented candle burning on the small desk.

The wall is lined with posters from Black dance companies. Dance Theatre of Harlem. Alvin Ailey. Chicago's Deeply Rooted.

"How long have you been teaching?" I ask.

"Ten years. Ever since my ankles gave out." Eva sits down behind the desk. "But you're not here to talk about my dance career."

"No, Eva, I'm not. I'm just trying to find out what happened that night after homecoming."

"Who told you?" Her brown eyes are blazing.

"Somebody who was there that night. Somebody who heard that you were assaulted."

"Only the other person in that room knows what happened to me. I did tell my friend Floyd Whelan, but when he tried to write a news story about it, he was threatened into silence."

"You never told anybody? Never went to the campus police?"

"Do you know anything about Hanover twenty years ago? What it was like to be a skinny Black girl from Barbados? Nobody was going to listen to me."

"I know about Hanover. I was there not long after you were. I know what it's like to get the wrong kind of attention. Or no attention at all." Bob Woodward's comment about interviews suddenly comes to mind: "Let the silence suck out the truth."

Slowly, it comes...

"I went to the homecoming bonfire with some other first-year students from my dorm and had some vodka shots. Then somebody brought us all to a party off campus. I barely knew anyone there and I lost track of the people I came with."

"They left you there alone?"

Clarke shrugs. "People kept handing me drinks. I remember the music was really loud and I started feeling woozy. I was sitting on a sofa with my head between my knees. Then I felt a hand on my back. I heard a guy asking me if I was okay. I said I needed to lie down, which I know was a totally stupid thing to say."

"Not if you're about to get sick."

"I look up and see a guy in a Big Green football jersey. It wasn't until days later that I figured out it was Cole Wright. He picked me up like he was carrying a baby. I felt like I was floating. I didn't even know where we were going until he put me down on a bed. I was kind of in and out. Room spinning, that old cliché."

My pulse is racing. "What did he do next?"

"He put a blanket over me and left."

"He didn't..."

"He didn't touch me. It was somebody else."

"You're sure it wasn't Cole?"

"Yes. Cole was so big he filled a door frame. This guy was smaller. I thought maybe it was his room, so I started to get up and apologize for being in there. Then he came over and started kissing me. I told him I was feeling sick. And he said something like 'I'll make you feel better.' Then he pulled the blanket down and got on top of me. I struggled, but I was about ninety pounds, all arms and legs. He pinned me down and he covered my mouth with one hand and he pulled up my dress with the other...and he raped me."

"Eva, I'm so sorry that happened to you. Did you ever see the guy's face? Do you know who it was?"

It takes her a few seconds to answer.

"I didn't then. I do now." She looks right at me. "He works in the White House. His name is Burton Pearce."

CHAPTER 129

Kingston, New Hampshire

The whole drive back to the hotel, I'm seething. *Goddamn Burton Pearce!*

I'm thinking back to him calling me with his condolences after Garrett died. Giving me his private number. Playing Mr. Nice Guy. Bastard!

I wonder how Eva Clarke will sleep tonight. Is she relieved that somebody else finally knows her secret? Or is she worried about the whole world finding out?

In the hotel parking lot, I turn off the engine and open the Subaru's door, then reach over to grab my backpack.

As soon as I start to get out, somebody rips it off my shoulder.

I see two figures closing in. I raise my arms and start swinging wildly.

Somebody grabs my wrists and pins them against the roof of the car. "Brea! Stop it!"

My watchers!

The woman has my backpack. Her arm is inside it, digging deep. "Just making sure you don't have a gun in here."

The man has my wrists. "I'm letting you go now," he says. "Do not run."

"Or scream," adds the woman. She returns my backpack to me.

My gaze darts from one to the other. "What do you want? Who are you?"

The man pulls out a leather wallet and holds up his ID. "Daniel Fane, FBI." I look over at the woman. She's holding out a wallet of her own. "Kathy Schott, same."

"What do you want? I'm an attorney. I know my rights!"

"Relax, Brea," says Fane. "We're not here on official business."

Schott puts away her ID. "According to our office, we're not here at all."

"I don't understand." My pulse is settling a bit. "What is this about? You two have been tailing me since before this trial started. I know it. I've seen you. Why?"

"Dr. Graham sent us," says Fane. "He asked us to keep an eye on you."

This is getting weirder by the minute. "Dr. Graham is dead."

"We know," says Schott. "I'm the one who sent you the link to the story in the *New York Times*. But that doesn't change anything. Dr. Graham gave us this assignment and we're seeing it through."

I'm still not sure what's going on. "I thought Dr. Graham was retired from the FBI."

"Let's just say he had deep roots at the Bureau," says Fane, "and some chits to call in."

"Well, now you have a debt to me," I say with a bravado I don't actually feel. "Does this mean you're my bodyguards now?"

"More like guardian angels," says Schott. "Just hovering on the periphery."

"I don't get it. Don't you have real assignments?"

"We do," says Fane. "We're moonlighting."

"I have so many questions. For starters, did Dr. Graham have an online alias?"

Schott smiles. "You mean Doc Cams?"

I was right! It was him. "He was posting some pretty harsh stuff against Cole Wright."

"Dr. Graham was a mole," says Schott. "A digital mole."

"What does that mean?"

"Dr. Graham dug his way into radical groups to see what they were up to. That was his specialty in the Bureau. He could take on any identity or tone of voice he needed to earn somebody's trust. He broke into a lot of crime rings that way over the years. Drugs. Smuggling. Extortion."

"So he wasn't anti-Wright?"

"No. He was pro-truth. He was getting ready to expose the whole network."

"Do you think he was killed?"

Fane gives a wry smile. "Yes. But by his coronary arteries." He pulls a small flip phone out of his pocket. "Take this. The only number it can dial is ours."

"Same number for both of us," says Schott.

I'm suddenly exhausted to the point of collapse. I take the phone and toss it into my backpack. "I need to go to my room now."

"No problem," says Schott. "It's clear."

"Wait. You searched my hotel room?"

"Quick sweep," says Fane.

"Jesus! How many times have you been in there?"

Schott glances at Fane. He nods. "Twice a day," she says, "starting the day you arrived."

So much for my DO NOT DISTURB sign.

I walk to my room. My eyes are burning. My head is throbbing. I feel like crashing. But my cell phone is ringing.

"Hello?"

"Brea? It's Ron Reynolds!" He's practically shouting into the phone over loud music and a noisy crowd.

"Hi, Ron. What's up? Where the hell are you?"

"I'm in a bar in Brentwood. A woman here knows one of the bailiffs. Be at the courthouse first thing tomorrow. They've reached a verdict!"

CHAPTER 130

Rockingham County Courthouse, New Hampshire

Early the next morning, the demonstrators are already in place, sipping from thermoses and hauling their signs. The TV crews are working out of their vans, setting up lights and platforms for their stand-ups. There are more cops and troopers and Secret Service agents surrounding the building than I've ever seen.

I hear the squawk of a siren behind me. I turn and see Cole Wright's caravan coming up the road. There's a state police car in the lead, lights flashing, followed by two black SUVs with tinted windows. Two motorcycle cops bring up the rear. They all turn right at the parking lot and I watch them until they're out of sight behind the courthouse.

The line for the gallery starts early, and there are more cops than usual at the metal detector. One is holding a huge German shepherd on a thick leash. The dog gives everybody a sniff as we file past. The bag search is extra-thorough today.

When I get inside and take my seat, I see Ron Reynolds in the back row. He's in the middle of a scrum of reporters, all whispering and gesturing. Totally wired. Ready to witness history.

Cole Wright and his lawyers are already at the defense table. Cole is in his blue suit again. He's gotten a haircut. Tess Hardy looks confident, but the way she taps her pen on her legal pad betrays a hint of uncertainty. A fast verdict isn't always a good sign.

At exactly nine o'clock, the clerk stands up and calls, "All rise!"

Judge Dow walks out from chambers and motions for everybody to sit down. He turns to the bailiff. "Bring in the jury."

A side door opens and the jurors file in and take their usual seats. Like everybody else in the room, I'm studying their faces, trying to read them. Do they look worried? Excited? Determined? But I'm getting nothing.

Dow scans the gallery. "I'm going to remind everybody again that I will not tolerate any outbursts in the courtroom." He turns to the jury box and looks at a stout woman in glasses seated in the front row. "Madam Foreperson, I understand that the jury has a verdict."

The woman stands. She's clutching a folded sheet of paper. "We do, Your Honor."

"Please hand the verdict form to the bailiff."

The bailiff takes the folded sheet and hands it to Dow. The judge unfolds the paper and looks at it for a few seconds. No reaction. He looks over at Cole Wright. "The defendant will please rise."

The First Gentleman stands up. Tess Hardy stands up beside him, her shoulder practically touching his. Solidarity.

Dow hands the paper to the clerk. "The clerk will now read the verdict."

The clerk turns to face the gallery. His eyes do not wander from the paper.

"In the matter before this court, on the charge of murder in the second degree, we the jury find the defendant, Cole Wright… guilty."

There are no shouts, but there's a visceral reaction. We all just about jump out of our seats. I spin around and catch Ron's eye. He nods. I know he's thinking of Garrett. I am too.

The judge asks Tess Hardy if she wants the jury polled.

She does.

The word *guilty* hums through my brain twelve more times but all that registers is that this is the moment I've been waiting for, *hoping* for, for the past nine months.

Cole Wright has been found guilty.

Except I no longer think he is.

CHAPTER 131

Kingston, New Hampshire

I return to my hotel room in a daze. My phone vibrates with a text: Check email.

I power up my laptop and go to my inbox and there it is, a huge file ready for download. Daryna! I click on the file folder from Ukraine.

Daryna doesn't mess around. My screen erupts; windows open so rapidly that they overlap one another. Dozens of them.

The first thing I notice are posts from Doc Cams; some I've seen, some I haven't. Dr. Graham was worming his way into the operation, pretending to be one of them until he could blow the whole thing up.

Next I see a pageful of posts from the anti-Wright blog, posts that Daryna has identified as being written by Rachel Bernstein. Some of them are from the past few days. She's still stoking the fires against the Wrights from Berlin. I wonder if she's the one who arranged the anti-Cole demonstrators at the courthouse.

It looks like Daryna also found restricted police and FBI files. Could these be the case files documenting the investigation into Suzanne's disappearance?

The files the lawyers said were missing?

The files that somebody in the federal government requisitioned—because they might have implicated somebody other than Cole Wright?

I enlarge another window and see two prison-intake photos from the correctional center in Cranston, Rhode Island, both head-and-shoulder shots of men in orange jumpsuits. One is John DeMarco, and I recognize the name right away. He's the inmate Garrett talked to who tipped us off to the grave location. The other guy is Anthony Romero.

Jesus! Is this the Tony Romero who was Suzanne's old boyfriend? The one who Teresa says was the father of Suzanne's baby? The one who beat up Garrett and had him chased?

Daryna's files prove that DeMarco and Romero did time together in Cranston, and now I have a pretty good idea where DeMarco got his information about the location of Suzanne's grave. He got it from Tony Romero.

The hacker has included a lot of detailed documents, including records of arrests and prosecutions for both men, everything from pimping to drug peddling to fencing stolen merchandise. I check the conviction and sentence records. Romero never served more than a few years at a time, and he's been out for almost five years, free as a bird. It looks like DeMarco still has ten years to go on his current stretch. No wonder he was so eager to share info—it could shorten his sentence.

The next window is a series of photographs so grainy, I almost blow past them. They look like surveillance photos taken inside a bar. What stops me is the sight of Tony Romero. He's pouring drinks for patrons who register only as dark shapes. One guy is slightly clearer. He's at the side of the bar holding a beer bottle to his lips, and his head is tipped back so that his face catches the light. Barely visible. Like some kind of gray ghost.

Burton Pearce!

I recognize the face, but it takes me a moment to believe what I'm seeing. The president's chief of staff—and the man Eva Clarke says raped her—is also a known associate of Tony Romero.

Suddenly, all the pieces click into place.

CHAPTER 132

Number One Observatory Circle

Burton Pearce is sitting in Ransom Faulkner's elegant living room in the vice presidential residence when the verdict is announced on TV. His first thoughts are for Maddy, but they're immediately followed by thoughts for himself. He does his best to contain them all. He clicks the TV off and walks over to where the VP is standing.

A tailor is kneeling at Faulkner's feet, pinning the cuffs on the pants of an expensive suit. Pearce is not worried about Louie's discretion. He's been with the VP for years.

"Well, I guess we can save the money on the suit," says Faulkner. He's still gaunt, but his face has regained some of its color, and he's standing up straight.

"Don't be ridiculous," says Pearce. "Tess Hardy will appeal. The plan will go forward. We'll just delay the Grand Bargain announcement for a time. Let the news cycle on this thing blow over."

"Blow over?" says Faulkner. "The First Gentleman in jail for murder?"

Pearce puts a hand on the tailor's back. "Louie, you know what? You can head out. We'll send the suit over later."

As Pearce pulls the double doors closed behind the departing tailor, a knock sounds on an interior door. A young aide pokes his head in. He looks at Pearce. "Sorry to disturb, sir. The president is calling for you on line one."

"Thanks, Sean." The aide backs out and closes the door. Pearce steps to a side table and grabs the handset from a phone console. He takes a breath, then presses the blinking button.

"Madam President, I'm sorry about the verdict. But it's not the end. Not by a long shot."

"How's Ransom?" The president's voice sounds cold and flat.

"He's fine, Madam President. Disappointed about Cole, of course. He's right here if you want to speak with him."

"Is it just the two of you there?"

"Yes, ma'am."

"Put me on speaker."

Pearce presses another button and puts down the handset. "Okay, ma'am. You're on with me and the vice president."

"Hello, Maddy," Faulkner calls out from his chair. "How's Cole holding up?"

"I haven't talked to him yet. He's on his way to processing, if you can believe that."

"It doesn't seem real," says Pearce.

"Let me know if I can do anything," says Faulkner.

"You're going to be doing a lot," says the president. "I'm resigning."

CHAPTER 133

Rockingham County Jail, New Hampshire

Cole Wright doesn't remember much after the first *Guilty* was spoken. Tess Hardy put one hand on his shoulder and whispered something in his ear, but her words were no comfort.

The next sensation he had was the feeling of cold cuffs being clamped around his wrists. Then strong hands gripped his upper arms and propelled him to the exit corridor, where true tunnel vision limited his perception to only what was directly in front of him.

The ride to the county jail was a blur of traffic and signs and the *thump-thump* of news choppers overhead. And then the car slowed down and rolled through a garage entrance.

He thought about his wife. How did Maddy learn the news? Was she watching the verdict come in on TV like the rest of the world? Or did she wait for Burton Pearce to tell her?

And now, reality is setting in.

Not setting in, really. More like slapping him in the face.

Cole is standing in an antiseptic-smelling corridor surrounded by police and Secret Service agents.

It looks like his people have done all they can to smooth the intake. The forms have been filled out and filed. He's spared the indignity of having to give his address and the name of his spouse: *1600 Pennsylvania Avenue. President Madeline Wright.* They gave him the courtesy of conducting the cavity search behind a hospital curtain.

But in every other way, he's just another prisoner.

He sits on a metal chair while a technician unlocks the ankle monitor. The device is redundant now. Everybody knows where he is, and he's not going anywhere.

He's photographed.

He's fingerprinted.

He's led into a tiny room, where he takes off his bespoke suit and puts on an orange outfit stenciled with ROCKINGHAM COUNTY DEPARTMENT OF CORRECTIONS.

No more power. No more influence. Now he's just a number. And he doesn't even know what that number is.

Two guards lead him from the changing area through a series of doors and into the main prison corridor. The sounds of men shouting and metal banging remind Cole of a locker room. It's as if his mind is searching for ways to make sense of this, to relate it to a world he knows.

The guards stop and turn him. He's facing an empty cell. A buzzer sounds. The door slides open. The guards pull him to the threshold, then nudge him in. "Home, sweet home," one of them says.

Cole takes the final step himself. The door slides shut behind him.

The cell has two metal bunks, bolted to opposite walls. Each bunk has a thin mattress, a sheet, a small foam pillow, and two blankets. In one corner of the green concrete space rests a combination stainless-steel sink and toilet; on the wall is a mirrored sheet of metal.

Cole avoids the mirror. He doesn't want to see himself like this. If he doesn't look at his reflection, it's easier to pretend this is some kind of nightmare.

A guard outside the cell passes a paper bag through the bars. "Hygiene pack," he says.

Cole looks inside the bag: a cheap toothbrush, a small tube of toothpaste, a thin bar of soap, and a roll of single-ply toilet paper.

He puts it down, places his hands on the bars, and looks out as two guards lead another inmate up the corridor. Shaved head. Sharp eyes. The build of an offensive lineman.

The procession stops in front of Cole's cell. One of the guards raps his nightstick above Cole's knuckles. "Step back," he orders.

Cole retreats to the middle of the cell. The door opens and the man enters.

The door slams closed again.

Cole looks across the corridor to a row of empty cells. *Why the hell did they put this guy in here when there's all that room over there?* "Hey! Hey!" he shouts at the guards.

But the guards are already passing through the double doors into the outer corridor. They don't even look back.

His new cellmate says, "I don't think that's gonna help." He holds out his hand and says, his voice in a near whisper, "Jeremy Knox, Secret Service."

"Oh, Jesus," says Cole. He hangs his head and leans against the bars. "This is the detail they handed you? To babysit me in prison? What happens if I get life?"

"They trained a bunch of us down in Virginia just in case the verdict went this way. We got processed like normal prisoners. Nobody else in the system knows who we are. They plan to switch us out every few months wherever you go, like tag-teaming."

That this plan was already in place seems to Cole more depressing than reassuring.

He turns to Knox and asks, "Do you have a gun?"

"No, sir. But I can handle things." Knox flops down on one of the bunks. "I'll take this side. Better angle. And by the way, that's the last time I'll call you 'sir.' "

CHAPTER 134

The White House

Read it out loud," says Maddy. "I need to hear it."

Burton Pearce is standing in front of the Resolute desk in the Oval Office. He can hardly believe what he's holding. It's a handwritten draft of a resignation speech in Maddy's neat script. For once, he didn't contribute a single phrase.

"Nixon's resignation speech went on for fifteen minutes," says Maddy. "I want mine to be shorter than the Gettysburg Address."

Pearce looks across the desk. He's known the woman sitting behind it for more than twenty years, since their days as Dartmouth students. It seems impossible that this moment has come. "You really want me to do this?"

The president nods. "I do."

Pearce clears his throat and reads aloud from the paper.

"'My fellow Americans, I have made the most difficult decision of my life, which is to resign the office of president, effective at noon tomorrow. Vice President Faulkner will take the oath at that time.

"'You all know the burden that my personal life has been for the past nine months. I love Cole Wright and believe he's innocent of the charges. With the verdict two days ago, I have realized that I need to focus all my strength on seeking justice and vindication for my husband. I cannot do that and give the daily duties of the presidency the concentrated attention you deserve.

"'I want you to know that our administration has been driven by a new vision for America, one that puts us on the path of financial stability and makes the investments necessary to secure the future for generations of Americans to come. The responsibility for seeing that vision through now goes to Vice President Ransom Faulkner, a man who has turned from being my fiercest rival to being a steadfast supporter, loyal partner, and devoted friend. You will be safe in his hands. I leave this office with gratitude, humility, and a sense of peace. I know in my heart that I am doing the right thing for my husband and for the country. I wish you all well. Good night.'"

Pearce lowers the paper and slides it onto the desk.

"What do you think?" asks Maddy.

"Madam President, I've never said this before, but—I wouldn't change a word."

CHAPTER 135

Washington, DC

I have to see Burton Pearce in person. I spend the drive south formulating a plan to intercept him, but in the end, all it takes is a phone call.

When I arrive in DC, I pull out my phone, scroll to Burton Pearce's number, and dial.

It rings. Once...twice...

"Ms. Cooke, I'm guessing this is not a sympathy call regarding the verdict against the First Gentleman. Whatever the reason, is it important?"

I wait a beat. "Was Eva Clarke important?"

A long pause. Then he says, his voice low and intense: "What are you after, Ms. Cooke?"

"I'm after the truth. Just like Garrett Wilson was."

"You have no idea what you're doing."

"Prove it. Meet me. I'm in DC and I'd be happy to come to your house. I have the address right here. Or I'll come to the White House—"

"Don't be stupid. Meet me at Montrose Park near Georgetown in thirty minutes."

"Where in Montrose Park? You need to be more specific."

"The Rittenhouse memorial. There's a bench nearby."

He sounds worried. Good.

He should be.

CHAPTER 136

Montrose Park, Washington, DC

I leave my laptop in my car for safekeeping and catch an Uber to the edge of the park on R Street. I start looking for the landmark that I googled on the way, the Sarah Rittenhouse Armillary Sphere—interlocking bronze circles of the celestial spheres on a marble base.

It's a cool night, but I'm hot; my adrenaline is burning. A guy jogs past with his dog, but other than that, the place is pretty much deserted. In the glow of the streetlights, I see neat gardens and lawns and paved trails surrounded by dark woods. I walk past the monument and down the stone path.

Maybe twenty yards in, I see a man on a bench. Lanky, balding, wearing a suit.

It's him. The Gray Ghost.

Burton Pearce stands up as I get closer.

"You're alone?"

"Just you and me, Mr. Pearce."

"What's in your backpack?"

I toss it to him. "Have a look."

He catches it, barely. He seems distracted as he paws through the innocuous-looking contents, then he sets the pack on the bench. "Where's your phone?"

I pull it out of my back pocket and waggle it. "Want me to turn it off?"

"I do."

I power it down right in front of him and return it to my back pocket. I step up close and look him in the eye. "Go ahead, search me. See if I'm wearing a wire."

He blinks and turns away a second. Then he sits down.

"Tell me about Eva Clarke," I say.

"There's nothing to tell," he says. "It was twenty years ago and consensual."

"That's not what Eva says, either now or then. I think you saw Cole Wright carry her upstairs and spotted an opportunity. That seems to be your pattern.

"Tell me, Mr. Pearce, when did you steal Cole's watch? I'll bet Cole stopped wearing it when he started dating Maddy. Did you pluck it from his room when they went out? Did you keep it for years, just waiting for the right opportunity to frame him? Did you bury it yourself in Suzanne's grave or did you give it to someone else?"

Pearce swallows hard. "What are you talking about?"

"I'm talking about your time in grad school at Brown University in Providence. About your roommate Gino Ebano. And his cousin Tony."

"Tony Romero? That little thug? That's what this is about? Yes, I've had a few drinks at his bar once or twice—so what?"

"Right. Twice. Just before he went away to the Cranston pen for the second time for grand larceny. And just after he murdered Suzanne Bonanno."

Pearce is quiet for a few seconds. Then: "Suzanne's killer is behind bars, convicted by a jury of his peers."

"But the jury didn't know what you and I know. I have the case files you hid. I have them all. You played a very long game."

Pearce shakes his head. "You should be writing novels, Ms. Cooke."

"It was hard enough for you to handle it when Cole and Maddy dated in college. But you snapped when they got back together after Cole was released from the Patriots. You knew Romero had killed his ex-girlfriend Suzanne. You knew he had a vendetta against Cole. You saw a way for you both to get back at him: Planting the watch. Arranging for the hole on Cole's property. Finding somebody to dig up Suzanne's bones."

Silence.

"And anybody who got in the way of your plan got removed. Amber. Garrett. You're lucky Leo Amalfi died in his bed."

Pearce stands up. "Enough. If this is all you've got, I'm going home now."

"Don't you want to give me a quote, Mr. Pearce? An ending for my book?"

He looks at me. "I'll give you an ending, you bitch. Here it is: President Wright resigns. I become President Faulkner's chief of staff. I preside over the biggest policy triumph in American history. Cole Wright gets shanked to death in prison. And you never write another goddamn word."

Fifty yards away, the man still calling himself Jack Doohan eases his finger onto the trigger. The subject's halo of black curls fills the circle of the night-vision sight. He sets the crosshairs on her temple.

Simple shot. Just waiting for Pearce to get clear of the spatter zone...

His thumb moves toward the safety.

Suddenly, the rifle gets ripped away. There's a knee in his back, and his left arm is being twisted. Two people appear in his peripheral vision. A male and a female.

The woman leans down into his face.

"Kathy Schott, FBI. Don't move."

CHAPTER 137

Providence, Rhode Island

Against the protests of the patrons, at eleven p.m., the TV in Raymond's Tavern is turned to CNN. On the screen, a blond reporter is standing in a parking lot. Behind her, bright lights illuminate a high brick wall topped with razor wire. The reporter adjusts her earpiece and speaks into a mic.

"From the White House to the Big House—that's been Cole Wright's trajectory over the past nine months. The man convicted of second-degree murder is currently being held here in Rockingham County Jail. But it's as yet unknown where he'll serve out his sentence. One thing's for sure—he won't be spending any time in a country-club prison. Back to you, Kelly."

The camera cuts back to a woman at the anchor desk. Tony Romero picks up the remote from the backbar and switches to a football game. Cheers of approval from the patrons.

Tony holds up his hands. "Hey, you morons gotta follow the news once in a while! Learn something about the world!"

In truth, Tony couldn't be happier.

The reporter who was trailing him is dead. Ditto Amber Keenan. Amalfi and his goons are gone too. And now he has the ultimate karmic revenge.

Suzanne had told Tony she was pregnant with his baby. But she didn't want his kind of life. She wanted to raise the baby with her new boyfriend, Cole Wright, the fancy Pats player. Tony couldn't take the disrespect. He flipped out. Strangled Suzanne to death. Wrapped her up in the sheets he found in her car. Buried her in the park and had the car chopped up for parts. Later, he added the watch Pearce gave him to the grave site. Serves Cole right for trying to steal his girl—and his baby. Tony didn't do the grunt work himself. He had other people do it for him. Then he got rid of those people.

Romero turns to a heavyset man standing at the end of the bar. "Close up for me, Dino." He points a finger at him. "And keep your hands out of the cash register."

Dino gives him a crooked smile and a nod.

Tony's tired. He doesn't feel like making small talk with the patrons in the front room tonight. He walks into the corridor and heads to the back exit. Easy way out.

He pushes the metal door open. A blinding light hits his face.

"What the f—"

"Put your hands up and kneel down!"

Tony kneels and squints through the glare. He sees figures coming toward him, weapons drawn. Cops! One of them lifts him up and pins his arms behind his back. Another starts patting his beltline.

"Gun!"

The cop pulls out the compact Ruger and holds it up by the trigger guard. Tony feels more hands on his chest, his legs, his crotch. "Clean!" another cop shouts.

Tony is dragged up the short flight of concrete steps. He can see better now.

A woman steps out from behind an open car door and walks over to where the cops are holding him. She flashes a badge.

"Detective Sergeant Gagnon, New Hampshire State Police."

Tony twists and scowls. "I got news for you, honey. You're in the wrong goddamn state."

The detective holds up a piece of paper. "Then it's a good thing I brought an out-of-state warrant. Tony Romero, you're wanted for questioning in the murder of Suzanne Bonanno."

"Bullshit! They already got the guy for that."

The detective smiles at him. "Yeah. We think he might be the wrong guy."

CHAPTER 138

Rockingham County Jail, New Hampshire

Cole Wright barely fits on the metal cell cot. Since lights-out, he's been turning from side to side, pulling the tissue-thin blanket over his shoulders, trying to get comfortable.

It's not possible. His hip bones and shoulders press down hard on the thin mattress; he can feel the steel underneath. In the opposite cot, his cellmate is awake, keeping watch. It's difficult for Cole to grasp that these four walls now contain his life.

He gave Garrett Wilson all the information he had and told him to follow the trail wherever it led. But Garrett's dead. And whoever really killed Suzanne is still free.

Cole flops onto his back and stares at the ceiling. He finds patterns in the rust stains and watermarks until exhaustion slowly takes over, his eyes close, and everything fades to black.

He wakes to the sound of banging on the cell bars and the metallic grind of the door opening. Rough hands shake his shoulders, then pull him upright. A flashlight shines in his face.

He sees Knox jump off his cot across the cell. A huge guard with a nightstick holds him back. The guard tells Knox, "We're here for him, not you."

"Put on your shoes," somebody orders Cole. He sticks his feet into his prison sandals and is shuffled out of the cell and down the dark corridor.

Is he being transferred already? Taken for more questioning? "What's happening?" he asks. "Where are we going?"

"Not far," says one of the guards.

And then they're through the double doors and in the outer corridor, the same place he was strip-searched and processed just sixteen hours before.

An administrator in a rumpled suit holds out the handset of a corded phone. "For you," he says.

Cole takes the phone. "Hello?"

"Hey, sweetheart. Ready to bust out of the joint?"

"Maddy? I...they just grabbed me from my cell. What's going on?"

"I'll explain when you get here."

"Here? Where?"

"Put the administrator back on."

Cole hands the phone back to the man in the suit, who listens and nods vigorously. "Yes, Madam President. Understood, Madam President. Goodbye, Madam President." He hangs up.

He pulls a piece of paper from a folder and turns it toward Cole. He points to a signature line and holds out a pen. "Sign here, please."

Cole takes the pen. "What is this? What am I signing?"

"Pending official processing," says the administrator, "you're being released into the custody of the president of the United States."

One of the guards takes Cole by the arm. "This way." The other guards fall in behind them. They pass through a series of doors and corridors and arrive at a loading area with enough clearance for a semitruck.

When Cole is about ten feet from the loading bay's door, an earsplitting Klaxon sounds. In one smooth motion, the door, via a mechanism that resembles a bank vault's, appears to split in two, one part rising up and the other sinking into the floor.

Through the opening, Cole sees a floodlit road and a line of state trooper vehicles, lights flashing. A heavy black SUV roars up to the entrance and brakes to a stop.

Cole feels the grip on his arm release. He's through the doorway and standing free.

The rear door of the SUV opens. Agent Doug Lambert steps out.

"Good morning, sir. Air Force One is waiting in Portsmouth. We're here to take you home."

CHAPTER 139

The White House

Three days later, once Maddy and Cole have shared sighs of relief, tears of joy, and their determination to make the state of their union unbreakable, the president delivers a speech to Congress.

"Mr. Vice President, Mr. Speaker, Members of Congress, my fellow Americans: I want to speak to you today about trust."

Maddy faces the full Congress, the members of her cabinet, the Supreme Court justices, and the guests in the gallery, all arrayed before her. And through the TV cameras placed strategically around the chamber, she faces the entire country as well. All are waiting and wondering what she will say.

She knows she has to nail this one.

In preparing what she would say and how she would say it, she researched FDR presenting the New Deal and Social Security to the country in the wake of the Great Depression, and LBJ presenting Medicare while the country still mourned the assassination of President Kennedy.

She knew she'd have everyone's attention and only one chance to get it right.

"For most of the last year, my husband and I leaned hard on trust. Some days it seemed trust was all we had. And as you can imagine, it was sorely tested.

"We trusted the justice system, that it would eventually discover the truth and find the First Gentleman innocent of all the charges against him. We trusted the men and women who pursue and dispense justice every day of their working lives.

"In the end, our faith was justified, and we are both profoundly grateful for that.

"During that ordeal, I loved and trusted my husband, a man I've known since I was a college student and with whom I've built a life—lately one in which my responsibilities are immense and the time we can spend together limited and so all the more precious.

"My faith in him was justified. He's the same good man I've always known. Like all of us, not perfect but working every day to do better—not only for me but for our country."

So far, Maddy has avoided looking at Cole so she can be sure to keep her voice strong and firm. But she steals a quick glance. Tears are streaming down his face.

"Throughout this administration I have trusted and deeply respected our vice president and am grateful for the care given to him by his incredible team at Walter Reed. My faith in his strength, wisdom, and tenacity was justified, and there's nobody I'd rather have behind me"—she turns around and grins at the man sitting behind her—"including right this moment, come to think of it, than Ransom Faulkner. Welcome back, Mr. Vice President."

The entire floor explodes in applause, and Faulkner, clearly moved, rises to his feet, bows slightly, and sits back down with the air of a judge who wants to calm the court. But the ovation lasts minutes, and Maddy lets it go on as long as she can before putting on a graver air.

"And I also trusted my chief of staff, a man I've known—or thought I knew—for decades. To say that I was shocked and horrified by his crimes is a profound understatement. To the family of Suzanne Bonanno, words cannot convey my sympathies for your loss, for the years of uncertainty about Suzanne's fate, and for the pain caused by these past months of public spectacle, orchestrated so deviously by Burton Pearce. Let me assure you that the entire country shares your grief and outrage and hopes that with the truth known, as painful as it is, her memory can be a blessing.

"Yes, I trusted my chief of staff, but he deceived me and in doing so put the country in danger. He arranged or approved the deaths of innocent people who might have imperiled his plot and nearly sent my husband to jail for a long time. His cleverly concealed actions also misled the prosecutors and jury in Cole's case, who did what they thought was right based on what they knew. The sole blame is on Burton Pearce and those whose criminal conduct enabled him, especially the mobster who killed Suzanne Bonanno and continued to kill to cover it up and shift the blame.

"We'll never know when the dam of decency broke in Burton Pearce. I just thank God he didn't succeed.

"As stressful as the past few months have been, the American people have trusted me with a job that doesn't allow me to take time off. So I've been working every day. But, like Cole and all of you, I'm only human, so that work has been done with a hurting heart and a divided mind, still trusting and believing in justice and in people, still working hard to do the job you gave me, and still trying always to remember why I asked for it.

"I had a lot of help. During the worst days of his ordeal, Cole took me aside and reminded me of an agreement we'd made when

I decided to run for president. He told me, 'You promised me that if you were elected to the most important job in the world, you wouldn't major in the minors but have the strength and determination to do big things.'"

She glances back at Cole. He is beaming at her now and, like the jock he was and always will be, pumps his fist in front of his chest. Her heart beats a bit faster.

"The American people put me here and trusted me—as they did all of you—not to play petty politics with every issue but to do big things.

"This is a trust I hold sacred, as I believe you all do as well. To fulfill it, we must overcome our differences and solve the problems that sometimes seem unsurmountable. We must come together, trust each other to do the right thing, and do just that."

Maddy knows the next few words could put it over the top. She looks out at the assembled men and women and pauses. In the silence, with what seems like the whole world waiting on her, a confidence blossoms in her chest. They can do this, they really can.

"So, as I said, trust is why I'm here today. Mine has been, with one terrible exception, justified. But now I'm going to ask for yours. To trust me and my administration with your support for a Grand Bargain, one that will, at long last, let us face up to a catastrophe we've allowed to creep up to our very doorstep and vanquish it."

She takes another long pause and then, clearly and confidently, makes her case.

"Here's what I propose. It's not my own idea but a series of proposals crafted by the best minds in the country."

Over the next forty minutes, President Madeline Wright tells the entire country the truth about what is facing them and how they can turn it around, how they can save Social Security, Medicare, Medicaid, and the economy with new revenues, new savings, and, if they don't work, changes in the entitlement programs to extend the lives of their trust funds to thirty years out and keep them there while gradually lowering the national debt as a percentage of annual income.

Many see these same details spool out on their laptops and phones. Jessica Martin's *Washington Post* exclusive has been released to coincide with her speech, as has an entire administration website devoted to describing the effort in terms ordinary Americans can grasp.

Toward the end of her speech, Maddy recaps the important points. "To raise more money, the United States will increase the legal immigration quota by a million people per year for a decade; the immigrants who pass a thorough vet will be given immediate work permits and go only to states that welcome them. All their federal taxes will go into a lockbox for a decade, with total tax revenue divided equally between Social Security and Medicare until both are sustainable for thirty years.

"The United States will pass a fifteen percent global corporate tax rate, so even companies that put their profits in tax shelters will pay that. The increased revenue will also go into the lockbox to pay for entitlements, along with new revenue from repealing the carried interest tax rate, which currently taxes the fees fund managers automatically earn, usually two percent, whether they make or lose money or don't invest at all.

"The carried-interest funds can also be used to incentivize the owners of office buildings with lots of empty space to convert them into energy-efficient, multipurpose structures housing offices, shops, and apartments, including affordable apartments for those with modest incomes, with all the new taxes these activities produce going into the lockbox or a revolving fund to pay for more conversions. This program will create good jobs in all states, raise revenue for state and local governments, and reduce the harmful emissions from the built environment that account for most of the emissions in cities—seventy percent in New York City, for example.

"If these efforts don't produce enough money in the short run, Congress will be authorized to raise the cap for Social Security taxes for people with incomes above three hundred thousand per year.

"To save money, the government will be able to bargain for lower prices for all the drugs it buys in bulk, building on the 2022 Inflation Reduction Act, which permits it for the ten most expensive drugs in common use. The government will also replace the costly student loan system with a direct loan program, which in the 1990s saved both students and taxpayers billions with lower costs and fewer defaults, thanks to an income-based repayment system.

"The program will be available to all student borrowers for legitimate colleges and community colleges and other skills-based training. The Grand Bargain will also bring back Al Gore's Reinventing Government initiative from the 1990s, which made government function better and at lower costs, with the federal workforce at its lowest level since 1960.

"Finally, our future growth rate will be enhanced by creating a National Economic Investment Fund to more adequately fund the ARPA agencies, including DARPA, the Defense Advanced Research Projects Agency, which gave us the internet and GPS; and the ARPA-H agency, which supports transformative biomedical and health breakthroughs, including further advances in the Human Genome Project, which has already given us a return on investment of more than one hundred and forty-one to one.

"The National Investment Fund will operate the way university research programs that produce commercially valuable results have functioned for more than forty years. Universities can license their discoveries to the private sector in return for up-front payments or for stakes in new companies as long as all profits go back into further research efforts.

"For example, MIT charges nothing on the front end for the use of its taxpayer-funded research but takes a modest ownership position. New York University has earned a lot of money from contributing its discoveries to new companies. So has the University of Central Florida. Based in Orlando, its campus is now the third largest in the United States after the University of Michigan and Ohio State. UCF's creative software developments have been used by NASA, Disney World, video-game companies, and others.

"In addition to selling the software technology, UCF gives faculty members leaves of absence to help start-ups deploy new technologies and established companies integrate their advances into ongoing operations. This system has enabled taxpayer-funded creativity to generate an enormous number of new jobs that make America more competitive, and it provides money to the university to keep expanding its software work. It's time to take a system that works well with university-funded research and apply it to other taxpayer-funded R and D efforts, increasing government revenues and reducing the debt-to-GDP ratio without raising taxes above what's outlined in the plan."

Then Maddy says, "We know that big investment programs produce more tax revenues than they cost. But if we're short of our goal after five years, the Reinventing Government board will be empowered to make more recommendations on savings, beginning with a review of the recommendations in the Simpson-Bowles budget report from 2010 and a rigorous effort to bring health-care costs in Medicare and Social Security Parts C and D into line with inflation. The board's decisions, after public hearings, can be implemented unless they're blocked by Congress."

When she gets to that point, Maddy realizes that while she has been delving deeply into specifics, into policy and politics, the entire chamber has been silent. Unlike at the State of the Union, her Democratic colleagues haven't jumped up in applause to show support for certain line items, and the people on the other side of the aisle haven't murmured or blurted out opposing sound bites.

It unnerves her, but she finishes the details of the programs and pauses, preparing to deliver some rhetorical flourishes meant to convey solidarity and trust.

She doesn't get the chance. The chamber explodes with applause, and after many minutes waiting for it to subside, she gives up.

She leans forward and says, simply, "Thank you."

EPILOGUE

ONE YEAR LATER

CHAPTER 140

Manhattan

The morning news comes on my car radio as I'm searching for a parking space near Madison Square Park, just below Twenty-Third Street. As soon as I hear the first few words of the intro, I turn it up.

"And now, from Washington, DC, John Agro, the man sometimes known as Jack Doohan—among other aliases—has agreed to turn state's evidence in the case against Burton Pearce, implicating the former White House chief of staff in a web of murderous conspiracies. Meanwhile, former Providence Mafia captain Tony Romero is due to stand trial next month for the murder of New England Patriots cheerleader Suzanne Bonanno more than eighteen years ago, a crime for which First Gentleman Cole Wright was convicted, then formally exonerated."

Sounds like I might finally have my ending!

A van pulls out of a space just ahead of me and I swoop in to park against the curb. *Perfect timing.* I promised to be here at ten, and I'm just one minute late.

I head into an office building across from the park. The lobby has a worn marble floor and decorative pillars. Old-school New York. The elevator doors look like burnished bronze.

When I get to the sixth floor, I head down the hall to suite 605, the office of my literary agent, Marcia Dillion. After Nottingham chief Reginald Hamilton canceled the contract with me and Garrett, Marcia started her new career. She tells me ex-editors make the best literary agents, which is one way she justifies her 15 percent commission.

Fine by me. She earns every penny.

I see her waving from her office door like she can't wait to see me. Marcia looks ten years younger. Being her own boss obviously agrees with her. I appreciate the enthusiastic welcome and the big bear hug she gives me.

She puts her arm around my shoulders. "They're fantastic!" she whispers in my ear.

"What are?"

"The pages you sent last week! I love how this manuscript of yours is shaping up."

She leads me through a reception area and past a conference room where two earnest-looking young women sit tapping on laptops.

"Black coffee, right?" asks Marcia.

"That is how I take it. Thanks for remembering."

She ushers me into her private office, which boasts a spectacular view of the park. A fragrant flower arrangement rests on a table in front of several elegant bookshelves.

We sit down on her leather sofa. I can't wait to tell her what I just heard on the radio. "Guess what? Agro is talking to the feds!"

"The creep who worked for Pearce?"

"Yep. And Tony Romero is going on trial in a few weeks."

"Will you be there?"

"Wouldn't miss it."

Marcia's expression turns evasive. She starts wringing her hands.

I love Marcia, but I know her tells. "What did you do now?"

She blurts it out. "I sent out the first few chapters to a select group of editors. A little tease, just to test the waters. I had them sign NDAs, of course."

"Marcia! We agreed. No leaks!" I'm mad for only a second. Then, of course, I have to ask: "What did they think? People like it?"

"They *love* it." Marcia beams at me. "And I didn't even mention the interviews with the president and Cole Wright. Trust me, when we go to auction, we'll have publishers and film studios drooling."

"An auction?" I ask, but Marcia keeps talking, so fast I can barely keep up.

"You and your book, my dear, are going to be the subject of a massive bidding war! I expect we're looking at a price well north of a million."

"That's amazing," I say, trying to take in the news. "But you know I have one condition. There's one house that's not allowed to buy, no matter how much they offer."

"Let me guess," says Marcia. "Nottingham."

"Right. For the way they undercut you and the way they tossed Garrett and me overboard."

Marcia grins. "Good. I'll enjoy watching that English windbag Reginald Hamilton suffer the consequences!"

"One other thing. And this is important. Whoever we sign with, Garrett's name comes first on the cover."

Marcia nods, then reaches over and wraps her arms around me again. "He'd be so, *so* proud of you, Brea."

I hug her back. "I hope so. I really do."

I know I couldn't be prouder of him.

CHAPTER 141

I've got one more stop to make today, and my heart aches just thinking about it.

After leaving Marcia's office, I drive to lower Manhattan, where the grid system turns into a crosshatch of short streets and alleys. Slowly I make my way through the maze to Sammy's Music Shop.

I park across the street and lift Garrett's guitar case from the trunk. I walk through the door. It's early afternoon on a weekday, and the shop is filled with tourists and customers admiring the rows of beautiful instruments.

Sammy spots me, walks over, gives me a quick hug, and smiles as he looks down at the case I'm carrying. "You here for lessons?" he asks, though he already knows the answer.

I wave my manicured nails. "No, thanks. I don't want calluses on my fingers."

"I wanted to call you," says Sammy. "But I didn't know what to say."

"It's okay. I understand. Really. It's good to see you."

"Garrett was one of my favorite customers."

"I know. He truly loved this place—and you." I lift the case onto the counter. "I brought this back because I know this is where Garrett would want it to be."

Sammy opens the case. The Martin is in perfect condition. No one's touched it since Garrett died.

"He was pretty good on the guitar," says Sammy. "He's amazing on that video."

"What video?"

Sammy's brow wrinkles. "You haven't seen it?"

"Seen what?"

He pulls out his iPhone. "Garrett's on the internet. You both are." He taps his screen and scrolls to a YouTube video. He turns the screen toward me. The video has over a million views. When it starts playing, I feel my knees buckle. It's Garrett, sitting on a stool on a tiny stage. The Sunapee Roadhouse! Somebody posted his amateur-night performance!

Some researcher I am. I didn't even know the video existed.

Sammy hands me the phone then steps back. I watch the whole video, tears streaming down my face. When it's done, I hand the phone back. "Thank you so much for sharing that with me, Sammy."

"He really loved you, Brea," he says. "I can hear it in the way he sang to you."

With a Kleenex from a box on the counter, I dry my eyes and clear my throat.

"Now. Sammy. About the guitar. Garrett left it to me, and I'm giving it back to you—on two conditions."

"Which are?"

"You have to display it, put it out there, where anybody who wants to can play it. And you can never sell it. It has to stay here with you, forever."

Sammy lifts the Martin gently out of the case. "Deal." He

walks over and sets it on a metal stand near the counter, where a pin light hits the gems in the fretboard. "It'll be my star attraction." Sure enough, as soon as he puts it down, customers start wandering over to admire it.

Sammy walks me to the door, then turns to give me another hug. "Come back to visit anytime," he says. "I promise it will be here as long as I am."

I squeeze his shoulder. Can't really talk. I pull away and wave goodbye.

In the privacy of my car, I pull out my phone and search for the YouTube video. Once I find it, I play it all the way through again, touching Garrett's face on the screen and talking to him in my head. Somehow, I truly believe he can hear me.

I love you.

I miss you.

You are so beautiful to me.

CHAPTER 142

National Mall

Cole Wright's bad knee is aching this morning. It tends to happen when he sits too long in the cold—and on this late-January day, the temperature in DC is in the thirties.

But he doesn't mind. It'll be better when he stands up. He rises with everybody else on the platform when the Marine captain steps up to sing the national anthem. Vice President Faulkner stands close by, straight-backed, hand over his heart, singing along with every word.

As the applause dies down, Cole holds the Bible flat in front of him. He looks proudly at Maddy as she places her hand on top of it.

"Madam President," says the chief justice. "Are you ready to take the oath of office?"

"I am," says Maddy.

Cole smiles. That's an understatement. With her landslide reelection and the last votes finally lined up for the Grand Bargain, she's never been more ready. Neither has he.

The chief justice looks Maddy in the eye. "Please raise your right hand and repeat after me. I, Madeline Parson Wright..."

"I, Madeline Parson Wright..."

Cole gazes out over those gathered to witness the inauguration, the crowd filling the grounds in front of the US Capitol Building, far past the Reflecting Pool. He's having one of those out-of-body experiences he used to have during big games, when the energy flowed and he experienced nothing but the field ahead of him. A feeling of total, absolute freedom.

The next thing that registers is Maddy saying, "So help me, God," and the crowd erupting in cheers.

An aide takes the Bible from his hand. The First Gentleman wraps his arms around his wife. The Marine band strikes up. They play four ruffles and flourishes, then burst forth with "Hail to the Chief."

"I love you, Maddy," he whispers. "You did it. You made it happen."

"I love you too, Cole," Maddy whispers back, holding him tight. "And they ain't seen nothin' yet!"

ABOUT THE AUTHORS

BILL CLINTON was elected president of the United States in 1992, and he served until 2001. After leaving the White House, he established the Clinton Foundation, which helps improve global health, increase opportunity for girls and women, reduce childhood obesity and preventable diseases, create economic opportunity and growth, and address the effects of climate change. President Clinton is the author of a number of nonfiction works, including *My Life*, which was a #1 international bestseller, and *Citizen: My Life After the White House*, published in 2024. With James Patterson, he is coauthor of the #1 international bestselling novels *The President Is Missing* and the *New York Times* bestseller *The President's Daughter.*

JAMES PATTERSON is the most popular storyteller of our time. He is the creator of unforgettable characters and series, including Alex Cross, the Women's Murder Club, Jane Smith, and Maximum Ride, and of breathtaking true stories about the Kennedys, John Lennon, and Tiger Woods, as well as our military heroes, police officers, and ER nurses. He has coauthored #1 bestselling novels with Bill Clinton, Dolly Parton, and Michael Crichton. He has told the story of his own life in *James Patterson by James Patterson* and received an Edgar Award, ten Emmy Awards, the Literarian Award from the National Book Foundation, and the National Humanities Medal.